THE GARDEN
AT THE ROOF OF THE WORLD

W. B. J. WILLIAMS

Dragonwell Publishing

Cover art by Howard David Johnson

Published by Dragonwell Publishing
(www.dragonwellpublishing.com)

ISBN 978-1-940076-00-3

CONTENTS

I dedicate the Garden at the Roof of the World to my eldest daughter, Kayla, whose demands for a new story put the germ of the novel into my head, to my youngest daughter, Hannah, who cried with me over the death of some of the characters, to my beloved wife, Margo, who inspires me to reach for beauty through words, and to my father and mother who always encouraged me to write.

Shalom, salaam, om shanti shantihi om, pacem, paix, peace.

W. B. J. Williams

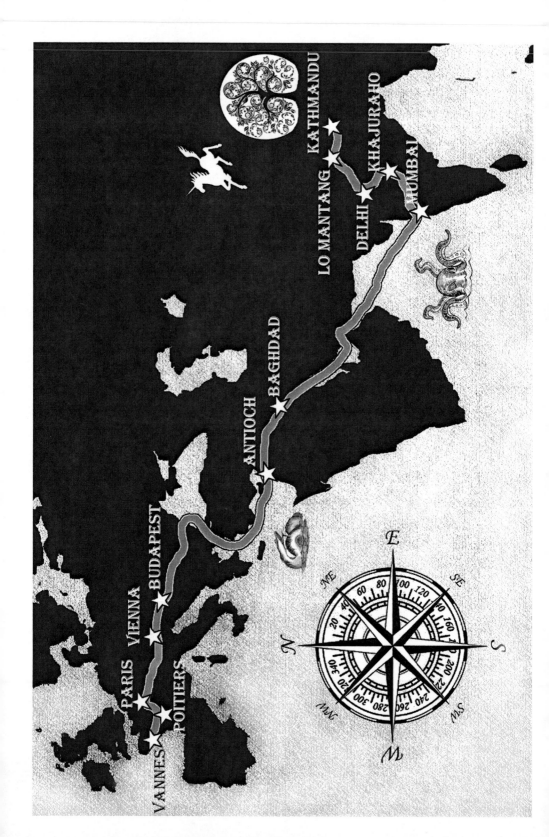

A LETTER

Namaste, Sri[1] Thomas of Aquinas, my most esteemed friend! I have reached the twilight of my years and at long last have the leisure to write to you in full about the women who accompanied the unicorn. Their story is a rich one, and I am glad to have taken the final steps of their journey with them.

After the bird brought your note, I went to wait for the maidens and the unicorn with two men of my village. Great was my joy when I saw them climb up the stone stairs of the mountain passes, and they accepted me as their guide. During the long nights of our journey to the Garden, and over the course of many weeks, I learned the fullness of their adventures. The Buddha has blest me with an excellent memory, so I hope to faithfully relate to you their stories in their own words.

It is the women who told most of the tale. The men would say little of their deeds. They once told me that only the women were called to serve the unicorns in their need, and the men followed because of their love of the women. I realized the truth of this myself when the Yeti came to destroy us. I count myself fortunate to have survived, if for no other reason than to convey to you their story.

I wish you well in your studies, my old friend, and look forward to renewing our correspondence of old.

Prince Jigme of Lo Mantang

---

[1]Translator's note: Namaste is Sanskrit for "I bow to the god within you" and is often used to recognize a common divinity within the other person. There is no English cognate, and it is commonly not translated. Sri is a title which means "Lord".

GWENAELLA

Gwenaella's call to serve the unicorns came from the First Woman herself.

Late and under the cover of darkness, she scrambled over the convent's wall, clutching the manuscript her dear love had given her in their tryst under the fig trees. Her heart raced at the memory of his embrace, his promise of marriage, and his kiss.

Gwen clutched the manuscript to her bosom as she pulled herself up the rose-covered trellis. Years of use by other students had provided a thorn-free path that she'd followed for her weekly trysts with Guillaume. She pushed herself up another rung and slid the manuscript onto the top of the wall, then pulled herself up beside it. She forced herself to lay still, to quiet her breathing. Below, she could hear the soft crunch of footsteps on the path along the wall. One of the nuns must be patrolling for students like her, hiding to avoid punishment for leaving the convent. Guillaume's gift would doom her to a dual punishment—not only for sneaking out, but also for possessing a romance. She smiled. Guillaume had written this romance specifically for her. Reading this would be worth any penance.

Finally only the sounds of crickets and tree frogs met her ears. She grabbed the manuscript and crawled along the top of the wall to where it met the roof of the dormitory that she shared with the daughters of wealthy merchants. Like her, they'd been sent here to learn how to be good wives to even wealthier merchants. Guillaume had promised to spare her that fate.

She grabbed hold of the gargoyle and swung herself down to the ledge just beneath the window, left open to the summer's cool evening air. She stepped through the window onto the soft rushes that the girls lay on the floor each evening to cover the hot stone and give warning of the nun's heavy tread. She moved as cautiously as possible but Rimoete sat up as she passed her bed, her dark tresses spilling out of her nightcap.

"Gwenaella," she whispered, "How did your tryst go?"

Gwen leaned over and whispered in her ear. "Guillaume is off to

Paris to seek his father's blessing for a betrothal."

Rimoete kissed her on the cheek. "God bless! You are a fortunate maid! What is this you hold?"

Gwen hugged the manuscript close to her bosom. "Guillaume wrote a romance for me."

"Oh, you are lucky in your love. I'm quite jealous, you know. Now go, Sister Switch is on the prowl."

Gwen kissed her for the fair warning. She slipped the manuscript under her pillow, undressed, and slid under the coverings. Her evening prayers were of joyous gratitude and pleas for Guillaume's father's blessing.

Gwen waited three hours before daring to light a grease candle and read Guillaume's romance. She sat on the edge of her bed, tracing each word with her finger as she silently mouthed them. Words he'd written with her in mind; a gift of undying love.

A soft shuffle on the rushes broke her rapture. One of the nuns. The smell of the burning grease must have given her away again. She quickly put away the manuscript, replacing it with another, left open for just this purpose. It was a brilliantly illuminated Psalter; with a magnificent drawing opposite each page to show some of the divine truth found in the sacred text. Gwen bent over it, her copper tresses mingling with the gilt of the illustration.

Gwen let the nun stand over her a moment before glancing up from the Psalter she pretended to read. She recognized the nun's scowl-lined face at once and tried not to wince as she said, "Sister Clair, what brings you to my side at this hour?"

The nun clicked her tongue, pulling the book off Gwen's pillow. "What are you reading, child? If this is another romance, your penance will be stiff."

Gwen remained silent, waiting for the text to answer the lie. Her rump still hurt from the last penance Sister Clair had administered.

"Why, Gwenaella! I'm proud of you. Psalm 8 is one of my favorites. '*Quid est homo quod memor es eius aut filius hominis quoniam visitas eum.*'[1] Wonderful, isn't it? Still, you should be resting." The nun closed the Psalter and blew out Gwen's candle. "I'm heartened to observe that my loving ministrations and prayers said in your benefit are having an effect. May the Good Lord bless you, my daughter."

---

[1] Translator's note: Sister Clair quotes from the Vulgate, Psalm 8 verse 5: For you have made him a little lower than the angels, and have crowned him with glory and honor.

As Sister Clair shuffled away, beads clicking in rhythm to her stride, Gwen smiled and pushed the manuscript she had actually been reading deeper under her pillow. Loving ministrations indeed. Gwen hugged the pillow, hoping Tadig[2] would consent to their marriage. While Guillaume was not the merchant he'd hoped for his daughter, perhaps being a scholar's wife would be permitted. She rose up onto her knees and prayed that she'd be permitted to marry for love.

The remnants of the night's rain glistened in the cold light of dawn as it dripped off the adjoining roof and slid down the spiral pillars of the cloister. Gwenaella hurried alongside Rimoete through the herb garden. They wore the shapeless white gowns of the convent students, though Rimoete had already pulled on the wimple Gwen had been struggling with.

Rimoete said, "I don't understand. How can it be that Guillaume wrote that the door to Pleasure's garden is opened by Idleness?"

Gwen, who was trying hard to straighten the wimple over her loose curls, said, "The girl's name was Idleness. What I don't understand is why there was an image of poverty alongside images of avarice and envy."

"Why that's silly," said Rimoete. "They're all images of things you don't want, things that keep you from pleasure. What a shame that Sister Clair should interrupt you. Has Guillaume already returned to Paris?"

Gwen's foot caught on a loose flagstone, and she tumbled to the ground. Annoyed with herself, she accepted Rimoete's offered hand and pulled herself to her feet. They both brushed the leaves and dirt from her gown.

As Gwen bent down to retrieve her wimple from the damp ground, she heard Sister Clair say, "Our Lord is also a stumbling block for the sinful, Gwenaella."

She looked up and saw the nun enter the cloister from the direction they were heading, face hidden in the bright light of dawn beyond her. "I don't know if finishing your dressing while you rush to matins is a sin, Sister," said Gwen defiantly.

"Sloth, my child, is a sin and a grave one at that. Well, I must say I'm going to miss giving you the whipping that such a remark merits. You've been sent for."

[2]Translator's note: Tadig is Breton for Daddy.

"Sent for, Sister?" Gwen felt the chills as she detected pity in the nun's tone. It could only be bad news. It was much too fast for Guillaume to have reached Tadig, or the word of an accepted approval of a marriage to reach her.

"Yes, follow me."

Rimoete embraced Gwen. "I'll keep you in my prayers."

"Thank you," Gwen whispered. She straightened her gown and followed the nun. Hurried footsteps echoed behind and someone gently pressed the wimple into her hand. She dared not turn to thank her friend, whose hand she briefly squeezed in gratitude.

The nun led her to the stone chapel where the priest would come once a day to say Mass. This was the only place where a man was permitted in the convent. Gwen's father might have found her a husband, some fat, rich, probably old merchant who would take her with her education still incomplete. Ah, Guillaume! So much for prayers answered.

The nun pulled open the brown wooden door carved with the words *"Petite, et dabitur vobis: quærite, et invenietis: pulsate, et aperietur vobis."*[3] She beckoned Gwen to enter.

Gwen hesitated; the dark of the chamber was foreboding. It took her a moment to adjust to the dim lighting afforded by the stained glass windows and see a man rising from where he knelt before the crucifix.

"Gwen, I'd had never known you, you've grown so."

"Uncle Boduuan!" She recognized the voice, his face was still in shadow. "I was told I've been sent for, but no one told me who, nor why."

"It's your brother. He's really sick."

"Sam's ill?" Gwen felt faint. "How so?"

"He's wasting away; he has no strength, and can barely keep down broth. I doubt he'll last a fortnight."

"Sancta Maria!" Blood rushed to Gwen's head like pounding surf.

She felt a soft hand upon her back and turned to see a familiar wrinkled face marked by years of scowls. The Mother Superior.

"Gwenaella, I heard about the summons and came as quickly as I could. While perhaps not all the Sisters agree with me, I will miss you, my child. In my heart, I had always hoped you would take up orders and join us."

Gwen bowed her head. "Mother, I must do my father's will. I will miss you as well." She felt a pang of guilt that despite the grave

---

[3] Translator's note: Matthew 7: Ask, and it shall be given you; seek, and you shall find; knock and it shall be opened to you.

situation she was secretly glad she was leaving.

"Yes, your father will need you to bring a son-in-law into his house, to take over with the boat and tend him in his old age. May you find joy in your husband." There was genuine pity in her old brown eyes.

"Thank you, Mother. Uncle, I will need just a moment to gather my things." *Pulsate, et aperietur vobis* indeed. The nun was right about one thing: the door from this joyless chamber led not to Heaven and love's promise fulfilled, but to bondage of a loveless marriage.

Through the cloister with flowers that no longer had any color to her, Gwen rushed to outrun her tears. Sam was ill. That lone fact hammered at her, making her grief at her broken marital hopes into a selfish ache. Whatever had laid her strong brother low?

Gwen returned to her room. Light streaming through the cracks in the shutters made the white plaster walls seem gray and shoddy. She walked over to the window and threw it open. A breeze caught her hair and blew the tears out of the corners of her eyes so they ran freely down her cheeks. There must be a way to open the door to health, to keep Sam from the grave. Perhaps some of the herb lore that Sister Clair had taught might revive him. If she could but restore him to health, surely Tadig would let her marry Guillaume.

She went to her pallet where her small chest of unvarnished wood stood, a contrast to the varnished and carved chests of the girls she had spent the last three years of her life with. They had learnt much from each other, these daughters of wealth and she, a fisherman's waif. She never understood how it was that Tadig had found the means to send her to the convent school, and always knew the price she'd have to pay would be a marriage to some wealthy merchant. She'd been content with this until she met Guillaume. Now life without him seemed a cruel jest.

She sighed and opened her chest. Sam was dying. The rest was not important.

Under her rags and shift, she found a blue woolen bliault[4] with a red velvet mantle and a white lace coif. She gently laid these on her pallet, and pulled off her gown as quickly as she could, tossing it to the corner of the room and replacing it with the clothes she had unpacked. Then she reached under her pillow and grabbed Guillaume's manuscript. Gwen's finger traced the handwritten title: *le Roman de la Rose.*[5] Remembering last night, when Guillaume had given his

---

[4]Translator's note: a garment commonly worn during the 12th century, it would have been out of fashion by the time Gwenaella wore it in the mid 13th.

[5]Translator's note: The Romance of the Rose. Guillaume is the author of the first part.

writing to her and professed his undying love, she hugged it as if holding Guillaume and his promise. After a moment she placed it in her trunk, wiped away the tears and took a deep breath. She knelt and brought her hands together. "Dearest Mary, ever a friend to women, let there be a way to restore Sam." She crossed herself and rose.

She placed the chest over her shoulder the way she often saw her father do. The weight of it made her stoop as she walked. She was glad when her uncle met her at the bottom of the stairs and took the chest from her. Rubbing the tears from the corners of her eyes, she followed him down the cut stone halls of the convent.

Sister Bodhicca, a young nun Gwen liked very much, waited for them at the wrought iron gate. Uncle Boduuan put down the chest while Gwen embraced the nun.

"I have a small present for you, Gwenaella," Bodhicca said, handing her the same Psalter she'd been pretending to read. "Sister Clair told me how you stay up at night reading it, and I thought that if you loved the psalms so much, you should have a Psalter of your own."

Gwen blushed and hugged Sister Bodhicca tightly, now shamed by her duplicity. Trying to sound sincere, she said, "This is a lovely gift, but it must have cost you a fortune. It should stay here, in the convent, where it may delight all your students."

"No, please take it. I insist."

Gwen took the Psalter and embraced the nun again. Its songs of loss would be a comfort.

Sister Bodhicca unhitched the lever to unlock the gate, and pulled it open with a screech. Gwen and her uncle each carried their burdens into the street. There waited a pony cart, a novice holding the tether. Uncle Boduuan put the trunk into the cart, then lifted Gwen into the seat. He took the tether from the novice and led the pony into the crowded streets.

The sun shone bright in their eyes as Gwen and her uncle made their way through Vannes. Neither knew the streets well, so they went slowly, meandering through the crowds of carts, horses and men.

"Way! Make way!" a man shouted from behind them, followed by the thunder of hooves. Boduuan guided his pony cart to the side of the street, along with many in the throng. Gwen watched as a knight galloped down the street. Dust covered his device; blood stained his surcoat.

A loud scream echoed through the crowd in his wake. Gwen jumped off the cart and pushed through the throng to the fallen old woman. She lay in the dust, her face a mess of blood from a large cut on her forehead. Gwen pulled her handkerchief from her sleeve and wiped the blood, trying to keep it away from the woman's clear gray-green eyes.

"Mother, pray tell, what happened?"

"A stone kicked up by the horse hit me," the hurt woman moaned.

Gwen slipped her arms under the woman and tried to lift her. Strange, the old woman smelled of a fresh sea breeze. Gwen shook off her confusion. What did it matter if the old woman did not smell of stale sweat and blood, the woman's green eyes were not clouded with age? She couldn't lift her alone. "Uncle Boduuan, help me carry her back to the convent. She needs care."

He scowled. "Gwen, that stone must be the Good Lord's warning to the witch, cast from the destrier's hooves. Leave her."

"Uncle, how can you speak ill of this poor woman?"

"Don't you notice, no one else is coming to her aid? Surely she is a witch. Now, let's go, your brother needs you."

"If you don't help me carry her to the convent, I'll carry her my-self!"

Her uncle looked into her face and turned away, his cheeks red. He grunted as he shifted the old woman's weight, lifting her gently into the cart. Gwen sat next to her, holding her hand as her uncle pulled them back the way they'd come.

"Child," whispered the old woman, "Seek a unicorn under the eaves of Brocéliande."

Gwen's heart skipped a beat. No mother of children would tell her to enter that wood. Perhaps her uncle was right and this woman was a witch. Besides, seeking unicorns was a quest for ladies, not the likes of her. "Why should I risk such a thing? What would a unicorn want with me, I'm no lady."

"Hush child, you'll know why soon enough. Go, seek a unicorn."

Gwen had begun to regret helping this woman, she must be a witch, but when they got to the gate, she hopped out of the cart and pulled the bell chain three times. Witch or not, the old woman was hurt.

Sister Bodhicca was soon opening the gate. "Bring her in! I'll get Sister Clair."

Uncle Boduuan laid the old woman down on the bench, backed away and crossed himself. The woman smiled at Gwen. "You've got a good heart. Thank you, dear."

Once Sister Bodhicca returned with Sister Clair, Uncle Boduuan and Gwen left the convent. Gwen silently pondered the old woman's words as they traveled.

In the three days it took them to travel from the Convent of St. Armel in Vannes to the village of Redon where her family lived, Gwen had plenty of time to think on ways to restore Sam to health. There were various herbs whose restorative powers she would try. If rosemary didn't work, perhaps ginger would. If he was in tremendous pain, some clove would help.

As the sun reached its zenith on that third day, they crested a hill and saw two rivers gleaming in the sun with Redon at the fork. Gwen, who had been leading the pony as her uncle rested in the cart, paused for a moment to look upon a place she had not seen in three years. From this distance, the stink of the salt houses pungent with the odor of fish could not mar the beauty of the peaceful town of thatched-roof cottages and the sun-bright river that ran through it. Beyond it loomed the dark shadow of the Brocéliande Forest. Gwen shivered. No way she was entering that wood—certainly not on some witch's urging. Tadig's home stood close to the forest, and she'd grown to womanhood in terror of its dark secrets and the enchantress that lived there.

She clicked her tongue and led the pony down the hill. Soon she switched with her uncle and sat on the cart, while he guided the pony through the village streets. The packed mud walls and thatched roofs brought a bitter sort of joy. She'd missed them so. She had often longed to flee the stone of the cloister for straw-swept dirt floors and the smell of fish stew. And now, instead of the joy she'd dreamed of upon her homecoming, she dreaded it. Did Sam still live?

Her parents' home seemed to have an aura of doom about it. The garden was overgrown with weeds, and the roof's thatching bare in more than one place. The shade from the forest made the walls seem gray and forlorn.

Uncle Boduuan brought the cart to a halt. Gwen hopped out, lifting the chest to her shoulder, and her uncle opened the door for her. "Tell your father that I will drop by in a few days to help out with repairing the roof. I've been away too long from your aunt and I want to look in on her, and then I'll need to work the boat before I have enough to spare another journey."

Gwen kissed him on his rough cheek. "Thank you so much, Uncle. I'll let him know."

She stepped inside to find the hearth cold, only embers left of the coals that should have had the evening stew simmering over it.

A smell puzzled her, something out of place. *Incense.* Fearing the worst, she put down her chest and opened the door to the extension Sam had built onto the house when he'd come of age, a room of his own.

BROCÉLIANDE FOREST

Inside, her mother knelt in prayer, facing the bed so that Gwen could see neither Mamm'[1]s face nor that of Sam who lay behind her. Next to her on the floor a small thread of smoke rose from the censer toward the rafters.

Gwen tiptoed into the room and slid a hand onto her mother's shoulder as she looked upon her brother. Mercifully, he slept. Pale where he was once bronze from days in the boat, his closed eyes were hidden behind the blackened lids. His breathing was phlegmy, his arms upon the sheets, once thick and muscular, barely more than skin-covered bones. Gwen's heart sank. No herbs would restore his health. He needed a miracle.

A unicorn's horn could heal... She shivered. No, the witch couldn't possibly have known. Besides, Gwen couldn't go into the woods. It meant certain death. Her parents needed her alive.

She leaned down and kissed Mamm on the cheek, wishing she dared kiss Sam as well, but fear both for him and of his illness restrained her.

"Gwenaella, thank goodness you've come," said Mamm. She rose from her knees and closed the censer, smothering the incense. They embraced, Gwen pushing the tears from Mamm's cheeks with shaking hands.

"Let's go where we can talk without disturbing his sleep," said Gwen. They left his room, and sat next to the hearth, Mamm taking up her mending basket and a shirt torn at the shoulder. Gwen saw that the basket also needed repair, and wondered if Mamm had done anything other than pray for weeks on end.

"We're at a loss what to do," her mother said, wringing her hands ceaselessly over the untouched mending. "Every day he slips further from us. Father Mathieux was here just yesterday to give him the sacrament of healing. We've tried everything—physicians, wizards, witches, priests, even astrologers, and all he does is get worse."

---

[1]Translator's note: Breton for Mom.

"Mamm, tell me how I can help?"

"Your father needs help on the boat. Someone to pull in the nets and tend the sail while he holds the tiller. He's getting too weak to do it all by himself."

Gwen sat up, knowing where this was going. "You know I'm not strong enough to pull in the nets."

"No, but your husband would be...Do you remember Iarnuuocon?"

Gwen let out a long sigh. So, it has been decided. Her doom fell, and she lived. She would not betray her anguish. She would honor her parents.

Besides, Iarnuuocon had been the least of those who had tormented her over her thin figure, her small breasts. If it couldn't be Guillaume, this was as good a choice as any.

She forced a smile. "Yes, I do. He was always kind to me when we were children."

That night Gwen cooked, letting her mother have the time to pray some more. While she prepared the food, she also prayed that there be another way. That they would find some way to save Sam. That she might yet be permitted to marry for love.

Her father came in late from the docks. He dropped his pitifully small catch on the table and collapsed into his chair without a word of welcome, staring into the embers. Gwen eyed him as she stirred the stew. His muscles sagged over his angular frame, shadows lay deep under eyes. Mamm said he had not slept much these last few days. He wouldn't come to bed, just sat and stared at the fading embers. Later, as they ate, he stared into his bowl, as if it were all the world to him. The emptiness in his eyes made Gwen shiver; he'd become so old since she'd seen him last. Gwen served him in silence and then Mamm. At last, she served herself and sat down.

After the meal father rose from his place and turned to Gwen. "My Gwenaella, my Gwen, I am so sorry." He started to cry, folding his face into brown splotched hands.

She was more troubled by his words than by his silence. A tremor in his voice told her more was wrong than Sam's illness.

"Now don't you worry it, Tadig, Iarnuuocon is a fine man." She rubbed his shoulders. "Perhaps Sam will get better when he learns of the wedding."

Father shook his head. "If he lives out the week, it will be all he can do." He took his place by the hearth and began to bore holes in

12

small rocks. Later he would tie them to his nets as weights. Knowing that he did not want to be disturbed, Gwen cleared the table. Her mother sat nearby, finally attending to the mending.

Gwen buried Guillaume in her heart deeper than she knew they'd be laying Sam. She would not trouble her parents with Guillaume's love for her. They did not need their hearts broken again.

After she finished cleaning the dishes, she kissed her parents, and went up to her old room. Tired, depressed and alone, she soon fell asleep.

A mist rose above the Lady's lake. The trees grew to the edge of the water, and the mist wrapped around each trunk. Gwen felt the coolness yet her feet didn't seem to be on the ground. The moon looked so full; its reflection in the lake was so vivid she could see its face looking upon her. There, what is that? As if a filament of the mist had taken form and walked, a unicorn came to the shore of the lake and looked at her. How beautiful!

"Seek out the unicorn. . ."

Gwen sat up in bed, her heart pounding. The dream was too beautiful to have been sent by a witch. The Blessed Mother must have sent it in response to her prayers. She knelt, thanking the Blessed Mother for a dream of hope.

Gwen rose, careful not to knock over the chamber pot. She swung out of bed, wincing at the cold air on her skin, and dressed in the moonlight. She felt her way along the corridor until she came to the kitchen door. To her surprise, a light was visible underneath. Gwen opened the door and saw her father sitting in his chair, staring at the fire.

"Tadig?"

"Gwen, what are you doing up?"

"There may be a way to save Sam yet. I just had a dream, as clear as tidewater, of a unicorn in Brocéliande. I'm going to find that unicorn and bring it here for Sam."

Her father's words were slow and tired. "Aye, a unicorn may cure what prayers have failed to heal, but I doubt it. Besides, what chance do you have of finding such a beast?" He hung his head, shadows hiding his face.

"I believe that the Blessed Mother sent me this dream. I know those woods. I know that unicorns dwell there. If one can be found, I'll find it. Whoever sought a unicorn with a cause more just than I?" She took the lantern from the peg where it hung and lit the oil, pushing back thoughts of Guillaume. There would be enough time to talk of marriage and love when Sam was well.

"Gwen, don't go tonight. There are wolves in those woods. Wait until dawn if you must go."

"I mean to go now, and I'll not be stopped." She looked at him; shoulders slumped, as devoid of joy as Sam of life. "Sam needs help fast. Every moment I delay could be a moment too long."

He straightened and looked at her, his face glowing red in the reflected light. "Gwen, sit down. There is something you ought to know before you go. If you are to take on the risk of a unicorn quest, you have the right of it..." He swallowed. "Sam's sick, but not without cause. While your Mamm was pregnant with you, I happened to catch a mermaid in my nets." He lowered his gaze. "I was surprised, and pleased. As she was comely and willing. I...I had relations with her."

Gwen blushed and turned her face away from him to stare at the flames. They flared, like her anger. "Does Mamm know?"

"Yes, I told her long ago. She, for her part, forgave me. What she never knew was that the last time I was with the mermaid I stole her mantle. I sold it for a small fortune, used the money to free us from bondage to the Lord La Roche-Bernard and establish us here. I had hopes that we'd be far enough from the sea so that we'd be safe from the merpeople."

Gwen would not look at her father, adulterer and thief. She wanted to strike him, scream at him. It could as easily be her, lying on that sickbed, dying. And yet, she remembered what Mamm had told her of Lord La Roche-Bernard. What Tadig had done was not an empty theft for gold...but that did not excuse the adultery!

"Sam was in the boat helping me, a month ago, when he fell from the tiller, clutching himself and shivering. I happened to look over the edge and saw that self-same mermaid with a wicked grin on her face. I knew it was her that did this to Sam, and it was done on account of my theft."

Gwen was quiet a long moment. Then, careful to keep the anger from her voice, she said, "Have you spoken of this to the priest?"

"Yes, I have." He rose and kissed her on each cheek. "It is my sin which is causing the death of my son and the ruin of my dreams for you. You were small in the cradle when I stole the mantle, so that you would never have to give your virtue to that bastard or his misbegotten heir. Perhaps you taking on this journey will restore Sam and lead to a better future for you. Go with my blessing."

He took a knit shawl from where it hung on a peg and wrapped it around her shoulders. She put her hand on his, confused about the wrong he had done to protect her, his betrayal of Mamm. Frowning, she stepped out into the dark night without a word of parting. How she wished her father was still honest and poor!

With each step from her house she remembered small things—her father's hand never raised in anger, her mother's fear when she talked about Lord La Roche-Bernard...the tender way Mamm touched her father on his cheek when she kissed him.

She turned back to the door, her father small in the shadows. "I love you Tadig." Without waiting for a reply, she ran from the house.

The full moon highlighted a gray path along the lanes she knew would be green and wholesome in the light of day. Through this colorless land she hurried until the trees of Brocéliande towered above her, gray pillars under a thick canopy that hid the moon.

A wolf howled in the distance. Gwen pulled her shawl closer with her free hand, and held the light up. She saw only twigs and leaves—not that she expected to see the wolf. She stood on the threshold of darkness, deepened by the small circle of light her lantern cast and offered up a silent prayer in the still recesses of her heart: *Blessed Mother, I'm willing to endure a loveless marriage to help my parents. I'll put aside all my hopes. Please let Sam live. Please, help me find that unicorn I saw in the dream. Please let it come home with me and cure Sam.*

Reassured by her prayer, and the hope that the Blessed Mother wouldn't have sent her such a dream if her fate was to be a wolf's meal, Gwen took a deep breath and stepped onto the path.

The woods loomed around her, the only sounds the whisper of leaves, her breathing, and the occasional crack of a twig. A loud rustle off to the right split the silence. Gwen froze. She held up the light, straining her eyes to see the source of the noise. As she was about to take a step, another rustle echoed to her left.

A deer?...Do wolves hunt quietly?

Crack. Gwen turned to her right and saw nothing. If it's a deer, holding still will keep it from running. If it's wolves, they'll give chase. Gwen looked around, straining to see into the shadows.

A shadow moved, and a howl cut through the forest's stillness. Gwen started to tremble. Another shadow shifted...

Fire! If she lit a fire it might keep wolves away! Gwen quickly bent down to gather some twigs and leaves.

Something growled, faint but clear.

She opened the door of her lantern. Hand shaking, she held a twig against the flame until it lit.

Another growl, deeper and closer than the first. Trying not to make a sound, Gwen gently held the small flame against the kindling until it spread into a small blaze. Licking her slightly singed fingers, she stood and looked around. Three pairs of eyes reflected the fire's light.

Wolves. They came closer, their open mouths pulled back into snarls.

Nowhere to run. Gwen pulled a burning branch out of the fire and held it in front of her, ready to swing it at the first wolf to spring. The lead wolf howled. In a blur of shadowed gray fur they sprang... past her. She felt the wind on her face and whirled to see the three large wolves fighting six other, smaller wolves.

Teeth flashed, bared in growls and snapping jaws. Blood glistened in the firelight. The smaller wolves, yipping in protest at their stolen prey, turned and ran into the dark night.

Gwen stood, clasping the burning branch in her shaking hands, facing the three wolves that had won the right to her slaughter.

Oh God, please have mercy.

Slowly the wolves approached, one straight at her, the other two circling round. Holding the fire before her, Gwen shouted, "Go away! I don't taste good! Go away!"

The wolves sat down, mouths open in a pant. The one in front of her started to wag its tail.

A melodious voice from behind Gwen made her jump. "What brings a young woman to Brocéliande at this time of night?"

Gwen turned to see a lovely woman wearing a long gown of deep green, her long silver hair braided with a blue ribbon. She swallowed hard. "My lady, I had hoped to find a unicorn."

"Why?" The woman's smile reminded Gwen of Mamm.

"My brother, Sam, he's very sick. I hope to ask one to cure him."

One of the wolves lay down at the silver-haired woman's feet, panting. The woman glanced at it fondly. "My pets told me you smelled different. I'm glad to learn it's true."

Gwen's eyes widened. "Your pets?" Her thoughts raced. Could this be the sorceress rumored to live in these woods? Perhaps the witch sent the dream to lure Gwen here, to snare her soul for hell through the temptation of a cure for her brother.

The sorceress smiled. "Yes. These three do me no end of favors." Another wolf moved to her side and sat. She caressed it behind the ears. "What makes you think you'll find your unicorn?"

Gwen fought back tears. "A dream came to me in answer to my prayers. In the dream, I saw a unicorn drinking from a lake within these woods."

The woman's eyes narrowed and then her face softened. "So, you are the one Mother Lilith sent me to look for. What is your name?"

Mother Lilith. Was Lilith the name of the witch? How could she have sent word? Gwen frowned. "My lady, I'm Gwenaella, a fisherman's daughter from Redon."

16

The woman nodded. "I will help you find your unicorn—if you agree to help me."

Here it was, the damnation of her soul. Gwen longed to say no, to run from this dangerous beauty, but the memory of Sam's labored breathing kept her in place. She would bargain with the devil himself for Sam's health.

"What must I do?" she asked slowly.

The sorceress shook her head. "If the unicorn agrees to help you and your brother, I'll send word of my need. Wait here until daybreak and then follow this path to the first split. Take the right path to my lake."

Gwen curtsied. "Thank you. I will do whatever you need at the peril of my soul." She met the woman's eyes. "You're the sorceress Nimuë, the Lady of the Lake. Why are you helping me?"

"I have my reasons. You're going to have to decide if you trust me, that's all. My pets will guard you while you sleep." Nimuë tossed her hand and the fire began to shimmer as if a rainbow rose from its flames. "Sleep, young maid, and choose well, come daybreak."

When Gwen awoke, she was startled to find the fire had burnt out. She hadn't meant to sleep. Confused, she looked at the ground. No tracks, or other evidence that a woman had stood there and talked to her the night before. Did she dream of it? Where were the wolves?

She forced the questions away as she scrambled to her feet and hurried along the path.

The sun was high when she came to the split. A narrow path ran off to the right. She looked at the ground, finding only the deer tracks printed into the soft damp soil. She definitely would have missed this path in the night.

After what seemed like hours of walking, Gwen found herself in a small clearing. A basket and a clay bottle sat in the middle. Opening the basket, she saw a note resting on top of a round loaf of bread and a piece of cheese wrapped in a cloth. Gwen read the note as she uncorked the bottle: "Next time you come into my woods, remember to bring food. Help yourself to this. Just leave all you don't finish on the ground for the forest creatures." It was signed Nimuë.

Gwen knelt, gave thanks to God for the food, and offered up a blessing for Nimuë in gratitude. Hopefully God would protect her from any ill humors in the food if the sorceress meant her harm. She ate as she walked, not wanting to waste time. Gwen was surprised that the bottle contained cold water, not wine, but as she drank, she felt joyously refreshed.

After another long walk, Gwen came to the clearing she had

dreamed of. She recognized the fallen tree, the mossy slope to the shore, the willow branches brushing the surface of the water. But no unicorn.

She sat on the log and began to cry. The failure of the dream's promise emptied her of all but sorrow. She clasped her knees to her chest and shook with sobs.

Suddenly the pain and the sorrow disappeared, like a weight lifted off her shoulders. Unreasonable, unbridled joy filled her.

From behind her, a musical voice said, "What is it that pains you so?"

Gwen lifted her head and saw a unicorn's reflection in the quiet waters of the lake. Its white coat shimmered with the colors of the rainbow, the white horn glowing softly in the sun. She turned, looked into the unicorn's eye, and saw what she could be, an uplifting vision that filled her with happiness. Then she remembered her true self, muddy and unkempt, selfishly clinging to her desire for Guillaume, her wish for Sam's miraculous cure entangled with the want for a marriage of her own choosing.

"If it pleases my good unicorn, my brother Sam is very sick and. . ." Gwen's lips trembled, forcing her to stop. She craved to be the woman she saw in the unicorn's eyes. She couldn't bear to ask this dear creature to risk itself so that she could have a marriage of her own choosing. But Sam—

"Girl, I will go with you and see what can be done," said the unicorn.

Gwen looked at the creature in wonder. "You would risk your life to do that?"

"Lead me to your brother. I will touch him with my horn."

Gwen stood up awkwardly. "Oh thank you, thank you!" She threw her arms around the unicorn's neck, and kissed her, once more breaking down in tears, clean tears of a grief relieved.

When she had cried herself calm, she lifted her face from the unicorn's fur, which smelled like the air during a storm.

"Our house is this way." Gwen pointed to the path she'd walked in hope and selfishness that morning.

It was dark when they reached the edge of the forest. In the moonlight she could make out the thatched roofs of the village houses. The smell of fish stew mixed in the smoke of the chimneys made her aware of how hungry she was, the cheese and bread of her breakfast now but a memory.

Gwen led the unicorn to the threshold of her home. Her parents rose to meet her. Mamm's cheeks were wet and her eyes red. She started to speak but saw the unicorn and fell back into silence.

Gwen led the way to Sam's room. He looked close to death, so frail. His skin was pale, his cheeks sunken, his lips devoid of all color. Gwen could barely see him breathe. "God, please, let us have come in time," she prayed. "I promise to marry whomever my father wishes. Please let us have come in time."

The unicorn pushed past Gwen and placed her horn to Sam's chest. Sam shuddered. Color spread across his body from where the horn lay, like fire across a dry field. His breathing strengthened. As the unicorn lifted her horn, Sam opened his eyes and smiled.

"Thank you," he said, his words dry and raspy but clear.

Without a word, the unicorn turned to leave. Gwen's father bowed to her, and her mother curtsied.

"You have our thanks," Gwen's father said. "If ever you need anything we can give, consider it given."

Gwen shivered, remembering her promise to Nimuë. She'd given it without thought of what that meant. But even if her soul was in jeopardy, it seemed a small price to pay for Sam's recovery.

The unicorn leaped through the open door. Gwen watched her run, a brilliant white flame in the dusk of the woods. She found herself missing Guillaume, regretting that he was not here to share this moment. Remembering her promise to God, and her promise to Nimuë, she put aside her thoughts of him. Sam lived, surely that was worth the sacrifice of her love, and whatever Nimuë would require of her.

Even her soul.

VOCATION

Gwen sat in her mother's abandoned garden, clearing out the weeds faded from summer heat. The earthen smell filled her with peace; the nuns of her school had always said she would find peace in prayer. It was good to be home.

She looked up to watch her brother as he worked on the roof, tying fresh threshing to fill a hole. She smiled and waved to him as he climbed down to get more branches. It was good to see him up and about again. In the weeks since the unicorn's visit, his health had been restored—along with Gwen's hope of escaping her arranged marriage. She longed for Guillaume's return from Paris. Thankfully Tadig hadn't mentioned marrying her off since Sam's recovery. God willing, she may yet marry for love.

Turning her attention back to the garden she was trying to rescue from her mother's neglect, she did not hear Sam approach. She jumped when he said, "Gwen, from the roof I saw a nun enter Redon. I'm going to her, to tell her about the miracle of my healing, and ask that they pray for Tadig."

"No, wait." Gwen hastily rose to her feet, wiping her hands on her apron. "Don't tell her about me. It doesn't feel right." The last thing she needed was for a nun to know about her conversation with the Lady of the Lake. It would be too easy for an accusation of witchcraft to be made by the village gossips.

"It took great courage to go into those woods, Gwen. Why won't you let me ask them to remember your deed in a novena?"

Gwen hung her head. "It is very kind of you, but I feel that this sister will bring me nothing but sorrow if she learns of what I did. Remember, Nimuë is a sorceress. The nun may accuse me of witchcraft in the restoration of your health."

"You're being silly." He took her hand in his. "Come with me. I can testify for the touch of the unicorn. She'll believe my tale if she sees the light of the unicorn in your eyes."

"No, Sam, please don't," she pleaded but to no avail. He would not let go of her hand as he began to walk toward town, and she gave in and walked beside him.

When they crested a small hill, Gwen stopped as she recognized Sister Bodhicca coming up the lane.

"I know her," she said to Sam. "She's from St. Armel."

Sam's hand clasped hers tightly. "Why would she come all the way here?"

"Let's save her some of her walk." Gwen tugged his hand, rushing toward the one sister that had been her friend.

"Sister Bodhicca." She embraced the nun. "This is Sam, my brother."

Bodhicca smiled. "I am most relieved to find you well, Sam. We had heard dire tidings concerning you. Gwenaella, I see that Adam's steed has graced you."

Gwen blushed. "Sister, it is a joy to see you again. Come with us to my father's house. We'd be honored if you share our poor fare."

The nun shook her head. "That is kind, but won't be necessary. Now that I have found you I might as well be giving you what I bear. There is no need to trouble your parents, and I long to return to the convent. Sam, would you be a good brother and let me have a private talk with your sister?"

Sam looked at Gwen who nodded her ascent, concern rising in her chest as she noticed Bodhicca's pursed lips and a line or worry between her tightened brows. "Sister, what brings you here?"

"I now know, seeing you, that you've been graced by a unicorn; that I've come on a fool's errand, so I sent your brother off. Why have him hear things that can't be true? I can see from the glow of your skin and the light in your eyes that you've had no lover."

Though the sun continued to shine brightly, Gwen felt as if all the warmth had gone out of its light. What could this mean?

"After you left, a message came to you from Paris. One of the sisters broke the seal and read it. I assure you that her penance was severe. In any event, I thought it best that you learn its contents as soon as possible. I wished to bring it to you myself so as to prevent further gossip."

The nun pulled a well-folded parchment from a pocket in her scapular and handed it to Gwen. "Take it, though I imagine you'll be puzzled as to how a man could address you so."

Gwen began to read.

> Gwenaella,
>   I write to you, my dearest love, from a bed from which I will never rise. As I entered Paris, I found the whole city engulfed

21

in a conflict over the lack of housing between the students of the university and the crown. I did my utmost to stay out of the riots but on my way to my chambers last evening, my fellows and I were attacked by members of the city guard. My wounds are grievous, and I am beset by fever. I've entrusted my copy of the poem I wrote for you to Jean de Meun, my dearest friend, who has promised to see it published. I beg of you to pray for my soul and look to a life together in the hereafter. Please forgive me for not being able to keep the promises I made to you.

Yours, with undying love and fidelity,

Guillaume de Lorris.

The thin parchment felt heavy like a lead weight in Gwen's trembling hand. At the bottom of the letter was a short note, written in the spidery hand of a local priest. She knew enough French to understand it. Guillaume was dead.

Gwen's hands crumpled the parchment as she cried out "No!" and fell to her knees, sobbing.

She felt Sister Bodhicca's hand on her shoulder.

"Child, how can this be? I knew you had no lover when I saw the unicorn's light in your eyes. "

Gwen looked up, her eyes misty with tears. "Guillaume spent a summer in Vannes. We met by accident, and came to love each other. We often met—"

"Gwenaella!"

"Yes, I know the rules we broke, but we were chaste. He—he wrote a poem for me. He went to Paris to make arrangements to take me as his wife, and return to ask my father's permission—" The words choked her and she broke down in tears.

Sam hurried up to her side, worry lining his face. "Gwen—" he began, but the nun shushed him.

"Help this poor child home, and do not ask of her why she cries. She'll tell you herself when she is ready."

Gwen let Sam pull her to her feet; let him support her as she tried to stifle the sobs that shook her. She'd been justly repaid for harboring selfish motives when seeking Sam's health. "Sister, you came all this way for me with this news. Please pray for my soul, as I fear I will not live out the night."

Sam helped her walk. Mamm greeted them with worries and questions, but all Gwen could do was wail. Though her promise to God to marry the man of her father's choice kept nagging at her, Gwen realized she couldn't keep her word. Guillaume was dead, and so

22

was she.

Sam brought her into her room and laid her on the bed. She curled up, dimly aware of tearful pleas from her mother, of food placed gently beside her. The thought of food made her sick; she could not look at it.

That evening, as dark clouds gathered on the horizon, Gwen sat at her open window, adding her tears to the rainfall. With sundown, Tadig returned as the storm arrived in force. She watched as he strode up the rain-drenched path and entered the house. She did not turn from the window when he entered her room. Nor did she struggle when he lifted her from her seat by the window to place her onto her bed.

He took her hand in his. "Gwen, Sam told me that the sister from St. Armel gave you a message which seems to have broken your heart. You've told us naught of your life at the convent. Please, tell me, what is this news that has torn all joy from you? I once told you of my sin so that Sam's life might be saved. Please tell me what it is that has broken your heart."

She sniffled. "A man who loved me is dead."

He placed his arm around her and pulled her to him. He smelled of the salt houses. "Tell me of this man."

Gwen told him of how she met Guillaume, of how they arranged to see each other despite the convent walls. She told him of their chaste walks, and of the poem he wrote for her. "He told me before he left for Paris, that he would soon come to you and ask you for my hand in marriage. I thought I could put aside my promise to him to marry as you wished, for Sam's sake..."

"He sounds like a good man," father said. "A man like that would not want you to go to the grave over him, but live. He loved you. Live that love." He kissed her on the top of her head, and then left her alone.

Drained of tears, she opened the chest she had packed that bright morning in the convent. Gently putting aside her clothes, she found the book Guillaume had stitched together with his own hand. She hugged it close, kissed its leather cover, and lay it down on the bed next to her. Lighting an oil lamp with an ember fished from the bed warmer, she sat and re-read his last letter to her. Kissing the letter she put it aside, picked up his manuscript and began to read.

Later that night, while the wind whipped the rain, a loud knock on the door startled Gwen. She could hear her father curse and the creak of the floor boards as he rose from his bed and went to answer. Closing her book, she rubbed her tired eyes, and opened her door a crack.

Father carried a lit lamp into the entrance hall and opened the door. The wind threw it wide open to reveal a stately woman standing behind. *Nimuë.*

The memory of her promise to the sorceress shook Gwen back to her senses. She must do her duty before she could let herself die.

"What brings you, witch, to darken my door on a night like this?" asked Gwen's father.

Nimue smiled, but her eyes were cold. "You opened your door readily enough when you sought my leech craft for your son. Is it naught to you that your daughter has made a promise of service to me in exchange for my aid in finding the unicorn that cured him?"

"I know nothing of this promise. I will fetch my daughter, but you should know that she is deeply grieved. She just learned a dear friend is dead."

Gwen threw a mantle over her shift and hastened from her chamber to the hearth. She approached the sorceress and curtsied.

"My apologies, my lady. I'd forgotten my promise to you, made sincerely that night."

Gwen's father squeezed her hand. "My daughter may have made a promise, but such a promise was not hers to make. She is pledged in marriage, and my agreement with her betrothed was made before she sought your aid."

The sorceress shrugged. "I have it in my power to take your daughter from you. You know this. Why do you seek to oppose me?"

The hairs on the back of Gwen's neck stood up, as if she could feel the sorceress getting ready to curse her family.

She felt she stood on the edge of a precipice as her father said, "Please, my lady, I almost lost my son; I'll not willingly lose my daughter to purposes unknown and potentially ungodly. If my lady would be so kind as to tell me what service she seeks from my daughter, I will be happy to bless her in your endeavor if it is not contrary to the laws of God or man."

"Fisherman, I chose to send your daughter to the unicorn because she is not only a chaste and honest maid, but placed herself at risk performing a charity to someone even her uncle called a witch."

Gwen startled at hearing Nimuë mention the old lady in Redon. She had been right in her misgivings. God forgive her, what had she promised?

Nimuë continued, "The service I require of your daughter is another work of charity, but not for me. The eldest of the unicorns is dying. He was foaled in Eden, and his loss would be a tragedy immeasurable. The friar, who has his cell in the forest, has given me hope. He tells me that if someone brings back fruit from the Garden at the Center of the World, and feeds this to the eldest of the unicorns, it will restore life and vitality to this noble beast. I will send your daughter to find this Garden and return with the fruit."

Gwen felt life return to her. This was a chance to take up a pilgrimage, redeem the selfishness that blackened her heart that morning when she looked into the unicorn's eye. Neither her life nor soul was forfeit. Rather, this was a chance to live up to the promise she saw in the unicorn's eyes.

Tadig looked into the fire. His voice trembled as he said, "My lady, all creatures die, and all the others that walked in Eden have long since gone to their maker. Why should I risk my daughter for this quest?"

"Father, may I speak?" Gwen felt the eyes of the sorceress burn through her.

He kept his gaze on the flames. "Gwenaella, I should have you whipped for your impertinence, but I'll allow you this time."

"Thank you, father." Gwen swallowed. "The unicorn who saved Sam risked her life doing so. We should return this grace."

"Gwenaella, I agree that we are in debt to the unicorns. My lady, I wish to offer you the service of my son, who should repay the life debt with his deeds. What you ask is too dangerous for a woman."

Gwen saw nothing but worry in his eyes. "My lady, may I speak with my father alone for a moment?"

"Yes, of course," said Nimuë.

Gwen took her father by the arm and led him back to her chamber. "Tadig," she whispered, "Why won't you let me keep my promise?"

Her father looked down at her feet. "Gwen, I fear you wish to use this errand as a way to seek your death. You know how dangerous such a journey would be. I would not lose you. Let Sam repay the debt of his life."

Gwen embraced him. "When news of Guillaume's death came, I felt dead already. But this, Tadig, this I want to do. I felt the weight of my sins when I looked into the unicorn's eyes, but she accepted my plea. I would repay her trust, and redeem myself."

"What mean you, redeem yourself? This sorceress is not God."

She lowered her eyes. "I sought Sam's healing in no small part so that I might be free to marry Guillaume. This was selfish of me. I feel the guilt of my sin and wish to set it right."

"Gwen, nothing we do is without sin. I fear those nuns have taught you all the wrong things. You're much too worried about sin. I'll let you go, but—"

"Thank you Tadig!" Gwen kissed him.

"—but, please, don't be so harsh on yourself."

They returned to the hearth where Nimuë waited.

"My lady," Gwen's father said. "Thank you for your patience. My daughter has convinced me to let her keep her promise. She may enter into your service on this task."

"I am glad, good fisherman. Your son's service would not have been acceptable in any event, for I intend to send your daughter in the company of the same unicorn that healed your son, and no unicorn would willingly abide the company of a man."

Gwen felt her blood pounding in her temples. That unicorn would go with her? This would be a joy, not a pilgrimage of penance.

"I would like to leave this evening, the matter is urgent. Gwenaella, the friar is expecting you at dawn, and will instruct you in how to find the Garden. I will take you to him."

"With your leave, my lady, I would gather some things to take with me," said Gwen.

"Take little, and only what is truly needed."

Gwen hurried back to her chamber to find her mother already there with an oilcloth sack. "Gwen, I've packed some needful things, and what little coin we've got. Let me help you change into warmer clothes."

Gwen embraced her mother, "Thank you so much, Mamm."

"I love you, Gwen."

"I love you too."

Gwen stripped off her shift and put on a warmer one. Then her bliault, her mantle, and finally a warm coif over her hair. She opened her chest and removed the book Guillaume had made for her. "Mamm, this is the book my darling made for me. It contains my heart and my love. Please keep it safe until I return."

Her mother took the book to her bosom, holding it tight. "I'll keep it safe. Do come back quickly."

"I will." Gwen took up the oilcloth sack and slung it over her shoulder. With her mother's hand in hers, she went back to the hearth and Nimuë.

Nimuë opened the door and stepped outside. Gwen followed her into the storm. She turned to wave and saw her parents holding hands as they watched her leave. Smothering an urge to run back to them, Gwen turned away and hurried to walk at Nimuë's side.

Soon after they entered the dark forest, a light spread from the sorceress, illuminating their path. Gwen recognized the three wolves that fell in pace beside them, escorting them along the forest paths.

After walking for a while in silence, Nimuë said, "I owe you a better explanation than I gave your parents of what this is about, why it is so important. Let me start at the beginning. Eve was not Adam's first wife. Lilith was Adam's first wife, his equal, created at the same time. Lilith, bold and beautiful, began to feel that Adam treated her as an inferior and left him, left Eden. Only the unicorns followed Lilith in her self-imposed exile. Only the unicorns stayed with her when your God created Eve. Only the unicorns stayed with her through the long years. The unicorn mare died in the ages past, mother to all her kind. The stallion lives still, the eldest of the unicorns. He is dying, and Lilith is heartbroken. She had decided to seek amongst the children of her enemy for someone to help her, when she met you."

"Met me?" Gwen whispered. The witch she helped on the day she left the abbey. *Mother Lilith.* When Nimuë first mentioned her, Gwen thought it was just a name. But her smell, her eyes—Gwen should have known right then that the woman was not of this world.

Nimue nodded. "It was Lilith whose forehead was hit by the rock, Lilith you defended and tended unknowingly. She sent me to find you, but it was you who found me in the forest. Lilith asked me to beg you help a unicorn, and there you were, seeking a unicorn's aid."

Gwen shivered and pulled her mantle closer against the night air.

"It was too much of a coincidence," Nimuë went on. "Too much that the friar who has a cell in these woods had also sought me out. He had told me to expect you. I am a sorceress, damned in the eyes of your religion—why would a friar seek me out, except to burn me? Why would he promise aid, the very aid that Lilith begged me to provide? It was too much. I had to test you."

Gwen wondered what this test had been, but didn't interrupt as Nimuë continued.

"The friar told me that the unicorn needs to eat the fruit of the Tree of Life, which was hidden when Adam followed Eve into sin. He claims to know where this fruit may be found. I am taking you to him. The unicorn who healed your brother has agreed to meet you there. She will take you to where the tree of life has been hidden."

The sky had begun to lighten, turning a rich blue against the dark canopy of the forest.

"I can't go myself." Tears echoed in Nimuë's words. "This is a journey to find where your God hid the Tree of Life, a journey to paradise. I rejected your God long ago." She stopped and turned to face Gwen. "The eldest unicorn is my friend."

Gwen embraced the Lady of the Lake; let Nimuë sob into her shoulders as she patted her back. "I promise, if this can be done, I'll do it," she said, trying to reassure herself as well as the sorceress.

They arrived at the friar's cell just as dawn was breaking through the clouds. The rain stopped. Gwen's heart beat in exhilaration when she saw the unicorn waiting in a small garden.

She curtsied to the creature. "I am glad you will be coming with me. I am Gwenaella."

The unicorn dipped her horn. "Thank you for agreeing to help. I am Britomar."

Gwen walked to the door of the small cottage and knocked. A man's rich and deep voice came from inside, "Please come in, my daughter."

Nimuë said, "This is as far as I come. I'll be sending what help I can, and Lilith has promised to find others willing to travel with you. If you would accept the blessing of a sorceress, I would be glad to extend it."

Gwen flushed. "My lady, you honor me beyond my worth. I would be most gratified to accept your blessing."

"I bless you in the name of mother Lilith, the first woman, unstained by sin."

Gwen curtsied, then put her hand to the door and entered.

A thin old man in a simple brown cassock stood near a table holding two cups in his hands. "Welcome, my daughter." He put a cup on the table and motioned for her to sit.

Gwen removed her mantle, hung it on a peg next to the door and then took the indicated seat. She sipped the red wine, sweet after the long walk.

"I am Friar Maeldoi."

"I'm Gwenaella. The Lady of the Lake tells me that to cure the eldest of the unicorns, we have to bring to him some fruit from the Garden at the Center of the World."

"Yes. Many of the trees in that Garden bear fruit, but only one can give the healing the eldest of unicorns needs. That fruit is born by the only tree in the Garden that has silver bark. The Tree of Life. The fruit is soft when ripe, and very fragrant. Pick one, and bring it to the eldest of unicorns to eat."

"Please tell me more about this Garden."

"It was planted by Saint Isa, a builder. He woke one day from a dream where the Lord was showing him Eden untended. He came to the conviction that he was called to build a garden for the people of the world where they could find peace and healing. He traveled far, until he found a barren place that was known as the world's center, the source of the four sacred rivers. There he broke ground and began careful planting. Others came to him to join his toil, and he established a monastic order of gardeners to tend this Garden.

"Around the Garden they built a wall; its gateway is open and has no door. An angel with a sword guards it. No animal will pass this gate, and no birds will nest in the trees inside the Garden. Shortly after the wall was finished, a tree appeared in the middle of the garden, a tree with silver bark.

"The monks welcome all who come in search of the peace found in walking its lanes. Any quest for this Garden must start and end in prayer, and the seeker must go there knowing that the Lord will sometimes refuse entry. The devil will set up snares along the way to prevent the seeker from reaching the goal. While the Garden's location is not exactly hidden, it is not publicly known. Ask along the way, and be prepared to find the truth in strange places."

"However are we to find this place?" Gwen wondered.

"Gwenaella, pray, follow your heart, and never give up hope. I know of no other way to find it."

"Then, I must find a quiet place to pray. Friar, may I use your chapel?"

"There is a grove in the forest, not far from here. I've erected a small altar there. Come, let me show you the path."

Gwen followed the friar to the beginning of the path. From there she went alone. The sun had risen enough to provide some warmth.

The path opened into a grove, where the friar had carved a tree stump into an image of the Lord in his mother's arms. She looked up and realized how absurd this was. She knew nothing of the world. How would she provide for herself on her journey? How would she find this Garden? Still, she'd given her word. Besides, what matter if she died? At least this way her death would serve some purpose. She knelt and thought of the prayer Tadig had taught her to say each time she was going to sea.

Father, I am so small, the world is so large. Please keep me safe as I seek to do this thing for the eldest of the unicorns.

As she crossed herself, she heard the words in her heart: *I too started as a child, small and weak.*

Gwen opened her eyes in wonder. There was no one around her, just the empty grotto. Refreshed and somehow confident, she strode back to the friar's house.

"Child, are you ready?" asked Britomar.

"Yes, I believe I am. Let me just gather my things." Gwen went inside, gathered up her mantle and her pack. When she returned to the unicorn, she curtsied. "I am ready now."

"Then mount," answered Britomar.

Gwen mounted and waved to the friar, who waved back. As the unicorn sped off, Gwen looked back to see the friar tending his own small garden.

ADELIE

Adelie's call to serve the unicorns began the day her mother was killed.

She'd gotten word that the baron's seneschal had sent his men into the duke's city in search of them both, and desperately sought her mother to warn her. Her mother was a whore, and once upon a time the baron's mistress. He had made her mother all sorts of promises; promises his seneschal had made certain would never be kept.

Unfortunately, news of the seneschal's brashness had reached Adelie late. She'd have to hurry. She needed to find her mother before she left her rooms to walk the streets, before the soldiers got to her.

She kept to the shadows as much as she could, sprinting across streets, shunning any open space where a soldier might catch a glimpse of her face. She headed for the pilgrimage house where she knew she'd find her mother. There it was, just a final sprint away, its dismal and broken door open with a false promise of welcome.

She glanced at the setting sun. She'd gotten here in time, her mother never left her rooms before dark that hid her age from her customers. Adelie gathered her courage for the beating Jean, the keeper of the house, had promised her should she darken its premises again, and stepped into the hall.

Things hadn't changed here since she had served Jean's poor food to the pilgrims that passed through the city. The hard-packed earthen floor was still muddy with spilt beer, the tables slick with rancid grease, the fire in the hearth too meager for the chill of the open door. Jean still ran this house as if the pilgrims deserved nothing better than the wild dogs that prowled the alleyways.

Not a single pilgrim looked her way as she slid past the downcast eaters, making her way to the kitchen. She expected to find Jean there, hoping he'd grant her access to the boarding rooms to find her mother. He owed her that much. He owed her mother that much.

She dodged the door as it swung open to reveal a wench carrying a tray of half cooked meat, and slipped past her into the dimly lit kitchen. She spotted Jean in the back and made a beeline to him.

His eyes locked with hers well before she'd traversed half the length of the kitchen. "What the hell are you doing in my house?"

She didn't lower her gaze. "The baron's seneschal sent his soldiers to find my mother and bring her to him—dead. I have to warn her before she walks the streets tonight. Let me up the back door stairs, Jean, and I'll be out of your house before the sun sets."

Adelie expected an argument, expected insults; she never expected Jean's face to crumble as it did. "Forgive me, Adelie. Your mother left some time ago with Dumb Jacque, she's been working a different part of town."

"Where? I've got to find her."

"I don't know, Lord help me Adelie, I don't know."

Adelie's fists clenched. She longed to hit Jean, beat him to a pulp, but that wouldn't find her mother. "Can you send—"

Her words were cut off by screams from behind her, followed by the slam of a door.

Lips drawn taut, Adelie wheeled to find Dumb Jacques stumble in, with a body cradled in his arms.

Mother.

Wishing that Dumb Jacques could speak, Adelie rushed forward as he lay her mother on the floor and knelt over her.

Her mother's once beautiful face was now purple and bloody, her breathing shallow and raspy. Her left arm hung at an impossible angle, Tears blurred Adelie's vision, but she swallowed the rising sob.

She crept forward and cradled her mother's ruined head in her lap. "Mama, can you hear me?"

"Addy, is that you?" The words were barely audible.

"Yes, Mama, I'm here. Who did this to you?"

"Soldiers." She coughed, bloody phlegm bubbling in the corners of her mouth.

"Don't die Mama, Please don't die."

"Addy, I..." Her mother's body shook. Then, just as suddenly, she went limp in Adelie's arms. Her eyes rolled and stopped, staring at a point past Adelie's shoulder.

"Mama!" Adelie shook with her scream.

She barely registered when a hand gently squeezed her shoulder. It took her a while to realize that the sounds she was hearing were words. People, pleading with her. Adelie shook her head and rose, forcing her grief down to the floor, next to her bloodied mother.

They were right. She needed to get out, to leave, before the soldiers found her too. She pulled a pouch off her belt and passed a whole le puy[1] to Jean. "Give her a decent burial."

He handed her back the coin and closed her fingers over it. "I will, but not with your coin." He walked to the back door, and unlocked it. "You'll remember your mother's room. It is still the third door on the left. Take what you can and never come back here."

Adelie swallowed. "Thank you Jean. I won't forget this." Without a second thought she dashed up the stairs to the room she had shared with her mother until Jean had thrown her out on the street, indignant because she wouldn't lift her skirts for him. He had never understood: she was not like her mother. No man would ever touch her that way.

Once in the dark of the old room, Adelie felt underneath her mother's pallet until she found the loose board. She carefully lifted it and reached under the floor to find the ring. So deceptively smooth, like her father's word; a sign of his promise to acknowledge her once the baroness was dead. She slid the ring into the small pouch at her belt. One day she will find him and shove it down his throat.

She heard loud banging below and peered through a crack in the wall, which sufficed for a window. Two men at arms pounded on the door calling for the innkeeper. Had they followed the trail of her mother's blood?

Realizing she had no time to lose, she pulled up her skirt, tucking it into her belt. She shimmied up a pillar until her head felt the press of the threshing above. Holding on with her knees, she pulled her knife from her belt and cut away at the threshing until she'd had a hole big enough to squeeze through. Long practice in slipping into homes to steal her meals had taught her how big a hole to cut. Once only her shins dangled through the hole, she looked to either side of the alley and saw no one. Adelie pulled herself up the rest of the way, slid to the edge and dropped to the ground. After a quick look around, she took a moment to pull her skirt out of her belt, letting the tattered cloth fall.

Knowing it was only a matter of minutes before the guards decided to search behind the inn, she slid along the edge of the building until she could see the street. Making sure no one was in sight, she darted onto the road, keeping close to the walls. As she scampered from shadow to shadow on the narrow streets she heard screams and swearing, broken pottery shattering, children sobbing, as if all Poitiers shared her misery.

---

[1]Translator's note: That was a small coin of little worth, however a whole coil would imply that it hadn't been filed down, thus still having its proper worth.

Laughter and a man's voice in song halted her flight. She stopped, trying to catch her breath, heart pounding to the song's rhythm.

> *"Sweet friend, to me she'd plead:*
> *Come here and meet my need.*
> *While my husband plants grain,*
> *Please sow in me your seed."*

His voice was joined with many others who all sang out, "Please sow in me your seed!"

A new roar of laughter set her legs in motion again. A man's song, as if some woman would actually beg for him. She'd sooner cut off a man's prick than let him touch her.

She turned a bend and saw the long square, with the cathedral on the other end. A pair of soldiers marched across, and Adelie's heart began to pound. In the morning, the square would fill with the carts of the merchants, and the noise of the market. She knew she would be able to hide in the crowd. The trick would be to stay nearby and hidden until dawn.

She pressed again the wall, waiting for the crunch of boots on the crushed stone to die out. After waiting what felt like forever, she peered into the square. Empty. Scanning the streets that opened into the square, Adelie saw one that looked small enough to discourage folks from taking a cart along its twisted path.

Looking again to make certain that she could see no men at arms, she darted to that street, entering an alley between two buildings that leaned toward each other, like drunken men. Several men lay asleep along the sides of the alleyway, wrapped in patched, dusty cloaks. She looked back to see if anyone was following her and tripped over someone she hadn't seen.

He sat up. "Damn you! Trying to steal my treasure, eh? I'll make the streets sleek with your blood!" He pulled a boat hook from his jacket and swiped at her.

Adelie grabbed the arm that held the hook as he bore down at her, and kicked up at his groin. He groaned as her leg hit his crotch, and curled up in the dirt next to her. She ran, the echoes of her own footsteps haunting her. She needed to find another hiding place, and fast, before the sounds of the fight raised an alarm.

As she rounded a corner, she crashed into three guards. One of them grabbed at her. "It's that brat! Get her!"

Adelie dropped to a crouch and rolled away from his groping hand, unsheathing her long knife as she came to her feet.

"Girl, you'll come with us," said one of the guards, taking a cautious step toward her. She slashed at him and he pulled back, his arm red with blood.

Another guard drew his sword. "Girl, you just made it harder on yourself."

Adelie backed up as the three men advanced on her. She lashed out at the nearest one. Her knife caught his blade and she pushed off it, jumping over the second one's sword. The third guard slashed at her, his blade grazing her side. She fell, forcing away the stinging pain, rolled over the ground, came up to her feet and began to run.

Her blood, dripping from her side, gave the guards a clear path to her capture. Adelie clutched at the cut, not daring to look and see how deep it ran. With the sound of their pursuing feet drowning the pounding of her heart, she darted into an alley, thankful for the sewage trench where urine ran putrid but golden in the sun's dawn. Keeping to the center so her blood dripped into the waste where it would leave no trail, she ran on into the maze of the alleys ahead, until the only sound was that of her rasping breath.

Finding a dark recess, Adelie hiked up her skirt and peed into her hand. She splashed the urine onto the wound on her side as her mother had taught, wincing as it stung. To her relief, the wound didn't seem bad, no more than a cut. She tore a strip from the hem of her tattered skirt and pressed it to her side to stop the bleeding.

With her wound taken care of, she turned her attention to her other immediate needs. Food. She was in no shape to slip into a house and steal as was her custom, so she'd have to scrounge.

Her search soon yielded a promising pile of recently discarded food behind a well-tended house. Most of the bread was mold-free and some of the bones had plenty of meat left on them. She gathered up what she could find and tied it into a bundle. Stepping around some broken pottery, she crept behind a row of empty barrels that had once held beer. She turned a corner sheltered by a pile of rotted crates, and froze.

A young girl huddled behind the crates. Her skin and rags were smudged with gray ashes and her greasy hair had straw sticking out of it, but sunlight danced in her eyes, clear and calm as she watched Adelie approach.

Strange, the girl smelled like fresh wind, with a slight touch of salt.

Adelie squatted, bringing her face level with the girl's, wondering again at the way the child studied her—calmly, without fear. Her eyes were green like spring grass.

35

"Hungry?"

The girl nodded.

Adelie handed her the bundle of food. "Where's your mama?"

"Don't got one."

"You should go to the convent. They'd take care of you."

"Convent?"

"Do you see the house on the hill with the bell tower?"

"Yes."

"Go there. The nuns will clean you up, give you food and a place to stay. You'll be safe there."

"Thank you!" The girl took the food, clutched it to her chest and ran off. Adelie listened to the echo of her steps with a strange uplifted feeling. Helping this little girl somehow made her feel there was still hope in this world.

When the cathedral bells began to chime vespers, she crept back toward the market, ignoring the hungry growls in her stomach. The square was now filled with the market crowds—good wives bartering, merchants crying their wares, and common folk passing through. Looking to all sides for the guardsmen she dreaded, Adelie stepped from the shadows into the glare of the waning sun.

Here her luck failed her, as did the charity of strangers. As she moved through the market, merchants shooed her away from their stalls, and customers turned from her in disgust. She worried; would they call the soldiers?

Scorned and chastised by merchants and customers alike, she soon found herself on the other side of the market, staring at the great oak doors of the cathedral. She'd never been inside a church, but the nuns that had taken her in had told her the priests would shelter someone seeking sanctuary. In any case, she didn't have much to lose.

She climbed the stone steps, pushed open the doors and stepped through the rounded archway.

The inside of the cathedral was so quiet she could hear her footsteps. Light streamed in through the stained glass windows, bathing the pillared chamber in reds and blues. One window showed a rag-clad man carrying a log, the next showed him stumble and fall, followed by a third where the man was hanging from that log by his hands as a soldier thrust a spear in his side. She briefly wondered who that was, some saint perhaps.

How to ask for sanctuary when there was no one in sight? Adelie searched throughout the church until she found an old bald man kneeling before a statue of a woman holding a child, his black robe spilling over the smooth stone floor. This had to be the priest.

Adelie waited until the man rose and crossed himself before she approached him. Her heart pounded as if she was still running from the guards. "Father, please, I need sanctuary."

The man's eyes showed concern. "My daughter, have you anything to confess?"

"No, father. Men killed my mama and want to kill me. I need help."

"Who are these men?"

Adelie froze. If she told him the truth, would he abandon her to her fate, or perhaps betray her whereabouts to the baron? Then again, would he believe her if she tried to lie?

She sighed. "The city guards."

"And you have nothing to confess?"

Adele lifted her chin. "I don't know of any sin but my birth. I'm the baron's bastard. His soldiers killed mama and now they're after me."

The old man lifted his eyebrows, then frowned. He leaned forward and squeezed her shoulders, staring into her eyes.

"Child, you are in a house of God. Is this the truth?"

Saints, she had nothing to lose. If this man didn't help her, she had no one else to turn to.

She dug into her pouch and pulled out the ring her mother had hid.

The priest silently took it, turning it over in his long, bony fingers, looking at the baron's seal and the heavy gold that adorned it. He rolled it on his palm, staring, then handed it back to her.

"Come with me." He turned and led the way through a door behind the altar into a dusty small room, illuminated by a narrow arched window. The walls were lined with shelves, holding candles and folded robes.

The priest gestured to a small bench beside the window. "You can wait in here until dark. Then I'll take you to a convent outside the city walls, and they'll give you the sanctuary you need."

That night he handed her a woolen mantle with an ornate badge stitched onto it. "Here, put this on, it will let you pass as my accolade."

"What is this badge?" she asked as she pulled it over her head, marveling at the feeling of soft wool. This cloth was richer than any she'd ever known.

"That is a pilgrimage badge; I had the mantle made with the

thought of taking a pilgrimage. It looks much better on you. Follow me."

As she followed the priest toward the city gate, she gazed into each shadow, jumping at each sound. Though her hood hid her face, Adelie feared the guards would recognize her and slaughter her on the threshold of freedom.

"Who goes there?" challenged one of the guards.

"Father Jacques and an accolade. We've communion to bring to the Convent of Eternal Mercy. Please open the postern and let us pass."

The guard leaned closer and Adelie edged away quietly, not to appear obvious.

"Father, would you come by my mother's house and bless my sister? She's to be betrothed, and your blessing would lift my mother's heart."

The priest nodded. "I'll come by on the morrow."

The guard put a large key into the lock, turned and opened the postern gate. Adelie followed the priest beyond the walls that up to now had been the horizon of her world.

After briefly explaining Adelie's situation to the nun who answered the bell, the priest said, "Fare thee well, Adelie. May the Lord watch over you."

"Thank you father." Adelie pulled off the mantle. "Here, take this, its too fine for the likes of me."

"No, Adelie, keep it. I can always get another. Besides, something tells me you'll be needing that pilgrimage badge. There are places on the king's highway that will stand you a good meal just because you wear this. I'll sleep better knowing you have it." He held up two fingers and made the sign of the cross over her, saying something in Latin that she could not understand. "Go in God's peace."

Adelie followed the nun into the cloistered courtyard where two young women dressed in blue habits were planting seeds by the light of an oil lamp. As they left the cloister, she saw a third woman quietly beating her bare back with nettles. Adelie shivered.

After a length of hallways and doors, the nun led Adelie into a small chamber with a wooden pallet for a bed and small clay pot under it. The nun showed her in and left, shutting the door behind her. Adelie heard a click and tried the door to find it secured from the outside.

Too tired to wonder if this was a convent or a prison, Adelie lay down on the wooden pallet and slept.

Adelie drifted between trees thicker than church columns. The large silver moon peered through the canopy of dark leaves. The darkness felt warm and wholesome, but Adelie felt an urge to go onwards, until she came upon a moonlit glade.

A unicorn lay in its center.

The creature looked at her and she laughed in child-like joy, something she had not done since she was little. She wanted to run, to embrace the unicorn, to bury her face in its mane, but could not speed up her steps. And then—

A darkness formed out of the shadows behind the unicorn. Adele's heart froze in horror. She wanted to scream, to warn the unicorn who continued to look at her calmly, but no sound came. She tried to run, but though her feet moved, she continued to float at the same heart-wrenching pace as the darkness neared its prey.

Suddenly two knives appeared in her hands and Adelie grinned as she raised them in a challenge to the dark. . .

Adelie sat up on the pallet, clutching her knife in her hand. A unicorn. This dream couldn't be an accident.

She had been called. She had to go.

Feeling her way in the darkness, she grabbed her pack and crept to the door. Still barred. No matter. She carefully slid her knife between the door and its frame until she felt resistance under the blade, and pushed up. The door swung open, letting Adelie out into the hall. She swung her pack onto her shoulder and noiselessly slid along the silent stone corridors.

A unicorn needed her, and she was going to find it.

ÉLISE

The Lady Elisabeth du Chauvigny didn't like to admit that it was her servant, Garsenda, who had received the call of the unicorns.

The Lady Elisabeth, who preferred to be called by her pet name Élise, loved Garsenda. She wasn't shy to take Garsenda's arm as they walked home that night after seeing a drama staged at the cathedral. She enjoyed this particular one from the book of Tobit, and she'd even helped with the music. Her cheeks still blushed with pride from the hearty applause.

"I can't get over how frightened the audience had been when the demon crept from the trap to threaten the newlyweds at prayer," Élise chattered, closing her cloak tighter against the night chill, "My music master had been right; the wedding night from Tobit had made for a very successful play."

"Yes, mistress."

"The best part of the night was that Papa was in the audience! Did you know he'd be there? No one told me. He came to the musician's box to congratulate me on my masterful harping!" She squeezed Garsenda's arm. "I was masterful tonight, wasn't I?"

"Yes, mistress." Garsenda seemed distracted. "Please excuse me for a moment." She removed her arm from Élise's and scampered after a woman in a patched skirt, huddling with two children against the cold evening air. She removed the fur mantle, a gift from Élise just the other day, and wrapped it around the woman's shoulders.

Élise's cheeks flushed. What a nerve! That mantle had cost her dearly! If Garsenda must give to the poor, she could have spared her old woolen mantle instead. She'd just have to have a talk with the girl tonight.

Garsenda returned to Élise's side. Odd, she smelled differently, as if a fresh sea breeze had washed over her. Élise inhaled, noticing the smile on the poor woman's face as she gathered her children under the furs, blessing Élise and her maid from across the road.

Élise recoiled as Garsenda tried to take her arm again. "Don't touch me, you silly girl, you'll give me fleas you must have picked up from that pauper. Whatever were you thinking? I *gave* you that mantle."

"Yes, mistress, but I already have a mantle. These children looked so cold and—"

Élise shrugged and turned away. Somehow, she just couldn't feel angry. The fading sea smell was so peaceful, so... warm. She pursed her lips. "Well, what's done is done, but it will be some time before I give you another present. Now let's get back to the Château before you freeze. You'll just have to make us both some hot wine when we get there."

Someone called her name. She looked up and saw her mother's chambermaid running toward them. She clasped Garsenda's hand and waited, suddenly frightened as it dawned on her that Mama hadn't been at the performance at her father's side.

"Mademoiselle! Hurry!" gasped the chambermaid.

"Hortense, what is the matter?" asked Garsenda, hurrying in Élise's wake.

"My lady is ill and calls for Mademoiselle."

Élise didn't remember how they got back to the Chateau, to her mother's chamber. Only when she saw Mama, pale on her bed, a surgeon bleeding her arm into an urn, did she regain her will. Dropping Garsenda's hand, she rushed to the bedside.

"Mama!"

"My dearest Elisabeth, I fear I won't last the night."

"No, Mama, please." Élise started to cry as her mother stroked her cheek.

"I'm entrusting your Aunt Marie with your care. Be a good girl and listen to her."

"Mama, you're not going to die," she sobbed.

"Don't be silly, listen. I've chosen a husband for you, Lord Bertrand. He's of a noble house, and his father has good things to say of him."

Élise raised her tear-stained face. "But Mama, I love Martis d'Hyères."

"I'm certain he's a good man, but his estate is in the north. He'd never understand your ways. No, you'll marry Lord Bertrand."

"Please, Mama—"

Her mother put a finger on her lips. "Remember, you're a woman now, you've got to be strong. Now, go, so the surgeon can take care of me."

Élise looked at the surgeon holding Mama's other arm over a basin as blood dripped out. "You'll make my Mama better, won't you?"

"My lady's humors are out of balance, and I'm bleeding out the excess blood," he said without looking up from his work.

"Go, Elisabeth, let the good surgeon work his cure." Mother's voice was so faint, so weak. *Dear Lord, let her be better by morning.*

Élise turned around as she reached the door. "Mama?"

"Yes?" The word was barely a whisper.

"I love you."

Silence.

"Mama?"

The surgeon lifted his head sharply. "My lady?"

"Mama!" Élise rushed to the bedside and clutched her mother's limp hand.

Élise let her fingers trace the flowers carved into the spine of her harp, her thoughts drifting to the day her mother gave it to her, with a kiss on each cheek. Now her cheeks glistened with her tears. That day was a lifetime ago. Élise lifted the harp, knowing well the beating she'll take from Papa who had forbidden any music in the hall, and held it tight as she made her way down the worn stone steps. Through the halls stripped of tapestry and banners, cold gray stone echoing her grief, Élise strode to the chapel where her mother lay.

Élise leaned over the gaunt shell that had been her mother, now still and wrapped in white gauze. Pushing aside the cloth, she kissed the cold folded hands that had once danced across the strings. She sat on the floor, and put the harp upon her knee. Softly, as if her mother lay sleeping, Élise played the simple notes of a lullaby her mother had hummed to her when she was small. She let her fingers take the song and interweave a hymn, the melodies entwined by a rhythm that echoed her heartbeat.

She let her eyes close as she turned her tapestry of song into her mother's favorite dance, and then into a madrigal. Song upon song flowed with her tears, until she felt a hand rest upon her shoulder.

Her hands fell away from the harp. She opened her eyes to see her Papa, eyes red from tears.

"You're not angry, Papa?"

He pulled her to her feet, into a tight embrace. "My little Élise, no, I'm not angry. Look, your fingers bleed. Let us find your nurse."

Élise looked at her crimson fingertips. "Papa, I no longer have a nurse."

Her father took a step back, looked her over and frowned. "I can see why, you've grown so. Well, let's have this tended to." His hand on her shoulder gently guided her out of the chapel. "It seems I must find a husband for you. Did your mother mention anyone to you?"

"Yes, Papa," she lied. "Lord Martis d'Hyères." She suddenly became very aware of her mother's gauze-wrapped face. Was she betraying her mother's last wish?... But wouldn't Mama want her to be happy? If she was alive, Élise would have convinced her Martis was the right choice, Élise was sure of it. If Mama watched her from heaven, she would approve of Élise's decision to take her destiny into her own hands. Mama was always telling her to assert herself.

Father looked thoughtful. "The handsome youth at the cathedral school? Well, then, I will have to meet the young man."

Head pounding, wet with her own sweat, Élise woke in the darkness of her curtained bed. Her solitude enfolded her like stone. Was she entombed like Mama?

"Garsenda?"

"Yes, mistress?"

"Hold me, I'm frightened."

"In your bed, mistress?"

Remembering her mother's lessons on how to speak to servants, Élise quieted the quiver in her voice. "Yes, Garsenda. Come, do as you're told."

She heard faint rustling and a gentle tapping of bare feet on the cold stone floor. The curtains pulled apart slightly, Garsenda's frame silhouetted by the moonlight that slid between the slats in the shutters. Élise sat up and pulled back the covers, guiding Garsenda under them. She cuddled into her maid's arms. There was nothing to be frightened of. She was not dead, she was not alone.

"Élise?"

"Yes, Aunt Marie."

"May I borrow Garsenda for a moment, my servants are all preparing for my rendezvous, and I would begin to prepare myself."

"But of course."

"Child, help me undo my bodice."

"Yes, Madame."

Élise tried not to blush as she watched Garsenda unlace the strings of her Aunt's baudequin bliault and stand back, awaiting further instructions.

"Thank you child," Aunt Marie said, massaging her breasts. "That feels so good to be off. Élise, in the olden days, when your great

Aunt Aliénor held court at Poitiers, we ladies would often go about bare-chested in the rose garden in summer months. So much more comfortable. Now, Garsenda hand me that rouge."

Garsenda handed her the clay jar. Élise suppressed a giggle as her aunt gently dabbed a rouge-covered finger around her nipple, slowly rubbing in the pigment until both nipples were a deep pink.

"Out with your question, Élise."

"Why put rouge there? No one will see it."

"Oh, the right man will see it, no fear of that. If you want a man's love, you must charm him. Make him unable to think of anything, of anyone but you. Some color on your cheeks is nice, but a nipple allowed to slip from the bodice will entice him closer. Some women go so far as to let gems hang from their nipples as from their ears, or to dip a finger into their con[1] and dab the scent behind their ears, between their breasts."

"No!" gasped Élise.

"Oh, yes. Men fall for that so very quickly, Mademoiselle."

"Aunt Marie, did you ever try this yourself?"

The old woman chuckled heartily. "Child, such a question for your saintly old aunt."

"I'm sorry." Élise hung her head.

"You never admit to these things, especially not to the men. You want them to think that they've chosen you, not you them. Make your choice wisely, Élise, and you'll have very devoted lovers. Now, does anyone spark your young heart?"

"Martis." Élise blushed.

"D'Hyères?"

"Yes."

"Well, I must compliment you on your taste. Let's get me back into this thing and we'll talk about just how to secure Martis as a lover."

"Why not as a husband?"

"My dear child, your mother told me she'd made arrangements with Lord Bertrand. The young lord will make a fine husband. Parents choose one's husband with wisdom and care, and you are fortunate indeed that your father left this matter in your mother's capable hands. You are so much more likely to have joy in your husband. However, a lady should always choose her own lovers with delight after making certain of his devotion."

Élise blushed and turned away from her aunt. She now wished that she could undo the letter she'd forged in her mother's hand to

---

[1]Translator's note: I've deliberately not translated this French word for a woman's genitals.

Lord Bertrand, breaking the betrothal. Perhaps it would get mislaid. If not, then she would just have to marry Martis.

Élise looked up from the poem she was writing, quill paused in her raised hand as she tried to find an appropriate rhyme, when she heard the door to her chamber open. She smiled as she saw Garsenda enter, clutching a sealed note in her hand.

Garsenda curtsied and presented her with the note. "My lady, the servant for lord Martis d'Hyères gave me this to deliver to you."

Élise lay down her quill. A light breeze fragrant with lilac pushed the feather until it rested against the inkwell. She sprinkled sand across the text, gently lifted the parchment, and shook the sand into a small rosewood box. "Thank you, Garsenda, just leave it on the table."

"My lady." Garsenda dipped her apron in a brown pitcher of water and used the damp corner to rub the ink from Élise's face. "He said it was urgent, and I was to bring an answer right away."

"Well, why didn't you say so?" Élise took the note, broke the seal, and unfolded the parchment. She then proceeded to read the note aloud.

"Dearest. I must meet with you at once. Please instruct your maid with a rendezvous and I will meet you when next the angelus rings."

"Will you meet him, my lady?"

"Yes, though he does not give much time for a lady to dress. One might think he wishes to see me in my shift."

"But my lady is already dressed." Garsenda stood back to take a good look at her mistress's face, and then began to rub at a spot she had missed.

Élise chuckled, looking down at her long silk surcoat with a red velvet girdle. Fingering the belt as she quickly thought of all the advice her aunt had given her on managing a lover and snaring a husband, she said, "Yes, but not for a rendezvous. Still, I suppose this will have to do. Tell his servant that I shall see his master in the rose garden."

"The rose garden, mistress?"

"Yes, Garsenda. Why do you ask?"

"Isn't that where ladies meet their lovers?"

"The rose garden of Poitiers has been the preferred place for a rendezvous for ages. Why should I not meet him there? Does he not aspire to be my lover?"

"My lady, perhaps you've had assignments in the rose garden

without informing your faithful servant?"

"Garsenda, will you get to the point?"

Garsenda blushed and looked out the window for a moment. "Lewd things happen there, my lady. It is not a place for chaste women."

Élise stood up. Her aunt had insisted that a meeting in the rose garden would ensure the undying devotion of any man. "Well, let us hope that lord Martis d'Hyères is as familiar with the meaning of my choice as you seem to be. Go now, and give him this from me." Élise leaned over and kissed Garsenda on the lips.

"Mistress?"

"Yes, Garsenda." Really, the girl was becoming tiresome.

"Last night I had a dream."

Élise picked up her quill, hoping the hint would not be lost on her servant. "What of it?"

"In my dream a unicorn seemed to need me, mistress. It wanted me to come."

"Don't worry Garsenda, just entering the Rose Garden will not make you unchaste. Now go, like a good girl." Élise turned her attention back to the parchment. "It does not do to be early for these things, after all," she mused out loud. After a moment, however, she put it down, got up and began to pace.

A breeze lifted the parchment and, unnoticed by her, swept it into the wash basin, where the ink rose in smoke tendrils until the water became dark.

Élise did her best not to hurry as she timed her steps to the ringing of the angelus. She so wanted to arrive as the last chime was echoing in the walled garden where she hoped to snare Martis d'Hyères as her lover, just as her aunt had taught. She paused at the door, pinched her cheeks to bring out a blush, and opened it as the last of the bells sang.

The large garden greeted her with budding rose bushes, thorny vines woven into trellises and lattice walls breaking the line of sight. Garsenda was right. Élise had never been in the rose garden before and she blushed furiously when she walked past a lady sitting in a man's lap, kissing him, his hand unlacing her girdle. She didn't know that Lady Genevieve had taken a new lover. It was unseemly to stare, so she only glanced at the various couples while searching for Martis.

Finally, she caught sight of him pacing, with his manservant standing nearby. She took a moment to take in his well-muscled arms, his graceful walk, the delightful way his brown hair curled ever so slightly as it hit his shoulders. Her eyes inadvertently traced down his torso, his shapely legs under the soft cloth of the pantaloons. She forced her gaze up again and met his dark eyes, startled. His expression was not that of a lustful lover waiting for a maid. Martis's brow was deeply furrowed as his eyes registered his recognition of her.

Élise hid her unease behind a bright smile as she approached. "My lord, it is good to see you again."

He gave her a stiff bow, "My lady, thank you for granting me this audience."

She stepped closer, alarmed. "Are you all right?"

He lowered his eyes. "I am most grieved, but my father has commanded me to leave this place at once. I had written him, requesting permission to ask your father for your hand in marriage, but he has formed an opinion that the ladies of Poitiers are not—" he hesitated.

Elise searched out his gaze. "Not what?"

He averted his eyes. "Not of good repute. Forgive me, my lady. I'm afraid he would not hear of our marriage."

Élise blanched, her ears filled with a roar as if privy to the winds of a tempest. The sweet smell of the lilacs nauseated her. Ill repute? Could he be implying...

She heard her own voice as if coming from afar. "My lord, I don't know what to say."

He continued to look away. "Please forgive me. But I'm afraid that if he were to learn of your choice of a place for a rendez-vouz—" He wordlessly glanced around, at the bushes hiding joyful couples, and the giggling from behind a nearby trellis.

"And you thought that I—" Élise's knees buckled, her eyes darkening. Oh Lord, and here she was, thinking lustful thoughts, looking at his legs, anticipating... while he—he—

She ran from him, through the garden, past the romances of her daydreams, through uncounted doors, down corridors, up the stairs, until finally, tripping over her own feet, she curled up where she landed on the floor of her room, shaking in tears.

When she finally became aware of her surroundings, Garsenda was fanning her. Élise looked around, the familiar furnishings of her room coming into focus.

"Martis?" she asked weakly.

"My lord sent for me when you ran from him. He is most concerned."

"Oh, Garsenda, what am I to do? The dear boy asked his father for permission to marry me, and his father told him I'm a wanton strumpet. And now, I'm afraid Martis may be convinced his father is correct. Why did I have to listen to my aunt instead of my mother? You were right, we should not have met in the rose garden."

"It is like that story my lady was telling me, Eric and Enide. You have to find a way to convince him of your faithful devotion, like Enide did Eric."

Élise wiped her eyes with her sleeve. "Garsenda, Enide was already Eric's wife. What hope do I have to prove myself chaste?"

"My lady could have her physician—"

"Chaste, not a virgin, Garsenda. I could be as virginal as snow and he'd still believe me unchaste. Wait a moment, your dream. . . We can go and find that unicorn of yours. He'll have to believe me chaste if I'm seen in the company of a unicorn."

"My lady—"

"Do not say another word, Garsenda. My father will certainly provide us with the escort we need. We just have to tell him that it was me who had the dream, he'd never believe it of a servant."

"My lady—"

"No need to thank me, Garsenda. Go off with you, and start packing. Father should be in his Château; we'll leave for Chauvigny in the morning. Oh, I almost forgot, I need you to take a message to Martis. Is he still in Poitiers?"

"I will endeavor to find out my lady."

"Please do, and ask him to come to my chambers. I'd rather make amends privately."

When Garsenda left the room, Élise rose from her bed and began to pace. She remembered how she used to play at being married and becoming a mother, before her mother died of fever, before her aunt took over the rearing of her. Perhaps a petition to a saint would bring help, but which saint? Was there a saint for women desperate for their men to marry them? She fell to her knees, brought her hands together, and began to sing a hymn to the Blessed Mother.

> *Quant voi la flor novele*
> *Florir en la praele,*
> *Lors chant chançon novele,*
> *Qui dou lait de sa mamele*
> *Le roi alaita*
> *Qui de sa char digne et belle*
> *Touz nos rachata*

She heard her chamber door open but would not turn to see who the silent visitor was. She closed her eyes, wincing slightly as a tear rolled down her cheek and finished the hymn.

> *Pucele digne et pure,*
> *De qui toz biens depure,*
> *Qui de pechié n'as cure,*
> *De moi te praigne cure:*
> *Vers ton chier fiz m'asseüre*
> *Par tel covenant*
> *Qu'es ciels en joie seüre soie parvenant.*

When she finished the final note, Garsenda said, "My lady, lord d'Hyères."

Élise wiped her tears and rose.

Martis bowed as he walked in, then reached up his sleeve and handed her a handkerchief. "I would be honored if you keep it, my lady. A small token of my love for you."

Élise clutched the handkerchief, not wanting to marr it with her tears. His love. The words made her feel weak with pleasure. And yet—

She looked into his eyes. "If you love me, why can't we be married?"

He lowered his head. "I can't disobey my father who forbids this marriage."

"If I could prove myself chaste?"

He smiled, looking at her tenderly. "I don't doubt it myself."

She held his gaze. "If I were to come to Hyères, having been touched by a unicorn, would that remove your father's doubts?"

His eyes widened. "You would risk that for me?"

How hard could it be? Élise smiled. "Yes."

He stepped back, looking at her with wonder. "I am certain that even my father could maintain no doubts of a woman touched by a unicorn."

SENECHAL

T he next day, after Martis departed for home, Élise and her maid returned to her father's Château in Chauvigny, only a few hours from her aunt's house in Poitiers. She sent Garsenda to make ready what they would need for their journey and then went straight to her father's chambers. She slowly pushed open the thick oak door, expecting to find him pouring over planting records, but found his bench empty, his table neat, lamp cold and dark. She rushed off in search of a servant and found the chambermaid making her father's bed.

"Hortense, do you know when my father will return?"

"The baron? My lady, he departed for Paris yesterday."

"Paris? Why?"

"My lady, he is off to join King Louis on a holy crusade."

Crusade? Élise frowned. Crusades were long and perilous, or so she heard. Why didn't father write her that he was leaving? Why hadn't he visited to say farewell?

When will she see her father again?

"Do you know where I may find Hervé?"

The maid giggled, "My lady, you may find the Lord's seneschal in the city baths." The maid curtsied and left Élise in her father's empty bedchamber.

Élise sighed. One thing was clear, if she was to go off in search of this unicorn of Garsenda's, she'd have to seek out her father's seneschal. She'll send for him at once.

Élise looked up as she heard a knock on the door. "Garsenda, do answer that." When the knock repeated, she remembered that she'd sent her servant to fetch more ink for her. Annoyed that she only had one servant, she put down her quill and went to answer the door herself. She pulled it open just a crack to see who it was, then swang it the rest of the way when she saw Hervé with two men at arms.

"My lady sent for me?"

"Yes, good Hervé, thank you for coming so promptly. Do come in,

I wish to talk to you in private."

"As my lady wishes." The seneschal bowed, taking off his cap, then followed Élise into the room.

Hervé looked older than Élise remembered. His gray hair was thinning on top, and his waistline definitely looked broader. He winced as he settled into the deep armchair, but his small sharp eyes bore into her with the same intensity she remembered from years before.

"I wish to venture on a quest to seek out a unicorn. I will need two horses, my jewels, and an escort. Would you be so kind as to make the arrangements?"

His eyebrows rose in surprise. "My lady, a quest for unicorns is extremely dangerous. Why does my lady wish to find a unicorn?"

Did she dare tell him? The truth was probably best. "I find that doubts upon my virtue stand in the way of an offer of marriage from the house d'Hyères. I wish to remove these doubts."

Hervé leaned back in his chair, a thin smile worming on his lips. "Lady Elisabeth, you need not worry about the opinions of the house d'Hyères. Your father made arrangements for you to be married before his departure and left me with clear instructions. Your bridegroom and his father are quite convinced of your virtue."

Élise realized her jaw was hanging open. Why hadn't father come to her with the news?

"I'm certain that when my father learns that—"

The older man's glance stopped her. "After your father learned of the deception you enacted regarding your mother's arrangements for you to marry Lord Bertrand and how angry Lord Bertrand was at the broken betrothal, he was furious with you. He swore that he'd throw you into a convent before he'd see you marry. However, he received a most advantageous offer of marriage and has affixed his seal to it a just days ago. Your father had planned to tell you himself, and left just this morning to find you in Poitiers, on his way to Paris to join the king."

Élise sat up straight. "Then, let me speak to my father myself. I am certain that when he hears about—"

Hervé shook his head. "I'm afraid this would be quite impossible, my lady. Your father has taken the crusader's vow, and will not be returning for some time. My lady can relax; she will be a bride rather shortly."

"To whom am I betrothed?" Her aunt had always advised stealth, not overt opposition.

"Prince Leon of Armenia."

"I am honored that I will be the means to link the house d' Chauvigny with that of Armenia." *Dear God, please, I know I'm lying but keep this serpent from knowing I'm lying.* "Will His Highness be coming to Chauvigny to fetch me?"

"You will be sent to him."

"Very well. But before I do, I must seek my father upon the road and wish God's blessing upon him. Arrange for a horse and escort at once."

The older man bowed his head, but his eyes remained fixed on Élise. "My lady, since your brother, the heir, is not yet of age, your father has left me in charge of his estates in his absence. He instructed me that upon your return to Chauvigny, I was to make arrangements for your journey to Armenia, not anywhere else. While you've arrived earlier than I expected, and regrettably missed your father upon his road, this does not change the very clear instructions I have. You will remain here, and I will see to the preparation for your journey."

Élise but her lip. "I will be happy to see to these preparations after I've returned from seeking my father upon the road."

"I will have nothing go wrong with these arrangements, my lady. Your father's instructions were most clear, and I can ill afford to earn his displeasure. I will also be making certain that there are no further rendezvous with d'Hyères."

Élise flushed, but did not let her confusion as to how he knew about her rendezvous color her voice. "You overstep yourself, steward."

"No, my lady. Your father was quite clear that he'd be sending you back to Chauvigny under guard, and that you were to leave Chauvigny for no reason until you departed for Armenia. I am just following his instructions very carefully. The two men I brought with me will see to it that you remain in your chambers until preparations are complete. Good day to you, my lady."

Drying her tears, Élise rang the bell for Garsenda. As she waited, she found some parchment and began to write. After the third ink blotch, Élise crumpled the parchment and threw it toward the door where it hit Garsenda in the face as she opened it.

"Oh, Garsenda, I'm sorry. I didn't mean to hit you. I was trying to write something for you to take to Martis, but I'm so agitated about what that demonic seneschal said that all I get is blotches."

"You spoke to Hervé? What did he say?" Garsenda gently rubbed the ink off her mistress's cheek.

"My father, before he left for the King's crusade, arranged for my marriage to the prince of Armenia, and Hervé won't hear of breaking the arrangement. He's locked me in this tower to keep me from fleeing. Oh, Garsenda, how can I defy him? In my heart I know my father would never force this union."

"You could look for the unicorn, then go straight to Hyères, and elope."

"He's posting guards, to protect my virtue. I'll never get out of the tower."

"I know. They've told all the servants. I'm only allowed to come because I'm your maid."

Élise hung her head and sobbed. "Then all is lost!"

"My lady," Garsenda said as she opened the shutters, "They saw your maid come in; they'll expect her to leave. There is no reason why you could not leave in my stead."

"Garsenda, that is very sweet but would never get me out of the city. And what about you? I can't do this alone. Besides, it is *your* unicorn."

"When they find you gone, they might whip me, but they'll let me go. I've had whippings before. I'll tell them that this was all your idea, and I had to listen since I'm your maid. Why not go to Poitiers, say you're on an errand from your mistress, and go to the cathedral school. Perhaps you can get the help you need from one of your teachers."

A breeze lifted a strand of Élise's dark hair and pushed it onto her wet cheek where it momentarily stuck until her hand brushed it aside. If she stayed, she'd marry a prince, one day be Queen of Armenia and have no end of lovers at her beck and call; just like what her aunt had promised. A queen, just like Blanche of Castile! If she left, she'd have no station, no resources and have to endure who knows what hardship. To go through hell, live like Enide for a man who loved her... Why, it was just like a story.

"I'll do it. I do hope you'll be able to get out of the Château soon"

"I'll come," Garsenda said as she began to undress. "I'm haunted by that dream, by the thought that a unicorn needs me. If you could be so kind as to wait for me for a few days, I think I could get back to Poitiers.

"You're about my height, and my wimple will hide your hair—I doubt anyone will recognize you. I've told the one cook who is my friend what I planned, and she's agreed to help cover for us. She'll greet you as me when you enter the kitchen, pretend you're me. Now, let me give you a few pointers on how to behave as a servant when your mistress is not present."

"You planned all this? Garsenda, you are a marvel!"

Élise felt relieved when the two guards stationed outside her chamber door did not challenge her. As Garsenda had instructed, she walked with head bowed and curtsied when she saw any aristocrat.

As she entered the kitchen, which Garsenda had assured her was the proper way in and out of the Château for the servants, Élise realized how hungry she was. She had not eaten in hours, but was not certain if, as a servant, she was permitted to sample.

"Garsenda! What idiot errand does your mistress send you on this time?" asked one of the cooks, handing her a piece of cold poultry. This must be the cook Garsenda told her about. As Élise took a bite, thinking of how to reply, another cook laughed.

"Is she sending for Hervé again?"

"Hervé must be a lucky man!" bellowed an old woman who didn't look up from a washbasin wherein she was scrubbing a pot.

Élise decided that a small twist on the truth might serve her best as she stepped around the table where the cooks were cutting various roots. Talking with food still in her mouth to better disguise her voice, she said, "Hervé has my mistress locked in her chambers until she can be sent to the Kingdom of Armenia to be married. My lady is sending me to the cathedral school to inform her music and scriptural masters that she'll not be attending lessons, and to inform her aunt that she'll not be returning."

The cook who had handed her the poultry leg said, "Oh, the poor dear." She turned away from Élise and started to chop carrots.

The old woman said, "I'd love to be a fly on the wall of their bridal chamber! The way that woman goes on about love and all, while her nose is covered in ink and she's never uncovered herself for a man."

One of the boys turning a spigot of ham over the fire said, "I'd like to go and remedy that."

Élise hoped that her blush would not be too visible as she held her poultry to her face, taking another bite as she edged around a large trough into which the blood from a hung boar was being gathered. The sharp smell of it made her queasy.

"I bet you would!" shrieked the old woman, "But she'd lift a quill to you, not her skirts, praising your manly peach fuzz!"

As the women laughed at the blushing spigot boy, Élise reached the postern door to the keep. Torn between her worry for Garsenda and embarrassment at the conversation she just overheard, she forced herself to walk calmly through the door and not to run across the courtyard to the Château's gate. She could hear the kitchen staff behind her laughing as the old woman said, "I bet even her con is covered in ink!"

At the Château's gate one of the sentries stopped her. "Who are you and where are you off to?"

Élise lowered her head like Garsenda taught her. "I'm Garsenda, servant to Lady Elisabeth du Chauvigny, taking a message from her to the cathedral school."

"You don't look like Garsenda," said the man.

Élise fought down an urge to cry, but thought of a quick lie that might help her. "Please, I also have a message for Hervé from my mistress's aunt."

The second guard said, "Let her pass, we can't afford any trouble with that demon."

They stood aside, letting her through the gate tunnel.

Once Élise set foot on the well-traveled dirt road from Chauvigny to Poitiers, she relaxed a bit. She was more than a little disturbed by the lies she had found herself telling ever since meeting with Hervé. She also began to wonder how Garsenda spoke of her with the other servants when she was not around.

Élise was not used to walking. After a while she found a boulder on the roadside and sat on it, fanning her face with her wimple, her dark hair a sweaty matted mess. The sound of approaching voices mingled with the clopping of hooves on the dry pounded dirt road. Élise looked up. A knight and his page were making their way to Chauvigny. Each rode a hackney while the knight's destrier followed closely, lead by a tether tied to the page's saddle. Élise figured the knight must be down on his luck, having only a hackney to ride, not a palfrey or roumsey. The destrier did not look like it had much spirit either; he'd not be found on the lists, that was certain.

Remembering what Garsenda had told her, she rose and curtsied, lowering her eyes. She was quite surprised when the clopping sound made by the hooves stopped in front of her. She did not dare to raise her eyes. The crunch of the boots on the ground made her skin crawl. Forcing her voice to be meek, she said, "May I be of service?"

"You can lift your skirts for me," said one of the men. Élise took a step backwards, wondering if this was a test of her faithfulness to Martis. Strong hands gripped each arm.

"Please, I've never known a man!" she cried.

"A comely wench like yourself! Ha! I'll believe that when I feel your sweet hymen's surrender. Now, lift your skirts or you'll regret it."

"No... please don't... uhf!" the words were knocked out of her as he hit her in the stomach. Doubled up in pain, Élise felt the hands of two men pushing her to the ground. When she finally found her breath, she choked on dust mingled with her tears.

Élise screamed, kicked and thrashed as she felt the weight of one of them, and his gritty calloused hands on her legs.

"The damned bitch pissed on me!" the man on her legs said as he pushed off the cloth covering her buttocks. She felt the other man force a gag into her mouth, pushing her head to the ground. She clenched her legs together as hard as she could, trying to twist herself from under the man. As she felt the heat of him slide between her legs, her thoughts raced in a desperate prayer, *Oh God! Please don't let this happen!*

As if in response, she felt a swoosh and a wet hot spray on her bare skin, followed by a haunting silence. Something landed next to her with a thud. The man who was holding her arms let go with a cry, "Mercy!"

Again, a swoosh, and again she felt a hot liquid hit the back of her bare legs. A pungent smell filled the air. *Blood.*

Not daring to open her eyes, she screamed into her gag as she felt the motionless weight on her legs removed.

"My lady," a familiar voice said, as unseen hands lowered her skirts. A rough finger brushed gently against her cheek, pulling out the cloth clenched between her teeth.

Sobbing, Élise rolled over and opened her eyes, recognizing Sir Ogier from her father's court. Thank God! But how?

He offered her a hand, and she took it as he helped her to her feet.

"How did you know?" she sobbed.

"My lady, the cook sent me to look after you on the road. As you learned just now, the roads are not safe for a servant to travel alone."

Élise wiped her eyes with her sleeve and took a deep breath. She had wanted to suffer to prove her chastity to Martis, but not this way. Thank the mercy of Sir Ogier.

"When you return, please give the cook my eternal gratitude. I'll arrange for a Mass to be said in her honor... and yours."

The knight offered her a handkerchief, which she used to scrub the mud off her face. Her heart quivered as she looked down at her two assailants, their heads lying in great pools of muddy blood.

"God bless, you have a mighty arm, Sir Ogier."

"Some knights feel that they can demand anything of a peasant. The world will not miss these two."

She returned his handkerchief, thinking of how often Garsenda would rub the ink off her face, and wondered if Garsenda had faced such dangers running the many errands she'd sent her on. Her resentment of the rough words she'd heard in the kitchen softened when she thought that no knight would have been sent to Garsenda's rescue.

Sir Ogier took the reins of all three horses in hand. "Come, my lady, let me walk next to you. There is a stream nearby. I'll water the horses and you can wash off that blood."

It was evening by the time they entered Poitiers. The crowded streets filled with merchants taking their empty carts from the market, and members of the court making their way through the street. She lowered her eyes and curtsied as the three daughters of a local count passed by, wearing square white caps and long white dresses, their hair hidden demurely under skin-tight wraps, proclaiming themselves to all the world as the pure women Élise knew them not to be, the harsh selfish shrills. They'd always delighted pulling rank on her at the cathedral school; she had no desire to catch their notice dressed as a peasant. She recognized Sir Hugo with his gold lace cuffs and gold-feathered hat hurrying off with his retinue in tow, thankfully too busy to do more than hail Sir Ogier in passing. That man was such a bore, though he backed his boasts with a mighty arm. Her eye was quickly caught by some bright cloth, laid out in a cart a merchant was pushing through the rutted dirt streets. A brilliant blue, which would go so lovely with Garsenda's eyes, lay on top of other fine rolls of damask, cotton and, to Élise's wonder, silk. She forced herself to look away and continue on. Her love for Martis was worth the sacrifice.

She discreetly led the way to the cathedral, trying to not let others see that she, a peasant, was leading the knight. Once she was on the steps, Élise turned back to Sir Ogier. "I owe you my virtue and perhaps my life."

The knight bowed. "I can only hope that my deeds today lessen my time in purgatory. Keep me in your prayers, my lady. I hope to God that you find Martis."

Longing for a bath and the tender care of Garsenda's gentle hands, Élise made her way into the cathedral school that had become her home whenever she took up residence in Poitiers.

The school was a large solid building of wood and plaster, just like a merchant's home, a fitting residence for the masters that lived there. In front of it stood a large platform, where plays were performed on feast days. Élise smiled as she remembered the play they had been working on, the struggle of the groom with the demon from Tobit. This place was home, safety.

Sunlight streaming through large lead-framed windows of diamond-shaped glass panes illuminated the large hallway inside. The white plaster made this place seem so joyful compared with the dull gray stone of the cathedral. As Élise walked the halls, she felt as if the walls welcomed her home.

She went straight to Master Raolett's studio, where she knew he would be sitting at his desk, writing.

The old man's smile of greeting dissolved into concern as he glanced over Élise's clothes. "Élise! Where are you off to, dressed like a filthy peasant in torn rags? Are you hurt?" His eyes rested on her torn sleeve. Following his eyes, she noticed it had a smear of blood on it. She must have missed that spot.

Élise stammered, momentarily flustered as to how much to tell. Her adventures would not be easy to relate, especially to a man. "Master Raolett, I'm off to find a unicorn, and I need your help." She briefly described her flight from Chauvigny. He winced when she talked about the attack along the road, but said nothing as she continued her narrative, for which she was grateful. "I need to leave in disguise, so that my own father would not recognize me."

"So, you not only wish to prove your virtue, but in doing so you would risk defying your father?"

"Yes."

"You realize that you may be violating one of the Ten Commandments, committing a mortal sin? Even if you are right about Hervé overstepping the authority granted him by your father, could you not go to Martis and submit to an exam by his father's physician?"

"Master Raolett, it is not my virginity his father doubts. It is my chastity. He does not think highly of the games of love played at Poitiers. He thinks every woman here is a flirt and a strumpet. I can't think of any way I can prove myself chaste other than a unicorn. Besides, there is also Garsenda's dream. After her aid in escaping that rascal, I owe her the chance to find it."

Master Raolett's thoughtful gaze made Élise's heart race. Anyone in his place would be much more likely to send her back to Hervé and a forced marriage than to help her. She offered a silent prayer that Master Raolett sees in her deeds a righteous act.

Master Raolett leaned back into his chair. With a hearty laugh, he slammed his fist onto his desk. "Then, you and Garsenda will travel as men."

Her eyes widened. "As men?" If caught, she'd be killed. It was forbidden for a woman to dress as a man. Well, if she was to risk damnation for not respecting her father, dressing as a man was not so great a sin.

"You want to go unnoticed, don't you?"

"But how? I lack a man's build and strength. I suppose Garsenda could pass for a boy."

"Let me worry about that. First, let me find you quarters, and a private bath."

Over the next few days, Master Raolett's staff set onto the task of transforming Élise from a slim young woman into a pot-bellied man. She had to cut her hair, shaving a good part of it off to make it look as if she was bald. She cried while he cut her tresses, secretly grateful that there was no mirror in his chambers. Those were the only tears she allowed herself, though she woke each night screaming. Her nightmares were of the blood spilled, that of her maidenhood. Afterwards, she lay awake under her sweat-soaked blankets, curled into a ball, listening to the monks chant the hours, shaking in the fear of remembrance. She missed Garsenda most during those times, Garsenda's gentle hands had often helped her when ridden by nightmares, rubbing away tension and worry.

The clothing they found for her would not look right unless she wore padding underneath to hide her womanly curves and breasts. The padding made her look barrel-chested, with a large belly and rolls of fat over her hips. In a strange way, Élise enjoyed the transformation. Those rolls of simulated fat made her feel safer than the stoutest hauberk of mail. No one would think of raping the portly man the costume turned her into.

They dressed her as a master troubadour. It was a role that fit her well, with her love of music and poetry. The found her a small knee harp with a case fitted with a strap for easy portage. The best thing in this costume was that it had her clothing and pack sewn into it as part of the padding, including a wig made of her own hair which she could wear until it grew back, once she felt safe in resuming the mantle of womanhood.

"What do you think? Will I pass?" she asked Master Raolett when it was done, pitching her voice deep and low, like a man's.

The master shook his head. "Good question. You should live in the costume for a few days before your departure. Get used to acting as men act."

One morning, as she broke her bread with the Masters, the doors of the dining hall opened to admit Garsenda. Élise's heart raced with joy.

Garsenda looked thinner, and there were dark circles under her eyes. Still, her dress was dry and clean, so she obviously managed to make the journey without being beset with danger.

Garsenda curtsied and said, "Pardon me masters, but I'm looking for my mistress, the Lady Elisabeth du Chauvigny."

Élise jumped up from her seat and laughed, speaking in her natural voice for the first time in days. "Garsenda, I'm right here!"

Garsenda's eyes widened and her mouth fell open, "My lady! What strange enchantment has befallen you?"

Élise rushed to her maid and clutched her hands, their familiar touch sending relief through her body. She missed Garsenda, but only now did she realize how lonely she had been without her. "No enchantment Garsenda. Rather, to escape my father's seneschal and permit me to travel without an escort, Master Raolett has disguised me as a man."

"But your beautiful hair?"

"Will grow back. However, now I can leave the city without my father's seneschal being able to stop me. Have you broken your fast?"

"Yes, mistress, I ate."

"Garsenda, until it is safe to drop the disguise, you must call me Master Guion. Did they let you go easily? Were you able to leave the Château without being molested? You must tell me all the details."

BROUGHT

Gwen would never talk about how she came to be possessed. All Britomar would tell me is that one day Gwen started acting oddly, frightening the small animals that had always brought her food. Even the wolves began to whimper when they approached with an offering in their mouths. They would no longer get close enough for an ear rub, but drop the food and run off, tails between their legs. Britomar realized something was wrong but didn't know what. Nor did she know what to do about it, until the day Gwen tossed off her clothes and complained about the heat as cold autumn rain began to fall.

Britomar waited until Gwen's back was turned and forced herself to approach her, something that had been so easy just days before. When Britomar touched Gwen with her horn, Gwen shouted out, "Stop it, you silly beast, that hurt!"

"I'm so sorry. Are you ready to depart?"

"Do we have to keep to the hills and woods?"

Britomar rolled her eyes and pawed at the ground. Instead of running, she answered, "Yes, it is too dangerous for me to be seen. You know men will want my horn."

"Yes, yes, I'm sorry, I forgot. It's just—well, let's get going then." Gwen approached her, naked without the pack that lay near the still-smoldering campfire.

"Don't you need your pack?" Britomar found that looking away from Gwen allowed her to slow her breathing. "And shouldn't you dress?"

"Dear, how forgetful of me, yes, of course I need my pack." Gwen turned to pick it up. "But if you don't mind, I'll stay as I am; it's so hot, I don't know how you stand your fur."

Britomar clenched her teeth as Gwen climbed upon her back. The moment the maid was seated, the unicorn bolted. Trees blurred as she raced the wind.

Whatever had happened, Gwen needed help, help Britomar couldn't give. She needed to find other humans. She only hoped they would help Gwen, not seek to kill Britomar for her horn.

61

Tired and damp from hours of trudging through a thick fog, Adelie crested a hill, relieved to find that up there the mists thinned. She saw a sprawling building up ahead, with many windows and a large stable. An inn? Her stomach growled as she caught the scent of baking bread. She had used up the food in her wallet the day before, and had not yet found anything to eat. With any luck, they'd honor her pilgrim's badge. If not, she'd just take what she needed. Adelie knew from her dreams that the unicorn needed her soon. God would forgive the thefts.

At this hour the inn would probably be quiet. Adelie quickly descended the hill, headed straight to the door. As she stepped into the building, she shook the raindrops off her mantle and draped it over her arm.

The hall was warm and spacious. Three old men sat next to the hearth to her right, two playing a game of chess while the other watched. A maid in a brown dress with a dirty apron carried three tankards of ale to the men, placing them on the table next to the chessboard. As she turned to leave, Adelie called after her, "Could you fetch me the innkeeper?"

The maid wiped her hands on her apron. "He's busy and I'd not disturb him right now for any coin. I'd get a good thrashing if I did."

Adelie smirked. If he was anything like the owner of the last place she'd worked at, he was probably lifting the skirts of a chambermaid. "Where may I wait for him?"

"You wait right here, he'll be down before long. Where's the rest of your entourage?"

"My what?"

"Are you simple, girl? Where are the other pilgrims?"

"I got separated from the main group. I'm hoping to rejoin them."

"They were here two days ago. How did you get so—"

Adelie was grateful as a bellow from up the stairs interrupted the chambermaid's question. "Excuse me," said the maid, "that'd be the master. Wait here."

Adelie did not have to wait long before he came down the steps, a burly man with thin black hair and a fleshing chin, pulling the belt tight around his midriff.

"I'm Thomas, the keeper of this inn. What do you want?"

"Master, I'm Adelie. I need a room to stay for a night. I'm trying to catch up with my group, we got separated." She hated the lie as she spoke it, but she hated the emptiness in her stomach worse.

"Another damned pilgrim eh? All right, you can stay the night and eat in the common room. Now get out of my sight. Too many more pilgrims and I'll have to close up."

Élise was cursing like a knight of station by the time they had crested the damp grassy hill. She looked ahead and saw what she'd been told to expect, a large building with shuttered windows and white plaster walls. It had to be the inn the peasants had told her about. Good, at least they didn't lose their direction in the dark. Garsenda was already heading towards the inn, so she hurried to catch up, leaning heavily on her staff.

Even with their goal in sight, travel was slow and painstaking as neither woman could see much by the light of their tin lanterns. When they finally reached the oak door of the inn, Élise's heart quivered as she failed to hear any sounds inside. If the patrons had all retired, the innkeeper might not let them in until morning. Still, no harm in trying.

She banged on the door with her staff until she heard shutters thrown open above and a rough voice call out, "We're shut up for the night! Go sleep in the stables!"

Forcing her voice into a deep, resonant timbre, she shouted, "I need a good fire to dry my harp's strings."

"A troubadour?"

"Yes. I'm Master Guion."

"I'll be right down."

Élise tried not to chuckle as she heard the innkeeper swear as he struggled to close the shutters flapping in the wind. After a long silence, the latch clicked and the inn's door swung open. A fat man, candle stump in his hand, beckoned her and Garsenda inside.

"Follow me," he said, and the two women followed him through the dark halls and stairs until into a large chamber. He stooped next to the hearth and removed a piece of kindling, holding it to his candle until it held a good flame. He then tossed the kindling back into the hearth, blowing gently until the flame had spread.

The room, revealed by the faint red light from the hearth, was spacious enough, with a curtained bed in the center large enough for them both to sleep comfortably.

The innkeeper swept the room with a welcoming gesture. "Master Guion, the room and board are yours, if you grace my common room with song."

Élise smiled. She'd like nothing better. "You can expect me at dusk."

Adelie was surprised to find a few knights in the common room, along with the more usual crowd of merchants and pilgrims. The presence of these noble soldiers made her nervous. Perhaps some of them swore fealty to the Baron du Chauvigny? Still, it was unlikely that they would know her.

Could she afford to stay the day to hear the troubadour everyone talked so much about? Troubadour music ranked chief amongst the few happy memories she had. Still, she did not relish the beating she'd get if Thomas caught her staying for more than just breakfast. She had to blend in.

Adelie found a dark corner and settled in for a long day of waiting.

As the afternoon wore off, she managed to join up with a group of pilgrims that arrived soon after the midday. They treated her like a lost member of their group and entertained her with many tales of the last few days of their journey, some of them quite amusing. While no one remembered her, there were enough of them that no one thought this odd.

Shortly after the evening meal was served, the room became quiet in a reverent hush. A portly man carrying a battered harp meandered to a bench that three patrons quickly vacated.

The troubadour was the ugliest man Adelie had ever seen. His potbelly, rolls of fat, and saggy arms stood strangely at odds with his thin boyish face. He moved with awkward uncertainty as he collapsed on the vacated bench, his young assistant next to him taking out a tambour and a flute.

Without fanfare or introduction, the troubadour began to play.

The melody took hold of Adelie's heart. She forgot about the unicorn's need, or grief for her mother. She could feel the rhythm of the strings echoing in her chest, easing her worries, bringing out a smile where only weariness had been for too long.

She wished her mother could be here.

The troubadour's assistant took up the tambour and began to drum out a lively beat matching the cadence of the harp. As Adelie's heart danced with the music, she realized that she was happy for the first time since she sat on her mother's lap, tracing the letters her mother had tried so hard to teach her.

Then the troubadour began to sing. His voice surprised her, high and lilty, clear like a robin's song, refreshing like a cold wind on a summer day. Not at all the voice of any man she'd ever heard before.

He was singing a joyful song to the blessed virgin:

> *Virgo sola existente en affuit angelus.*
> *Gabriel est appelatus atque missus celitus.*
> *Clara facieque dixit: Ave Maria,*
> *Clara facieque dixit: Ave Maria,*
> *Cuncti simun concanentes: Ave Maria !*

Adelie joined in with the rest of the pilgrims, singing along at the top of her lungs: *Cuncti simun concanentes: Ave Maria!*

The merchants began to clap in rhythm with the tambour, even some of the soldiers joined in, tapping their feet to the beat of the music.

> *Clara facieque dixit, audit karissimi,*
> *En concipies, Maria: Ave Maria !*
> *Cuncti simun concanentes: Ave Maria !*
> *Cuncti simun concanentes: Ave Maria !*

As the song went on, more voices joined in, until the entire common room erupted in the final chorus of *Cuncti simun concanentes: Ave Maria!*

Élise did not wait until the applause had died down before she began to pluck a martial beat on her harp, to which Garsenda added the deep resonance of the tambour.

> *"Chevalier, mult estes guariz,*
> *Quant Deu a vus fait sa clamur*
> *Des Turs e des Amor—"*

Slam!

Élise stopped singing in mid word, her hands frozen against the strings of her harp as she looked up at the sudden noise. There was an echoing clang as Garsenda's tambour fell to the floor.

The door to the inn swung wildly in the wind, filling the room with a fresh smell of a thunderstorm.

Beyond the threshold stood a unicorn. A slim young woman lay on her back, naked as a newborn babe, her copper-brown curls plastered wet to her face, neck and shoulders.

Élise slowly put aside her harp and rose. She shivered with gratitude for the miracle that brought a unicorn to her. She desired nothing more than to kiss the miraculous beast, let the beautiful creature rest its head in her lap.

As she took a step to the door, the woman on the unicorn's back fell to the floor with a groan.

Élise rushed to the woman, pushed aside her wet curls, and touched her forehead. The woman was burning with fever. Élise frowned. Something was amiss; unicorns were well known to cure illness with a touch of their horn. What could feign such sickness?

"I can't help her," said the unicorn, as if hearing Élise's thoughts. "I tried this morning. I'm so worried."

A young pilgrim girl slipped to Élise's side, covering the shivering woman with her cloak.

"Please," said the unicorn, "Can you help Gwenaella?"

Élise turned to Garsenda. "Pierre; come here. We need to bring this maiden to a warm room where we can have a fire. Get the innkeeper!"

She could think of only one thing that would make a woman so sick even a unicorn couldn't cure her. Élise just hoped she remembered everything the priest had taught her about what they'd done in the book of Tobit to be rid of a demon.

The pilgrim girl rose and whispered something in the unicorn's ear. To Élise's annoyance, the unicorn nodded, then turned and slipped into the shadows before she too could speak to it, could ask for the favor of a touch of its horn. No matter, once the maid was tended to, the unicorn was bound to aid her in repayment. She turned impatiently, spotting the fat innkeeper hurrying up to their side.

"Thomas," she said, trying to make her voice sound calm, deep and manly, "A unicorn brought us this girl. She's being tormented by demons. I'll need you to bring me the liver and heart of a fish, and something to burn them in. Bring them to my chambers at once."

"Who are you to tell me what to do in my house?" the innkeeper demanded. His eyes narrowed in suspicion. "What would a troubadour know about getting rid of demons? There is no way I'm letting you—" his words fell into a grunt as the pilgrim girl suddenly appeared at his side, with a knife to his throat.

"You were saying?"

"You wouldn't dare harm me, these good knights will pro—" a prick of a knife at his throat cut his words short.

Élise raised her voice, "What say you, good knights? Does not our pilgrim have the right of it? Shall not our host take in the maiden that the unicorn brought to us, seeking the cure for what ails her?"

"Bring her in," bellowed a dark man with a rich mustache.

"But my good knights, my holy pilgrims, would you have me aid this maid to drive away the demons that torment her?"

"By all that is holy, yes!" shouted one of the other pilgrims. "Our good troubadour has the right of what is needed to save the dear maid's soul. Stop being such a fool, innkeeper, and fetch what the troubadour demands."

Two pilgrims helped Adelie to carry the maid behind the troubadour and his apprentice. The woman still shivered under the thick mantle, but to Adelie's hands she felt hot enough to burn. After laying her down on the mattress, Adelie brushed a sweaty curl from the forehead of the maid. She longed to go after the unicorn, find out if this was the reason behind her dreams, but whoever this Gwenaella was, she needed Adelie's protection lest that fat innkeeper try to throw her out again.

The innkeeper hurried in, setting a heavy iron skillet and two jars on a small table near the hearth. He then retreated along with the pilgrims, throwing fearful glances at the sickly girl, as if the demons possessing her would come out and devour them any moment. Adelie stayed, hoping to remain unnoticed in the shadows by the bed.

The troubadour placed the skillet on the hearthstones, lifted the organs and whispered over them—likely a blessing, though Adelie couldn't follow the Latin. He then lowered them into the skillet. Soon a thick foul smoke began to emerge from the skillet, its smell making Adelie gag. The room became hazy. She did her best not to cough as the troubadour lifted the skillet, brought it to the bed, and drew the curtains shut.

Gwen couldn't breathe, a foul smell choking her, pushing down on her chest. She began to writhe and flung up her hands to push it away.

Someone near her pleaded, "Breathe!"

How could she breathe when someone was pushing on her? She struggled, her lungs screaming in protest. Then, when she couldn't hold in anymore, she let out a gasp.

She was convinced that this one breath would kill her, filling her with the poisonous smoke. But to her surprise all she felt was relief. She felt as if the cold hand grasping her chest faded from her, leaving her body to rest peacefully on the mattress.

Memories of the past few weeks flooded her thoughts. Oh God! What had she done! What had she been thinking? Could Britomar ever forgive her?

Gwen opened her eyes, to see a portly man standing beside her bed. When the man met her eyes he nodded briefly, then turned and threw open the bed curtains, revealing the rest of the room.

A thin young woman in tattered clothes stood in the shadows behind the bed holding a knife. Her short flaxen hair was tangled and matted, her thin, freckled face frowning in concern as she watched Gwen. She also nodded as she met Gwen's gaze, the tension in her face dissolving into relief. Gwen looked further to a young man on the other side of the room tending a roaring fire. A crucifix hung nearby and Gwen felt comforted as her eyes fell upon it. *Dear Lord.* He had promised forgiveness even upon His death.

Gwen completed her prayer and sat up in bed. The questions that came to mind spilled out of her.

"What happened? Where's Britomar?..."

The portly man frowned. "I must assume Britomar is the name of the unicorn that brought you here." His voice sounded odd, forced somehow.

"Yes." Gwen wringed her nose. "What's that horrible smell?"

"Burning fish entrails." The man waved away Gwen's questioning glance as he continued. "Britomar left after she brought you in. I assume she will be coming back for you."

"How did I get well, then, if Britomar wasn't here?"

"Burning the liver and heart of a fish will drive out some demons."

"*Demons?*" Gwen blanched. Had she been possessed?

"Yes. A demon had taken hold of your body and was trying to kill you."

Gwen sat back, looking at the strange man in disbelief. "How would a troubadour know how to drive out demons?"

The troubadour's giggle was light and musical, and definitely feminine. "Since you're the unicorn's companion, I feel no need to hide from you. I'm neither a troubadour, nor a man, though I'm disguised as one. My apprentice who tends the fire is actually my maid servant, Garsenda. I am Lady Elisabeth, but please call me Élise."

"I'm sorry, I'm being rude. I'm Gwenaella, please call me Gwen. Who is she?" Gwen's eyes traced over to the pilgrim girl, still silent in her corner.

Élise shrugged. "All I know is that she covered your nakedness with her mantle and defended you from that fool, the innkeeper."

The pilgrim girl stepped forward. "I'm Adelie." Her eyes darted to Elise. "What could cause you to travel as a man, when you're a lady and all?"

"My father's seneschal tried to force me into a marriage. The disguise served to get me and my maid out of the city. I am on a quest to find a unicorn to prove my chastity to my beloved's father, so he'd allow us to marry."

Adelie's mouth softened, the set of her shoulders relaxing a bit as she glanced from Élise back to Gwen. "That is odd, I was also looking for a unicorn. I've been having the oddest dreams about a unicorn who needs me to protect her from a disaster."

Garsenda whirled and stared at Adelie. Now that Gwen could see her standing, she wondered how anyone could mistake that delicate smooth face for that of a man. She leaned forward, letting out a sigh of relief. "Then you must be one of the people Nimuë promised to send to help us! Please, Adelie, you must come with us and help the unicorns."

"What help can I offer to the unicorn?" asked Adelie.

"Her king is dying. We're trying to get to the Garden at the Center of the World, and bring him some fruit from this Garden to restore his health." Gwen stared at the shuttered window as if her eyes alone could thrust them open. "I have no idea where it is."

"Why?" asked Élise, "Why risk your life, your soul for him? The unicorn is beautiful, but they're only beasts. Can't they choose a new king?"

Gwen and Adelie both turned to her, their faces showing impatience.

"Their king walked with Adam in the garden of Eden," Gwen said. "He remembers men from before the fall. We can't let that last bit of innocence die. Besides, I made a promise to a sorceress. A promise I must keep even if I risk losing my soul."

Élise gasped. "That is a task worthy of a song. But it is just as likely to bring about your death as his salvation."

Gwen shook her head. At least if she died, she might be with Guillaume again.

"I don't know. I have no idea how I'm supposed to do this. God knows I'm no saint."

"Well it seems obvious that Adelie is sent to help you, and perhaps I can be of some help as well. I'm certain meeting Gwen and her unicorn is not a coincidence and I, Lady Elisabeth du Chauvigny—"

Adelie shrieked, pulling out her knife in a flash. "You're his daughter!"

"Adelie, what is wrong?" Gwen asked as Garsenda rushed forward to shield her mistress.

Adelie's full lips curled in a snarl. "Baron du Chauvigny's soldiers killed my Mama. He wants me dead too, he sent soldiers after you. And you—you're his daughter!" She spat out the last word as if it was a curse.

Élise stood back, with a dumbfounded expression. Then, slowly, her own lips curled into an expression that resembled Adelie's. "Hervé. My father's seneschal. That son of the devil! Papa would never do such a thing!" She turned to Adelie, her expression softening. "I'm sorry about your Mama. Was she a lady?"

Adelie lifted her chin, her eyes meeting Élise's with a challenge. "She was a whore."

"What makes you think the baron would wish you dead?" Garsenda asked.

Adelie's lips twitched again. She continued to hold Élise's gaze. "I'm his bastard. I've been running from his sergeants for as long as I can remember. Each time they find me, they've tried to kill me."

Élise raised her hands and swept past Garsenda to Adelie's side. "We're sisters! Papa would never kill any of his bastards, never. He loves his children, all of them. And he is on a Holy Crusade now. It must be Hervé. He locked me in my rooms to force me to marry the Prince of Armenia, knowing full well that Martis loved me and sought my hand. I could see him doing what you say to keep the line of succession under his control. Now, please, put down the knife. You wouldn't stab your own sister, would you?"

Adelie lowered her knife. "I'm sorry. I've been running from your father's soldiers for a very long time. And, whether Hervé or our father is responsible for my exile, I shouldn't blame you, my lady."

"We shall be like Le Fresne and La Codre," said Élise.

"Like an Ash and a Hazel my lady?" asked Adelie.

"No." Élise giggled. "Like the two sisters in the Lai le Fresne. Garsenda, could you help me out of this costume? Time to become women again. Adelie, please call me Élise."

Garsenda helped Élise out of the hidden lacing that held the costume together, revealing a shapely woman with full breasts and short raven-black hair.

Élise said, "In Paris, the Church has recently founded a new University. I understand that they are sending their best and brightest to teach there. I can gain you access to the court and get you a letter of admission so that you can ask one of the doctors how to help the unicorns. In fact, I am heading in that direction myself, and would be delighted to journey with you and do you this favor. In the morning I will seek out Thomas and arrange to purchase some mounts for us. I imagine the unicorn, Britomar must be in a hurry to bring the fruit back to her king."

Gwen's heart lightened. Perhaps the Lord had used her weakness to bring her to the very people who could help her and Britomar. She threw open the shutters to let out the remnants of the stench of the burnt fish livers.

In the distance, a unicorn galloped through the rain, its coat shining like a moonbeam. *Britomar.*

"We must go down to Britomar at once," said Gwen. "Our quest is urgent. Besides, I must seek her forgiveness."

Adelie glared at Lady Elisabeth but nodded her ascent. Gwen couldn't blame Adelie for her mistrust of her newly found half-sister, but right now, she was glad to have company. Perhaps if she was not alone, perhaps she could avoid—no she wouldn't even think of it. The remembrance of the demon was too horrible. Anything would be better than facing the demons alone.

Translator's note:

This is one of the spots in the manuscript where the text had become damaged, and the dialog between the women and Britomar can't be made out.

WAYLAID

Adelie looked at the shadows between the trees, hesitant to leave the clearing and search for firewood. The paths Britomar took them on were far away from the villages and towns, and Adelie was surprised at how much she missed the crowds and how much she resented walking in the forest alone.

She glanced at Garsenda unpacking the saddlebags, Lady Elisabeth rubbing down the horses, and Gwenaella gathering stones in a circle to create a safe place for a fire. They had all seemed content. Adelie was surprised she couldn't feel this way.

After she joined up with Gwen and Britomar her dreams had stopped haunting her, confirming that she must have found the task she had been called to do. She was happy to do something meaningful for the first time in her life, but to learn that the dreams had originated with a sorceress, and that demons lurked in the shadows hunting for her soul, made Adelie shiver just by thinking about it.

Demons had always seemed to be nothing more than the threats given by churchmen who used it as a means to get her to lift her skirts. Seeing Gwen in the grips of a demon made Adelie realize how serious it could be. She didn't want to face such things. She was nothing special, just a whore's beget, and if a person like Gwen could become possessed, what chance did she have?

Besides, she didn't think she could be of help to either Gwen or Britomar. Lady Elisabeth—no, she would not think of her as a sister—seemed to be giving them all the help they needed, between buying the horses for everyone, having her servant do all the cooking, and promising the access to the University. All Adelie ever did was gather firewood.

She pushed through the brush. It was not easy to find dry branches and by the time the pile in her arms grew to the size that she knew would last them the night, the sun was already setting. She stopped for a moment, adjusting the wood, and froze. Her skin prickled at the unnatural silence. She couldn't remember the last time she heard a bird sing.

Something was wrong.

Trying to move as quietly as she could, she crept back to the clearing where she had left the others. As she got closer, she smelled smoke, a fire plainly visible through the trees. How? With what wood?

Fighting the urge to pant, Adelie quietly put down the wood she carried and stalked around the clearing. There. As she crept closer, she saw the women, bound and gagged, in the center of the clearing. Her eyes darted further, noting the two men warming their hands over the fire.

Bandits! Were there others? And, where was Britomar? Looking around, she spied another man at the far edge of the clearing, near the stream where they had hung some wash. He was looking into the forest as he walked the perimeter.

The lookout. This meant that with any luck, that was all of them. But Adelie had to make sure.

She sat down quietly to wait.

As the sun began to set, a fourth man emerged from the other side of the clearing.

"It's no use, I can't track those horses in the night," he said.

"Damned shame it is, they would've brought us a lot of gold!" answered another, poking the fire with his dagger. "Guess we'll have to take our coin from selling these women then."

"They'll fetch a good price, especially the fine lady."

Adelie watched as they ate some dried meat, and drank from their flasks. Then two of them wrapped in cloaks and settled down to sleep on the opposite sides of the fire. Another man remained sitting, tending the fire. The fourth stepped over to the bushes, pacing to patrol the perimeter.

Adelie slipped her knife out of her belt, knowing that this was her best chance.

She waited until the one man's patrol took him within paces of where she was hiding. As he passed her, she could smell his sweat. She waited, then stepped out of the bush, taking great care not to make a sound. Taking a deep breath, she sprung forward, her hand over his mouth, pulling his chin up and back as she dug her knife into his throat.

She let out a breath and dropped the body to the ground.

"Jacques?" The bandit by the fire called, peering into the forest. Adelie slid into the bushes, her heart pounding, trying hard not to puke. She had just killed a man. Dear God.

"Get up! Something took down Jacques!"

Damnation! They were all awake now, her one advantage gone.

One of the men picked up a branch from the fire, and held it in front of him as he walked to where Jacques lay on the ground, the yellow glow deepening the shadows around him.

As the bandit leaned over his fallen comrade, Adelie sprang from the bushes, knife at ready. His knife met hers as he rose. She parried and slashed at his side. Behind him she could see his fellows running to join the fray.

The bandit crouched, knife in front, beckoning with his free hand. She tossed her knife to her left, feinted a stab, taunting with a grin, "I'm gonna feed you your balls!"

He growled and sprang at her. His arm hit her knife hand, brushing it aside. She used his momentum to pull him past her and down. She landed on his back and slashed his throat.

She moved like a lightning as she snatched up his knife, leapt backwards and landed on her feet in one fluid move. The two remaining men reached her, clubs raised. They swung widely and she skipped back, dancing between them. Pain exploded in her shoulder as one of the clubs connected. She bit back the cry, her left arm limp, and focused on dodging the blows.

Head to the forest. She skipped back again, arm burning with each movement. In the woods she was just as likely to trip over a root, but they'd have trouble with those clubs, and the trees would protect her back. Swing, leap. He's off balance! Adelie threw her knife and caught him in his stomach. He doubled over in pain.

She reached for the knife that she still held in her useless left hand. The last bandit cautiously stalked her. Now it was almost even—if only. Swing, skip—ooof! He caught her on the leg, and she fell. With a prayer in desperation she threw the knife, and missed.

With an evil grin on his face, the bandit raised his club over her. Adelie braced for the blow, her heart pounding so loud she could hear it. Wait, it wasn't her heart. The sound came from the outside, and it was getting louder. *Hoofs!*

A flash of white streaked through the air. The bandit's grin faded to shock as a white shape landed between him and Adelie. The sharp horn burst through his abdomen with a spray of blood. *Britomar!*

The unicorn pulled her horn from the fallen bandit, wiped it on the grass, and then touched it to Adelie's shoulder. Joyous warmth spread through her body, melting away the pain and the numbness in her arm and leg. She shivered, wishing for this joy to last forever, but Britomar leaned away and it passed, leaving an emptiness behind.

Adelie clamored to her feet, hugged Britomar, and then rushed to the others.

The three women looked horrible, their faces bruised and smeared with blood and dirt. Tears glistened on Élise's cheeks. Wrinkling her nose at the smell of urine, Adelie removed their gags and asked, "Are you hurt bad?"

"No," Élise sobbed, "Just frightened and bruised. You are the bravest woman I've ever met. How did you ever learn to fight like that?"

"Dodging our father's soldiers all those years taught me a thing or two." That, and a kindly nun in the convent she'd run to when Jean had thrown her on the street. Sister Catherine had learned to fight before she gave up her station and took her vows. She had taught Adelie everything she knew. Thank God. Suddenly woozy, Adelie sank on the ground, staring at her hands. Blood. So much blood. What had she done? In all those years of fighting for her survival, she'd never killed.

She was only vaguely aware of Britomar brushing past to lay her horn on Garsenda. The purple blotches on the maid's face lightened to a bright pink, and then faded. Britomar then did the same for Élise and Gwen.

Garsenda stooped in front of Adelie and offered her hand. "We've got to clean you up. Let's move camp, and then see to it."

"But—the horses—" Adelie started to say when she saw the horses enter the clearing and prance over to Britomar who greeted them each, nuzzle to nuzzle.

Adelie glanced back at the dark forms of her fallen enemies. It would be good to get away from them. "Yes, let's get out of here."

Garsenda helped Adelie to stand. They quickly loaded their horses and made their way upstream until they found another clearing. There Garsenda and Gwen led Adelie to the stream, where Garsenda washed her clothes while Gwen helped Adelie scrub herself clean.

Naked, Adelie emerged from the stream, cold and shivering. Britomar trotted over and laid her horn first on one shoulder, then the other.

Adelie shivered, watching the water disappear from her skin. Her hair dried, a flaxen cloud shrouding her shoulders in warm, silky folds. She hadn't felt this clean and refreshed in years.

"There you are, my brave one," said Britomar. "Climb on me and rest there while your clothes dry by the fire."

Gwen held out her palms, with her fingers clasped together. Adelie placed her foot in Gwen's hands and swung the other over Britomar's back. *I just killed three men and maimed another. Why do I feel so happy? I'm so full of life, I feel like I'm in love with the whole world! Is this what Gwen felt as she rode Britomar through the storm?*

Is this how the demons got to Gwen? Through joy? I want the whole world to see me up here! Naked beautiful me! Ah, that's what happened to Gwen. Pride. What a delicious way to fall.

Élise held the skillet over the flames, watching Adelie sitting on the unicorn's back, Garsenda scrubbing her bloodstained clothing in the river. The smell of the frying sausage mingled with that of her urine-soaked skirt. Élise wished she had washed herself clean of her shame, but that would mean getting Garsenda to stop helping Adelie. No, she'll wait until her famished, exhausted companions had eaten and rested near the warm fire.

Ow! That fire was hot! Élise put the pan down briefly, wrapped her hand in her skirt, and returned the skillet to the flames. Her nose wrinkled as she realized the sausages were burning. *Damnation! Can't I even cook a simple meal?* She pulled the skillet off the fire and set the pan on the ground.

She looked at Adelie on Britomar's back and noticed that her face was drawn, wearing a worn and haggard look. *My poor sister.* Pride rose in her chest when she thought of how Adelie defended all of them against four men. Father would be so proud of her if he knew he had a lioness as a daughter. She should be singing her praises, not sitting here idly over burnt sausages...

Singing? Why not? Élise went and found her harp among the packs. She spent a few moments testing the tuning, closed her eyes and began to play. After finding a melody that pleased her, she began to sing.

> *I sing to you of a maid who defied death*
> *Her triumph over bandit's designs*
> *Who did in the dark forest flowereth*
> *Into a chevalier like the Leonine*
>
> *With her long knife her cunning rescueth*
> *Of fellow maidens caught in evil's snare*
> *Bound and battered, their spirits languisheth*
> *Until their bold rescue which she did dare*
>
> *Having no more light than fading moonshine*
> *The life from their leader's throat she did tear*

Roused the wicked with hopes to undermine,
Those left alive rose to fight, devil-may-care

The first to reach her died fast from her knife
His knife cut the belly of his fellow
Thus did the maid deprive each of his life
To hell she sent them, well welcomed below

The last bandit thought this strife would endith
With him as the victor as the maid fell
He raised his club cruelly to give her death
Heaven sent her aid so all would be well

A unicorn, friend of the maid who fought
Slew him in his moment of conquest
For with Gods grace the best help was brought
This worthy maid saved the unicorn's quest

Élise plucked the final notes on her harp and opened her eyes. In front of her sat Gwen, staring at Élise with the awe that brought tears to her eyes. Adelie slid off of Britomar's back and knelt in front of Élise. "That was beautiful, thank you."

"What was beautiful was how you fought."

Gwen smiled at them. "You both did something beautiful here."

Garsenda, who had just finished hanging Adelie's clothes on some nearby bushes joined them but said nothing of the song. She picked up the skillet and gave it a shake. "Let's eat these before they get cold."

Élise said nothing, but noticed Garsenda grimacing as she cut the burnt sausages open.

After they ate, Élise finally took the bath she longed for, submitting to Garsenda's capable hands that scrubbed her back and rinsed her clothes in the stream.

As Élise finished putting on a dry shift, there was a sudden fluttering of wings, and a large raven landed in the clearing. It hopped over to the women, tilted its head and said, "kraak."

Élise backed away from it as it hopped, and started as it lifted into the air, and landed on Gwen's shoulder.

"Whatever do you want?" Gwen said to the bird.

It kraaked again, adjusting itself a few times.

Adelie shook her head. "Well, it seems you have a friend."

"When Britomar and I were alone, many creatures came to us

bringing food. What do you bring?" Gwen ruffled the shaggy black feathers on the bird's neck. This it seemed to appreciate, shifting so her hand ruffled a spot on its breast. "And why do you come to us now?"

The raven shot back into the air. Élise's eyes followed its flight as it swooped down stream towards where Adelie had fought the bandits. It flew over the bare treetops to disappear from her sight. She stared at the horizon for a moment and then shrugged her shoulders. That raven was the oddest thing, but it was gone.

She called Garsenda over to help her get into her dress when she heard Gwen exclaim, "Look, it's coming back!"

This time the raven landed straight away on Gwen's shoulder. It had something in its mouth.

"Why it's my pouch!" gasped Adelie. "It must have fallen off my belt. In our rush to leave, I never noticed it was missing. "

Élise took a long look at the raven who dropped the pouch into Adelie's hand and puffed up its feathers in response to her thanks. She'd long thought that ravens must be creatures that preferred the company of sorcerers and witches. She could not trust anything that feasted on carrion. Gwen had mentioned a promise to a sorceress. Perhaps, the raven was her familiar? Élise would be glad when their journey to Paris was over and she could present herself to Martis as the chaste maid she was.

As they traveled through the woods, Élise felt a tightness in her throat each time Britomar left to scout out the land ahead. She didn't feel safe without the unicorn by their side, especially with that raven always about. As Britomar faded into the woods, joy seemed to go with her. Traveling as a woman again made her feel so vulnerable. Would that they hadn't discarded their troubadour costumes.

Finally, Britomar came back one night to tell them that the edge of the forest was within a day's travel. They were getting close to Paris.

"This forest must be Fontainebleau," said Élise as they all gathered round the fire. "I know that the king has recently completed the fortification of Paris. We'll not be unable to bring Britomar into the city unobserved."

"I'm not eager to enter the city anyway," said Britomar, "I'm still not certain that we'll find what we seek there."

Élise smiled. "The university must have someone who has heard of the Garden, and perhaps knows of its location. I think it a worthwhile gamble."

"I don't want to enter Paris either," said Gwen, looking down at the ground. "I would stay with Britomar, here in the forest."

"Would that be safe?" asked Adelie.

"Safer than a country girl in a large city," said Garsenda. "I think Gwen has the right idea. The main problem we'll have is how long does she wait for us, and where will we meet with her?"

"Your scents are distinctive and known to me," Britomar said. "I'll know you are coming hours before you arrive, if the winds are right. Come a day's ride into the forest and wait three dry days. Gwenaella and I should not be far. If we have not found you, we are no longer here."

Élise, sat up, her heart beating fast. Ever since the attack in the woods, she'd been having trouble sleeping. Every shadow held a bandit, every sound betrayed a rapist. She heard someone walking. Carefully turning, she saw Gwen pacing by the fire.

"Can't sleep either?" Élise said softly.

"Élise! You startled me."

"Sorry," she said as she rose and wrapped herself in her blanket. She joined Gwen by the fire. "What is bothering you?"

"Somewhere in that city is the man who killed my Guillaume. I can't bear the thought that he is so close... What keeps you awake?"

"I'm terrified of being attacked by more bandits. What if Adelie hadn't come back just then? What if they had moved us before Britomar came back?"

"But it ended well, we're all fine."

"I keep telling myself that, but I don't think I could bear a third attack."

"Third?"

"Yes. Gwen, I've never told any of the others this, but I was nearly raped fleeing my father. I had dressed as a peasant woman, and ran into a Chevalier who tried to take me."

Gwen's hands covered her mouth, her eyes widened in horror. "How horrible! How did you escape such a terrible fate?"

"Another Chevalier, who was looking for me on the road, came to my rescue."

Gwen reached out and took Élise's hand. "Don't you see? You're being watched over. Twice now, you've been saved from a terrible fate at the last minute. This errand we're on is important to the Lord Himself, and all who aid it will be kept safe by His strong arm."

"Do you really think so?"

"Why else would I have found you, just when I needed you most? I know you want to be with Martis, but I can't keep myself from wishing that you'll find a way to stay with Britomar and I throughout our journey."

"But I'm a coward. How can I help you?"

"A woman who would risk defying her father to seek her true love is no coward. A woman who would risk being stoned to death for dressing as a man is no coward. Come, let us lay here near the fire and both try to forget our troubles. Perhaps you'll dream of Martis and I of Guillaume."

WRONG IMPRESSIONS

Adelie woke before dawn, shaking from a nightmare of running naked through the streets of Poitiers, chased by guards armed with swords. She rose, stretched, and walked over to where Britomar stood with the horses. The horses had such a wholesome smell to them, and just standing near them as she saddled them for the ride lifted her spirits; the cold terror from her nightmare dissipated.

She found Gwen by the campfire blowing into the embers, returning life to the fire while Élise rolled up the blankets.

"You're up early, Adelie," Gwen said, putting a pan over the glowing coals.

Adelie lowered down on the ground at the other side of the fire. "I want to make certain Élise gets back to you with the answers she claims she'll find there."

"You don't trust her?"

Adelie shook her head, stealing a glance to make sure Élise and Garsenda were out of earshot. "I don't. She is her father's daughter."

Gwen's eyes showed compassion. "Adelie, I can't know what you lived through." She threw some sausage onto the skillet. "But Élise saved my soul, and my life. I trust her. Try to see the woman who drove out the demons, not the father who drove you to a life in the gutters. Besides, she's not her father, you shouldn't hate her for his sins."

Adelie nodded. Gwen was right, of course. It was just so hard to distance herself from everything Élise symbolized.

After they all ate, Garsenda, Élise and Adelie mounted their horses and left for Paris.

Before long they merged onto the main road, joining other travelers going into the city by horse or on foot. A group of women traveling without escort drew some glances, but Adelie's grim look and her wicked dagger hanging on her belt in plain sight dissuaded further curiosity.

Late in the afternoon they rode over a small hill and saw the city walls.

"That's strange," Élise said, narrowing her eyes against the sun. "There're dwellings outside the walls already. The city must be growing faster than King Philip had planned. Why, it has become absolutely huge since I was here last!"

"I don't think I was with you then, mistress," said Garsenda.

"No, I don't think you were in my service yet. Oh look, they've put up signs on the street corners! Oh! Sancta Maria! What names!" She stared, her cheeks slowly turning crimson.

"What!" asked Adelie, "What do the signs say?"

"I don't know if I should say..."

"Mistress, please tell us."

Élise pursed her lips. "Let's see, we passed rue du Poil au Con,[1] rue Trousse-Puteyne and rue Grattecon...but rue du Chapon? Really, they go to far! Have they no shame? Posting such a sign! I know that most of the common folk can't read, but still!"

Adelie looked down that street as they passed. It was crowded with young men. Adelie looked away. Despite the shock, she felt oddly homesick. She missed her mother. It was too much to think she would never see her again.

They rode in silence until they could see the gate flanked by the guard towers on either side. The walls of rough cut stone rose far taller than any building they could see. The buildings themselves leaned into the street, as if reaching for what little light could be harvested. They had thatched roofs, small windows, and walls covered with roughly applied layers of plaster, often filthy along the base and beneath the windows.

The gates stood open and the guards did not challenge their entrance into the city. Once they rode through, Élise clapped her hands in delight.

"What is it?" asked Adelie, who kept glancing from side to side, peering into the shadows.

"The streets! They're paved! How wonderful!"

Adelie looked at her half sister not believing that someone could take such delight in stone roads. She shook her head.

As they moved through the crowds, Adelie could see that all the streets were indeed paved, even the side alleys. The homes, however, were of the same character as those outside the walls, just often larger and less dirty near the base.

---

[1] Today the street is called rue de Pélécan. The original name refers to the prostitutes who refused to comply with the law of the time and shave their privates. The names of the other streets are equally colorful: Whore's slit street, scratch cunt street, and the street of little boys.

It took them the better part of the afternoon to reach the bridge that would take them to the island in the middle of the city, where the royal palace stood. Beside it, workers were using ropes to pull large stones to the top of the scaffolding that stood next to the palace.

As they crossed the bridge and approached the palace, a guard stopped them. "What is your business?"

Adelie could feel her heart pounding, and put her hand on the hilt of her knife.

Élise spoke: "I am Lady Elisabeth du Chauvigny, and this is my sister, Lady Adelie. We have need to visit the university, and wish to apply to the queen for a letter of admittance."

"The queen is ill and does not take visitors at the moment. You must apply for an audience."

"But that will take days. Surely if you took word to the queen that our matter is urgent, she would see us."

He snickered. "Two women desirous of admittance to the university on an urgent but mysterious matter. Why don't you send your servant with a formal request? I'm certain if the matter is indeed that urgent, the queen will send her approval at once."

Élise pursed her lips, ignoring his insulting tone. "Where might we have lodging while we await the queen's reply?"

"The inns are overfilled with students. Ladies of your quality may find the Maison des Filles-Dieu[2] fits your need best. It is just outside the wall."

As they road from the palace, Garsenda moved her horse close to that of Élise. "My lady, I cannot believe that guard meant us well. Should we not seek out a convent?"

"Nonsense, Garsenda. I'm certain if that was not where ladies of station guested in Paris, the guards would not have recommended the Maison des Filles-Dieu. Paris must be very safe to house such an establishment outside the city walls."

It was nearly sunset by the time they found the house the guard had mentioned. The Maison des Filles-Dieu was a large house with many shuttered windows. An older woman, wearing an apron over her clothes and a shawl over her long grey hair greeted them at the entrance.

"Three of you, well, we've got the space for you, and we'll stable your horses. Do you all swear on all that is holy never to whore again?"

Garsenda shrieked. Élise, her face hot, realized exactly why the

---

[2]This house, established by St. Louis, was a home for former prostitutes.

guards hadn't sent them to the convent.

"There must be some mistake. I am Lady Elisabeth du Chauvigny; this is my sister Lady Adelie and my maidservant Garsenda. We need lodging, and were told we could find some here."

The woman giggled. "A real lady traveling by horse, in clothes such as those? Do you take me for a fool? A lady would go by sedan and wear clothes befitting her station. A lady would also seek lodging at a convent."

"My dear woman, our speech is that of Aquitane, and our clothes are suitable to our errand which is both secret and holy. We need an urgent audience with the queen," said Élise.

"Well, for fools, you certainly are persistent fools." She chuckled. "In any case, it's too late for you to be on the streets, unless you truly are whores. I'll find you a room for the night. You will want to consider a convent on the morrow."

She led them to a small unadorned and windowless chamber with a single large bed.

"Might a sheet of parchment, ink and a pen be placed at my disposal?" asked Élise.

"You can write?"

Élise nodded.

"Well, if any can be found, I will have it sent to you." She left.

"I can't believe that guard, thinking us whores!" said Adelie.

"It seemed to have to do with asking to go to the university," said Garsenda. "Perhaps this is not such a good idea after all."

"Nonsense, Garsenda. He just wasn't thinking. Imagine, whores riding horses, requesting an audience with the queen! Now, where is that woman?"

Élise soon had her parchment, pen, and ink along with a board and a candle. She spent the next hour writing her application to the queen for audience. Then she lay it down for Garsenda to take to the palace in the morning, and slid in next to Garsenda and Adelie in the bed.

At dawn, after they had eaten, Élise sent Garsenda with the parchment to the palace. A few hours later, the woman who had admitted them the night before came to their chamber. She kept her eyes on the ground, and trembled.

What's wrong? Did something happen to Garsenda?

"My apologies, my ladies for doubting you. The queen's sedan is waiting outside to take you to her at once."

Élise let out a breath. "It is no matter, good woman."

Adelie, shaking her head in disbelief followed Élise and the woman back through the narrow hall. Doors opened as they passed. Women of various ages stood at the entrances and stared at them.

Adelie longed to shout to them to close their doors, to close their legs, to get out of her life. She had never resented her mother's profession, but now, seeing all these women who had led lives like that of her mother's, she was surprised at her anger at how they lived.

Finally, they stepped through the door into the light and fresh air. For the first time Adelie refused to look for guards as she stared wide-eyed at the gilded sedan with four men wearing white gold-trimmed livery standing by the polls.

Today she would be treated as a lady. Today she would meet the queen. Somehow she no longer felt like the bastard daughter of a whore and an ignoble lord.

ACCUSED

As much as Gwen had enjoyed the companionship of the others, it felt nice to be alone again with Britomar. The quietude was a welcome change after the constant chatter. She ate her breakfast slowly, gazing at the sunrays streaming through the bare tree branches. Having always wondered about the delicate floating white specks oft found in sunlight, she asked, "Are those fairies dancing in the sunlight?"

Britomar looked up from the grass she was eating and said, "It is beautiful, but it is not the fair folk. It is just dust floating in the air."

"Then I will not mind so much when I return to the dust from which I came. I had no idea dust could be so pretty."

"Brawk!"

Gwen turned her face to the sky, and found a lone black bird speeding down to her. The raven, which had become Gwen's companion of the last few weeks, came to a hasty landing on Britomar's back.

"Brawk!" it insisted.

Britomar's ears sprung up.

"Caw! Brawk Caw Brawk!" spoke the raven; it took wing, flying back into the woods.

"She says a woman needs our help," said the unicorn. "Quick, get on my back."

Gwen, still not an experienced rider, climbed up on Britomar's bare back. The unicorn was off almost before she had a firm grip with her legs.

The wind whistled in Gwen's ears as Britomar glided through the underbrush. The branches they passed became a blur of brown . The wind in Gwen's eyes brought tears to their corners, but she did not dare brush them away for fear of falling. She leaned forward against Britomar's back and neck, clutching tightly.

How could Britomar go so fast and still not a twig hit them? Gwen wondered as she let herself become one with the wind.

Britomar leapt over a large bush, landing in an open field at the base of a hill. Gwen wiped her eyes against her shoulders and saw a hideous creature barreling down the hill at them. Huge horns curled from the sides of its hairless head, protruding from the folds of its fetid green skin. Its nakedness betrayed its intentions toward the kicking screaming woman it carried on its shoulder.

When the ogre saw them, it raised a large green fist and shook it at Britomar and Gwen. Horror pierced Gwen, a cold shiver running up her spine as the ogre let out a low growl.

"Get off!" said Britomar.

Gwen slipped to the ground. The unicorn reared up and screamed so loud that Gwen had to cover her ears. Britomar lowered her horn and charged up the hill.

She moved with such speed that Gwen did not see the horn strike. The ogre dropped the maid on the ground, as it howled in agony, reaching for where its left arm bled black ooze. Opening its mouth to reveal a nest of razors, the ogre roared in fury and bounded after the unicorn.

Gwen dropped to all fours and began to crawl toward the woman, hoping she could do some good, hoping not to be seen. She saw Britomar knocked to her haunches; the ogre roared in triumph. Gritting her teeth, Gwen crept onward, praying that Britomar would prevail.

As she neared the woman, the ogre's foul smell caused Gwen to retch. She doubled over, unable to control it.

"Brawk!" The raven darted over her. Through the haze of tears, Gwen saw the bird's wings beating, talons scratching at the ogre's face. She rolled away from the tepid pool of her vomit, and saw the ogre's sex, stiff and oozing red. Her stomach heaved.

"Brawk Caw Brawk!"

Gwen glanced up. Warmth washed over her as she saw Britomar rise. The ogre's fists flailed at the raven, which flew farther out of reach, drawing the ogre away. The unicorn regained her footing and hobbled back to the fight.

The ogre must have seen her coming, as it turned from its pursuit of the taunting bird and rushed toward Britomar. Britomar allowed it to approach, then leapt straight into the air as the ogre's fists pounded where she once had been. She landed and rose onto her hinds, striking the ogre on the side of its head with her hooves, pounding repeatedly. The ogre staggered under the weight of her blows. It swiped at her with the one arm, turning to pummel her. She lowered her horn and lunged, then leapt away. The ogre roared, clutching its face. Gwen saw black ooze gush down its cheek out of the misshapen eye socket.

Clasping a hand to his face, the ogre stumbled toward the unicorn. It moved awkwardly, like a drunken sailor stumbling from a tavern. Britomar backed up, taunting it, staying just out of reach. As it leaned forward, she struck, her hooves pummeling the ogre in the chest. Gwen felt the ground shake as the foul thing fell, its death screech hurting her ears.

It seemed like a long time before the scream stopped. Gwen lifted her head, covering the last few paces to the ogre's intended victim. Wings fluttered over her as the raven resumed its perch on her shoulder.

She knelt over the woman. Her breathing was shallow, and her left arm lay under her at an impossible angle. Gwen gently rolled the woman over. Her heart filled with sudden joy at the wholesome smell of the unicorn and she turned to see Britomar limping heavily toward her, the horn glowing golden in the sunlight.

"Does the woman live?"

Gwen nodded. "Yes, but her arm is shattered."

"Straighten it as best as you can. I'll see what I can do."

As Gwen straightened the arm, she felt the ground shake. She looking up at Britomar. The unicorn shook her head.

"Horses and men, many of them. They'll be here before I can bring health back to the ogre's victim." She leaned down and laid her horn on the woman's arm.

The woman screamed, though her eyes never opened. Britomar moved her horn to the woman's chest. Gwen stood over her, watching a river of mounted knights pour over the hill and flow around them. She turned back to the woman. A glow appeared on her chest where the horn touched her and spread across her body like wild fire on a dry field.

A man's voice boomed over Gwen. "Witch! Stand away from that woman!"

Unsteady on her feet, still lightheaded from the ogre's stench, Gwen peered at the speaker, a massive man in full armor.

"Lord Bryon, know you what you do?" another rider said.

Lord Bryon drew his sword. "All good men know that the unicorn is ferocious, except when tamed by a maiden of good virtue. That this pair slew that ogre proves she is not a woman of good virtue, otherwise the unicorn would have been too tame to battle such a fiend. That foul bird which rests on her shoulders must be her familiar. Besides, what does this matter? I would have that horn for my own."

Britomar stepped toward Lord Bryon. "Gwenaella is not a witch, and I am not her creature."

"Spawn of Satan, you dare to address a Knight of the Temple?" Gwen's eyes slid to the red cross of a crusader on his shield. He, like most of the others, wore his helm so she was not able to see the face of her accuser.

"I am not a spawn of Satan," said the unicorn, "and I challenge you to prove your word by the right of arms."

"What right has such a creature?" asked another knight as he shifted his horse to block Britomar's retreat.

"The girl has this right for herself," responded a knight who wore on his shield the image of an uprooted tree.

Gwen stared defiantly at Lord Bryon. "I claim that right. I will be proven innocent of this charge."

Lord Bryon laughed. "Who would stand as your champion, witch?"

A young knight rode forward, long sandy hair flowing below the base of his helm. His shield bore a red-white lion rampant sinister on a blue field with eight white six-pointed stars. "I'll stand champion for the maid and the unicorn."

To this there was at first general laughter, but the Templar held up a hand and said, "I accept you, Sir Wigandus, as a worthy champion for the accused." There was more snickering from some of the other knights. "Lord Gefroy, arrange a guard for the accused and the beast, while Sir Wigandus and I prepare for melee."

Two knights dismounted and stood guard next to Britomar. Two others came and flanked Gwen.

Sir Wigandus dismounted and approached Gwen. He took off his helm, and fell to one knee. "May I beg the favor of a woman so lovely that I would fight for your beauty alone?"

Gwen blushed and looked at her feet, not at his sky blue eyes. "Sir, please rise. I am but a poor fisherman's daughter, and have naught to offer a knight so brave as yourself, save for a small crucifix I wear around my neck." She removed it, and curtsied as she handed it to him.

He wrapped it around his sword arm. "I will prove you right, fair maiden, be it the will of God." Remounting, he rode back to where they had cleared a small area for the melee. Four knights were stationed at the corners of the field as marshals.

The two combatants dismounted and knelt before a chaplain. Gwen had to strain herself to hear the words:

"Chevaliers, know you that God himself will be watching this melee, as the fate of a virgin maid rests on its outcome. You will fight only with your sword, depending on God for your shield. You will fight until one of you yields the contest. But I urge you both to show mercy to he who yields. He too is God's agent in dispensing judgment on this maid. Do not seek to kill your opponent, nor render him unfit to fight against the heathen. May the Lord of Hosts bless you and this melee; so that the judgment it renders reflects the will of the Most High. Do you both solemnly swear that you bear no grudge against your opponent, neither public nor private, and that you will honor and do dignity to the results of this melee?"

Both knights drew their swords stuck them in the ground, and knelt before the hilts. Each said, "I do so swear."

The other knights cleared the field. Gwen, who had never before beheld a melee, found herself holding her breath as the two men circled, swords outstretched, each waiting for the other to make the first move.

It was then that she realized that if the young knight failed, not only she, but both Britomar and the eldest of unicorns would die.

THE UNIVERSITY

Élise looked at the closed sedan with regret. Its ornate doors would keep the onlookers from being able to see her—and keep her from seeing the streets of this wonderful city. Still, it might be best. To think that yesterday men had mistaken her for a common whore.

She let Adelie enter first and was about to follow when a familiar voice caught her attention.

"Élise!"

She turned to see a tall man wearing an ermine collar over a crimson doublet, striding majestically past the onlookers. *Martis!* What luck!... But what was he doing in Paris?

She smiled and enthusiastically waved to him "Martis, I am overjoyed! I never hoped to find you in Paris."

He frowned, looking past her to the doors of the house she just left, and back to her face in disbelief. "You—you promised me you would seek a unicorn. Not a *brothel!*"

Élise felt as if she'd been hit with an icy wind. How could he take her so wrong? Couldn't he see the sedan of the Queen of France?

She wanted to scream, to run away and bury her face in tears. But another, reasonable voice sounded inside her head. *Calm down. He is on the edge. And it does look suspicious, seeing her on the doorstep of a whorehouse. Those cursed men who sent us here!*

She took a step back and spoke, her voice reaching her through the ringing in her ears. "My lord, here is my sister who can vouch that not only have I found a unicorn, but have also been graced with a unicorn's quest. We are on our way to an audience with her majesty, Queen Blanche. If you would be so gracious to join us, you can learn the truth of these matters in detail in Her Majesty's presence."

His face contorted in anger, his expression forcing her to take another step back. Yet, she didn't stop smiling at him. She tried to calm him, help him hear reason. "Please, Martis, if you would not believe me, ask at the Palais du Royal. Garsenda awaits me there in Her Majesty's chambers."

Martis's lips twitched. "Liar! I know well you have no sister. I can see now that my father was right about you. Why I ever loved you is a mystery to puzzle even the Lord of Hosts! I'm certain your father will be most displeased when he hears of this."

He turned away, and stomped off. Élise began to shake, but calmed as Adelie's arms wrapped around her.

"Martis!" she called after him. "If you go to the forest south of the city, you'll find there a maid named Gwenaella with a unicorn named Britomar."

Martis paused for a moment, then hurried off. Élise watched until she felt Adelie tug her arm and lead her back to the waiting footmen. They stepped into the gold painted sedan.

"How can you be so calm after what he said?" asked Adelie.

Élise forced a smile. "This is just the way it had to happen. If I'm to prove my love for him, I have to be despised by him, discarded by him, otherwise my trials would seem empty."

"Élise, how can you love him when he treats you so?"

"I must love him, especially when he treats me so. Love does not show its colors only when things are easy, when we are in each other's arms. If I can't love him when he thinks he has found reason to hate me, then I can never truly love him at all."

"If he can't love you when he has found reason to hate you, did he ever love you?"

Élise shivered and forced herself to think of Garsenda's arms around her.

"He told me he loved me, a lifetime ago. He has never told me otherwise." *He nearly did, just now! But I mustn't think of it. I must hold on to our true feelings for each other, or my trial is pointless.* "In any event, let's not talk about it. We must be calm when we meet the queen."

Élise wished the sedan had a window that could offer a distraction from Martis's words, from the validity of what Adelie had said. Having no other refuge, she softly began to sing.

> *Ar em al freg temps vengut*
> *Quel gels el neus e la faingna*
> *El aucellet estan mut,*
> *C'us de chantar non s'afraingna;*
> *E son sec li ram pels plais -*
> *Que flors ni foilla noi nais,*
> *Ni rossignols noi crida,*
> *Que l'am e mai me reissida.*

She sniffled and wiped her eyes, once again forcing a smile. She sang to a different, livelier tune, hoping to lift her spirits.

Ab joi et ab joven m'apais,
E jois e jovens m'apaia,
Que mos amics es lo plus gais,
Per qu'ieu sui coindet' e guaia;
E pois ieu li sui veraia:
Beis taing qu'el me sia
Qu'anc de lui amar nom m'estrais,
Ni ai cor que m'en estraia !

The sedan stopped and lowered to the ground. After a gentle knock, the door opened and one of the men helped the ladies out. Élise took Adelie's arm and together they walked forward into the palace as the footman beckoned.

Each corridor, each room they passed stood in stark contrast to the richly draped halls she so loved in Poitiers. Here the walls were bare, save for one large hall decorated with the banners of the counts and dukes who had sworn their fealty to Louis, the king of France. She had heard that the king didn't take highly to warmth, light and comfort, preferring a stark ascetic life.

Élise brought to mind all she'd learned about Queen Blanche from her aunt. The king's mother, had been quite a woman in her youth, leading her husband's army to victory against the English in Normandy. She was devout and artistic, having composed a beautiful song to the Blessed Mother. "She is a formidable woman of good heart," she said quietly to Adelie as they reached the final set of doors, carved with fleur de lis. "I'm certain of her help."

The servant they followed knocked on the door. After a moment it opened from within, and the servant indicated they should enter.

Inside, they saw Garsenda sitting on a bench. Élise glanced past her, sweeping the room with her eyes. A massive four-posted bed dominated the right side, covered with magnificent gold-embroidered woolen curtains. The wooden crucifix in the corner was painted so realistically it appeared as if blood was dripping from the Savior's wounds. A large oaken desk by the window was piled with scrolls, parchment and a large book, all pushed to the edges to clear a space.

A silver-haired old woman sat at the desk, absorbed in her writing. Her emerald green dress fit her loosely, as if she had shrunk to her present size since it had been made for her. Élise smiled as she looked on the old queen, remembering her own grandmother, a frail woman that nonetheless emanated so much authority. If only grandma hadn't died when Élise was still so young.

The queen put down her quill, spread some sand on the parchment and shook it gently. Then she then turned to her visitors and smiled. "Lady Elisabeth, Lady Adelie, how sorry we are that we were not made aware of your arrival until this morning. I had heard from your father of your beauty, Lady Elisabeth. He speaks honestly."

"Thank you, Your Majesty. Is he still in the city? I would seek him out in his chambers."

"He has a room here in the palace. I can have him sent for, if you wish?"

Élise reached out and took her sister's hand. "Your Majesty, first I must complete a most sacred errand. In the wood south of Paris awaits the maid Gwenaella, who has been chosen to accompany a unicorn to the Garden at the Center of the World. We crave admission to the university, where we hope to learn where this Garden may be found. I promised I would bring her word of the Garden's location, and I would keep this promise before even seeing my father."

The Queen rose. "A unicorn? You wrote as much, but we didn't think, especially when you mentioned you were disguised as a—what was the word? ah yes—a troubadour. Still, there is a glow about the three of you. We wish our old bones permitted us to travel so far; we'd love the sight of a unicorn. However, we must preserve our strength so we can rule in our son's stead when he leaves on this crusade of his.

"As for the university, I'm inclined to grant your request, but I must warn you: it is not a fit place for ladies. There is no building to house the lectures, so the doctors and lecturers rent rooms, often above brothels, in which to share their learning with students who often pimp for the whores beneath."

Élise felt her face flush; she hoped the queen had not heard of where she had spent the night.

"Your Majesty need not worry much on our account, my sister is most proficient in the arts martial."

"Yes, your servant told me some of your adventures. Come, as I write your letter of introduction to the doctors of the university, it would please us much if you would entertain us with a song. We used to be a trouvère in our youth."

Adelie shifted restlessly on her feet as Élise unpacked her harp from its oilcloth sack. She had tuned it recently, so the strings needed only a minor adjustment to sound true. Élise sat on the bench, placed her harp on her knee, and began to pluck a tune with a lively tempo.

Amours, ou trop tart me sui pris
M'a par sa signourie apris,
Douce Dame de paradis
Ke de vous væill un cant canter:
Pur la joie ki puet durer
Vous doit on servir et amer.

Et pour çou ke nus n'a mespris
Tant vers vo fill n'en fais n'en dis,
S'il s'est en vo service mis,
Ke vous nel faciés racorder:
Pur la joie ki puet durer
Vous doit on servir et amer.

Virge roïne, flours de lis,
Com li hom a de ses delis
Ki de vous amer est espris,
Nus hom nel saroit reconter:
Pur la joie ki puet durer
Vous doit on servir et amer.

Mout fu li vaisaiaus bien eslis,
Douce Dame, ou Sains Espris
Fu ix mouis tous entriers nouris:
Ce fu vos cuers, dame sans per!
Pur la joie ki puet durer
Vous doit on servir et amer.

The queen smiled and clapped her hands. "You have a lovely voice, and it is pleasing to our ears to hear our song sung so beautifully. The letter we gave to your servant will gain you admission to Master Albertus, who, as we have learned, has much knowledge in matters of nature. God bless you, and please keep this old woman in your prayers."

Élise curtsied deeply. "Your Majesty's words have become part of my own prayers. It will be an honor for me to pray for you."

My dear Thomas,

First, I must apologize for never telling you I was of the order of monks charged to protect the Garden. Had I shared this with you in our correspondence, you could have sent the women straight to me, and saved them much trouble. However it was a secret I was charged never to share, except with those searching for it in earnest.

I also hope it causes you no embarrassment to read how Lady Adelie depicted her meeting with you, along with your master and dear friend. If it is true that you are called the dumb ox, I do not know how you bear it. I myself find my patience sorely tried by two dolts who were assigned to me as servants. Their comments are far from flattering, but not so base as what you are called freely and openly by even your master. Great must be your sanctity to bear it with the patience that was evident in the telling of their meeting with you. I include this only because you requested I spare not a detail of the adventures that the women related to me.

Prince Jigme of Lo Mantang

When the door to the sedan opened to let out Élise, Adelie and Garsenda, they found themselves in front of a sizable house whose timbers had yet to darken with age. Even the paper on the windows looked new, with no scratches or tears marring the white surface. One of the footmen knocked on the paneled door, and handed the queen's letter to a black-frocked monk inside. The monk read the letter and opened the door wide, bowing to the three women.

Élise practically tripped over a large shaggy dog that she did not see at first in the dim parlor. She bent down to let it sniff her hand, and then scratched it behind the ear. It panted, staring at her with its odd eyes, one glassy white, the other brown as earth. It wagged its tail as she scratched its head, licking her in the face when she stopped. Élise drew back just as she heard a man bellow from inside the house, "Brother Benedict, if this request is another of the idiotic questions Her Majesty has been sending, I'm going to throw the fools waiting in the parlor into the street muck myself!"

Brother Benedict's reply was too quiet for her to hear, but the result must have been favorable, as a moment later he re-entered the parlor and said: "Please follow me, my ladies."

Élise did not know where to look first as they entered the large back room. Along one side hung a long sheet of paper covered with flies, plants, and beautiful flowers, some of which Élise had never seen. More flowers sat on shelves also occupied by scrolls, loose sheets of parchment, and misshapen piles with oddly colored rocks on top. On a table in the middle of the room an array of glass vials rested on iron tripods. One, round with a narrow spout, stood beneath a wheel which had fans attached to it at periodic intervals.

Underneath, a small brazier blazed with a bright blue flame.

A thin bald man in the black habit of the Dominican order huddled over the wheel. He spun around as he heard the newcomers.

"Am I going to have to wait all day for you to introduce these women?"

Brother Benedict bowed. "Most humble apologies, I did not want to interrupt you again. Allow me to present Ladies Elisabeth and Adelie du Chauvigny, and their maidservant Garsenda."

A white mist emerged from the spout, accompanied by a shrill whistle. Garsenda covered her ears and screamed. Élise clasped a hand to her mouth to hold back a shout of delight as the wheel began to spin. On the wall opposite, an image of a black bird appeared, wings flapping. Master Albertus moved the candle from underneath the vial, causing the mist to stop rising, the wheel to slow, and the image of the bird to come to a rest.

He picked up a quill and made some notes on a sheet of parchment that lay on the table. Then looked up and smiled. "Please excuse me, my ladies, you came in just as I was finishing my studies of the motion of birds' wings in flight. Brother Benedict tells me that you are seeking to bring aid to the eldest of unicorns?"

Élise lifted her chin. "Indeed we are, my lord."

The man clicked his tongue. "Please tell me how you know that the eldest of unicorns is dying?"

Élise briefly glanced at her companions. "We are traveling with a unicorn, Britomar and with the maid Gwenaella, who has been chosen by the unicorns to find the Garden at the Center of the World. Therein, we've been told, is a fruit that will heal what ails the eldest of unicorns."

Master Albertus shook his head. "My ladies, I myself know only the rumors of the Garden's location, and that only from the research by one of my students. Brother Benedict, bring Brother Thomas here."

The monk frowned. "That dumb ox? Is there no one else who..."

Albertus's glance interrupted him. "Yes, Brother Thomas, him and none other. Now, please."

Brother Benedict gave a curt bow and left the room.

"A dumb ox?" Adelie asked.

Garsenda shrugged. "That is what he said. Perhaps, he meant a magical but humble creature?"

Master Albertus laughed, "Some of the students call Brother Thomas that. In truth, they are all idiots, not fit even to tie his boot-lace. Brother Thomas will shake the world one day. Let us see if he can tell us more of this Garden you are seeking."

97

Brother Benedict soon returned with a younger man, also dressed in the black frock of the Dominican order, but large of girth and dark-skinned. Master Albertus let him in, then pushed Brother Benedict back into the hall and closed the door in his face.

"Ladies du Chauvigny, may I present to you my favorite student, Brother Thomas Aquinas. He greatly surpasses my poor self in both knowledge and understanding. Please tell him of what you have told me, and in greater detail."

Élise told Thomas about Gwen, her brother's illness, and Britomar. Friar Thomas was intently quiet as she told about the plight of the eldest of unicorns. But when he heard of the Franciscan friar in the wood near Brocéliande, and of the Garden at the Center of the World, he lifted his head sharply.

"Please forgive your servant's interruption, my lady, but I had despaired until now of being able to help you on your journey. My studies have been elsewhere, and I have little knowledge of this Garden. The only thing I know about it is that it is not to be found at the world's center."

"How can that be?" asked Adelie.

"The world's center is Mount Sinai. There is no garden there. I know nothing about the rest of what the Franciscan told you, other than the Garden exists."

Élise could not believe her ears. Mount Sinai is the world's center but there's no garden there? Was there no hope for Britomar and her king?

"I have a good friend, however, who greatly surpasses me in piety and knowledge. He is Brother Bonaventure, and like your monk, he is also of the order of St. Francis. With your gracious permission, I will take you to him."

"Thank you, Brother Thomas," said Adelie.

"Brother Thomas, is it wise to take them to Bonaventure?" asked Master Albertus.

"I would trust him with my very soul."

"It is not your soul I'm worried about. He is, after all, a..."

"A Franciscan? Yes, Master Albertus, but so was the friar in the woods. The Franciscans have a special mission regarding the beasts of the world."

"Thomas, what do you make of this woman who claims to be Lilith's priestess, Nimuë?" asked Master Albertus.

"While not recorded in scripture, the Jews maintain that Lilith was in Eden before Eve, if the eldest of unicorns walked with Adam, then it is likely that Lilith knew him too. If it is true that Nimuë is... well,

98

let us talk more of that later. These good women have been most patient as we've debated. Ladies, please follow me."

After they left Master Albertus' chambers, Adelie asked, "Is Master Albertus always that cross?"

Thomas smiled. "You must not mind his gruff manner. The king's ministers have been sending him very trivial questions, which keep him from being able to convince those who think it is impossible to know God that we are all born with the desire to learn, and are driven from this nature to learn of God."

"Trivial questions?"

"Yes, such as, would the seraphim write the mystic name of God in the sky."

They had no time for further questions. It was hard enough to keep up with Brother Thomas, who, despite his girth, proceeded at great speed through the tangled Parisian streets. Eventually he led them to a small building and then through its dark corridors until they found themselves at a plain wooden door.

He knocked with three short raps followed by two taps. A gentle voice said from within, "Brother Thomas, by all means enter."

Thomas opened the door to reveal a simple room, devoid of all decoration except a crucifix on the wall and a mat for sleeping. A man dressed in the brown frock of the order of St. Francis floated, in a sitting position, about a hand's breath above the mat. His smile widened when he saw Friar Thomas accompanied by three women.

Élise could have sworn that he smiled directly at her. Hearing him speak made her feel much the same joy she felt when Britomar was near.

"Brother Thomas, you bring a vision of rare beauty into my cell. I am grateful to you and indebted to the cause that brings such loveliness into my humble dwelling. May I be blessed by your names, ladies, and your reason for seeking His most unworthy servant?"

"Brother Bonaventure," Thomas said. "I am honored to be accompanied by Ladies Élise and Adelie du Chauvigny, and their maidservant Garsenda. I will let them tell you themselves of their errand."

Élise told Brother Bonaventure what she had already related to Brother Thomas. He listened intently, the emotions on his face following the sadness and joy of the tale and becoming more and more troubled as the tale drew to it's end.

"Daughters," he said, "I have heard of the Garden, and it is known to my order. Its location, however, is hidden. Only one who can answer a riddle will learn of its location."

"A riddle? What riddle?" Élise asked.

"Hidden at the roof of the world is an echo of what was lost. Enter freely those who are truly repentant, as if through the needle's eye."

"The roof of the world?" Élise felt troubled. Why were they all talking about the roof of the world? How could it be that the Garden would not be found at the world's center on Mount Sinai? Could these friars be mistaken? Perhaps Mount Sinai was not the center of the world? Or perhaps it was actually there, but hidden as the riddle mentioned? It made sense. Mount Sinai was a mountain, and what else but a mountain could be the world's roof?

Brother Bonaventure spoke, disturbing her confused thoughts. "I believe the roof of the world in this riddle is referring to a chain of mountains north of Persia. There used to be a Christian Kingdom near there by the name of Georgia, but since the defeat of the Greeks by the Saracen Turks this part of the world has become isolated from Christendom."

Brother Thomas said, "Forgive the contradiction, but there are higher mountains than this—north of the Indus River, where followers of Siddhartha Gautama have many monasteries. I would not be surprised if the world's roof is there."

Élise's heart pounded, her hope fading into panic. If these two wise men could not agree, which one should they listen to? Should they seek a hidden garden at Mount Sinai or in these mysterious distant lands Brother Thomas mentioned? Mount Sinai seemed easier, at least she'd heard of it before. But where was it? In the Holy Land for certain but where?

Brother Thomas continued, "However, the needle's eye could be a reference to an ancient gate in Babylon, so perhaps the garden is one of their fabled hanging gardens. Besides, legends refer to Eden at the place where four major rivers meet, and Baghdad is between two of them, the Tigris and Euphrates...I would look first in the court of Al-Musta'sim, the Caliph of Baghdad, which is near to Babylon's ruins. Even if they don't know of the Garden, they have a vast library that could help you in your search."

"Baghdad?" Élise's heart raced. Baghdad was so far, in the heart of the ungodly lands, even further than the crusade her father was headed for. However would they reach it if even their trip to Paris had proven so perilous?

"I correspond with some of the scholars in Baghdad, and with some of those who follow Siddhartha," Thomas said. "I will send a letter to each alerting them to your need. This is a dangerous journey, and may well lead you into lands controlled by Hulegu, grandson of the great Khan. I will pray for your safe return."

Which is it? Baghdad, the mountains of Georgia, or the mountains of this Siddhartha? Élise realized that she had twisted her fingers so much they ached, and forced herself to unclench her hands.

Brother Bonaventure said, "I would think that the reference to the needle's eye is an instruction to the person who would answer the riddle to place themselves in a state of grace. I will also pray for you, ladies, and for Gwenaella who I long to meet. She must be filled with grace to be the unicorn's chosen."

Élise said, "But good friars, the friar of the wood was clear that the Garden will be found at the world's center."

"My lady," said Friar Bonaventure. "The Lord of Hosts *is* the world's center. Wherever the Garden is, so is He. "

Élise rose, trying to suppress the turmoil in her thoughts. "Thank you, good brothers. Please excuse our haste, we must bring these tidings to Gwen and Britomar as soon as possible."

"But of course Lady Elisabeth," said Brother Bonaventure, "and give the maid Gwenaella our blessings as well. One word of caution: on this journey you will all be challenged in your faith. Not only faith in God, but faith in yourselves. Don't forget that each of you was chosen for this. Our Lord does not give to us burdens we cannot bear, if we just keep our faith."

But you've given us choices not direction! What are we to believe in? Élise wanted to protest, but kept her worries private. After all, her own quest was nearly finished. All she had to do was to find Martis and get him to Britomar, then her part in this was done. Hopefully Gwenaella would choose her path wisely.

A KNIFE

Adelie breathed a huge sigh of relief as they stepped into the street. They now knew where to go! They would find further directions in Baghdad.

As she followed her sister back to where they'd left the sedan, a cold shiver ran up her spine as she realized that she had not checked the streets for guards. She forced herself to calm down. After all, how could her enemy know that she was in Paris? She was safe with Élise and Garsenda, and shortly would be safer still.

Garsenda reached out and took her hand, "She did it! My mistress found the path we must follow!"

Adelie gave her hand a squeeze, "Aren't you nervous about going to Baghdad?"

"Terrified, but after talking with these priests, I feel like I can accomplish anything." Garsenda looked back at Bonaventure's residence.

Adelie followed her gaze. "Yes, they made me feel that way too."

Garsenda's hand on hers froze. Adelie looked ahead and saw Élise talking to a lord.

He wore a rich fur mantle, polished boots and a bright green hat. As she stared, trying to recognize his features, he turned and Adelie saw his face.

Father.

Adelie's heart raced. Élise had almost convinced her that their father wasn't to blame for her mother's death, but as she looked at his face, her fear came back, her worst fear realized. This was the face of her tormentor. The man who betrayed her and left her an orphan.

The man who ordered her death.

She put her hand on her knife hilt.

The baron met Adelie's gaze and, against reason, his face softened as he nodded to her. "Lady Adelie, I am the Baron Cristoffle du Chauvigny. Come and join me at my board, I would hear more of what brings my beloved daughter Elisabeth to Paris unescorted, though in such lovely company."

Adelie let out a sigh. Clearly he didn't know who she was. Perhaps it was best this way. She exchanged glances with Garsenda, then nodded slightly.

They followed the baron, who had linked arms with Élise, over the bridge to the Ile de la Cite and into the main hall of the Château.

The hall was draped with the emblems of the realm, three white fleurs-de-lis on a blue field, alternating with white banners with a single red cross. Élise later told her that those banners had been borne by French crusaders since the fall of Jerusalem to Saladin. The baron led them into a windowless side hall lit by torches hung on sconces, their flame staining the walls with soot, the ceiling above them black. The hall led them to a large stone stair, lit from narrow slits in the right wall. The steps were well worn from the passage of mailed feet, and Adelie slipped more than once in her soft shoes. Garsenda caught her, whispering in her ear, "If my mistress's thoughtlessness gets you in trouble, I'll protect you at the cost of my life."

Adelie had no chance to reply to this, as a young woman of their age, dressed in white with gold lace at her cuffs and a golden wimple framing her dark face, approached them.

The Baron bowed. "Your Majesty, may I present my daughter, Elisabeth, and her companion, the Lady Adelie?"

The queen smiled. "Baron du Chauvigny, I have heard much of your two daughters from the queen mother. I am charmed to make their acquaintance."

The baron shook his head. "Your Majesty is mistaken, the third woman is my daughter's maidservant, Garsenda."

"Oh, no. Her Majesty was most clear that she had met with two daughters du Chauvigny, one who was a most accomplished trouvère, the other a most accomplished cavalier. You must be most proud of them both."

Adelie's heart raced as the baron's gaze paused on her, his eyes widening in surprise. *Here it comes.*

But the baron only smiled and turned away, bowing to the queen. "No father could be prouder, Your Majesty."

"Good. I'm told of the urgency of their errand, so I'll not delay you any further. Good day, baron."

"Your Majesty." The baron bowed again.

After the queen disappeared around the bend of the stair, he led them down a long corridor with many doors, a torch by each. Adelie followed on stiff legs, noting each detail, the cracks in the stone, the rancid oil in the torches. She felt for the reassuring firmness of her knife on her belt. Whatever her father planned for her, she won't go down quietly.

She prayed Élise had been right about him. If not, she was likely headed for her own execution.

They soon came to a stout oak door strapped with iron bands that had their ends beaten into a fleur-de-lis. The baron pushed this door open and stood aside for them to enter.

A large table piled with maps and letters dominated his chamber. Beyond that stood a bed with crimson drapes, a large wooden chest at its foot. He sat on the chest and pointed at the three chairs, "Please, sit. Garsenda, you too. I'll have my servants bring up refreshments." He clapped his hands and a valet emerged from a side door.

"Bring wine, bread and meat! My daughter and her companions require refreshment!"

The valet bowed deeply and withdrew.

The baron's gaze swept over the three ladies and Adelie's skin crept as he, once again, paused on her face before moving on to Garsenda.

"I wish to discuss the nature of your service, Garsenda," he said. "Not only was I uninformed of my daughter's presence within Paris, but I just learned that she took lodging within the Maison des Filles-Dieu? For that alone, I should have you flogged."

Garsenda's lips trembled. "My lord, I—"

"Father, it is not Garsenda's fault," interrupted Élise. "I did not have her secure lodgings for us, as it was not my intent to spend a night within Paris. It was only a failure to obtain immediate audience with Her Majesty that required a night's stay. The Maison des Filles-Dieu was recommended to us by one of the palace guards. He played an ill joke on us, and if you must have someone flogged, it should be him."

The baron shook his head. "Never in all my days have I been so humiliated as to learn from his majesty, Louis of France, that my daughter is traveling with her maid and a—" he paused, looked at Adelie, shook his head and continued, "and is staying at a home for retired prostitutes."

Adelie fingered her dagger.

"Father, I gave Garsenda no choice," Élise insisted. "Do not punish her for her faithfulness and obedience."

The baron sighed. "She is supposed to be looking after you, Elisabeth."

"I can look after myself."

"That remains to be seen. What is this errand the queen spoke of? What brings you to Paris, without proper escort and in the company of the likes of her?" He looked at Adelie, who was staring at him lips drawn taught, her hands clenched.

"Father! Did not the queen tell you that I was on a sacred errand for a unicorn?"

The baron stood abruptly. "Explain what brings you to Paris and explain your choice of companions or I'll flog you and your thoughtless servant!"

Adelie made to stand, but Élise held her shoulder. "Father, first, I must know if it is true that you have issued orders for the destruction of any of your bastards."

Adelie felt sweat trickle down her back. Her clenched fists were beginning to lose feeling. *He's going to kill me!*

The baron's eyebrows flew up in surprise. "Who could have been so audacious as to tell you such a horrible lie?"

"Her Majesty spoke true, amongst us you have two daughters. May I present to you your daughter, Adelie."

Adelie turned white, but kept her hand on her knife hilt. If he but drew—

The baron lowered back into his seat, eyes fixed on Adelie. His lips began to tremble. "Adelie, my child. When the queen mentioned two daughters, I thought you were a fiction invented by Élise for some unknown purpose." He cast Élise a sad glance. "She's been untruthful with me much recently. I meant to deal with you later. I thought..." He leaned forward, looking at her closely. "I should have known. I should have recognized you at once...Oh, Adelie. I had tried so often to bring you and your mother into my household. When I had heard of her death, I wept for a week. I was told you perished too. How can this be true, that you live and I am accused of attempting your destruction?"

Adelie took a deep breath, her strained muscles slowly relaxing. Weakness swept over her as Élise let go of her shoulder. She fought back unwanted tears. "My lord, the soldiers came when I was small, with orders to kill me. The sergeant took pity on us. I have feared you my whole life. My mother and I lived as fugitives, until your soldiers butchered her."

The baron shook his head. "My child, my child, I don't understand, I never gave such orders. I told Hervé to..." He frowned. "Hervé, could he have?...No, no no." He pounded his fist on the chest. "I'll have that bastard..." He lifted his eyes to Adelie, his gaze softened. "Forgive me, my child, I had no knowledge of the monstrosities that have been done in my name. I'll have that man...His head shall hang on the gates to the city as a warning to all who would be traitorous to their lords, I swear it!" He hesitated. "But why are you in Paris? Did you come here fleeing my soldiers, only to find me?"

Élise said, "No, Papa, but that is one of the reasons I did not seek you out right away, though my heart was torn about your leaving on a crusade with out saying a proper fare thee well. We are traveling with the unicorn and her chosen maid, Gwenaella, on a quest to the Garden at the Center of the World. She needed information we came to Paris for, and we cannot delay in bringing it to her."

He smiled. "Papa! I like the sound of that. Hopefully I'll hear that one day from your lips, Adelie." Looking again at Élise, he asked, "What is this Garden and why did you join such a quest? Who is Gwenaella? Not another daughter of mine?" He laughed.

Élise shook her head. "No, she's the daughter of a fisherman from Redon in the Duchy of Bretagne, and it is she who found the unicorn. We are helping her. She must bring back a fruit from this Garden to heal the eldest of unicorns. I myself have no intention of taking the journey to the Garden; I just gained admittance to the university to help Gwenaella learn of the Garden's location."

"The eldest of unicorns? No, don't explain further, I'll speak to the Queen Mother and learn the tale. Adelie, I would have you take this ring." He pulled off his left hand a ring, which bore his device. "If ever you seek to enter my household, you would be more than welcome." Adelie took the ring, uncertain if it were rude to let him know that she already carried the ring he'd given to her mother.

There was a knock on the door, and the valet entered with two servants, carrying wine, glasses and food. As they ate, the baron asked them about their experiences on their journey to Paris.

"You took on four bandits by yourself?" he asked Adelie.

Adelie looked down at her food, pushing her meat with her knife without eating.

Élise said, "You should have seen her, she was brilliant!"

"With what? That knife you're eating with?"

"Yes sir," said Adelie, keeping her eyes down.

"Don't call me sir, girl. You are definitely Barza's daughter; I see it now in your face. I fully acknowledge you as my own get. Let me see that knife."

Adelie suppressed a gasp. Those simple words just changed everything. She was no longer an unacknowledged bastard. With these words, she now had a place within society. Adelie looked up at the baron and handed the knife to him, hilt first.

Baron du Chauvigny looked it over, and tested its balance. "This is a good knife for carving your meat with, but it is short and not well set in the hilt." He handed it back to her and he drew a long knife from his belt. "I was planning on using this to run through a good many payeen, but I'd rather see it in your hands." He held out the knife. "Take it, Adelie, I want you to have it."

In disbelief, Adelie reached out and took it. She balanced it in her hand, admiring the feel of it, the lightness and elegance, the way the hilt fit so naturally into her hand. The blade was long, a weapon for killing.

"Thank you." She paused, and then said, "Father."

A broad grin spread across his face. "Father? Hmmm. A good beginning. I hope one day you too will think of me as Papa."

There was another knock, and again the valet entered. "My lord, the ladies' horses are waiting."

The baron's smile slipped into a frown. "I will see these mounts of yours. My little Elisabeth, purchasing horses!"

They all followed the valet back through the building down to the stables. The baron busied himself checking the teeth and hooves of their horses, grunting in satisfaction with each.

"Elisabeth, I'm impressed. These are good healthy mounts which will last you on your journey."

Élise smiled. "Thank you, Papa, but the credit should go to Britomar. She talked to the horses, and found us four who would be willing and able to make the journey to Paris."

"Britomar is the unicorn?"

"Yes, Papa."

He nodded. "A useful beast. I wish my men could have a unicorn aid them in choosing their mounts." He turned to Garsenda, suddenly serious. "One other thing. Garsenda, I release from your mistress's service."

"Papa!" protested Élise.

"No, not another word. You should go as a free woman, and help this Gwenaella find her Garden, if you so wish. If you, as Élise says, received a unicorn calling in your dream, it must be the quest you were chosen for. I'm certain that Élise will find her betrothed has provided her with many servants."

Adelie looked at Élise who stared at her father with tears forming at the corners of her eyes. The baron continued. "I know something of the lands you will travel through, I will pray for all your safety."

"Baron, there is one thing that Lady Elisabeth did not tell you—"

"Don't Garsenda," said Élise, putting her hand on Garsenda's arm.

"Shut up, you. Out with it, Garsenda," commanded the baron.

Adelie could not take her eyes off of Élise as Garsenda told of

Martis and their flight from an unwelcome match. Élise seemed to be on the verge of tears but she kept a smile on her face.

When Garsenda finished, the baron was silent for a moment, and then looked at Élise with a frown. "You have spoken of this d'Hyères before. I contacted his father, who emphatically did not approve of the match. So much so that his reply was insulting. I then sought and found a very prestigious match for you with the Prince of Armenia, and left instructions with Hervé to send you there. Was he also faithless in this?... Your face tells me otherwise." He shook his head. "You are, and always were, a willful child, and I understand that you have some affection for the young d'Hyères. But what is done is done, and I will not break my word to any man, especially to a prince who has estates in the Holy Land. His people, the Tartars, are fierce, and would not easily accept an affront. You will go to Armenia and marry this prince."

"But Papa—"

"No 'but Papa'! I will not break my word, especially to forge a match with a man whose father disparages my daughter. You may travel with Britomar as far as Armenia, which is on the way to Baghdad. I was going to have you sent there in any event. I could not pay for a better escort for you than a unicorn. At least her company will keep you chaste."

He helped the women into their saddles, seemingly oblivious to the stares he was getting from passers-by and from his own valet. "Were your errand less urgent, I'd forbid you to leave." The baron looked at the sky. "If you hurry, you'll be out of Paris before they close the gates. Go, with God speed and with your father's blessings, on your journey and to your marriage!"

"Papa, may God bless you on your crusade." Adelie's heart broke at the tears in her sister's voice. "May you return with Jerusalem liberated and Christendom vindicated."

Adelie swallowed. "Father, God bless you."

"God speed you on your journey Adelie. Upon your return, I'll seek a husband for you."

POETRY AND MEN

The Templar screamed, rushing at Wigandus, sword cutting through the air. Wigandus blocked and thrusted at Sir Bryon. Gwen winced at the clang of steel on steel. Repeatedly the two men slashed at each other. The blows fell fast and furious, causing Gwen's ears to ring with the din. They separated, circling around each other, swords lowered as they sized each other, composing for the next attack.

Gwen's labored breath echoed their panting. She prayed that Wigandus could continue to hold up under the Templar's fury.

Again Sir Bryon sprang, sword dazzling in the sunlight, but Wigandus stabbed at his arm, knocking Sir Bryon's sword to the ground. The Templar fell to his knees, blood gushing from his arm.

Standing over him, Sir Wigandus said, "Do you yield?"

"Yes, by God, I yield."

Gwen felt Britomar nuzzle her, the warmth of the unicorn's touch spreading over her body. Britomar stepped forward, but the guards drew their swords to bar her way.

Britomar spoke, her voice echoing clearly across the meadow, "Stand aside and let me approach the wounded knight."

Lord Gefroy nodded to the guardsmen. "Let the unicorn pass, she and the maid are proven innocent before God."

Britomar pranced to the wounded Templar. "I can only heal your body. I suggest you seek a priest to heal your soul." She then bent her head and touched him with her horn.

The bleeding stopped. Sir Bryon looked dazed as he flexed his arm in wonder. The other knights watching the scene in awe crossed themselves.

Sir Bryon rose, picked up his sword, and handed it to Sir Wigandus. "I am vanquished in mind, body, and soul. I have no further need of my weapon. I will now seek my penance." He walked slowly to his horse. Mounting, and without a word from his fellows, he rode up the hill and disappeared from view.

The chaplain called out, "We stand in witness to the innocence of this maid, known as Gwenaella, and the unicorn." He turned to

Gwen. "Gwenaella, please forgive us our doubt."

Gwen wondered if she could forgive Sir Bryon, but let her voice promise what she did not feel in her heart. "I forgive you, and your present company."

Sir Gefroy approached the ogre's victim who lay unconscious on the grass, and picked the woman up. "Fair maid Gwenaella," he said. "My heart tells me that whatever has brought you to Britomar is more than the conceit of a woman. May God be with you."

Sir Wigandus stayed with Britomar as the other knights mounted, helping Sir Gefroy to get the woman secure on his horse. Britomar touched her once more and she woke.

She looked at Britomar in wonder. "It wasn't a dream then, you're real."

The unicorn smiled. "Yes, I am real."

"Bless you, dear unicorn." She nodded to Sir Gefroy who climbed up on the horse behind her.

Gwen turned to Sir Wigandus who alone of the knights remained unmounted. "Noble knight, you fought valiantly. I thank you for risking yourself for my sake."

The knight held her gaze. "It was my honor, fair maid Gwenaella. My sword is yours, if I can offer you further assistance... I see that you are far from home. May I escort you hither so that your family may rejoice in your finding of this magnificent beast?"

Gwen wished that her head would clear. It felt light and she was still slightly nauseous. Besides, the young knight's gentle gaze was so disconcerting.

"Britomar and I are on a sacred quest," she heard herself say. "I'm not going home until that is done."

His eyes lit with delight, "Let me join with you on this errand. I had come to France to join in your king's Holy Crusade, but I'm certain he has enough brave knights to accompany him. Your quest seems most worthy and noble. It would be my honor to be of service."

Gwen wished to plead with him to leave, but figured the unicorn's fear of men would accomplish the same end. She had no desire to have a man around, especially not one that seemed interested in her, no matter how handsome. "As the errand is not mine, but that of Britomar, the choice is hers to make."

Britomar lifted her head and spoke solemnly, "Sir Wigandus, if you wish to join with us, you must swear a vow of chastity. You must also know that Gwenaella is not the only maid who accompanies me on this errand."

He drew his sword and knelt, holding the hilt of his sword with his right hand.

"I will be that most chaste of knights, to rival Sir Parzifal himself," he said. "I this most solemnly swear, that I will defend the chastity of all who accompany Britomar with my life. I swear that I will live chaste and virginal in the service of this errand until such time as it's completion." He then rose.

Sir Gefroy waved and said, "Sir Wigandus, it was a good day you joined our company. You saved us from ignominy and sin. We are proud to stand witness to such an oath. You will find great glory in serving the maid Gwenaella. God be with you!" He and the rest of the knights rode back up the hill toward Paris.

Gwen sighed as she climbed up on Britomar, eyeing her new companion from the corners of her eyes. Traveling with a man? She wasn't sure it was a good idea. Especially not with a handsome man like Wigandus.

She wasn't sure if her vow of chastity precluded her from admiring the man's looks, but she found his presence disconcerting. She dug her hands into the reassuring softness of Britomar's silky mane, fighting hard to suppress the blush spreading over her cheeks. How could just being around a man affect her so soon after Guillaume's death? The girls at the convent school had always been going on about how there was nothing more romantic than a man fighting for your honor, perhaps that was all this was. Either way, she was being silly.

"We have a camp in the wood," she said. "Lets go there and wait for my companions to return." It should be easier once she had other women for company, shouldn't it?

Sir Wigandus looked at her sideways with the expression she could not read. He patted his horse, whispered softly, and then mounted. As they rode back to camp, Gwen wondered how the unicorn could tolerate a man. She had always thought that unicorns feared and avoided them. Perhaps Sir Wigandus was a knight of exceptional chastity and virtue? She stole another glance at him, and once again blushed to the roots of her hair and hastily averted her face as she found him looking her way.

Disconcerting or not, this man has just risked his life to save her and Britomar and committed himself to their sacred cause. He was a superb fighter, and apparently a virtuous soul. She should feel nothing but gratitude for his company and protection. If only that was all she felt. *Oh Guillaume, can you ever forgive me?*

As they arrived at the camp, the raven flew out of the trees and settled on a branch near her horse. Gwen hurried to tend to the animal, which seemed nervous at having been tethered and alone for a few hours. As she did so, she told Sir Wigandus the details of their errand and of her companions.

Sir Wigandus listened attentively.

"It is a rare and noble quest that you undertake," he said. "I am honored that you would permit me to join with you on this errand."

Gwen lowered her eyes. "Sir Wigandus, thank Britomar, not me. It was her decision, it is her errand."

Britomar regarded him calmly. "This brave knight was willing to stake his life on the innocence of strangers. I deem him worthy of our trust. Besides, the friar said to accept help as it is offered."

"Please, could you tell us about yourself?" asked Gwen as she settled down to mend a tear in her skirt. "Your speech is of a foreign land."

Sir Wigandus leaned his pack and armor against a tree and sat on the ground across from Gwen.

"I am from the Langrave of Thuringia in the Empire. I have long heard the meister-singers praising the great deeds of goodly knights. My boyhood companion was the son of a famous poet, Sir Eschenbach, and I heard the tale of the deeds of Sir Parzifal from the poet's own telling. Inspired by his tales of chivalry, I have longed to do my part in the defense of Christendom. I trained to be competent with the noble weapons of war, and have spent long hours at the knee of those who understand its strategies. Word came to me that King Louis of France was preparing a Crusade to free the Holy Lands from the infidel. I begged and was given permission to seek out your king and to offer him my sword.

"I have not yet taken the vows of the crusader, and today I am glad of it. It does my heart good to serve a woman of such beauty and nobility of heart."

Gwen blushed, and turned away. His intense gaze made her feel like a fish out of the water. If only he wouldn't look at her that way.

They spoke little through the rest of the day. Gwen spent the time mending garments. He cleaned the stones from his horse's hooves, brushed its brown coat, and tended to his weapons, all the while singing or speaking to her in verse. Gwen listened to the wondrous songs of chivalry, to his soft, melodious voice. She was afraid to admit that his closeness, his protection, was making her feel so warm inside, safe for the first time since she had embarked on her quest with Britomar. She sent a silent thanks to the Lord for granting her such a companion. If only he didn't make her blush every time his gaze fell on her. If only he was a little bit less attractive...

That night, as they settled down to sleep, he laid his sword between them. Gwen went to sleep, acutely aware of his still form by her side.

She couldn't believe how silly she felt. She had heard of such things in songs, but she'd never expected to live them. *Dear Lord, give me strength.* With that, she sank into a deep, untroubled sleep.

When Gwen awoke, she found Sir Wigandus had already risen and was stretching near the fire. She watched him stretch, muscles rippling on his back as he moved. His torso was perfectly sculpted, his skin so smooth she wondered what it would feel like to touch it. *Dear lord.* She forced her eyes away before he could realize she was watching and jumped to her feet, busying herself with preparing breakfast.

Gwen continued to feel awkward for the next several hours. Wigandus showed her how to take care of horse's hooves. In turn, she taught him to sew so that the stitches were tight and would bind the cloth as if it had never been torn. While he worked on mending his surcoat, she again found herself staring at his shoulders.

This was going to be a long and difficult trip.

She welcomed the sight of Britomar, who emerged out of the wood and came toward her.

"Garsenda, Elisabeth and Adelie are returning. We should go to meet them, and bring them back here."

Gwen asked Sir Wigandus, "Would you prefer to stay with the camp, or join me in their welcome?"

He smiled. "While my heart will be empty with your absence, fair Gwen, I see the wisdom of you telling your companions of me without me present. I will stay."

Gwen went to her horse, unfettered it, and mounted. She flushed when she noticed him looking at her bare lower leg as her full skirts pulled up somewhat, and hastily covered it with her cloak. She followed Britomar through the undergrowth to the meadow north of the forest. As she rode, Gwen forced her thoughts to the leaves, the trees, the ground in front of her, the smell of horse, anything but the adoration she saw in his eye.

They waited under the forest eaves, not far from the hillside where Britomar fought the ogre, and then Wigandus fought Sir Bryon. Gwen shivered at the memory.

As they waited, she saw a lone man riding fast along the skirts of the hill. He seemed to be scanning the woods, as if looking for something, or someone. Gwen was about to ask Britomar if they should retreat further under the cover of the forest's shadows, when the unicorn said, "He has something of the smell of Élise about him.

Let's see what he's about."

Gwen's horse followed Britomar out of the wood without prompting.

Soon the stranger rode up to them. He reined in his mount hard, but expertly kept to his saddle as it reared up, whinnying its protest.

"You come from the woods like a vision to accuse me! Do you know of a lady—"

"We know Élise," interrupted Britomar. "You have her scent about you. What news do you have of her?"

He shook his head, looking forlorn. "That she has visited with the queen, and that she has reason to find me a fool! Pardon me, but I must be off to Paris and see if I can amend my folly!" He urged his horse back into gallop, away, and back around the hill.

Gwen frowned. "That must have been Martis. Élise told me of him. Something must have happened in Paris between them...Oh, why must Paris be the death to love?" She sniffled, unbidden tears running down her cheeks. After a moment she felt Britomar's warm breath and smelled the lightning in her fur. She wiped the tears away. "I'm sorry, Britomar, but I miss Guillaume so much."

"There are some hurts that I can't heal," said the unicorn.

"Being in your presence helps, it does. But the chevalier...Sir Wigandus...he..."

"I'm sorry, I didn't know that having a man amongst us would cause you pain."

Gwen sniffled again. "It must be because he keeps praising me the way Guillaume did...Oh, Britomar, why did you let him come with us?"

"The raven told me to."

Gwen's eyes widened. "The raven?"

"Yes."

Gwen wondered if the raven was Nimuë's familiar, but was afraid to ask. It was bad enough to know that the sorceress had a part in getting her together with Britomar. She still wondered about this Lilith she had helped. Nimuë's story about Lilith being Adam's first wife couldn't be true, and even it were, how could Adam's wife still be alive? Why wasn't she mentioned in the stories Gwen heard in the convent? But, no sense dwelling on unanswered questions. A promise she'd made, and a promise she'd keep, even if it was to a sorceress.

"Shouldn't we be getting back?" she asked the unicorn.

"The three women are on their way, and will be here shortly."

"But I thought..."

114

"...that I was confused by Élise's smell on that man? True, her smell was stronger than the others, but I also smell Garsenda and Adelie. They are not far from here."

"Then Élise will meet Martis along the way?"

"Perhaps. I hope so. He seemed so disturbed by what he has done. It would be good to give him a chance to ask her forgiveness."

They did not have to wait long before they could hear Garsenda and Élise in a heated discussion. Gwen soon saw them, Adelie riding off to one side, while Élise and Garsenda rode next to each other, both red-faced in their argument.

As they got within earshot of Gwen, Adelie shouted, "Élise was right! The scholars told us where to look!"

"That's wonderful!" said Gwen. "But first, did you see Martis on your way here?"

Élise winced. "No."

"Then you may want to ride after him, he was here not long ago, asking for you."

"It's pointless."

"Why?"

Élise pursed her lips. "Little miss perfect here had to go and inform my father that—"

Garsenda shook her head, "How was I to know that you wouldn't want—"

"Stop it!" screamed Adelie. "Enough, both of you. Anyone might have made this mistake. Garsenda was only trying to act in your interests, Élise."

"Like she acted in my interests when she sent me to be assaulted and raped on the king's highway?"

Garsenda gasped. "I did nothing of the sort! I had no way to—"

This time Gwen interrupted. "Will you all be quiet for a moment! I don't know what you are all going on about, but Martis feels terrible about something he did or said regarding you, Élise, and he was looking for you. That has nothing to do with your father, or with any of us. If you love him, go to him and hear him out."

Élise lowered her head. "No. Britomar's errand is more important." Adelie and Gwen both started to speak but she waved them into silence. "He couldn't forgive me for things I didn't do, he couldn't believe me. Adelie, you asked me in Paris if he could act that way if he loved me. I thought about it a lot. And I know the answer now. No. If he loved me, he would have come with us to the queen when I asked him to. He would have trusted me that much."

"Élise," Gwen protested. "He's broken-hearted about how he

treated you."

"Enough. As we stand here bickering, Britomar's errand waits."

"It can wait for love," said Britomar.

"No, Britomar, I'm not certain it can wait, certainly not for Martis. Love, if it is in his heart, will have to find me. If I am his true love, he will find me. Besides, my father has forbidden me to seek him. I am supposed to marry a prince of Armenia or something."

Gwen raised her head. "Élise, would you not ask him to join with us? Wouldn't that be the greatest possible test of his love for you?"

Élise's mouth fell open. "Ask a *man* to join us?"

Gwen sighed. "It's already been done. A knight of the Empire waits for us at camp."

Gwen registered the shock on the other woman's faces, but she kept her eyes on Élise. If Guillaume could be here, she would have asked him to join her quest without hesitation. She wanted Élise to be happy.

But Élise only shook her head. "Gwen, you have obviously had some adventures of your own while we were in Paris, but no, I will not go to Martis. If it is meant to be, love will find a way to triumph." She glared at Garsenda. "I am promised in marriage, and Martis is forbidden to me." She nudged her horse, urging it back for camp.

As the others followed, Gwen maneuvered her horse so that she rode next to Garsenda. "Is there that much anger between you?"

Garsenda shrugged. "She accused me of setting her up to be raped, when I was only trying to help her escape an unwelcome marriage— at her request, too. My master set me free of her service. I'm done with her."

Gwen didn't know what to say. She was grateful when Adelie picked up the thread of Sir Wigandus. "What happened while we were gone?"

Gwen told them about the ogre, and then the trial. "When the fighting ended, he offered himself as my escort home. I told him I was not going home, that I was on a sacred mission, and he asked to come with us. Britomar accepted."

"What will we do with a man amongst us?" groaned Garsenda.

"He has sworn an oath of chastity," said Britomar.

"That may be, and he may even keep it," said Garsenda, "but we'll have no more privacy for baths, for relieving ourselves, for anything!"

Gwen wondered if Garsenda was always that petty. "He never intruded on me during the past day. In fact, I was surprised by his courtesy." *If only he'd stop quoting poetry at me. Or looking at me with that tender admiration in his eyes.*

Britomar shook her head and snorted. "We will need someone to protect you all in situations where Adelie's knife does not suffice. Besides, the raven was rather insistent that Sir Wigandus be allowed to come."

When they neared the camp Gwen caught a smell of roasting fowl. Then wings fluttered and a familiar weight settled onto her shoulder. She couldn't turn to look at the raven, but she could tell it was preening in delight at her return.

Wigandus stooped over a makeshift spigot, turning two large birds over the fire. Gwen smiled as she saw him shift a roasting leg, burn his fingers, shake them while muttering what must be German oaths, then sticking his fingertips into his mouth. Apparently he had more about him than poetry and chivalry.

The raven cawed and the knight stood up, met Gwen's eyes and smiled. She felt a warmth inside her, and suppressed a blush, busying herself with introductions.

After exchanging pleasantries they settled down to their meal. As they ate, Élise told Wigandus, Britomar, and Gwen of what they had learnt from Brothers Bonaventure and Thomas.

"I am so excited to think that the world's center is Mount Sinai and that we'll stand on His holy mountain."

"But Élise, they were all certain that the Garden is elsewhere." said Adelie.

"But they did not know where, and only gave hints of mountains east and north of Jerusalem. Why not look on Mount Sinai first?"

"Brother Thomas seemed to think we would learn in Baghdad where the Garden is," said Adelie. "I feel that we should make our way there first."

"I know that the Italian cities have trade with the Holy Land, and the infidel. We could gain passage on a ship of theirs," suggested Wigandus.

Britomar shook her head. "After seeing the greed of Sir Bryon, I fear to spend much time on a ship. Overland routes, while slower, remain open to us."

Wigandus clicked his tongue. "The passages north of the Danube are beset by a new barbarian horde. The rumors of the Great Khan and the terror of his army have reached Thuringia. We may find the overland route closed to us as well."

"Why can't we travel through Constantinople?" asked Garsenda.

"The Greeks make war upon the excommunicates to recover their city, so we would be in great danger," said Wigandus.

"Let us attempt the overland route, and we can always head south if needed," advised Élise.

"I agree, but how should we go?" asked Adelie.

"That is a good question. Should we travel north through the Empire, or go south of the Alps and through Italy? South of the Alps would mean avoiding the armies of the Great Khan, and would offer us more hope of supplies. North has less roads, and therefore less chance of being noticed. I would go the northern route, were I to go alone," said Britomar.

Wigandus nodded. "I know my way through the Empire, and I know it to be safe. I also understand that King Wenceslas of Bohemia is keeping the barbarians at bay. I too would recommend the northern route."

"But which is to be our destination, Mount Sinai or Baghdad?" asked Gwen.

"The world's center is Mount Sinai," Élise said. "Let us go there."

"But Brother Bonaventure said the world's center is wherever God is," said Garsenda. "Both of them were clear that there is no garden on Mount Sinai. Let us go to Baghdad and learn more. After all, didn't the riddle hint that we must find the roof of the world?"

"I agree with Garsenda. We should go to Baghdad," said Adelie.

"Then it's decided," said Britomar. "Let us prepare our things so that we may depart at dawn. We will go to Baghdad through the Empire via the land route."

FOR EVERYTHING THERE IS A SEASON

Translator's note:

This is one of the few places where pages of the manuscript were impossible to read. Every technique was tried, including looking at the fragile original under a microscope. I was able to continue with Jigme's manuscript with the company high in the Alps, with no knowledge of how they got there, or what adventures they faced upon the way.

Gwen looked up through the breaks in the forest canopy at the cold glare of the sun on the white caps of the mountaintops. Just above the peaks, though hard to see in the blazing light, a large bird circled. She watched it until its flight was lost in the snow-flecked canopy of tall pines. She felt the raven tighten its grip on her shoulder, and realized that the bird had also seen the flight of its brethren, and was somewhat anxious about it.

When she lowered her eyes, she had to blink for a moment before she could see again. The path before them was again in the shadows, and her eyes saw brilliant spots in its place. It had been days since they had seen a cultivated field, and there were few signs of other travelers on the snow-splattered road.

Sir Wigandus moved his horse next to her.

"I saw you looking at the peaks," he said. "Those are the Alps. That village you can see at the base of the mountain must thrive on trade over the passes. We'll be able to replenish our supplies there."

Gwen, who had not noticed the village until he pointed it out, let her eyes follow his hand. The village, not far away, was enclosed by a stockade and seemed rather large.

Gwen felt the raven's wing brush her cheek as it took off from her shoulder. She gasped as the bird flew back in her face and then upwards again. She followed its flight and saw a shadow falling upon them. "Look out!" was all she had time to cry out, echoed by a loud screech from above, "Kreeee!"

Gwen heard the metal sing as Wigandus drew his sword. Élise screamed. Britomar reared, her horn flashing in the sunlight.

Gwen nearly fell off her horse as it bucked and tried to run. As she frantically pulled back on the reins, a blast of foul-smelling ice-cold air hit her in the face.

"It's a griffin!" shouted Sir Wigandus. "Off your horses!"

Gwen leaned over and embraced the bucking horse's neck, "Easy girl! Easy, Britomar's here." The horse shook its head but the bucking became a prancing. Gwen slid a leg around its side, took a deep breath, and leapt. She fell and rolled forward, scrambling to her feet, grateful for the lessons Wigandus had given them all.

Neither the griffin nor the raven was to be seen in her anxious scan of the sky. Wigandus looked at the sky as well, sword at ready, as did Adelie with her knife. Britomar took off, chasing after Élise's horse.

"Garsenda!" cried Élise.

Garsenda was hanging from her horse, her foot caught in her packs, her chestnut hair dragging on the now bloody snow. Trying to control the panicking horse, Élise held the reins with one hand, frantically pulling on the saddle straps with the other.

Gwen began to run to help Élise when she saw Britomar gallop past. Distracted, she slipped and fell into the snow. As she rose to her feet, she gasped.

The griffin had landed on Garsenda's saddle. The poor horse screamed in agony, knocking Élise to her haunches. The griffin's claws closed on the horse's back, lifting its prey into the air, with Garsenda dangling limp by her leg where she was still entangled.

Britomar leapt at the griffin, knocking it off the horse. Together they rolled, horn stabbing, hooves flashing, claws cutting. The griffin's massive beak tore Britomar's side. The unicorn fell to the ground. From the blood and snow, the griffin rose.

With a flash of steel Wigandus sprang at the griffin, hacking at its wings. Adelie leapt next to Wigandus, catching a claw with her knife, bending under the weight of the monster's paw. As Wigandus pushed in under the beast, stabbing at its soft underbelly, one of its claws hit Adelie, cutting her shoulder.

Élise pushed herself off the ground and ran to Garsenda. The maid lay limp on the ground, blood gashing out of the gaping wound in her side.

Gwen's heart quivered as she scrambled to her feet and rushed to Britomar. The unicorn's wounds were dirty and deep. They smelled wrong. She grabbed a handful of snow and melted it in her hands to wash the wound. Packing more snow over the rent on the unicorn's side, she pulled her cloak off and wrapped it around the unicorn's neck, pressing it against the torn flesh. She frantically tore strips of cloth from her skirt, tying them together into strips long enough to hold the cloak in place.

Wigandus said, "There may be more griffins around. We must find shelter."

Britomar opened her eyes. "Gwenaella, you must take me to the village over there. I spoke to a girl there yesterday, they have some there skilled in tending the wounded."

Just then Élise started to sob. "No, no, no! Garsenda! Come back!"

Adelie and Wigandus rushed to her side. Gwen turned to look. The knight picked up Garsenda's hand and felt her wrist. His face looked grave as he gently lowered the hand on Garsenda's chest, folding her other hand over it. Then he reached over and closed her eyes.

Tears rolled down Gwen's cheeks as she sat by the unicorn's side, watching Adelie wrap her arms around Élise's shoulders, trying to lead her away. Élise screamed, throwing her arms around Garsenda's still form. Gwen pressed her head against Britomar's side. The clean smell of a summer storm she had come to love had been replaced by sweat and blood. The wound smelled foul, as if infected.

Wigandus unstrung a small hand-ax from his belt and rushed into the woods, chopping down a sapling. He lay it down and started at another nearby. Gwen shook off her grief and ran to his side. She took the first sapling and dragged it onto the road. Soon, Wigandus joined her, laying the two long poles down side by side.

Gwen took a knife from her pack and went to Garsenda's dead horse. She cut the straps to remove the packs, saddle and halter, bringing them to where Wigandus was stripping the saplings of their branches with his hand-ax. She cut and tied two strips to the lower ends of the poles. Wigandus then helped her tie the straps to the harness of his destrier. He spread his cloak over the two poles as Gwen tied it to the poles with a length of rope, wishing she had some of the good flaxen rope Tadig used to use to make his nets. She secured the rope with a knot Tadig had taught her to secure a sail to a mast.

Adelie sat nearby, cradling Élise in her arms.

"We need both of your help to move Britomar onto the gurney," Gwen said.

Élise looked up, eyes red and hollow, and nodded.

Wigandus had moved his horse and the gurney as close to Britomar as he could. He put himself near her shoulders. Gwen supported the unicorn's hind, Adelie and Élise by the legs.

"Don't lift until I give the word," Wigandus said. "We're going to shift her onto the gurney in one motion. Ready?... Lift!"

Britomar was surprisingly light. Gwen held her breath as they lowered the unicorn onto the frame, glad that the cloak did not tear, and that her knots held. She looked around for the raven, but the trickster was nowhere to be seen.

Wigandus walked to Garsenda and lifted her broken body, draping it over Élise's horse. He handed the reins to Élise. Gwen and Adelie put the packs from Garsenda's horse on theirs, tying them down as best as they could with what leather and rope was left. Then they all began the slow walk uphill to the village.

SALVATION IS FROM THE JEWS

Gwen looked back at Britomar anxiously. She could see the unicorn's breath in the cold night air, which provided a measure of reassurance for her. If Britomar died, the whole trip, Garsenda's death, Élise's broken heart, and all their suffering were meaningless.

They traveled slowly, so she had been able to put fresh snow on the wound, slowing the bleeding as much as she could. Dusk had fallen, and so did her hopes. She prayed that the village would open its gate to them. This must be a dangerous land for a village to have built a stockade, no matter Sir Wigandus's assurances that the Empire was secure and well defended.

At long last they approached the village gate. Gwen could hear voices, screaming children, laughter, and argument. She couldn't make heads or tales of the words, but the language sounded so very different from the German she had heard Wigandus use sometimes.

Wigandus handed her the reins and strode to the gate. Pounding on it, he shouted, "Gott im Himmel, ließ uns hereinkommen. Wir haben verletzt!"[1]

After a long moment the gate opened to reveal two men holding torches. They wore thick fur cloaks and strange pale-yellow caps.

Jews!

"Hurry!" whispered Britomar.

Sir Wigandus talked to the guards. One of them ran off while Wigandus and the other pushed the gate open wide, both gesturing that they were to enter.

Two sturdy looking women ran toward them, open mantles flowing from their shoulders. One rushed to Britomar, the other to Adelie. Gwen dismounted and stood next to the unicorn.

One of the women approached her. She had dark curly hair, sticking in unruly strands from under her head scarf, her large black eyes glistening in the torchlight. "I am Ruth. The woman looking at your friend is Esther. I'll take your beast to a place were men are gathering

---

[1]Translator's note: "By God in Heaven, let us enter. We have wounded!"

to tend its wounds. Esther will take good care of the maiden."

Gwen nodded. "Thank you, Ruth. I'm Gwenaella. May I come with you and Britomar?"

"The unicorn?"

"Yes."

"Come. Our rabbi will be along in a moment to help with your deceased friend, and find suitable quarters for the good knight, if he would be so kind as to wait for him here."

"I will wait." Sir Wigandus lifted Garsenda's body from the horse and laid it on the ground. Élise silently walked over and lowered to the ground by Garsenda's side.

Gwen led Sir Wigandus's destrier after Ruth through a wide street toward a stable, not far from the village gate. Three men with lit torches stood outside the stable's open door. More torches moved inside. The men helped Gwen to guide the destrier and gurney inside.

The stable was spacious and well lit. A table in its center was set with tools, laid out on a soft white cloth: small and delicate knives, tiny shears, and white silken thread.

One of the men unhitched the destrier and led it into a stall. The others leaned over Britomar. After a moment one of them turned and spoke in halting Provençal, "We must know: does she chew her cud?"

Gwen frowned. In all the months of her journey, she'd never paid attention to how Britomar ate. "Why does it matter?"

Another man said, "A beast with cloven hooves could make us all unclean in the eyes of the Lord."

Gwen looked back and forth between the surgeons in disbelief. God wouldn't let it all end here, in the hands of these damned Jews, would he? "Please, you must help, our mission is a holy one!"

The first surgeon said, "Shall I fetch the rabbi?"

"Yes, and quickly!" replied the third man, who till this moment kept quiet.

The first and youngest of the surgeons ran out of the room and after a few minutes returned with an old man, his thick beard grey with the years. He paused to catch his breath and shouted: "Fools, this is a unicorn, not a pig! Healing her will be a Tzedakah!!"

At those words, the men renewed their efforts, cleaning Britomar's wounds. They worked quickly and efficiently, their deft movements speaking of experience.

Gwen couldn't take it any more, now that the strain of urgency was released. She began to cry, first quietly, and then in loud sobs, covering her eyes with her hands.

The old man approached her and said, "Young woman, it is not fitting for you to stay here while they work. Please, come and walk with me."

She followed him outside, into the clear night air.

"I am Rabbi Efraim," he said. "Welcome to our humble village. I am sorry that Levi, Natan and Shlomo did not begin the work on your friend before I arrived. They were confused. You see, the unicorn has cloven hooves. Such beasts are unclean to us, if they do not chew their cud."

"But, Britomar would die if they did not tend to her wounds."

"Yes, but they were afraid for their, what is your word, souls. There are worse things than death."

"It's so typical for your people to feel that healing could ever be wrong," she said in disgust.

The rabbi sighed. "Child, what is your name?"

"Gwenaella." She looked down at her feet as they walked, guilty for giving voice to her feelings, realizing she'd just insulted the man who had saved Britomar with his words.

"Gwenaella, you are wrong about us. True, there are some of us that do not understand what the Lord wants of us. They do wrong without knowing they do so. No people are without their fools, and no person is without their failings. It is my job to teach those who live in my village to better understand what is expected of them. Healing is so important that we are permitted to do so, even on Shabbat, if doing so would save a life."

Gwen shook her head. "Yet we are taught that the priest and the Levite would not touch a hurt man, only the Samaritan would help him."

She sensed a smile in his voice. "Ah, yes, I know the story." He paused. "If you were of my people, this is what I would say to you: the priest and the Levite in that story were too self-important. They placed their worries about becoming ritually unclean ahead of the possibility of giving aid to those who needed it. The Nazarene was one of many who spoke against these hypocrites. He used the Samaritans as his example because these hypocrites, and others, despised the Samaritans. He was trying to shame the hypocrites into remembering their Torah."

"I thought you Jews hated Jesus."

The rabbi winced. "You say you Jews as if we are one in our thoughts. We have no more unity than you Nazarenes have. Some of us hate the Nazarene rabbi, some find him and his teachings troubling." He grinned. "Some wish that his followers were more like him. However, to be honest, most of us do not think of him, and we do not teach our children anything of him or his teaching."

Gwen wondered what else had she heard from the pulpit that had been false. "Rabbi, I am sorry, I did not know that what I had been taught was so wrong."

"It may be some time before your friends and Britomar can travel...Now, tell me, what drives a unicorn to travel with people?"

"The eldest unicorn is dying, and we're traveling to the Garden at the Roof of the World to pluck the fruit of the tree of life for him."

The rabbi stopped and looked at her in surprise. "The eldest unicorn?"

"Yes. He was foaled in Eden."

"A creature from before Adam's fall still walks? And you hope that feeding it fruit from Eden will restore it to health?" The old man clicked his tongue. "This is a good thing you do." He glanced at the rising moon, a bright crescent in the dark sky. "Now, let's get back to the stables. I suspect that Britomar is already on her feet."

When they arrived back at the stables, Britomar was standing up, chewing some of the oats that she had been given. The surgeons were gone, but Ruth and Esther were there. So was Élise, brushing Britomar's back with a faraway look in her eyes. The rabbi exchanged a few words with Ruth and Esther and left Gwen and Élise in their care.

Ruth said, "Please come with me to my house. Your friend Adelie waits for you there and I have rooms enough for you all. I hope you won't mind staying with me. My husband, a cantor in the synagogue, is able to afford one of the houses in the village which is large enough to have a guest room."

"Ruth," Gwen said. "You are very kind, but we would be fine in an inn. There is no need to place us in your home."

Ruth chuckled, "Mademoiselle, there will be enough gossip said against you without adding to it. To be traveling so freely with a man who is not your husband is scandalous to some amongst us. If I let you three stay in the inn, they would think you were prostitutes and have you driven from the village lest you seduce our men."

Gwen gasped, but Élise nodded. "We have the same prejudices in our villages, and good Christian folks would treat us the same, but for Britomar."

"She is a remarkable beast."

"Did I understand you correctly that your husband is the cantor?" asked Élise.

"Yes, he has such a beautiful voice."

Élise's face unwound into a sad smile. "I was taught Hebrew so that I might learn to sing the Psalms in their original language. I would love to hear him sing. Do you think he would be willing?"

"I will ask him tonight after we dine. Here we are, please consider this home until Britomar is well enough to travel." She opened the door and they entered into a richly furnished room, with curtains on the windows as well as the shutters, woolen cushions on the bench and chairs, and candle sconces hung on the walls with polished metal plates behind them.

Adelie was sitting on a bench under the window, where she had been watching for them. The two women went to her, as Ruth excused herself, "I must attend to the kitchen."

"How is your shoulder?" Gwen asked sitting next to Adelie.

"It is sore and stiff, but they tell me I won't even scar. How is Britomar?"

"Last we saw her, she was on her feet and eating."

Élise paused for a moment, and then said, "The Jewish nation is known for its surgeons. I understand that Saladin himself used a Jew as his own physician."

"Are we in any danger, staying in a Jewish house?" asked Adelie. "The only Jew I had known was rumored to take Christian children to the Infidel for use as slaves."

"They appear to be honest enough folks," said Gwen, who then relayed to Adelie what the Jewish matron had told them regarding staying in an Inn.

Adelie laughed. "To be accused of whoring by a Jew! Well, let us make the best of our stay here. They are treating us as honored guests, the least we could do is to trust them."

"But what of Garsenda?" asked Gwen quietly. "How will we do a funeral properly without a priest?"

"Sir Wigandus made the arrangements with the rabbi. He's sent for a priest from a nearby monastery." Élise looked out of the window, as if she would say no more on the subject.

Adelie moved to sit next to Élise on the bench, "I know how you feel, to lose someone you love. You wrote a song for me, write a song for her."

Élise looked back at Adelie. Tears glistened on her cheeks. "I don't know words to write the torment I feel... I almost had her free of the straps... If only I'd had a moment... she always helped me when I needed her and I couldn't even... Please, leave me alone." She turned back to face the window.

Shortly Ruth returned to the room and bade them join her family for dinner.

Four children, all girls, were waiting in their places. Their dark eyes glistened with curiosity as they stared at their guests. Ruth smiled, beckoning everyone to their seats. "My son is with his father. They'll come home later, so as not to intrude upon your modesty."

The meal of roast goose with carrots and bread seemed delicious after the day's hardships. While they ate, the youngest girl, no older than four, kept looking at Adelie. Whenever Adelie would return her glance, she'd blush and quickly look back at her food.

After the cake had been served, this girl went to Adelie and asked her if it were true that a griffin had hurt her. Adelie said, "Yes, it is true, and your aunt Esther fixed my shoulder right up."

"May I see your shoulder?" asked the child. Adelie looked at Ruth for permission. She nodded, so Adelie opened her blouse. The young girl kissed the bandage, and solemnly said, "When I have a booboo, my Papa kisses it and it feels better."

Ruth smiled. "Children, run along to your rooms. I'll be up in a few minutes to tell you stories."

"Mama, could the pretty lady tell us a story?" asked another girl, pointing at Gwen.

"She may, if she wants to, but then up to your room with you all."

The youngest girl went to Gwen, and tugged on her skirts. "Please, would you tell us a story? Please?"

"What is your name?" asked Gwen.

"Deborah."

"Well, Deborah," said Gwen, picking the child up and placing her on her lap. "I'll tell you a story I heard growing up in my village.

"Once there was a fisherman who had been out to sea for a long time. He had not caught much, and was determined to bring back to shore a worthy catch. He cast his nets again and again without catching a thing. Then, after one such casting, he brought in a young mermaid. He untangled her from the nets, and said to her, 'I'm sorry miss; I was trying for some fish. I hope you're not hurt or anything.' The mermaid tried to talk, but he could not understand her. She gestured wildly toward the shore, but still he could not understand her meaning. Finally, she dove back into the water.

"Not long after, and with little warning, a storm brewed up, catching the small boat in its grasp. The fisherman fought bravely, but a tall wave tossed him overboard into the stormy seas. In his floundering, he was surprised at the feel of strong hands grasping him and he felt someone pulling from behind. Try as he might, he could not see who it was. Finally, exhausted, he fell asleep.

"When he awoke, he was on a beach with many seals. He rose

and began to wander, hoping to find a village. When he did, he was surprised that it was his own village he had found. His boat was never recovered, so he had to seek work on another. No one would take him, they all considered him unlucky. Finally, he went down to the beach with the seals and cried out to the ocean, 'It would have been better to have drowned in your sea than to live unwanted amongst my own kind!'

"All at once, a large wave knocked him to the ground. A hard object hit his stomach, knocking the wind out of him. When he regained his breath, a small chest lay next to him on the sand. Opening it, he found it filled with pearls. Amazed at this great fortune, he shouted to the sea again, 'Thank you!'

"He used the pearls to purchase a new boat. From that day forward, his nets were always full. He knew that he was in debt to the mermen, and wondered how he could repay.

"One day he came back to the harbor to find a mermaid on the dock. Another fisherman had caught her in his net was showing her off to his comrades. Without a word, he pushed through the crowd and hit the fisherman hard in the stomach. Caught off guard, the man dropped the mermaid and our fisherman quickly scooped her up and tossed her into the water. She waved to him before she dove; he stood there watching. He then reached into his pocket and found some pearls. He handed these to the man he had slugged, who was still struggling to stand. Then he returned to his boat and unloaded his cargo. He knew his debt was paid.

"The other fisherman went weeks without a catch. Finally, he took his boat to the place where he had caught the mermaid and dropped the pearls he had in his pocket into the depths of the sea. When he returned to shore, his nets were full. He immediately sought out the first fisherman, and from that day forward, they were the best of friends."

The children listened to Gwen with their mouths open. When the tale was over, they thanked her and then ran off to their room.

"Your children are darlings, Ruth," said Adelie.

The woman smiled. "Thank you. Please excuse me while I get them into their beds."

The three women cleared the table and washed the dishes. When Ruth returned to the kitchen, she exclaimed, "If you will forgive me for saying so, I had always heard that Nazarenes were cruel and heartless. I am delighted to learn otherwise and have you as my guests."

At that moment, the door opened to admit two men, one a strong youth with a long black beard and curly ringlets flowing from under his yellow cap, the other a somewhat portly gentleman, his beard scraggly and grey.

"Élise, Gwenaella, and Adelie, may I present my husband Yosi and my son, David," Ruth said.

"Welcome to our home," said the elder man as he handed his cloak to Ruth.

The women helped Ruth serve the two men their food, and then excused themselves.

Ruth led them up the stair in the back of the house. It was too dark to make out any details by the light of Ruth's lamp. "I am sorry, but there is only one bed."

"Don't worry, we'll manage." said Gwen. She was not likely to sleep much anyway. Why had she chosen that story?... Why couldn't Tadig be like the man in the story?

Élise sat down on the bed and began to cry. "Before we started fighting all the time, Garsenda used to undress me each night. Is it wrong of me to remember her hands on me?"

Gwen took her hands; Adelie sat by her side, leaning Élise against her. Gwen said, "This morning, I rode away from the two of you because I couldn't bear your bickering a moment longer. Now the silence hurts."

She worried about the missing raven, hoping the bird would find her again. It had tried so hard to fend off the griffin.

Élise lifted her head off Adelie's shoulder. "I realized while standing vigil over her with Sir Wigandus that she only wanted me to be a better person, and that I just wanted her to keep caring. I'd rather have her scorn than not be in her thoughts. I've been so angry with her ever since she told my father the truth of why we left home. I realize now that she thought that if he knew about Martis, that he'd fix things so that we could be together."

Gwen shifted so that she too sat next to Élise. "You loved her, didn't you?"

"Yes, I..." the rest of her words dissolved in sobs.

INFERNO

Adelie woke coughing. Her eyes stung, and the room was dark and blazing hot. She got out of bed, surprised at the strong smell of smoke, and staggered to the door. It was hot! "Wake up! Wake up! Fire!"

She had to shake the other two girls before they woke. Gwen tossed her a blanket, which she wrapped around her naked body. Élise's hands shook as she covered up as well. Gwen glanced at the pitcher of water next to the wash basin, and shook her head as she tucked in a corner of the blanket in front of her to keep it closed.

Adelie pulled the blanket's edge over her mouth and nose, opened the door, and stepped back, coughing. The walls were beginning to smolder, and thick black smoke billowed into their room.

They dropped to their hands and knees, crawling under the curling tendrils of death, breathing the hot air through their blankets. Once they reached the stairs, they were able to stand; the stairs were still free of flames. They raced down and then out through the open front door.

Ruth was in the street, kneeling as she held two of her children, both crying.

"Where are the others?" Adelie asked, coughing.

"Yosi and David went back to get them," she sobbed.

Adelie looked at both Élise and Gwen, words sticking in her throat. Gwen turned her head to stare at the thick smoke filling the void of the door frame and grimaced.

Adelie saw the bucket brigade forming, and had an idea. She ran to a pile of buckets and lifted one over her head, letting the water pour over her. Gwen and Élise did the same, and then they ran back to the inferno.

Covering their noses with wet blankets, they crawled through the parlor in the direction of what they hoped was the girls' bedroom. Flames had begun to lick the walls. Adelie could feel panic rising as she moved further into the oven the house had become, praying fervently that they reach the children in time, forcing herself to repeat again and again in her head, *please let us save the children.*

She gasped in relief when they saw Yosi, surrounded by flames, kneeling. He was holding one of the younger girls in one arm while he pulled on David's leg, caught in the collapsing floor boards. David held Deborah.

"Give us the children!" Élise shouted.

Élise and Gwen each grabbed a child and rushed outside. Adelie knelt to see what could be done to free David. She pushed down on the floorboards to keep them away from his leg. Yosi waited for his son's leg to come free and pulled him up.

David's leg was bleeding badly. He tried to walk, but could not put much weight on it. He put an arm around his father's shoulder, and the three of them headed toward the exit, coughing in the thick smoke.

At the end of the passage they had to stop. The main hall in front of them was an inferno, tall flames rising up to block their path. Remembering how her mother once smothered a fire, Adelie unwrapped her blanket and threw it down to cover the flames. They raced over the path she had created to the door.

Adelie shuddered as she looked back and saw that the house was completely engulfed. The bucket brigade was wetting down neighboring homes, so that the fire would not spread. Coughing badly, she felt a cloth fall over her shoulders, and turned to see Esther.

"I'll go and fetch you poor girls some clothes," she said.

Adelie looked down and saw that beneath the cloak Esther had covered her with her skin was black with soot and covered in raw oozing blisters that she was only now beginning to feel. Grateful for the covering, she wrapped herself in it, wincing as it pulled across the blisters. She glanced at Gwen and Élise, and saw they were also marred, both coughing and gasping for air.

Gwen frowned. "I'm going to make certain Britomar's safe." She rushed off into the shadows.

Adelie sank to the ground, wincing at the pain in her blistering skin, spreading the cloak so that it covered her legs. Deborah came over and hugged her, then curled up in her lap. Adelie rocked her, humming a song she learned from Elise on the road. She couldn't stop thinking how close they had all come to joining Garsenda.

All through the night, men passed bucket after bucket to toss water upon the flames. Esther had taken Ruth's younger children, though Deborah would not be separated from Adelie. Once David's leg was bandaged, he limped over to help with passing the buckets. At some point, Adelie glanced up from rocking Deborah in her lap and noticed that Wigandus was standing next to David in the bucket chain.

By dawn, the house was a smoldering ruin, but they had kept the fire from spreading.

Wigandus sought out Adelie and Élise. He looked weary, but his face was stern and eyes alert. "I visited Gwen in the stables. She's safe; the rabbi has posted a guard." He lowered his voice; "I have a boy in my room, tied up. He snuck in and tried to slit my throat. What should I do with him?"

"Let's go to their rabbi," suggested Élise, who looked odd in the Judaic dress she'd put on.

Adelie agreed, "First, let me dress." She reluctantly handed the sleeping Deborah to Esther and took the garments. "Where can I do it, Esther?"

They found the rabbi talking with Yosi and David, who were sifting through the ruins of their once fine house. As they approached, Yosi looked up from the cinders and smiled. "I owe you all the lives of my children. I bless you and the mothers who bore you!"

David looked only at Adelie, who lowered her eyes and blushed.

"Rabbi," said Élise, "Sir Wigandus was attacked in his room, a boy tried to slit his throat, but Sir Wigandus tied him up. The innkeeper is guarding him at the inn."

The rabbi's shoulders slumped and he looked at the ground. "To think that my own people could..."

Yosi stepped from the ruins, took the rabbi's hand and said something in Hebrew. The rabbi nodded sadly. "Come with me." He headed toward the inn, staring at the ground as he walked.

Shadows cast by their lanterns danced like vengeful ghosts on the walls of the sparsely furnished room. The innkeeper was sitting beside a boy with sand-colored hair, who seemed more sad than scared as he lay on the floor, tied hand and foot. "This boy is not from our village, rabbi. I've never seen him before".

Rabbi Efraim nodded. "You're right; I've never seen him before either. Still, that may mean nothing. Ungag him, and let him up."

The innkeeper obeyed.

"What is your name? Who sent you, boy?"

The boy looked back and forth between them, and then said, "I'm Hans. Master Nechemiah told me to burn the house and kill the knight. He told me that if I made certain that the foreigners were killed, he'd spare my sister."

"Master Nechemiah?" Wigandus asked.

The rabbi frowned. "He is a merchant who I've long suspected of being in the slave trade with the Mohammedans."

"Let's take the boy and pay a visit to this Nechemiah," Adelie said through clenched teeth.

When they got to his house, they found it empty. Chests stood open, cabinets bare. In the study, under a chair, the rabbi found a large leather-bound book with age-darkened pages. He flipped through it, muttering under his breath.

"It is as I suspected," he said. "Here is a document detailing his transactions, I guess he forgot it in his haste to depart. Let's search the cellar."

In the cellar they found a girl shackled to a ring in the wall. She was very thin, and covered with purple bruises. As Sir Wigandus busied himself with setting her free, Rabbi Efraim walked along the wall, lined with many other such rings, chains hanging empty over the scruffs in the urine soaked floor. He took up one of the chains, weighted it in his hand and let go. Hanging his head, he said, "I myself hold the boy blameless, he did this to spare his sister. I will find some one to adopt these children."

Sir Wigandus shook his head. "I still don't understand why would he try to murder us and our hosts." He grunted as he pulled on the end attached to the ring. The room echoed with the metallic twang as the ring snapped. The girl ran into her brother's arms, shaking.

The rabbi said, "Nechemiah has long hated Nazarenes. When the king drove us from our homes in Paris, he lost his wife on that journey, and swore to kill any Nazarene he met. I always hoped those were just words."

Adelie stole a glance at David and was surprised at the anger his face showed. She shivered, and for the first time since she was a girl she started to cry.

Élise put an arm around her. "Come, we're all tired. Let's find a place where we can sleep in peace."

The rabbi said, "I'm terribly sorry, this has been a hard night for us all. Let me find you all a place to rest."

Outside, they saw Esther running to them, beaming, her hair falling out from her kerchief. "Rabbi, I have found housing for the three Nazarene women."

"Well done Esther, well done. Where?"

"Sara will take Gwenaella, Miriam will take Lady Elisabeth, and I will have Lady Adelie under my own roof."

"But Esther, you've already taken in Ruth and her children. Where will you find room for yet another?"

"Ruth insists, Rabbi. Adelie saved David's life, risking her own and sacrificing her modesty. Ruth wants Adelie with her family."

"And you, Esther?"

"We'll make do, rabbi, we always do," she said, lowering her eyes.

"You are a good woman, Esther. Go to the stables, you will find Gwen there."

The rabbi took Élise with him, while Adelie followed David through the shadows as the sun turned the eastern sky pink. While she found his silence awkward, she could think of nothing to say herself, too embarrassed by being alone with him.

David had barely opened the door when Ruth threw herself through it, embracing Adelie in tears, kissing her on both cheeks.

Adelie pulled away, "Please, I don't deserve..."

"Deserve! Had I riches to shower upon you, you would deserve more. Adelie, you gave me back my son! You helped save my other children. Now, no more words. Come in."

Adelie slept on the floor with Ruth and her daughters. Her dreams were filled with flames and griffins. She woke before they did and found a well at the back of the house, private enough for her to wash herself. She scrubbed gingerly at her soot-stained skin, ignoring the way her blisters stung when opened.

By the time she returned, the others were awake. Deborah jumped around her shouting "Addy! Addy! Addy!"

Ruth poked her head out of the kitchen. "Quiet, child! You'll wake Papa!"

"Papa is already awake!" yelled Yosi from an adjoining room. Adelie could not help but grin as Deborah and two of the younger children began to chant "Papa Papa Papa!", when a bang on the door to the house stilled their voices.

Yosi emerged from the side room straightening his skullcap. He opened the door to find the rabbi, accompanied by a short and stout monk in a blue cassock.

Yosi turned to Adelie. "Adelie, you had better come."

Adelie bent over and gave each of the children a kiss on their forehead. As she stepped toward the door, David emerged from the side room. Adelie's heart quickened as he followed her out the door.

Outside they found Sir Wigandus, his face haggard with grief, holding Garsenda's shrouded corpse. To either side stood Gwen and Élise. Élise had her harp strapped to her back. Wigandus placed Garsenda into a cart. Élise took up one of the handles, Wigandus the other.

It was a slow, hot walk from the village to the graveyard in the shadows of the monastery. After they climbed up to where the monks had cleared a space for a small cemetery, David joined Wigandus in the digging the grave. Élise's sobs were the only sound other than the shovels and the thuds of the tossed earth.

The monk said the prayers in Latin. Élise took Garsenda's feet, and Wigandus the shoulders, and together they gently laid her to rest.

Élise sat at the foot of the grave and played some hymns on her harp. Adelie noticed that David had been singing the words under his breath as Élise plucked the sorrowful tunes. She played hymn after hymn until she broke down in tears. Adelie embraced her and helped her stand. The monk blessed the grave, and then Sir Wigandus and David began to fill the hole.

"Thank you," Wigandus said to David when it was done.

"It is hard to bury someone so young," David replied. "Thanks to you and your friends, this is the only funeral we have today."

As they walked back to the village, Adelie glanced over at David and noticed that he walked with Sir Wigandus and not with the rabbi. She only dared to glance in the direction of Yosi once, and saw that his face wore a troubled expression, and that Rabbi Efraim was quietly talking to him.

Adelie spent the next few days helping Ruth with the children, who liked nothing better than to watch the men building them a new home. They would play nowhere else but in sight of the rising house, and took their midday meals there. The girls loved to watch Wigandus as he helped carry the huge logs that other men cut into the beams for the new roof. Adelie frequently played dolls with Deborah. Often she would look up and watch as David helped Wigandus put a beam into place. As if David could feel her eyes on him, he always turned around and waved to her, making Adelie blush.

At night, Adelie slept on the floor with Ruth and her girls. She'd frequently wake in the night from nightmares of the flames, only to hear David and Yosi arguing softly in the other room. Once, she woke from a nightmare to the sounds of chanting and found a faint light coming in from outside. She wrapped herself in her blanket and followed the light, and the voice. Outside, she found David, facing east, singing softly to himself. She waited until he was done, and then stepped out from the doorway.

"You sing beautifully. What do the words mean?"

David's smile made her blush. "Thank you," he said. "It is an ancient prayer we sing every morning, and again at night."

"It scared away my nightmare."

"His words do that... How are your burns healing?"

"They're fine, Britomar touched me with her horn."

"She is a remarkable creature. And you—you are a remarkable woman."

Adelie's blush deepened. She looked down at her feet, hoping to make it less obvious. "I'm just an alley rat. I ain't nothing special."

"I don't know. I'd love to have lived as you have, traveling, meeting new people, following a unicorn from one adventure to another to save the life of the eldest of unicorns."

"You've got a father who loves you and teaches you. You've a mother who loves you, and will choose for you the best of brides." Adelie's lips trembled. Why couldn't she have all these things too? She turned her face from him and slid back into the house so that he wouldn't see her cry.

One night she got up to find a chamber pot, and heard Yosi and David bickering in the other room. She stepped quietly, not to let them hear her. Adelie could not understand what they were saying, but caught her name in something David was saying. Distracted, she almost tripped over Ruth and realized that the older woman wasn't sleeping either. When she saw Adelie looking, she put a finger to her lips, but it was too late. The men must have heard Adelie stumble. The argument in the other room had ceased.

Ruth sat up to look into Adelie's face. "Child, have you feelings for my David?" she whispered.

"Yes..." Adelie paused, her lips trembling. Ruth hugged her and Adelie realized the older woman was shaking with sobs.

Adelie sniffled, swallowing her own tears. "You don't have to tell me it's impossible, I already know that. But I—I love him."

Ruth clasped Adelie's hands. "My grandmother, when she lived in England, met a knight. He had been badly hurt, and she tended his wounds. He came to love her, as many patients do those that heal them. Later, he saved her life, defending her when she was accused of witchcraft. He loved her, and she loved him. And then... he went off to marry his betrothed, and she moved to Spain where she eventually fell in love with my grandfather and followed him to France. She was happy, but she never forgot that knight, and taught her children and grand children how not all the Nazarenes are cruel."

Adelie lowered her head. "I know. I must move on too, and let David marry and be happy."

Ruth clutched her hands tighter. "It is hard for a mother to say such things, but you are a remarkable woman and I am proud that you find my son worthy of your love. But... as a mother I also worry that your love for him could destroy you both."

"Ruth, I—I don't know what to say..."

"Then don't. Let us both listen, and pray."

Within a week of their arrival, Britomar was ready to travel again. Gwen and Élise purchased supplies for the next stage of their journey east. Adelie, however, did not help them, but instead helped Ruth purchase new goods for her home. It was hard to bear a thought of leaving, now that she found a place she was so happy in. Could she abandon her quest and stay in the village with Ruth and her family?

Adelie sat on the porch sewing by the faint light of the setting sun when Élise came by.

"We're all set to leave with the dawn."

Adelie looked down at her sewing. "I don't know if I can leave. I—I want to stay."

Élise's lips stretched into a smile, but her pinched face spoke otherwise. She clenched her fists. "If you stay here to be near a man who can't have you, you'll be a fool."

Adelie put down her sewing and looked up at Élise. "But I—Oh, Élise, what should I do?..."

Elise strode forward and sat down next to her. "Papa gave you that knife to help keep Gwen safe. He acknowledged you as his own. If you don't come, you will also turn your back on Papa. One day we will miss that knife of yours. And every day I will miss the sister I have grown to love."

"You're right, I know you're right." Adelie wiped her nose with her sleeve. "I just never met anyone who made me feel this way."

Élise shook her head. "Before we came on this journey, Garsenda and I did not fight—well, at least not so much. She was once in love with a village boy. When I encouraged her to leave my service to marry him, she told me that he could never marry a ladies' maid, and she—she would never change who she was. Not for a man. Because if she did, she would never know if he truly loved her."

Adelie sighed and put down her sewing. After a long moment she nodded. "I'll meet you at daybreak."

As Adelie walked inside, Deborah ran to meet her. "Addy! I made you this." She handed Adelie a straw unicorn doll.

Adelie sank to her knees and hugged the girl tightly. "Thank you, Oh thank you so much, Deborah. I love it! It's so like Britomar." She gave Deborah another hug. "I have to leave first thing in the morning, and I don't know if I'm ever coming back."

Deborah's smile faded. "Then I will kiss you good bye." She kissed Adelie on the cheek and ran out of the room.

After saying goodbye to the other young children, Adelie entered the parlor where Yosi, David and Ruth were sitting. She went to Ruth. "Ruth, you have a wonderful family, and are a remarkable woman. Thank you so much for having me in your home."

Ruth rose and embraced her, but then sat down again without a word. Adelie wondered if she'd done something to put her off, but kept her concerns to herself and went to prepare for her journey.

She slept fitfully that night, and rose before the dawn. She was a little surprised to find Ruth, Yosi and David sitting at the table finishing a meal.

Adelie took a deep breath, careful not to step on any of the sleeping girls as she walked over to them. "Yosi, I cannot put it into words what it has meant to me to live with your daughters. I felt for the first time like I had a family of my own. Thank you."

David rose. "Father, with your permission, I would join them in their quest. They will need someone who can speak Arabic, and perhaps Pharsi where they are going. I have these skills, and the healing of the eldest of unicorns is an errand to which we should lend our aid."

Adelie realized her mouth was hanging open and closed it. David had been fighting with his father about joining their errand?

Yosi bowed his head. "David, we have talked about this for days. Since you still wish to go on this errand, I will not hold you back. You always longed to travel with your uncle, now you'll have your chance to see how much truth there is to his stories of buildings with roofs of gold. I just need to know, are your motives for joining their errand clear?"

Adelie glanced at Ruth, who would not meet her eyes.

"Yes I am clear as to why I am doing this," said David.

"Then, I bless you, my son, and I bless this endeavor."

David went to his mother, who hugged him and said, "David, the perils you will face are not to be found in just the sword. Be careful, my son."

"I will be, mother, I will be." He went into the back room and came out with a pack. After embracing his parents once again, he followed Adelie into the street, and to the stables.

The rabbi was waiting there with Sir Wigandus, Élise and Gwen. He held the reins of David's horse.

"David, I give you my blessing, and the blessing of our community. On this journey you represent the children of Israel. You are a soldier of the Lord now, and should not rest until your task is done. There will be Sabbaths enough when you are done. I am filled with pride at your courage, and will join my voice to the prayers for this errand's success."

He started to chant and Adelie recognized some of the words from Ruth's Friday night prayers. Her legs began to shake. She both wondered and dreaded at the thought that perhaps David was also joining their errand to be with her.

As they rode out of the village, Gwen's black bird swept out of the trees and landed on her shoulder. Adelie looked back as the doors in the stockade slowly closed. She was leaving the only real home she'd ever known.

RECONCILIATIONS

Élise turned to look back upon the cruel gray peaks that housed Garsenda's grave. She squinted, holding up a hand to shield her eyes from the steady rain, then lowered her gaze and pulled her hood forward. Garsenda's words from their recent arguments echoed in her thoughts: that she was cruel and heartless, that she thought only of herself.

How she longed to shout at her "No! I think only of you!" but nothing she felt would shut down that echo that Garsenda's death had fixed in her memory.

The rain became heavier, beating upon her hood, drowning the sound of the muddy plop of the horse's hooves. She looked ahead to the others, slumped in their saddles. Was this quest for the eldest of unicorns worth their lives?

Garsenda had always been so vigorous, so full of life. Élise remembered, when she was younger, how Garsenda pricked her finger on a rose Élise had given her. Back then she had kissed the soft wound, Garsenda's eyes shining in gratitude for the simple kindness.

When Garsenda had first become her servant, they were both so young, more playmates than a mistress and a servant. Elise remembered singing to Garsenda when the echoes of thunder kept them awake on dark stormy nights. She found herself humming the soft melody of that song. As she hummed, words formed on the edge of awareness, and she sang a new song.

> *I am glad of this rain,*
> *Though it drenches me,*
> *It hides my tears*
> *Does it fall on your grave,*
> *Turning bare earth green*
>
> *May God grant that your grave*
> *May grow wild flowers*
> *The morning dew*

Would be my tears for you,
My dearest beloved

Her voice started to break but she sang the words that hung on the edge of her heart.

Your beauty echoed by
Flower's open hues
Ever renewed
I am glad of this rain,
It brings me thoughts of you

The rough edge of her song cut her resolve and Élise broke down in sobs as the horse under her continued its merciless plodding away from Garsenda's grave.

Crack! Élise looked up from the pot of porridge she was stirring to see Sir Wigandus parry David's wooden training sword with a clean blow. She smiled as she watched the muscles in the knight's arms pulse. Parry, crack! Parry crack! Each time David swang his weapon at the knight, Wigandus's wooden blade was there to block it. Finally, breathing heavily, David backed off.

"Better this time," said Sir Wigandus. "Less predictable, but your eyes are still telling me where your sword will land. Now you, Adelie."

Adelie came at the knight with two wooden knives. Élise wanted to clap as the knight's sword became a blur in his parries.

"Good!" said Sir Wigandus. "Good! You nearly caught me this time."

Adelie stepped back, her mouth set firm. "Come at me, then."

Without warning, the knight's sword was in motion, slashing, sliding, cutting, as Adelie parried each move he made until he slid his blade over her knives in a thrust that knocked her to the ground.

Élise started to rise, but David beat her to it, helping Adelie to her feet. Élise's eyebrows rose in surprise. Wasn't that a bit too familiar of David?

Something's burning... What? The porridge! Élise wrapped her hands in her skirts and lifted the pot off the coals. Taking the spoon, she quickly stirred it, hoping to rescue the bulk of it. Phew! Only the very bottom was scorched.

Garsenda would never have burnt the porridge. Garsenda was

right; Élise was selfish. She should never have looked up from the pot to watch the lessons that Sir Wigandus gave, no matter how much fun they were. She permitted herself a small smile at the thought of his arms and the speed of his blade, and set to scoping porridge into bowls for their breakfast, leaving the burnt portion for herself as a penance.

Élise shaded her eyes with her hand. For miles they had been following the river, hoping for a place where they could cross before they reached the large city Britomar had told them lay ahead. She did not want to enter the city, not after all joy had been torn from her in the last city she had entered. Paris. *Martis.* Should she have gone after him? Was Garsenda right about that too?

Feh! Adelie was right about Martis; he had never loved her. Garsenda didn't have a clue about love. Damn her and her presumptions! If only she didn't have Garsenda's death on her conscious. If only her father hadn't commanded her to marry the Prince of Armenia...Feh! Why think about what might have been? If Martis had truly loved her—

"I think I can see a city," said Gwen.

Élise looked to where she was pointing. Thin tendrils of smoke rose over a jagged line of rooftops, barely visible in the afternoon haze.

"Yes, I see it too," said Sir Wigandus. "If I'm not mistaken, that's Wien. At least it will have bridges we can use to cross the river."

"Are there any other bridges that we may use?" asked Britomar. "I am loath to enter."

David said, "Most folks who want to cross the Danube do so by boat. Merchants are constantly traveling by river from one city to another."

"Are these boats sea worthy?" asked Gwen. "If we're to take a boat, perhaps we could take it all the way to the Holy Land?"

"Not those which come this far in," said Sir Wigandus. "Britomar, how high can you jump?"

"Fairly high, why?"

"There is no need for us all to enter Wien together. If you go by yourself and leap over the city gates at night, with your speed you can be through the city before the guards blink their eyes."

Britomar laughed, "I may be able to leap high, but that would be flying. Still, you give me an idea. While you need the bridges, I can cross the river by swimming it. It is too deep and swift for horses, but I can make it. I will wait and watch for you on the far bank."

David said, "While we're in the city, I would like to find a local synagogue."

"David, you shame us," said Gwen. "We have not sought out a priest almost since this journey began. Yes, seek out your synagogue, and we will find a church. How and where will we all meet again?"

"If we go with David to his synagogue and wait for him there," said Adelie, "he can then come with us to church. This way we won't need to separate."

"I will not enter a church," David said gently. Adelie blushed.

"It is no matter," said Sir Wigandus, "I will go with David while you maidens enter the church. By the time we get to the church, you should be shriven, and so can wait with him while I pray."

Britomar said, "Then let us proceed. I will know when you have left the city, and meet with you there." She then started to run to the river. Élise watched her as she galloped, a flash of white across the golden fields of wheat. She felt like a tremendous wall against the sea of her grief had been yanked from her heart. She too should see a priest, but how could she ask God's forgiveness when she'd not forgiven herself?

Élise looked at the other two women as they rode to the city, and saw that they both hung their heads. Sir Wigandus and David rode at the front so she could not see their faces. There was no sound except for that of the horses' hooves on the turf.

Unable to bear the silence, she began to hum a song. Words flooded into the music and she let them take voice.

How can you have ever
Claimed to have loved me
When you so easily
Distrust me, then dismiss me

Either your love allows
Doubt to be put aside
Or your doubt will prevent
What you thought was love

Am I as dear to you
As you claimed with kisses
Or a pariah you shun
In the cold light of day

Empty are your words of love
But malice filled what you said
When we met unexpectedly
Not in your careful rendezvous

Her face burned with embarrassment as she noted that Adelie and Gwen were staring at her. She kicked her horse so it moved past theirs. How dare they judge her! Neither of them had lost their loves. She'd lost two—no wait, Gwenaella had once told her about a man who had loved her but died. Once again, Élise realized she'd been selfish.

The city before them was smaller than Paris, and the walls less high. However, as they approached, it became obvious that the gates were much better guarded. The armored men lowered their spears as the travelers approached and said something that Élise did not understand. Sir Wigandus replied. At once they raised their swords and stood aside to let them pass.

"What did they say?" asked Élise.

"They wanted to know what business is this, that Christians travel with a Jew into the city of Wien?" he replied. "To which I answered, 'We are on a Holy pilgrimage, and he is to be both a guide and translator'."

Those few people they met on the narrow and muddy streets glanced anxiously in their direction, and then moved away from them. Far from the friendly and welcoming people that Sir Wigandus had always represented they'd find in the Empire.

It did not take them long to find the cathedral, though getting though the market square to the entrance took a bit of effort. Élise looked wistfully at the displays of brightly colored cloth, and then stopped herself. It was not right of her to be thinking of the fine cloth on her way to a confession.

When they reached the church doors, Sir Wigandus said, "I'll take David to the synagogue. We'll meet you here later."

Élise watched Gwen's raven flit from her shoulder to his. "How lucky you are to have such a good knight as a devoted lover," she said when he was out of earshot.

"A lover?" said Gwen, her face full of surprise. "If that is how knights love women, you can have him."

Élise looked up again at the men, and smiled at the sight of Wigandus's broad shoulders and towering form. She'd love to have him, but her father's word to the court of Armenia was binding. Pity to waste such a man. Strange, she'd always thought that Gwen liked Sir

Wigandus.

None of the women ever told me what they confessed to the priest, and from what you have told me about your Dharma, that is appropriate. What they did tell me was that when they left the church, they found Sir Wigandus and David waiting, with a third man that neither Élise nor Adelie recognized.

The man wore a sackcloth over what appeared to be a hair shirt. Upon seeing them, he rose and threw himself at Gwen's feet.

"Please dear maiden, please forgive me! My soul is torn in grief for my ignoble deeds. Please look upon me with mercy and extend me your forgiveness."

Startled, Gwen drew back. She didn't remember this man and had no idea how he knew her.

SHADOWS AND BLOOD

The man at Gwen's feet raised his dirt-smudged face to her. "Forgive me, please forgive me. My soul cries out to Heaven and is bleeding from the wrongs I have done unto you! Please, fair maid, please forgive me!"

Gwen frowned, struggling to regain her composure. "Who are you and what wrong have you done me, that you seek my forgiveness?"

"I am Sir Bryon, who lately and falsely accused you of witchcraft."

Gwen thought of her own sin and her penance which hung upon her like the stones on her father's nets. To be thinking of a man, a man far above her station. To be longing for a man before a year of mourning had passed on the death of her betrothed. That knight had turned her into a lustful woman. How strange that her protector had turned into her tempter. She must stop thinking about him. Her errand depended upon her chastity.

This knight was wearing a hair shirt in penance. He must be sincere.

She heard a flutter of wings and felt the familiar grip of her raven's talons through her mantle. Words rose within her with a warmness that came from the depths of her soul. "I forgive you, Sir Bryon, for both your false accusations and the fright you caused."

Sir Byron remained kneeling, "I would join your errand, to serve out my penance."

Gwen took a deep breath. She most definitely did not want him, nor any other man for that matter. But they already had men traveling with them. And, she had to admit, their strength and skills came in handy...No, she could not bear his presence.

She lowered her eyes. "Sir Bryon, that decision is not mine to make, or that of my companions. The errand is that of the unicorn. I am but her maid."

Sir Wigandus handed Bryon a small purse. "Go and outfit yourself with armor, weapons, and a sturdy horse. We will look for you on the road to Pest. There you may present yourself to Britomar."

Gwen looked at Wigandus, her eyes open wide with disbelief at what he'd just done.

Sir Bryon grasped Wigandus's hand, "I will not be far behind you."

Gwen wanted to tear that purse from Sir Bryon's hand and throw it at Wigandus's face, demanding an explanation. Could he not take the hint that this knight was not welcome? Instead she clenched her fists, her nails digging into her palms as she watched Sir Bryon make his way into the crowds, and through the market. She turned to Wigandus, but the knight mumbled something indistinct and disappeared into the church. Gwen gazed at the empty space where he stood a moment ago. How could her protector welcome her accuser? She did not understand that man.

No one talked while they waited for the knight to return from the church. Gwen turned to watch the market, looking for some sign of where Sir Bryon had gone. Tents with striped canopies in the large square rippled in the wind. Beneath them was the turmoil of the dealings, the customers, the goods. Élise had spent many hours along the road telling her the wonders she had missed by not entering Paris. What did she see in such a place, so noisy and confusing compared to the wind and water she was used to? How did one find the rocks that hid beneath the waves of those tents, how did one find the sharks amongst that sea of people?

Gwen started as she realized that an older woman in a dark head scarf was staring at her from underneath the nearest tent, frowning as if in disapproval. Gwen took a step forward to speak to the woman when she heard the door to the cathedral squeak. She whirled and saw Wigandus emerge from the dark doorway. She wanted to fly at him, pound him with her fists, demand his explanation, but the look of consternation on his face dispersed her anger. Something was wrong. She saw the same pain she remembered in his eyes when they'd worked together to form a gurney from sticks and rope.

Wigandus quickly made his way down the steps. "We should leave Wien at once, and try to meet with Britomar by dusk."

"Is there a problem?" asked Adelie.

Wigandus lowered his voice, "I'll tell you what I learned later. It is not safe here."

"Yes, let us leave at once," Gwen agreed, wondering at what he was hiding.

Élise said, "Don't we need to purchase provisions?"

"We can get what we need on the road," said Sir Wigandus. "We must hurry."

Gwen gathered the reins of her horse and followed Wigandus as he led his courser and hackney through the market to the far side of the city.

Walking through the crowded, slippery streets made Gwen long for Redon with its open lanes. Women carrying baskets and men pulling carts made the muddy lanes hard to move through quickly. They stuck to the center of the lane, walking single file, under the shadows of buildings that drew closer to each other as they grew taller. Scowls from women they passed, many crossing themselves as they shook their heads, reminded Gwen of her penance. A night's vigil on her knees in silent prayer waited for her like the ocean—cold, dark, and foreboding.

Above the din and reek of manure that had begun to give her a headache, she heard the higher pitch of children shouting. Hoping to see some innocents at play, she looked for the children. There— a small group running toward them, shouting something…wait! Gwen ducked as the children started to throw stones. Sir Wigandus grabbed one of the boys, lifting him up by his leather pants. As soon as he set him down again, the boys ran off, but Gwen thought she understood one taunt, "Judenlieber!" She suddenly connected all the scowls with David in their midst.

David strode forward and put his hand on Wigandus's arm. "Don't worry, my friend. I can't be hurt by taunts or stones thrown by children."

"I know," said the knight lowering his voice, "but I have learned that this city has left the Empire, and that its Duke is about to force all Jews to leave the Duchy. We must get you out of here, and then find a way to send a message to your people in the city."

"The rabbi is already aware of this, and my people are leaving this very evening," said David.

"That may not be soon enough," said Wigandus. "If only Gwen's raven could carry him a message."

Adelie said, "I'll take the message if you tell me where to go. I can move quickly through city streets."

David quickly related to her where the Jewish quarter was and she ran off. Gwen watched her disappear into the shadows, wishing she had Adelie's courage. The shadowed streets they walked no longer reminded Gwen of her penance, but of the hatred she once felt in the inferno of David's home, the worth in the grateful tears of David's sister Gwen had carried to safety through the smoke and blistering heat.

The brightness of the open sky momentarily blinded Gwen as she stepped through the city gate. Gwen closed her eyes, offering a prayer of thanks for their escape and a plea that all who hate God's chosen people to remember how Jesus forgave those who tortured him even as his blood flowed to mingle with that of thieves. Gwen hoped Adelie would be in time with her message, and rejoin them safely on the road to Pest.

They found a small wood with a stream running through it just before sunset. They passed under eaves until a meadow opened up before them, covered with white flowers that looked pink in the fading daylight. Gwen hoped Britomar would be waiting for them there, in the peace under the trees.

"Lets set up our camp for the night here," she said.

"It's as likely a spot as any," Élise agreed.

As they set camp, Gwen remembered her meeting with Britomar in Brocéliande. She had been so afraid of the dangers of the woods, and now she felt more at home in a forest than in a city full of people.

She sat next to Élise and began deboning some pickled fish. Her raven skipped over, trying to steal a meal. Her laughter at the bird's mischief was interrupted by Wigandus shout, "Bandits!" She looked up. The knight had drawn his sword and was putting on his helm.

Gwen grabbed the meat cleaver. David stood next to Wigandus, holding one of the pans. Élise grabbed a branch from the fire and stepped to Gwen's side.

Men with hard-set grime-covered faces rushed into the clearing, ragged clothing hanging loosely on their bodies. Gwen huddled closer to her companions, gripping the cleaver so hard that her hand felt numb.

One of the men, with an angry red scar on his scalp, shouted, "Hast du sie lebendig! Ihr Lösengeld ist die Mühe wert."[1]

"Gott als mein Zeuge, sterben Sie, wenn Sie Ihre Hände auf die Maid legen!"[2] shouted Sir Wigandus.

Gwen did not understand the words, but the newcomers' intentions were clear. Some of them rushed Sir Wigandus; the rest encircled her and the others. They did not look like they were about to fight. They stood there with clubs at ready, as if guarding prisoners already theirs.

One of the attackers swung his club at Wigandus, who sidestepped it and slashed out with his sword slicing into the bandit's abdomen.

---

[1]Translator's note: "Take them alive! the ransom will be worth the trouble." I've deliberately avoided translating these battle cries and insults, as Gwen would not have understood most of them.

[2]Translator's note: "God as my witness, you will die if you but touch the maiden!"

The bandit cried out in agony and fell to the ground, twitching. A bandit who was behind him swung his club, but Wigandus spun, his sword slicing the man's wrist off. That bandit screamed and dropped to his knees, clutching his arm.

One of the bandits called out: "Die Geiseln genehment!"[3]

Gwen raised her cleaver as bandits closed on her and the others around the fire. She wished she knew how to use weapons properly.

"Buauseant!"[4] came a bellow from the road.

The bandits turned toward the road as Sir Bryon rode hard upon them, sword raised to strike. Gwen's spirits lifted as she saw Adelie behind him, knives at the ready. Blood splattered over her as Sir Bryon's cut took off the head of the nearest attacker.

"Johann! Hilfe!" called one of the bandits. He dodged Sir Bryon's sword and caught Gwen's arm as she tried to hit him with her cleaver. Gwen winced as he twisted her arm, forcing her to drop the cleaver. He pulled harder, causing Gwen to overbalance, but just as she was about to fall, his grip slacked and he collapsed. Adelie rose behind him, pulling her knife from his side.

Gwen grabbed the cleaver and brought it up just in time to catch a knife that slashed at her other arm. Her new attacker crumpled as David hit him on the head with a pan, but a blow sent David to his knees. Gwen gasped. A horse screamed at the side, but she had not time to glance in that direction as another bandit swung a club at her. She dodged it and slashed at him with the meat cleaver.

"Merde dans tes dents!"[5] screamed Adelie as her long knife sliced into the thigh of the bandit whose staff had hit David.

Gwen dropped to the ground to avoid another blow, rolled over, and grabbed a club from the hands of a dead bandit. Rising, she glanced over at Wigandus and Sir Bryon, who were standing back-to-back, swords hacking at men wielding clubs. She had to look away again as another bandit hacked at her, knocking her club out of her hand. She tried to dodge as he swung again, but he smacked her hard on her side and she fell screaming. The bandit put one foot on her and pressed down on her back to keep her from rising, while swinging his club at Adelie.

Behind Adelie, Gwen saw a club connect with Sir Bryon's head. Sir Bryon swayed but recovered, taking off the arm of his nearest

---

[3]Translator's note: "Take the hostages!"

[4]Translator's note: This is the battle cry of the Knights Templar, it means: "Be Glorious!" Originally French, Beau Seant,the battle cry of the Templars eventually became a word and the name of the Templar's banner.

[5]Translator's note: "Shit in your teeth!"

attacker. He took another blow to the head. Blood splattered. Gwen heard a nasty cracking sound and gasped as she saw the Templar collapse on the ground.

She was barely aware of the fight between Adelie and the bandit holding her. The bandits were winning. Was it the end?... And then, just as suddenly, she felt a rush of joy and knew Britomar was here even before the unicorn leapt into the clearing, screaming her challenge, tossing a bandit into the air with her horn.

Gwen felt the man on top of her loose his balance, and shifted, forcing him to topple over. Adelie jumped on top of him. Blood from his neck sprayed into the air like a fountain.

Gwen scrambled up to her feet and saw Sir Wigandus stumble forward. His face was grim and blood-stained. He cut down two bandits with one mighty stroke, shouting, "Zur Hölle schicke ich sie froh!"[6]

Gwen shakily stood, dimly aware that any bandits still living were running for their lives. Adelie rushed to Élise who was sitting on the ground, her arm at a strange angle. Gwen hobbled to Sir Bryon. Britomar joined her a moment later, shook her head, and walked over to David, who lay a few yards away moaning.

Kneeling, Gwen took Sir Bryon's broken head into her lap. His blood began to pool on her skirt. He opened his eyes. "My penance is complete; I am yours again, oh Jesu!" His eyes became void as a small streak of blood oozed out of his mouth and stopped.

Shaken, Gwen looked up again, to see Britomar lay her horn on Élise. Élise laughed oddly as she raised her arm. Gwen's eyes welled with tears as she watched Adelie help Élise to her feet, and walk toward her. She felt the warmth of tears bite into her cheeks. *Why can't I stop crying?*

"Was there nothing you could do for him?" she asked Britomar, who had come back to her, standing beside the exhausted Sir Wigandus.

The unicorn shook her head. "No. He was hurt too badly. To heal him was beyond my power."

Sir Wigandus knelt and crossed himself. "He must not be deprived a proper burial. I will go and seek a priest."

"Are you well enough to ride?"

"Ach, ja, mine liebchen."[7]

He limped to his hackney, untethered it and mounted. Gwen watched him ride away, brushing a tear from her cheek; the beat

---

[6]Translator's note: "To hell I'll gladly send you!"
[7]Translator's note: "Oh yes, my darling."

of the hooves on the ground echoed the pounding of her heart.

Gwen lifted her hand to stroke Sir Bryon's blood-crusted hair. Shaking with tears, she lowered it again. His arrival had brought Adelie back to them, kept Wigandus alive, kept them all alive until Britomar found them. He rode fearlessly into the fray without regard for his own safety, and now he lay dead in her lap. True, he had tried to have her killed, accusing her of trading her soul with the devil, but it didn't seem to matter anymore... She did not want to cry over him. Why couldn't she stop?

She closed her eyes and saw again the blow from behind which had split open Sir Bryon's head. She saw the anger in Wigandus's eyes as he turned to slay the man who wielded that club. She saw the blood spray from the sword slicing through flesh and she opened her eyes to see the bloody mess in her hands.

She remembered her mother cradling her brother when he was sick with fever. She was rocking him gently and humming a song, a hymn.

Gwen sang, no longer minding the tears, the sobs that she couldn't hold back anymore. She sang and sobbed, until the squeal of a cart's wheels interrupted her. Only then did she realize that David's and Élise's voices had been added to her dirge. She opened her eyes to see that her tears had washed the blood away from Sir Bryon's face, which now seemed at peace.

Sir Wigandus lifted the large man from her as if he were a child, and set him on the cart behind the young priest who drove it. Gwen rose and kissed Sir Bryon's cheek. The bandits' bodies were then placed onto the cart. For the first time Gwen saw them not as bandits but young men, thin with hunger. She asked the priest to pray for them.

When the priest drove off, she made her way to the stream and stripped off her blood-soaked clothes. She found a flat rock and scrubbed. She scrubbed and cried, not noticing that she bruised her hands. She then lay the clothes out on the ground to dry and knelt on the soft grass, gazing at the cold light of the stars as the dark blue sky turned to black.

She began the prayer the priest had charged her to say as part of her penance, but stumbled over the words, breaking down into sobs. As she sobbed, she felt more than heard a voice ask, *Why do you cry? Can't you even now forgive and let go?*

Her skin prickled, a strange calmness descending onto her. She stopped sobbing, and wiped her eyes. Her grief was tainted by the shame of her anger. It was not enough to say words of forgiveness.

He had died for them, not for their errand. At last she felt nothing but sadness for the loss of a man capable of dying so that others may live. First Garsenda, now Sir Bryon, how many more would lay down their lives to bring her to the Sacred Garden?

Refreshed, empty of anger, Gwen offered up an honest and heartfelt prayer for Sir Bryon. A cool breeze made the small hairs on her back stand up. Remembering that she was naked, she called out, "Adelie? Élise? Can you please help?"

Élise came running. "Gwen, what is the matter?"

"I need dry clothes. I should have brought some clothes when I went to bathe, but I did not think of it."

"Gwen, it would have been a wonder if you had. Adelie and I were worried sick when you wandered off. I'll have what you need in a moment."

After Gwen dressed, she strolled back to camp, wondering that twice now He had spoken to her.

That night, after the others lay down to sleep, Gwen rose to her knees and once again began to pray.

TO ASHES YOU SHALL RETURN

Adelie clenched her teeth as they entered yet another burnt village. The bitter tinge of cold ashes clinging to the rising breeze made her nose itch. She glanced at a heap of blackened human bones spilling from the cinders of a nearest ruin and turned away. She felt for her knives, wishing to find those responsible, as she led her horse through the deadly silence.

After seeing two other such villages, she had no hope of seeing anyone alive. Not a single building had been left standing, not even the small church. The smell of wild flowers that dominated the air told her that this village had been destroyed some time ago.

Adelie forced back tears and rising bile. She remembered how she rushed through the flames to save Deborah. The children in this village had not been this lucky. No one was able to save them from an earthly hell. She glanced at her companions, hoping to find some comfort in familiar faces. Élise had a haunted look about her, hollow-eyed from the lack of sleep since they passed through the first burnt village. Gwen stared straight ahead, her lips pressed into a tight frown. Even the raven that had become a fixture on her shoulder was quiet, making none of its usual clicks, awks and caws.

Sir Wigandus looked about him like a hunter searching for a dangerous beast. David, whose voice had long gone raw from singing funeral hymns, continued to hum the dirges under his breath. His face looked worn, and his eyes had lost that playful sparkle that she loved so much. Only Britomar seemed unfazed by the death and destruction.

Adelie's head was beginning to pound as she rode out of the village into the fields overgrown wild with weeds. She broke the kernels from the stalks of rye as she passed. The harvest they took from the ghosts would keep them alive. Searching along the rows for grain not damaged by crow or mouse gave her something to do, and she welcomed it.

That night, after they had all eaten, Adelie took up her wooden practice sword and followed Wigandus to a flat area on the side of their camp. A moment later, David appeared at her side.

Adelie let the two men start the melee. David brought the edge of his blade so that it crossed in front of him, balancing on the balls of his feet. Wigandus stepped forward and swung at David. Parry. Swing. Parry. Swing. Adelie watched the exchange, admiring how far David had come in the months since he first took up a practice sword.

Wigandus's speed was increasing; each parry echoed a louder crack as the knight's blows grew in force. Adelie's jaw opened. Swing. Parry. Cut.

"Wigandus?" she said.

Swing. Parry. Cut. Parry. Swing.

David backed up as he brought his blade up, forward, down.

"Wigandus!" Adelie screamed, leaping forward, bringing up her sword to parry the knight's weapon that cut the air like doom even as David lost his footing. Wood met wood and shattered. Adelie crashed to the ground, clutching her burning hand.

Panting, the knight stood over her, blade raised, face twisted in a snarl. She raised her hands and he stopped mid-swing. Reason returned to his eyes as he tossed aside the wooden blade, covered his face and fell to his knees next to Adelie.

Adelie pulled herself up from the ground. David had already righted himself. They stood and watched Wigandus, sobbing, speaking words that had no meaning for her. After a moment, Adelie stepped forward and gently pulled his hands away from his face. "It is alright, neither of us were hurt."

Wigandus averted his eyes. "I lost myself to grief and nearly killed David. How can that be alright?"

"Because I forgive you," said David. "It was not me you attacked, but those who created the ghosts we've all been haunted by."

The sound of hooves made Adelie turn; peace and joy enfolded her as Britomar approached.

"Is anyone hurt?" the unicorn asked.

"My hand hurts a bit," Adelie said, "but it's not bad."

Wigandus lowered his gaze. "Britomar, I am afraid I have failed you and your errand. I must return to Thuringia and join a monastery."

"Wigandus, look at me," said David. "Do you value me so little that you would discard my forgiveness?"

"No, but—"

"Stop it," interrupted Adelie. "You made a mistake, that's all. I might have done the same, I am so full of anger over what we've seen."

"Thank you for coming to my aid," said David.

Adelie's cheeks felt hot. It felt so good when he spoke to her.

"Wigandus," said Britomar, "You have not failed me, nor my errand. Without you I'd be dead today. Please stay."

Wigandus looked up at the unicorn. "I thank you, noble creature. My heart has ridden with you, and will again. And yet...does it matter that I serve you out of love for another?"

Britomar slowly shook her head. "No matter your reason, you are here, and for that I remain grateful." She briefly touched her horn to the knight's shoulder, and then cantered to where the others waited.

"David, I offer you my hand," said Wigandus. "I may have saved your life, but you saved my soul."

David clasped his hand with vigor. "It is good that you and I stand as brothers."

Days later, as they crested a hill, Adelie heard what sounded like blows. Her throat tightened. She glanced at Sir Wigandus, who was reaching for his sword. Then, realization dawned on her. "Hammers?"

They all strained their ears. They could now dimly hear men's voices. It did not sound like men in battle, the tones were calm and jesting. Sir Wigandus sheathed his sword.

As they rode closer, David said, "I think they're speaking Hungarian."

The road brought them up and past the hill that had blocked their view. Adelie now saw scores of men working near a river that she hoped was the Danube. They halted and looked upon the men as they worked.

The men were lifting large stones from a barge, using a rope flung over the tall scaffolding next to the river. One of the workers gestured toward them and said something to a knight who was standing by, watching the proceedings. The knight nodded, then mounted, and rode to meet them. As he did so, the hammering stopped, and all the workers turned to look.

Sir Wigandus said, "His device has the bars of the royal house of the Arpáds."

The knight slowed his horse as he approached and called out in *Langue d'oc.*[1]

---

[1] Translator's note: Langue d'oc is the way French was spoken in the south of

"Were it not for the Jew amongst you, I'd take the arrival of a unicorn as a sign from God himself."

Adelie winced, wondering if she should make David some clothes that were not bordered in yellow, a cap for his head in a less damning color. Would he welcome such clothing? Would he wish to hide what he was? *I know so little of him, and his thoughts.*

"I am Bela Arpáds, King of Hungary, or what is left of it. What brings a unicorn, three maids, a Knight of the Empire, and a Jew to Hungary?"

Gwen answered him, "Your Majesty, our errand is sacred, and is that of healing. We desire to pass through Hungary on our way to Persia. There we hope to learn the location of the garden at the roof of the World. This noble Jew, David, will be our guide there. He knows the language of the Mohammedans."

"What has happened to Hungary, that its villages are in ruins, and the city of Pest is destroyed?" Sir Wigandus asked.

The king's lips twitched. "Five years ago, the Tartars struck without warning or mercy. They burned everything that would take flame, putting my people to the sword. With the help of my neighbor, good King Wenceslas of Bohemia, we resisted as best we could. We had little hope. When Mary, my queen, became with child, we prayed to God, dedicating our child to His service if the Tartars could be taken from us. Our prayers were answered, and the hoard disappeared as suddenly as it had come. When I saw the unicorn amongst you, I hoped that you were a sign that peace and joy had returned to our Kingdom, that we offered little Margaret to God rightly."

Britomar smiled. "We unicorns are not messengers or agents of the Most High, Your Majesty. Rather, we look to men for such guidance. If you have dedicated your daughter to Him, I would look upon your child, if I may. After the sight of the ruin and devastation in your lands, I fear my companions and I are sadly in need of a glimpse of the hope for Hungary."

The king nodded. "She is in a convent now, and in God's hands. I will gladly take you to her myself, but first we should go to my queen who may wish to accompany us." He turned his horse and rode into the hills. They followed him up a poorly marked path.

As they rode, Sir Wigandus asked, "What is it you are building, Your Majesty?"

"I am building a new fortress, to protect my people. I will erect a large keep here, and build a city under its protection. It is my hope

---

France. Most of the crusaders spoke that dialect.

that I can entice many to come and settle in its walls. Our land is fertile, and the Danube connects us with the Empire, the Kingdom of Bohemia, as well as the Kingdoms of the Bulgars and of the Greeks. We lost many souls to the Tartar hoards, as our defenses were inadequate. I mean for my people to never know such destruction again."

They rode above the construction site. The keep's strong walls rose above some of the nearby hills. A large cave opened in front of them. Two score of men at arms stood guard next to it, their armor gleaming in the sunlight. Their shields bore the white and blue bars of the Arpáds. They raised their spears in salute when the king approached.

The travelers left the horses in the guards' care, and picked up torches as they entered the caverns.

"We still dwell in these caves of refuge while we rebuild Pest," the king said. "The unicorn should have no trouble entering, as the caves are large enough to permit horses to pass."

Gwen's raven lifted off her shoulder, rising into the pale blue sky. Adelie stepped down into the darkness, scarcely lit by torches hanging along the walls. She longed to fly away like the raven, and await the others re-emergence. The rock loomed, so heavy, so near, she felt it could crash down on her at any moment. Could it be safe?

The passage soon opened into a large chamber, its low wide arches supporting a smooth roof of stone overhead. They passed through many such chambers; some of them man-made, with brick and mortar supporting the vaulted rock ceiling, others formed by nature, pointed pillars of rock rising from floor and roof—a maw to devour. Smell of stale excrement filled the air, echoes of voices carried under the ever-present rock hanging above her like doom.

In one chamber women and children were sitting on the edge of a large basin with a statue of a knight carved into the rock wall behind it. The women were occupied with sewing and caring for their children. These were ladies of station, but their fine wool clothes were stained and threadbare. They stared at the newcomers, conversations interrupted, faces lighting with joy as Britomar passed by. Some of the girls pointed and smiled.

The travelers stepped into a larger chamber, its ceiling hidden in the darkness above. In the center sat a woman in a red woolen cyclas, a gold circlet in her gray-flecked red hair reflecting the dancing torchlight. Her gown, though originally rich, was visibly worn, and the woman had a sad look about her. She held a nursing child.

The king stopped before her. "My queen, may I present to you these foreigners who wish to look upon our little Margaret."

The queen nurses her own? And in public? Adelie couldn't help but gape.

The king turned back to them. "May I present Queen Mary Lascaris, and the Princess Anna."

Sir Wigandus bowed deeply and said, "Your Majesty, I am Sir Wigandus of the Langrave of Thuringia. These are the Ladies Elisabeth de Chauvigny, and Adelie de Chauvigny. The maid is Gwenaella of the Duchy of Breton, the Jew is David ben Yosi, and the Unicorn is Britomar."

The queen nodded. "We are deeply honored by your visit. I sincerely regret being unable to receive you properly." She seemed about to say more when the princess gave out a shriek of delight, pointing at Britomar and squealing. She tried to rise from her mother's lap, reaching for Britomar with both arms outstretched, as the queen busied herself with trying to hold onto the twisting babe and maintain her modesty at the same time.

After the queen calmed the baby and covered herself, she rose and brought the princess close to Britomar.

"May I?" she asked.

"I would be delighted," Britomar said.

The babe reached over and touched Britomar's golden mane, chattering excitedly. Adelie couldn't help smiling, joined not only by the queen but by Gwen and Élise as well. She was glad to see her companions smiling again. David, however, merely looked thoughtful, and Sir Wigandus's face was stern and hard. Something bothered the knight, she wished she knew what.

"Mary," said the king at last. "I promised our guests that I would take them to Margaret. Would you care to accompany us?"

Adelie was a bit surprised at the kings' open familiarity, but the queen did not seem put off by it. "Bela, is it wise for us to visit so often? She's God's to take care of now."

"Yet I miss her." He winked. "Besides, I promised our guests, and I would not be a worse host than circumstances necessitate."

"Then, I will gladly come with you."

The queen rose, and handed the young princess to one of the ladies who attended on her. They then retraced their steps back to the open air and sunshine, the king and queen in quiet conversation. As they walked, Adelie found herself beside David, and slipped her hand into his. She immediately regretted the immodest gesture and pulled back, but he held her, giving her hand a gentle squeeze. She felt blood rush into her face, and her spirits soared.

One of the guards followed them with his eyes and said, "Your

160

Majesty, the Jew dog dares to touch the Lady Adelie. Shall I teach him his station?"

Before King Bela could answer, Sir Wigandus grabbed the guard by his surcoat, effortlessly lifting him off the ground with one hand. "Know this, knave, and know it well. I will defend David's right to hold Adelie's hand with my sword. Theirs is a true love! It is Holy in the eyes of all Christians. Know you not that the good Christian knight Gahmuret, and the heathen queen of the moors, Belacane, were married? Their love gave us Fairefis, brother to Parzifal himself! That same Parzifal whom Heaven blessed, he who held in his hands the Grail! More so will Heaven smile on love between a Christian maid and one of His chosen people, for a Jew is closer to Him than any heathen." He then tossed the guard to the ground, as if he were no more than filth.

Adelie stood, stunned by both Wigandus's anger and his words. Her heart was pounding and she grasped David's hand tighter.

The king and queen looked at David and Adelie, mouths open, but the king quickly put a smile on his face. "David ben Yosi, you are the most fortunate of Jews to have such a knight to defend you, and to have the love of such a beautiful maid." He turned to the guard and called, "Captain, teach this knave a lesson. Hungary's future depends in no small part on good Jews returning and living in peace and prosperity within our cities. I will have no unlawful hurt on any who come to Hungary, even though they are a Jew. Come, good knight and worthy Jew, my daughter awaits us."

As they rode, Adelie's mind spun questions she wanted to ask Sir Wigandus regarding Fairefis and his sire. She started in surprise when her mount came to a sudden stop.

In front of them stood a broken stone building, its roof missing in many places, and many of the walls blackened with a recent fire. In front of the building, a small group of sisters and a small child worked in the garden. They were all pulling weeds.

King Bela dismounted and approached the sisters. One of them looked up and said something to the girl, who ran to the King, with arms outstretched, her face alit with a bright grin.

He bent and embraced her. Then, hand in hand, they approached the newcomers.

"Anyu!" the girl cried. She dropped her father's hand to run to her mother, who had been helped out of her sidesaddle by Sir Wigandus.

After a long embrace, the queen said, "Margaret dear, we have guests. I would like you to meet Sir Wigandus of the Langrave of Thuringia, the Ladies Elisabeth de Chauvigny, and Adelie de Chauvigny, Gwenaella of the Duchy of Breton, David ben Yosi, and Britomar the Unicorn."

The girl looked straight at Gwen with bright brown eyes and said, "To reach the Garden, you must be pure of soul. Follow His beautiful commandments and be true. I will pray for you."

Adelie's eyes widened. How could this girl know of the Garden and Gwen's errand? This girl must be in God's care.

Gwen curtsied, "I am grateful for your prayers. May I ask your blessing on myself and my companions?"

Margaret looked at David, "Son of Yosi, would you receive my blessing?"

He smiled. "A blessing from a child who serves the God of Abraham, Isaac and Jacob would be most welcome."

"Then I will gladly ask the Lord to bless you all." She held up her hands. "May the Lord bless and keep you, may His face shine upon you. May He protect you on your journey and speed you to a swift completion of your quest."

David bowed. "Baruch atah Adonai elohaynu melech ha'olam sheckalak me'chochmato lirey'av. Amein."[2]

"Thank you, David ben Yosi." Margaret's smile fell. "I have to get back to my gardening." She gave her mother a kiss, her father a hug, and raced back to the nuns who stood and watched her.

"She is a most charming child," said Gwen. "Is it true that you pledged her to God while she was still in the womb?"

The queen nodded. "Yes. Hungary was being destroyed by the Tartar hoards. We did not want our child to come into such a world, and knew that all mothers must have felt this way. So when we returned from our exile, we gave her to the convent." She smiled to the king, who covered her hand with his. "Our sacrifice has brought peace to Hungary. Now we hope that people will return, and Hungary will prosper again. My husband is inviting all peoples to settle here on the land of their own and live in peace."

"I will spread the word in the Empire upon my return," said Sir Wigandus.

"And I will spread the word through those of my people that I meet," said David.

"David," King Bela said. "For your people, I will build strong walls around their quarters in the cities, and give the key to the gates to your Rabbis. This way Jews will be safe and prosperous in Hungary."

---

[2]Translator's note: "Praised are you, Oh Lord our God, King of the Universe, who has given wisdom to those who revere God. Amen."

"Your majesty is most generous," said David. Adelie noticed that his eyes did not carry the smile his lips showed the king.

"Please, as you take leave of us, do not take to the roads," said the queen. "While His Majesty's troops are doing their best to restore order to the land, I fear that there are still bandit groups preying on our people. I beg of you to take one of the larger river crafts down the Danube to the Black Sea."

"Your Majesty's concern is most touching. I will consider your advice," said Britomar. "However, the craft would have to be large enough to carry not only myself, but the horses of the others as well. Do vessels of this size come this far up the Danube?"

"Yes they do, Britomar," answered the king. "It is not uncommon for pilgrims to the Holy Land to take such crafts down the Danube, and knights on Holy Crusade have used such portage as well. Merchants tow them upriver using horses kept by the riverside. In the dry months, if their vessel is too large for the ancient Roman canal, they unload at the Iron Gates and take a land route around. After you have passed the Iron Gates, you should have easy passage down river to the Black Sea.

"Now that the Tartars have been driven out of Hungary, the merchants are returning. There is one such vessel at the dock, which has just offloaded oils, spices, Egyptian cottons and a most precious splinter of the True Cross. They had intended to go further upriver in search of pilgrims to take to the Holy Land, I think they will be willing to take you instead."

They rode back down river to where the soldiers were unloading the cut stones from the boats. Following the king they came to a group of men dressed in bright green doublets and large plumed hats.

"Don Antonio!" shouted the King.

"Yes, Your Majesty!" replied a swarthy skinned man, who also wore a sword.

"I have here people of high station who desire transport to the Holy Land. They have an errand there which is most pressing, and would take passage on your vessel."

"Your Majesty is most kind to bring us such passengers. I trust he will not be offended if I inquire as to their credit?"

The king said, "I will cover the costs of their passage."

Don Antonio bowed. "I will make the arrangements. I will be ready at daybreak tomorrow, please be here then so that we may leave."

"You should have no fear of us being tardy, Don Antonio," said

Britomar, stepping forward. "We would leave now if that were possible."

His eyes widened as he saw her, "My God! A unicorn! I am terribly sorry, but with five horses and a unicorn on board, we must take on as many provisions as our ship can hold. With all respect to His Majesty, Hungary is very much a wasteland, and we will not be able to restock until we come to the ports of the Greeks."

The king said, "I will pay you handsomely for their delivery."

Adelie overheard Élise quietly ask the king, "Your Majesty knows this Don Antonio to be an honorable man?"

"He is almost as bad as a Jew when it comes to money," he whispered, "but he carries an honest cargo and those pilgrims he has taken to the Holy Land have never complained of his treatment."

Again, Adelie heard the complaint against David's people, and felt as though she was also subject to this rough judgment. If only there was a place for her and David to sit and talk privately.

That night, their group slept in the caverns. None of them talked much; the din of the echoes reminded them both of how they were far from alone, and of how easily voices would carry. Adelie did not sleep, for each time she closed her eyes she saw Deborah, bright-eyed and smiling, running through a field of bone and ash.

BETRAYAL

É lise lay awake in the dark of the cavern, afraid to close her eyes and see again the dream that had woken her, a dream of Garsenda burning into ash. From the flame of an oil lamp hanging by a chain from the ceiling, she could see the others in their slumber. She rose on an elbow, and looked for Sir Wigandus. Perhaps she could sleep if he held her, perhaps in his arms she could feel safe. Perhaps he'd like to hold a woman instead of a hope?

If only he would. If only he'd take her as a man takes a woman, she could see a way out of her marriage. To think that her betrothed was of the same people that burned those villages; that burned the children. She must find a way to make herself unwanted by him. She was certain that her father, if he knew what she'd learnt that day, would never have made the arrangements for her marriage to such a butcher.

She rose and stepped over Gwen where she slept, looking down on the sweet an innocent face of her rival for Wigandus's affections. Did she not see the value in the poetry the knight had recited, the worth in his mighty arm? Chaste, virgin, and so naive.

Élise lay down next to Wigandus and wrapped his arm around her, sliding his hand under her shift. As she began to drift asleep, Wigandus stirred. His hand grasped at her breast, then pulled back with a jerk. He sat up and stared at Elise next to him.

"What are you doing, my lady?"

Elise sat up and wrapped her arms around herself. "I can't sleep. I'm being plagued by nightmares. Garsenda used to hold me, comfort me. I would love to have you hold me, comfort me, help me feel safe and loved."

"My lady, this is not right—"

"What is not right? Are you not a man? A knight? No knight would refuse a lady in such distress."

Wigandus lifted his head, his face in shadow. "I love another, my lady."

Elise leaned toward him. "The one you love has spurned you,

scorned your offer. She doesn't want you." She took his hands and placed them on her hips. "Accept my love instead, take me and all I'm willing to give."

He removed his hands. "Forgive me, my lady, but my heart is given and I will have no other."

"Even though I love you?"

"My lady, I do not want your love."

"Am I ugly in your eyes that you would spurn my offer?"

He shook his head. "No, my lady. You are beautiful. To feel you so close, to smell you—you make me want you, very much so. But it is Gwen that I love."

"Not even for a night? A night to quiet my tears and give me the illusion of love?"

"Tomorrow I may die in her protection, for I suspect the king of treachery. How can I betray her?"

"What she never knows can be no betrayal. Life is so short; should we not enjoy what we're given, take love where it is offered and live life like a song—beautifully. A blending of words and music. Be the words for the music I offer."

He drew away. "Lady Elisabeth, the songs you speak of are lovely but short, composed to delight and fade. The song I would live is longer and deeper of purpose. I take joy in righteous service, not in pleasures of the moment, no matter how delectable. Go and get some sleep."

She reached again for his hands but he grabbed her wrists and held them firm. Élise sobbed, "I can't live without you. If you won't be mine, I'll destroy myself."

"My lady, don't be absurd, no man is worth such despair. Go and pray that God send you a man who loves you." Wigandus let go of her arms and turned away from her. She rubbed her wrists and went back to her place by Gwen's side. She lay awake in the darkness, swallowing tears, wishing she had never left Poitiers.

After what seemed like ages, a soft glow began to appear, becoming a dancing gleam of torchlight as it grew along with the soft echo of footsteps. She sat up as a guard entered their chamber.

"My lady," he said, "The king would bid you rise. The river boat is ready for your transport."

She yawned, stretched, went to wake the others, eager to be away from the subterranean court of a king who could not offer the common hospitality of a bath. She jumped slightly when Adelie sat up as she approached her. "Couldn't sleep?" she asked, wondering if Adelie had witnessed her humiliation.

"I heard you talking and it woke me," Adelie answered, turning her face away. "Let's wake the others."

Together the two sisters set out to wake their friends. Élise paused briefly over Wigandus. It would be lovely to wake him with a kiss. Perhaps if she made one last effort. She leaned over him, all set to indulge in her fantasy, but he woke when a lock of her hair brushed his forehead.

"Time to leave?" he asked.

"Yes."

Gwen awoke a moment later, and they all lined up to follow the lone guard through the quiet chambers. They stepped from darkness to darkness; outside, the stars still lit the world's canopy.

David spoke in Hungarian to one of the guards who hurried off and returned shortly with the horses, saddled and ready. They mounted and followed a sergeant who held a torch aloft.

When they arrived at the river's edge, they saw a small group of sailors holding torches. One said something in a language that Élise did not recognize. David answered and then said to them, "The boat is downriver, we're to follow them."

Sir Wigandus grimaced. "Something smells wrong about this."

Élise wondered what the chevalier suspected. She saw Adelie draw one of her knives. Her skin prickled.

Dawn was brightening the eastern sky by the time they reached a large barge, a ramp leading onto it from the riverbank.

Sir Wigandus said, "Let me go first," and then muttered under his breath, "I do not trust these merchants." He dismounted, and led his horse up the ramp.

Élise patted the neck of her horse and heard Sir Wigandus's great booming voice from the barge, "Du schlecht Verräter!"[1] followed by clangs of steel.

Terror rose in her stomach. She turned to see the guards behind them dropping their torches and drawing their swords.

As Britomar screamed and charged, Élise tried to regain her mount. Someone grabbed her legs. She kicked, but lost balance and fell, screaming. She landed on top of her assailant and rolled off, trying to get to her feet. He grabbed her ankle, forcing her to land face-first in the dirt. His foot pushed her back to the ground. *Ow!* She struggled, trying to dislodge him, spitting dirt.

Hooves echoed nearby and suddenly the weight lifted off her back. Élise pushed up to her hands and knees and saw a man writhing near

---

[1] Translator's note: "You horrible traitor!"

her. An ugly wound gaped in his torso, blood splattering from his mouth. She glanced around, and was surprised to see the guards running away, upriver. Adelie stood panting over two dead men. David was clasping his bloodstained hand to his side, two more men by his feet. Gwen crouched on her knees, wiping vomit from her chin. A fallen guard lay near her, blood streaming from a hole in his chest.

Élise looked anxiously at the barge. The slow drumming of Britomar's hoofs made the only sound as the unicorn pranced closer to the ramp.

Gwen cried out, "Wigandus!"

A moment later there was a piercing cry and a sickening thud. A severed human head sailed over the outer wall of the barge. Sir Wigandus appeared at the top of the ramp. "Come up! The raft is ours! I only hope we can figure out how to steer this thing!"

Élise started to sob, but grabbed the reins of her horse and followed Gwen up the ramp. When they reached the top, Gwen suddenly stopped with a gasp. When Élise finally gained the deck of the barge she saw why, and her tears stopped as she gazed at Wigandus. Ten men lay dead on the boat's deck. Gwen handed Élise the reins of her horse and rushed to him, hugging him fast.

"Liebchen! It's all right, I'm fine." Élise moved away to give them some privacy. After she tied the reins to a peg on the barge's wall, she found a crate near the stern and sat. So, the maid finally saw the worth of that chevalier. So much for the hope that he might one day look upon herself as a woman, as a lover. Élise sighed. She would have to find some other man to gain the only release she could find from her father's promise.

She looked up at the lavender clouds and wondered if she would one day know love. She saw Adelie and David quietly talking, the wound in his side no longer bleeding, and felt more alone than ever. She buried her face in her hands and started to cry.

An arm wrapped around her. She picked up her head and met Adelie's eyes, filled with worry. "Are you hurt?"

Élise shook her head. "I'm such a coward; all I could do was run."

"You're no coward. You stood up to Papa, and you faced demons. You know you can't fight; so do what you can to save yourself, that's all."

Élise sighed and leaned against Adelie's shoulder.

Soon Gwen, David, and Wigandus guided the barge and set it adrift down the Danube. Sir Wigandus held the rudder while Gwen kept watch at the bow. David stood next to her, holding a long pole.

Adelie rose, broke out the feedbags, and gave each horse some oats. Britomar came and stood next to her, her golden mane swaying in the breeze.

As Élise watched them, her sorrow melted away, replaced by a melody. She got up and unpacked her harp. The smell of the oiled wood reminded her of all the times she played for Garsenda. If she could not live a song of love, she'd sing a song of love in the life she lived. She sighed, tested the tuning, and began plucking a sprightly song:

> Our captain is a merry merry maid
> She knows the water's ways
> She guides us through the river's course
> Past shallows and over hidden rocks
> Her heart's immune to siren's call
> A true course she shall set
> She keeps her crew looking sharp
> They dance to her command.
>
> With a yo ho, yo ho, our captain's heart is true
> With a yo ho, yo ho, and we dance to her command.
>
> Our pilot is a merry merry knight
> A rudder is his blade
> With mighty fist he carves a path
> Through cataracts down the open way
> He listens to his captain's call
> He loves her merry ways
> His mighty arm keeps us safe
> And answers her commands.

David joined her singing:

> With a yo ho, yo ho, our pilot's heart is true
> With a yo ho, yo ho, he answers her command.

He grew quiet, as she continued:

> Our unicorn's a merry merry beast
> In service to her king
> For her we will dare the river's course
> Neither Jew nor Greek, not slave or free

BETRAYAL

As one we heed a higher call
A true course to the garden
She keeps us all filled with hope
We strive on her errand.

She sang the chorus gladly, her voice mixing with David's, Gwen's and Wigandus's baritone.

With a yo ho, yo ho, the unicorn's heart is true
With a yo ho, yo ho, we strive on her errand.

Our guide is a merry merry man
He knows the tongues we'll need
He cuts through babel's curse
A scholar tending to the horses
Brushing them with wisdom and truth
His song for a foreign land
With gentle heart with the word
He sings at her command.

Even Adelie joined in to sing the chorus:

With a yo ho, yo ho, the scholar's heart is true
With a yo ho, yo ho, he sings at her command.

Our escort is a merry merry maid
Who knows the dance of knifes
Through fires blaze she strikes a path
Then she rocks to sleep a tired child
She'll bring us to the Garden's paths
Her strong arm keeps us safe
And warm our souls with her love
She'll dance to her command.

Élise noticed her sister blush but sing heartily with the others:

With a yo ho, yo ho, the maiden's heart is true
With a yo ho, yo ho, she'll dance to her command.

She now started to bring the melody to a conclusion, but David started to sing a new verse:

Our minstrel is a merry merry maid
In service to us all.

Élise' cheeks burned. Her fingers faltered, but found the tune again:

She kills sorrow with song
Sung a hymn or a bawdy tune
To keep our spirits high
With harp she makes our path
Light and filled with grateful joy
She sings to her command.

Élise grinned heartily as she lent her voice to a resounding chorus:

With a yo ho, yo ho, the maiden's heart is true
With a yo ho, yo ho, she sings to her command.

THE DANUBE

Gwen knew she was dreaming as she looked at herself sitting in the prow of her father's boat, her father sitting at the stern holding the tiller. There was a splash and a mermaid rose from the depths, her hair green like seaweed. Gwen tried to scream "No!" but her words held no sound as her father leaned to kiss the mermaid and was dragged into the dark, suddenly still waters.

She woke, relieved to find herself curled up next to Wigandus on the gently rocking barge, his arm wrapped around her like a blanket. She lay there, listening to his breathing and the quiet lapping of the water against the hull, enjoying the mingled smells of river mud and man, remembering all the times she had been with her father on his boat. She quietly mouthed the prayer her father used to say each time he went to sea. "Protect me dear Lord, for my boat is so small and your sea so large." As she said the prayer, Gwen realized how much she missed him. If her mother could forgive him, so could she. He had taught her to sail his boat on both the ocean's waves and through the river's currents. This barge was her responsibility, and the lives in it her charge. Hopefully her remembrance of how to handle a boat on rough water would translate.

She unwrapped herself from Wigandus, sat up and looked at him in the light of a full moon. It would be so nice to run her hands through his hair, caress his chest, pull his strong shoulders to her in a deep embrace, bury her face in his chest, smell him, nuzzle in and loose herself in discovering him. She shivered, trying to get these thoughts off her mind.

The moon, silver and full, hung above the far shore, enchanting in its beauty. Gwen sighed. Even this beauty didn't help her put aside her longing. She looked around the boat and saw Britomar, also awake. Gwen rose and gently stepped around Adelie and Élise, making her way around the bales and boxes to where the unicorn reclined at the prow.

"Couldn't sleep?" Britomar asked as Gwen sat on a box near her. The unicorn's ivory horn glistened in the moonlight, and her pale fur shone, as if the light came from within her. Gwen felt more alive than ever, as if she too bathed in the moon's radiance.

"No, a dream woke me." Not wanting to talk about her father's sin, she asked a question that had been nagging at her for quite some time. "Are we going fast enough? Will we reach the Garden in time? I'm so worried that had it not been for the rapids ahead, I'd have kept us going all night, piloting by the light of the moon."

"I have to believe we will, why else were you sent to me?"

"Sent?" Gwen's heart quickened. "I was not sent to you, I came to you for Sam's sake. I knew nothing of your king."

The unicorn smiled. "You were sent to me, as I was sent to you by the Lady of the Lake, with the hope that you might take on this errand."

"That's why you helped Sam?" Only sudden pain made Gwen realize her nails had cut into the palms of her clenched hands.

"No," said Britomar. "That's why I met with you in Brocéliande. If Nimuë didn't have the hope in you taking on this errand, she might have sent you down the paths that would have allowed you to find a unicorn, but not to me."

"So you only helped Sam to get me to help you?" Gwen's chest heaved.

"No. I helped Sam and left without asking for anything from you. I helped him, if only because you were the first ever to ask a unicorn to help someone else. I left, and waited to come back, though the wait was the hardest thing I had ever done. I never wanted you to think that I only helped Sam to gain your help."

The splashing of the river and the boat's gentle rocking muddled Gwen's thoughts, as if she was again in her dream, unable to help as hope drowned with her father. There was something in that splash, a smell she couldn't place, that made her nauseous.

She tried to ignore it, returning to more certain worries." What would you have done if I hadn't said I'd help?"

Britomar hung her head. "I don't know."

Gwen frowned. "I wish I had such confidence. I can't fight like Adelie, or chase away demons like Élise. What can I do, what is special about me that God will let me into Eden?"

Britomar touched Gwen with her horn. "Perhaps it is simply because you said yes."

The horn lifted as the words sank in, and Gwen found herself breathing again. For a while she listened to the gentle lap of the waves on the hull.

Britomar broke the silence. "It is not in my nature to question things. I was asked to go, and I went. I was told to ask you for help, and I did so. Your questions have unsettled my heart. I sense that I have tasted of your nature in this."

"I wonder," said Gwen. "Perhaps not of our nature, but of our failing. It is the doubt born of sin, of not trusting in Him."

Britomar shook her head, her mane silver in the moonlight. "It is a heavy burden. I never understood it before, I only felt its impact. I wonder what this means that I can understand sin?"

"I don't know." Gwen remembered her longing for Wigandus. "Britomar, I know that a unicorn can only abide a chaste maid, and I've begun to lust for Sir Wigandus. How do you bear to be around me?"

Britomar's horn once more glowed in the pale light of the moon. "You smell like love, not lust."

Gwen felt her heart lift; she had never imagined that love could also have desire. "May I curl up here by your side?" She yawned heavily.

"Yes."

When Gwen rose the next morning, she was surprised to see the sun already high up in the sky. Her friends were all about the barge, preparing for the day's journey. Strange, that until this moment she had not realized that they were friends, not companions.

Gwen stretched and yawned. Feeling in need of a bath, she looked downriver and saw a sheltered spot, well hidden from view by river grass. She past Adelie who was sweeping the desks of the manure, but had to stop when she saw Wigandus moving boxes so that they were better balanced. The muscles in his arms and shoulders rippled as he lifted a crate. She blushed and averted her eyes as she continued to the plank. David was not far upriver, walking one of the horses on the shore. He waved to her as she disembarked. He'd grown in breadth since joining them, become less the scholar and more the man.

Gwen began to walk downstream, and soon came upon Élise putting out a fire next to the remains of breakfast.

"Good morning," Gwen said.

Élise shook her head. "I've burnt breakfast again."

"No matter, it will still be better than what the nuns used to serve me in the convent. I'm off to take a bath, I'll eat later."

It did not take Gwen long to reach the secluded spot she'd spied from the barge. She undressed and stepped into the water, delighted in its cool freshness as it enfolded her. Swimming among the reeds, she looked up at the flutter of wings and saw her raven landing on the pile of clothes she left ashore.

Gwen shook her head. "Don't you dare."

As if the challenge was what it needed, the raven shook its feathers and clicked at her as it rose into the air, her dress and undergarment clutched in its talons.

She chased after it, half swimming, half running through the river grass. The raven would land every few yards, wait until she reached it, then lift into the air, mocking her with its clicks. Finally dropping her clothes in a clearing, it flew off with a loud brawk.

Gwen huddled behind the tall reeds, staring at her clothes and up the meadow to where Wigandus now walked his destrier along the bank of the river. As if adding a barb to its jest, the raven landed on the destrier. Gwen's cheeks burned, her heart pounding.

The knight scratched the bird as it preened, strutting across the back of the massive horse. The raven spread its wings, cawed, and flew back to the clothes, which it pecked. Gwen held her breath as the knight's gaze followed the bird. From behind the reeds, she could swear he looked her in the eye before he turned and continued to walk his destrier upriver, away from her.

As soon as he was out of sight, Gwen darted out of the grass, grabbed the clothing, and rushed back into cover. As she dressed, she was surprised to realize that she was actually disappointed that he'd not stayed.

As Gwen neared the barge, she heard voices raised in a heated argument. Afraid of another attack, she picked up the pace. Her worry melted into relief as she realized that there was no danger. The only people in sight were Adelie and Élise at the edge of the water, scrubbing pots.

"Must you be so obvious?" Élise yelled,

Adelie turned and pointed her pot at Élise. "What do you mean?"

Élise continued to scrub. "Your eyes follow him. Your hand holds his, even in front of the king! What will it be next? Kissing? Sharing his bed?"

"And who the hell are you to talk? I overheard everything that happened between you and Wigandus last night. I may be watching David, but I've never tried to seduce him."

Gwen froze in her tracks. *Élise* tried to seduce *Wigandus?*

Élise lifted her chin. "I love Wigandus, who is a good Christian knight. As a lady of station I'm entitled to maintain lovers. Why do you waste your attentions on a Jew, as if he's worthy—"

"Worthy! Why I—" Adelie began, before Gwen interrupted them.

"Stop it! Both of you stop!" Gwen ran to them, flailing her arms. "I know the past few days have been hard on all of us, but the last thing we need is to start fighting each other."

Gwen was gratified to see Élise's cheeks flush red. The woman was not entirely shameless. She took their stunned silence as a chance to catch her thoughts.

"If we start to fight over the men, if we start to fight over the desire they light within us, we're doomed, and so is the eldest of unicorns. We must act out of love, not desire, or we might as well go home right now."

Élise looked down at the pot dripping suds into the river. "You're not upset that I tried to lay with Sir Wigandus?"

Gwen sighed. "I want to be. Right now I want to hit you, tear your hair...but until yesterday I didn't let anyone know, least of all him, that I love him. We love the same man, and we're going to have to live with that, you and I. He'll either return your love, or mine, or choose neither of us. If he doesn't choose me, I'll let him go, because I love him."

Élise looked up, tears streaming down her cheeks. "That's easy for you to say when he holds you, wraps his arms around you. Would you feel the same if *you* had gone to him and he pushed you away?"

"I'd hope so," said Gwen. "As for David, yes he is a Jew, a Jew who chose to risk his life by joining us. Who are we to judge Adelie for loving him?"

"I'm sorry, Adelie, I'm sorry," sobbed Élise.

Adelie put down her pot and hugged Élise. "It's alright. I have been rather open in my affection for him, and we can never marry. I don't want to be like my mother, but when I'm near him, the temptation to wrap myself around him is so strong. Let's put this behind us."

"Good. Now, I've got a boat to run." Gwen walked away from the river to the ashes of the fire. She quickly ate the food Élise left for her, then boarded the barge. She waited for everyone else to return on board and spoke to David and Sir Wigandus. "Could you both pull in the plank and then take in the lines; we need to get going."

"I'll take the first shift at the rudder," said David.

Gwen took her seat at the prow and watched the men lift the plank and place it on the deck. It was fun to watch, but dangerous. She took a deep breath, turned toward the river and began to look for the eddies in the currents which could indicate hidden rocks. Somehow, searching for danger beneath the water felt safer to her than watching the men at work.

They had not gone far when Britomar came forward, her smell of thunder mixing with that of river mud.

"Can I help, Gwen?" she asked.

"Yes, please stay with the horses, and see if you can get them to lie down. If they're standing when we hit rough waters, they may get badly hurt—or fall overboard." Gwen shifted in her seat to get more comfortable. "Just keep them calm." She turned to watch the river again.

As she settled into the quiet rhythm of the boat's rocking, she felt more than a little at home. Sitting at the prow and watching the water reminded her of sitting in her father's boat, scanning the waves for signs of fish. She had spent many happy days there until he had sent her to the convent school. Their long hours together had prepared her well for the monotony of the ever-same river with its clear surface reflecting nothing but the hills and the trees.

As the hills grew taller, the river narrowed and the speed of the current increased. The rapids would not be far ahead.

"Wigandus! Take the rudder!" she shouted. "David, get up here and grab a pole!" She was glad that the raven alighted from her shoulder and came to rest on one of the many crates.

They rounded a bend in the river, and Gwen saw whitecaps and eddies boiling ahead.

"Hold to center!" She trusted Wigandus to do so. She moved to the left of the prow, pole in hand, scanning for eddies where there should not be. "David, look for changes in the water's flow. They show hidden rocks. If you see one, and it looks like we may hit it, shout, and I'll come and help you push away with the pole. If I shout out, come help me."

The boat started to pitch and yaw, and Gwen heard the horses whinny nervously. She hoped Britomar would be able to keep them calm.

"A rock!" David called.

She rushed over and together they reached into the water with their poles and pushed. Gwen's pole hit something hard, knocking her down. Pain pulsed in her shoulder, but she felt the boat shift as David held.

She jumped to her feet, grabbed her pole and called out, "Élise, Adelie, get up here and find poles!"

The boat began rocking heavily. "*Merde!*" Adelie shouted as she hit the deck. Élise rushed to Gwen's side, then Adelie joined them, standing next to David.

Gwen's heart pounded as they scanned the waters for rocks rising up in the center. *Sweet Mother of God. So many eddies.* The water was getting shallow. "Get ready, here they come!"

"A rock!"

They reached with their poles. The wood dug painfully into their shoulders, causing some of them to overbalance, but the boat shifted. It rocked as the water roared around them. The eddies became white-caps. Suddenly the boat lifted its prow and fell again, jerking to the right. Splattering water soaked their clothes and pooled on the deck.

"A rock!"

They pushed, as the prow raised and the boat shifted. *Crash!* This time they all fell, tangled together. Rolling, Gwen was on her feet again. She grabbed her pole and took her perch, eddy swirling. "A rock!"

It took Gwen more time to recover after the next blow that shook the boat and soaked everything in sight. She glanced around, instantly alarmed as she realized there were fewer of them this time. Where was Adelie?

Gwen's eyes quickly scanned the boat; Adelie was not there. She raced to the stern and glanced over. After a moment she saw a flash of cloth rise between the boiling crests of water. *Adelie!*

Without a thought, Gwen leapt into the water. Cold embraced her as she swam to where Adelie floated, face down, in the calm center.

Gwen rolled her to her back, slipped an arm around her shoulder, and kicked toward the barge, now drifting in calmer waters.

Something gripped her leg.

She let go of Adelie, kicking at it as hard as she could, but the thing would not let go. It pulled, and Gwen couldn't fight it off. She coughed as water slid into her mouth, frantically kicking as her trapped foot slowly went numb in the unknown embrace. She slid under the surface, her vision darkening as her face submerged into its turbid depths.

And then, just as suddenly, the grip on her foot was released. Gwen kicked herself to the surface and coughed, gasping for air. Britomar's head crested next to hers, with Adelie floating nearby. Gwen grabbed her with one hand, and Britomar's mane with the other, and the unicorn's strong legs moved them through the water faster than the barge on the swift current.

Gwen smiled at the sight of Wigandus's worried face peering over the tall wall of the barge. He tossed a coil of rope to her. She caught it and looped it under Adelie's arms, knotting it over her breasts so that Wigandus could pull her head-first out of the water.

Gwen treaded water as Adelie's limp body rose up the side of the barge, lifted over the edge by David and Wigandus. Another rope landed next to her. She grabbed it and used it to walk up the side of the barge, rolling over the edge down to the deck, landing with a welcome thud. She darted over to Adelie, pushing past David and Élise. Remembering how the sailors brought back the men rescued from drowning, she cupped her mouth over Adelie's and forced the air in. Breath in, force out, breath in force out—

She gasped in relief as Adelie coughed, splattering water. *Thank God!*

David helped Adelie sit as she coughed. Looking anxiously at Gwen, he said, "We'll need to get her out of her wet things and under a blanket, to keep her warm."

"I'll take care of her," said Élise.

David nodded, then picked up his pole and went back to the stern. Gwen returned to the prow, looking for more rocks in the calming waters around the barge.

She heard the loud clomping of hooves on wood, and the boat shook. Gwen turned and saw Britomar, prancing through the puddles to where Adelie lay on the deck, cradled in Élise's arms. The unicorn laid its horn on Adelie. Color spread across the girl's cheeks, her face relaxing into a smile. Gwen heard Adelie say something, but could not catch the words.

"Sancta Maria, Thank You!" she mouthed, relief washing over her. Adelie was safe. Everything was fine.

Gwen lost herself in watching the gleaming surface of the river and started when she felt a blanket being placed on her shoulders, quickly followed by the raven resuming its perch over it. Adelie sat down next to her, and stared out at the river that had nearly been her grave.

"Thank you for diving in after me," said Adelie quietly.

"Are you all right?" asked Élise, lowering down on Gwen's other side.

Gwen hesitated. "I think so. My head feels a little funny, but otherwise I'm fine."

The three women sat there, silent and still, watching the Danube quietly go past. Finally, Gwen rose and shouted to David, who was again at the rudder, "Pull to the shore on the right; there's a good place to tie up for the night!"

That night, as they ate around the fire, Gwen asked, "Britomar, what was it you chased away from me in the river?"

The unicorn looked thoughtful. "I don't know the human name

179

for it, and you wouldn't understand ours. I saw it take hold of your leg and pull you down."

"Its hand was ice-cold, colder than the river." Gwen shuddered at the memory.

They all ate in silence, broken only by the river's gentle lapping on the shore. After the meal, Gwen strode back to the barge and lay down on the deck. She couldn't stop thinking about the creature that nearly drowned her. Was it allied with the merfolk? Were they seeking revenge for her father's theft?

The next thing she knew, birdsong pulled her awake. It was morning.

From that point onward, she saw no further eddies. The next day, David pointed out a rock that had the name of the Roman Emperor Trajan carved into it. Next to it a narrow stream branched off the Danube. An old canal? Gwen wished she had seen the other side of it, above the rocks. A canal around the rapids would have saved them much trouble. Still, she felt satisfaction in having passed through the Danube safely, and in having saved Adelie. She had finally done something meaningful on this journey.

GALIANA

Galiana looked upon her reflection in the basin to make certain that the paint on her face was perfect and enticing. A mask of beauty stared back, painted pale like a lady of station; above her eyes a flawless blue hid the faint lines of age, red daintily enflaming her lips and livening her cheeks, framed by her long golden hair. A smile would ruin the effect, but she had no reason to smile. It was time to find another fool willing to pay for a moment of sex, her means to live. Those lines stealing the softness around her eyes warned her that her time to prey on men will soon draw to a close. This next catch had better be big.

She had hope of a fat purse. Last night she'd noticed a new barge coming downriver, the first in many months. That meant men who hadn't seen a woman in days. She intended to wait near the wharf, to show these men an enticing way to lose some gold.

Galiana glanced out of the window again, past the weathered grayed buildings, to the gleaming river and the barge. Something in the prow glistened in the sunlight. Most likely knights on a pilgrimage to plunder. They'll be good lusty fun, but were likely to have lean purses, younger sons of small estates. A merchant would be a better catch, though likely less fun. She dabbed her brush back into the red and painted her nipples, softly humming a song her last client had taught her. She needed money, not fun.

Grabbing a translucent silk shawl from her bed, she draped it over her left shoulder, so that it hung between her breasts, down to her crotch. She wrapped a silk belt around her waist and tied it, so that her pretense of modesty would not fly away with the breeze. Sliding her fingers gently between her legs until they were wet, she spread her scent on the nape of her neck, under her ears, the places where a man might kiss.

Sliding her feet into gilded leather sandals, Galiana made her way through the dusty streets to the warehouses, where the other whores stood, also hoping for some gold. Their jealous glances were all the compliments she needed. Today, she was the dainty morsel, the bait that most likely would snag a rich prey.

As she waited, a small girl came up to her, black hair pulled back, dirty white tunic torn at the hem of her skirt. Her dirt-smudged face was tear-streaked; yet her green eyes sparkled. Oddly, she smelled of the sea, a fresh smell that made Galiana inadvertently inhale deeper as the little girl stopped in front of her.

"Beautiful lady, aren't you cold?" the girl said.

A man's voice, deep and rough, shouted, "Milita, get away from her, she's a whore."

The girl didn't move. "That's my papa. He'll whip me if I don't listen." She held up a small copper coin. "Take this, and buy yourself some clothes."

Galiana took a second look at the child who was daring to brave her father's displeasure to give her unneeded charity. "Child, take me to your father."

The girl's small hand wrapped around two of the fingers of Galiana's offered hand. *Such a small child.* Galiana suppressed a smile, unwilling to embarrass the girl.

The girl led Galiana to a group of farmers, who had come with food-laden wagons to trade with the merchants about to set sail. Their clothes was soiled and patched, their faces dirty. They leered at Galiana as she approached, wrinkling her nose at the strong smell of manure.

"Papa, the pretty lady wanted to speak with you," said the girl.

The nearest farmer put down a sack of flour and looked at his daughter. "I thought I told you to get away from the whore."

"Papa, what's a whore?"

The other farmers chuckled.

Galiana said, "I insisted on meeting the father of a girl so kind as to offer me coin, thinking me cold. You should be proud of your daughter." She squatted and looked in the girl's brown eyes, folding the child's coin into her hand with another larger one beneath it. "You did a very nice thing, offering me your coin. I don't need it, and I'm not cold, but you are very sweet." She let go of the girl's hand and stood up. "If I ever had a child, I'd like her to be like your daughter, brave and charitable."

The girl's papa swept his daughter into his arms. A tear glistened in his eye and ran down his dirty cheek. "Her mother, God bless her soul, was like that. Thank you."

Galiana nodded and strode back, up the refuse-strewn lane, to her perch. Part of her wished she'd stayed with the man and the child, offered to help raising her. She pushed the thought deep, buried it beneath the hope of the money she'd earn that day. She could ill afford sentiment. Such thoughts had ruined many a whore, and more often led to starvation and early death than to a life as a mother and wife.

Soon she could see enough of the dock to observe a boy with curly copper hair and a raven on his shoulder tying the barge to the pier. She stood on tiptoe to get a better look, and a sharp sense of longing stabbed her like a knife.

A unicorn climbed from the barge to the pier, its golden horn gleaming in the sunlight.

Ignoring the tears that were ruining her makeup, or the smile that broke her carefully painted mask, Galiana pushed through the crowd and stopped. A knight with long flaxen hair, his torn, dirty surcoat baring the arms she'd love to... since when did she want a man?

The knight spared her not a glance. Behind him, next to the boy with the copper curls—*wait, that is no boy, that is a woman!* What she'd thought was a man's tunic was a ruined merchant's dress. A woman on a barge... no matter. The unicorn had stopped and was looking right at her! Galiana pushed through the throng, reached out her hand and touched it on the side. Joy seared through her, so bright it burned—and then, just as sharp, came the realization of what she was—what she had chosen to be.

Galiana's joy fell as she looked at the unicorn. This was a thing of purity and all her life had been an exploitation of lust for greed. The sudden awareness of the hard truth of a life without love sliced through her. She stroked the unicorn's fur, trying to say "thank you" with her touch for the one thing of purity that had come into her life, a life she could no longer bear.

She covered her face and wailed, running through the crowd, through the filth, straight into the river.

The cold water took her. Her lungs screamed in pain as she forced herself to breath in water, let the primal chaos take her into death from the ruin of her life.

Something strong wrapped around her shoulders and pulled her coughing into the air. She struggled to face her unwelcome rescuer. It was the young woman she'd mistaken for a boy, mercilessly pulling her to shore—and shame.

"Cruel, heartless maiden!" she spat, coughing up the words with water. "Let me drown my grief! Look at me, I'm just a worthless whore!"

"You are not worthless," said the maid who did not stop dragging her to the unwelcome safety of the land. "Just stop being a whore, and become a woman again."

Galiana sobbed. "I have no family who would take me in, and no man would marry someone like me."

"Then come with us. We will find you new clothes, and you can find a new life in a new place. No one need know your past, if you would not have them know it."

Galiana felt hope rise as the maid's arm wrapped around her and helped her stand. "I could do this?"

"Yes." Gwen offered her hand. "Come with me now, and leave this all behind."

Galiana grasped the offered hand. "Thank you. I'm sorry, I don't even know your name."

"Gwenaella. My friends call me Gwen."

"I'm Galiana."

In the time it took them to rejoin the others, Gwen told a little of their errand and then introduced the others who awaited them, but their names swirled in Galiana's head. Was this real? A unicorn, a knight, and a maid traveled openly with a Jew and a lady of station? Another maid came up to her and wrapped a blanket around her as they continued to walk to the ship.

Some men called out to her with vulgar words—words that defined her past. Galiana could not help but notice Gwen's face redden to their taunts. One man called out to Gwen, calling her a whore as well. Gwen lowered her head, but raised it again as the knight spoke to the crowd, "A pile of filth such as yourselves should be washed clean, not so? The next oaf who utters a comment about the women will find themselves getting a scrubbing."

A huge man with a bald head and a bare, hairless chest stepped forward and said, "So, what are you, their pimp?"

The knight unbuckled his sword, and handed it to the Jew. He then strode forward and said, "I gave no warning regarding comments about me. However, your insult is actually directed at the ladies, for if I am their pimp, they must be prostitutes. I demand an apology."

"Take this for my apology!" The bald man swung his fist at the knight.

Wigandus blocked it and jabbed the bald man on the jaw, knocking him to the pavement. As the bald man tried to rise, the knight brought his elbow down on the man's back, then grabbed him by his ankles, and dragged him down to the river.

"No! Have Mercy! Please! Stop!" the man screamed.

Wigandus dropped the man's ankles. "You asked for mercy, and mercy I'll grant you. Get yourself to church, you miserable fool." He turned and walked away.

The bald man rose and rushed him again.

"Look out!" Gwen called.

The knight wheeled, and hit the man hard in the belly with his fist, causing him to double over, then slammed his other fist on the bald man's chin. He did not bother to look at his fallen enemy as he rejoined the women. No further taunts followed them as they continued on their way.

As Galiana watched the Jew kiss a small metal tube which hung on the door of a house they were about to enter, she realized that she had no desire to return to her own chambers and retrieve the gold hidden there. A knight had just fought to defend her, a maid had saved her life, and a unicorn walked with her over the threshold of a Jew's home. She had always mocked the priests who pleaded her to give up the life of a whore and become a nun, telling them that had their God not wanted her to whore He would have sent her a husband, not a slaver and a rapist. And now, she suddenly felt that perhaps their God existed after all, and wanted something of her. Whatever the price, it would be worth that moment, when a unicorn looked at her and saw in her not a whore, but a woman.

REFUGE FROM A STORM

The wind howled as the ship rocked, tossed about by a storm that had lasted since dawn. Some of the dips had become severe, and Élise held on tightly to a rope that secured a barrel against the wall of the hold. The floor fell and Élise fell with it, only to rise again as suddenly. As this repeated again and again, each time more violent than the last, she wondered if she had died and gone to hell, trapped with the rats below the ship's deck with sun and fresh air forever beyond her reach.

A scream pierced the air, and a blast of wet wind hit Élise's face. She looked up to see the sailors pulling back the deck hatch. Rain pellets stung like bees, the wind pulling her hair into the storm.

Voices called down to them, followed by more screams from the deck. David translated, "Wigandus, a monster from the deep attacks the ship."

Wigandus rushed up the ladder after David. The hatch closed again after them. Élise grasped her rope as the ship rocked violently, wondering if this hold would be her tomb.

Suddenly the ship stopped moving. Its timbers groaned as it shook, and a loud crack echoed overhead. Élise held her breath, startled to hear Adelie's frightened sobs. Adelie had always been so brave.

Élise crawled to her sister and held her as Adelie rocked back and forth, calling David's name. Élise's heart echoed the misery, calling without words to Wigandus to be safe.

Crash!

Élise was tossed into the air, torn from her sister. A heavy sack smashed into her legs and she fell, crashing onto the deck. The ship trembled beneath her. An unearthly silence filled the hold as the screams from above ceased, and the ship once again began to rock, pitch, and yaw. The lamps had died, the wind's howl the only sound in the pitch-dark hold.

"Is everyone all right?" Élise asked.

"I'm fine," said Gwen.

"Just frightened," said Galiana.

"Élise, are you hurt?" asked Adelie.

"No, not really."

Britomar said, "I'm all right. The horses are frightened, but otherwise fine."

A gray light split the darkness as the hatch overhead slid open. David came down the ladder, followed closely by Wigandus. Both men were soaking wet. David slipped the last two rungs and collapsed on the deck.

Élise and Adelie rushed to his side, and Adelie cradled his head in her lap. David breathed shallowly, his forehead smeared with blood. As Wigandus stepped off the ladder into Gwen's embrace, Britomar laid her horn on David.

Élise turned away as the glow of health returned to David's cheeks and his breathing relaxed into an easy rhythm. Her sister's joy made her own loneliness harder to bear. She looked away from Wigandus as he held the sobbing Gwen.

"What happened up there?" she asked.

"A tentacled monster had wrapped itself around the ship," said the chevalier, his voice weary and sad. "David and I joined the sailors in hacking at it until it released us."

"That beast snapped the mast in two," David said. "We're not far from shore, so they're trying to rig a sail so we can make for land and repair the ship."

Élise sat in a huff, wishing for someone's arms to embrace her, destroy her value to this Prince of Armenia that awaited her.

Through the open hatch, Élise watched the fading light of dusk. The ship's rhythm had shifted a number of times in the past few hours, and settled into gentle rocking. A man leaned over the hatch and shouted. David responded, then translated to the rest of his companions, "They found a ruined harbor. The town around it is deserted, but it will be a safe place to repair the ship. The captain recommends we stay on board tonight, and asks for our help in the morning."

Sir Wigandus said, "That sounds like a worthy plan."

David called back to the man above and they settled to their evening meal.

Élise lay awake, listening to the men snore, wishing she had one at her side, wishing she had found a way to forgive Martis, wishing she'd never listened to Garsenda's plea to follow Britomar on the long journey from Paris that steadily took her into the arms of a butcher.

At daybreak she joined Adelie, David, and Wigandus as they climbed up the ladder. Gwen and the whore thankfully stayed with Britomar down below.

As Élise stepped into the fresh air and daylight on the deck, she found David in a heated discussion with the sailors.

"They don't want the women to come to shore," David said to his companions.

"Why?" asked Élise and Adelie together.

"They don't think you're strong enough to help."

Sir Wigandus said, "They may not be strong enough to help with the mast, but they can bring on fresh water and search for food."

David spoke to the sailors, one of whom laughed and said something, which David translated. "They want to know who can be trusted to guard them. I've told them that Adelie can guard you both, but they find it hard to believe."

"Tell them to get their best and strongest, and let him fight Adelie," said Wigandus.

"Do you think I'm up for this?" asked Adelie.

"When we spar, I see a warrior I'd rather not face. You'll put down their champion."

"You're certainly better at unarmed combat than I am," said David. "I think Wigandus is right."

David told them Wigandus's challenge. The sailors sniggered and talked among themselves, eventually pulling forward a muscular man with sunburnt face and a deep scar over his cheek.

Adelie measured him with her eyes as she put down her knives. The sailors made a circle around them, cheering and laughing.

The muscular sailor circled Adelie, fists at ready. He lunged and punched at her face, but Adelie adeptly stepped out of the way and hit him squarely in the jaw. The sailor grinned as he rubbed his face, circling again. This time he threw one fist, closely followed by the other. Adelie slid under and grabbed his arm, pulling him into his blow. He overbalanced and rolled past her onto the deck.

As he started to rise, Adelie kicked him squarely in his crotch. He doubled over, and she threw two punches up to his jaw, sending him back to the deck. He did not attempt to rise this time. Élise marveled that her sister was barely winded.

The sailors laughed and chattered as they helped their companion back to his feet. A few of them said something to David. He smiled and translated, "They've agreed, you can come ashore and search for food."

Élise pouted a little at this, and contemplated returning to the hold.

After all, part of her reason for offering to help was to be amongst men, not to stay apart under her sister's protection. Still, fresh air was better than hours with that whore, and the beasts... How did Britomar become just a beast to her? Élise frowned and grabbed a basket, joining Adelie in the boat heading to shore.

It took Élise a few minutes of walking on solid ground before she felt that the land was not swaying. She followed Adelie up the long path into the fields, once tended by men, now running wild. They each began to harvest what wheat they could find, snapping the kernels off the stalks and putting them into the baskets

After a while, Élise could swear she heard chanting. The sound grew stronger as they continued, the words within the chant slowly becoming apparent, though strange. They followed the sound into a clearing between the nearby bushes.

Two men in the clearing were whirling and chanting. One wore impeccable white robes with multi-colored trim and a richly colored hat. The other's robes were dirty and tattered, his head covered by a gray knit cap.

Élise glanced at her sister, who stopped with her mouth open, and dropped her basket.

The men came to an abrupt halt. Then, the better dressed one brought his right hand to his forehead, then his lips, then his chest as he folded in an elaborate bow. "May Allah bring you as much joy as he has given you beauty."

The second one said, "Make it a habit of shutting up. Ladies, may we be of service?"

"You speak Provençal?" asked Élise.

"No, obviously we are all speaking Urdu."

Élise blushed.

"I am Shams," the man continued. "This overdressed peacock is my persistent student, Melvana Jalal al-Din. Who are you and may we be of service?"

Elise straightened up. "I'm Lady Elisabeth du Chauvigny, and this is my sister Lady Adelie. Our ship was damaged. We're gathering food while the men repair the vessel."

"Then we shall help you," said Mevlana Jalal al-Din.

The men followed them through the fields of wheat, harvesting the kernels and placing them in the baskets. Since there were only two baskets, they harvested in pairs. Élise found herself with Mevlana.

"Shams said you are a persistent student of his," she said.

"Yes. He was sent to me by Allah to help me find the hidden Imam. Then he left me, before I had achieved that oneness of being, knowing Allah in the knowing of my true self. But I sought him out, and convinced him to return to me so I may finish my studies."

She snapped another kernel from the stalk. "When we arrived, the two of you were whirling."

"Yes, it is a way to experience the joy of His presence, to completely surrender to Allah."

"If he left you, why did you seek his return?" She dropped a kernel, and had to stoop to retrieve it.

Mevlana smiled. "His teachings are likened unto mother's milk. I suck on them to find my way back to Eden."

"Eden?" *Perhaps he knows of the Garden?*

"Yes, Eden," answered Mevlana. "Since my eyesight is flawed, I trust my insight. He has a way of showing me how to trade seeing for being. This will help me find the hidden Imam."

Élise held her breath. "Have you heard of the Garden at the Roof of the World?"

He stopped picking grain and looked at her. "Yes, this is where Eden is now. It was moved there by the Prophet Isa."

"Can you tell me anything about how to get there?"

Mevlana stopped, forcing her to stop with him. "Four men argued about the best way to get to Constantinople. Unable to settle their dispute and travel together, they each set out, using their own chosen path." He reached forward and lifted her chin so she was looking at him. "The Persian took a caravan along the old Roman roads, the Arab a boat, the Turk went by the mountain paths, and the Greek went along the coast. They all arrived at the Golden Horn on the same day at the same time."

"Are you telling me it doesn't matter how we go?"

"Only Allah knows the true path."

They began to walk and harvest again. Élise said, "We've already had such a hard journey and now you tell me that there is no way to know if we're going the right way to get to the Garden. That is a hard thing to say."

"The dove does not know if it will eat that night, but she'll sing anyway."

Élise reddened and she clenched the basket handle. "No dove is attacked by monsters, nearly defiled, or forced to watch her best friend die in her arms." *Or, to marry a man whose people kill wantonly.*

Mevlana turned to Élise and put a hand on her shoulder. "Allah has been frightening you, because in his loving kindness he wants you to rest in the true security of his undying love."

"You're telling me that Allah has let these things happen to me because He loves me? I'm glad I don't follow your Muhammad."

"That is sad. Muhammad is the best of His prophets because he alone has never stopped growing toward Allah and begging forgiveness for his prior ignorance."

They continued to harvest in silence for a while. Élise pondered all he had said. She knew her disquiet came from her desperation to find the release from her betrothal, which could only come from a sin she'd been unable to commit.

When the basket was full, she put her hand on Mevlana's as he dropped the last grains into the basket. "Thank you. Hopefully the men will have the ship fixed and we can leave tomorrow in search of the Garden."

He clasped her hand, his earnest gray-green eyes piercing her. "Don't wait for tomorrow. It has never existed, and never will. Now is all."

Uncomfortable under his gaze, she lowered her eyes and took up the basket with both hands. What did it matter to her how to get to the Garden? In Antioch she'd have to part with the others, get an escort to Armenia. Her betrothed waited. She caught up with Adelie and curtsied in farewell to the two men, haunted by the yesterdays she wished had never been, by tomorrows hoped for that she still had not let go of, and a future that hung over her like doom.

Her heart stormier than the weather their ship had faced, she followed Adelie to the ship. There they found the men erecting a new mast amidst the rubble of the deck. Élise paused before descending onto the ship, wondering what ruin lay in store for her.

What manner of man was the husband this ship would bring her to? The burnt villages of Hungary hung before her eyes as she climbed into the darkness of the hold.

ANTIOCH

*T*homas, *few parts of what I relate to you bring me as much sadness as what I must relate to you now. Your beliefs on sin and redemption are so very different than ours, and when I think upon the events I'm about to relate, I almost hope your tradition has it right; that sins are forgiven the repentant, and not the cause of suffering in the next incarnation.*

I've never journeyed yet by sea, and the account I was given of the cramped and foul conditions in the bowels of the ship do not make me long for the experience, but I can well imagine their joy of finding themselves sailing into the harbor. Such was the joy Élise felt as she looked up when the hatch to the hold was pulled open, confirming what the quieter rocking of the ship had told them all—they had at long last made harbor. The brilliant light that streamed through the opening blinded her; she closed her eyes and the light was still bright through her lids. She let the warmth soak into her and then reopened her eyes. Wigandus and David were already climbing up the ladder, with Gwen at the base.

Élise put her hands on the rungs and climbed up into the light and fresh air. Antioch! The first city that the crusaders had taken from the infidel. Surely a bath and civilized hospitality awaited her above. A return to civility, then the farewells that must follow, and her long journey to Armenia.

Her head crested and she had to pull her gaze back from the harbor to focus on climbing out of the hatch without tripping over her tattered skirts. With any luck she'd have time to have new clothes made in the city before she left.

Standing up on the deck of the ship, Élise quickly forgot all about her ragged skirts and promised husbands.

Masts rose in every direction like a forest with spars for leaves. Tanned, sweaty men scrambled on ropes and wooded decks. Further on, a large wooden crane stood at the end of a pier, lowering a stone twice the height of a man onto a ship. Élise held her breath. Would the ship collapse under the weight? She watched as the huge shape settled into the hold, barely rocking the ship at its moorings.

Élise was disappointed to see rotten piers and a shallow wall with broken square towers surrounding the city. Surely a place as grand as Antioch should have tall walls and towers rising high above the sea? Had their captain betrayed them and taken them to a wrong port? And how could it be that a port with more rotten piers than good ones could be so vibrant?

She stared closer at the city, realizing that no church rose above the walls. Her skin crept. What kind of a Godless place did they find themselves in?

A man cried out, "Karkadann!" and others echoed the cry. Sailors and dock workers abandoned their tasks to fill the pier. The crowd became so thick that some were pushed into the water. "Karkadann!" the men chanted, staring somewhere behind Élise. She turned and saw a sling lifting Britomar out of the hold.

Élise twirled a lock of hair. Karkadann must be their word for unicorn. And now there was a crowd blocking their way. How were they ever going to get through?

Their captain shouted orders to his crew, who lined up on deck with short swords in hand. Sir Wigandus stood behind them, his head towering over the sailors.

A shrill blast of a horn came from the city walls, silencing the throng of sailors on the pier. Glancing nervously in the direction of the broken towers, men rushed back to their tasks, but some held back, watching.

Boots echoed on the dock. Men marching. Élise stretched her neck to see a company, armed with halberds, approaching their berth. Sunlight gleamed on the polished steel of their blades.

One man stepped forward. His helm bore a square cross, the emblem of a crusader, his sun-ripened face dark against its frame of polished steel.

"Welcome to Seleuceia ad Pierea, the port city to Antioch ad Orontes. I am Captain Jacques, at your service." His eyes trailed toward Britomar with wonder.

Élise pulled on a lock of her hair, twisting it around her finger as she tried to figure out how it was that this man spoke native Langue d'oc, so far from Marsilha.

Gwen answered, "My companions are Sir Wigandus of the Langrave of Thuringia, the Ladies Elisabeth and Adelie de Chauvigny, David ben Yosi, and Galiana Passavanti."

Jacques laughed. "You forget to name yourself, fair maiden—or are you a nameless witch sent to enchant us?"

Élise felt Sir Wigandus's strong hand gently push her out of his way as the knight stepped forward. "By my word as a knight of the Holy Roman Empire, she is Gwenaella the maid, chosen companion of the unicorn Britomar on a Holy mission. I will hear an apology, or prove her innocence by right of arms!"

Jacques blanched. "My apologies, maid Gwenaella. I spoke hastily and in ignorance. The Prince of Antioch has sent me here to bid you welcome and escort you—and the unicorn—into the city, where he hopes you will stay to enjoy his hospitality."

Élise put her hand over her mouth to hide a smile. A prince? Things certainly looked better and better. Perhaps this Prince of Antioch will host a tournament in their honor? Perhaps she might yet find a champion and lover? She smoothed her once-white skirts, now gray with the dirt that resisted her scrubbing. Wishing she were properly clothed as a baron's daughter, she strode down the gangplank with her head high. It was odd that the captain had taken them to this rotten Seleuceia ad Pierea, but Antioch was at least nearby, with its hope of a bath and a night in a real bed.

Captain Jacques's men surrounded their group. Cheers erupted all around them as they walked, men calling out and singing. Every now and then Élise caught the word "karkadann".

She walked with an easy stride behind the marching soldiers. Before long, she found herself stepping to the easy rhythm of the crowd's chanting. Her feet felt odd after so many weeks on the ship. The street, paved with gray stone worn smooth by wagons, shone brightly under the hot sun. It ran straight, as if a giant hand had cut the way through the buildings with a hack of a sword.

The buildings they passed were built of square, bleached mud blocks, topped by flat mud roofs. Men worked on some of the roofs, rolling large cylinders across the top. They all paused from their work to turn and stare at Britomar.

The chanting that followed them through the city suddenly changed. While before it had been a joyous noise wrapped around "Karkadann", the chant now rose louder, words shouted quicker with a hint of a martial song. While Élise did not understand what she heard, she saw David grimace and lean to exchange words with Wigandus. He then strode through the company of guards to the captain. After a heated exchange he returned back to their group with a disgusted look on his face.

"That fool of a captain," said David, "he is letting the crowd get out of hand. They seem to think we're here to liberate Jerusalem. If this rumor gets out of control, we may be forced on the road to Jerusalem with an army behind us."

Élise's heart raced. Jerusalem had fallen? If so, why wouldn't they want to be the vanguard of such an army? How could even a Jew not want Jerusalem liberated from the murdering Saracens? Those butchers! Those unbelieving monsters should be slaughtered until the streets are cleansed in their blood—

The remembrance of Mevlana's gentle hand taking hers broke her thoughts. She shook her head, forcing the memory away. Her present was too real, too distant from the sheltered life inside the walled gardens of Poitiers where women had no other goal than to entice passion out of men.

The cool shadow of an arch fell over her and Élise realized they had passed through the city gate. She looked up and gasped, forgetting all but the towering walls and spires of the grand city that rose on the hill before her.

It was the largest city she had ever seen. To this city, Paris was just a town. It beckoned her, its multi-towered walls wrapped around the base of a hill, with palaces and churches rising above like diamonds out of the rough of the mud brick houses. The reception owed them, the hospitality she expected to be bestowed on them as the companions of a unicorn on a holy mission, made her heard quiver with anticipation.

A withered old woman in tattered black rags ran to them, slipping through the soldiers. "Such beauty! Such purity!" she shouted, "It is a sign! Go to Jerusalem! You will restore Israel!"

"Get down, old crow!" shouted a guard, raising his hand to her.

Élise winced, as though it were she that he struck. His blow knocked the old woman to the ground, her blood pooling on the gray stone. As Élise looked at her crumpled form, she remembered the poor woman Garsenda had given her mantle to, ages ago in Poitiers. She blushed at the memory of how she had chided Garsenda.

She stepped toward the woman, but Gwen beat her to it as she swept by, cradling the old woman in her arms.

"You, beast!" she shouted at the guard. "She is just a harmless old woman!"

Britomar came to Gwen's side. At the touch of her horn the woman shuddered, a rosy glow spreading over her face and limbs. She rose, giving Britomar a fond smile.

"You are a dear creature, touched by God's own hand."

One of the soldiers cried out, "Jesu Cristi! A miracle!"

195

The captain came over to them. "The prince is waiting for you." He glanced at the woman, then wheeled and marched back to the lead of the column.

"I wish there were a way to avoid seeing this prince," said Gwen as she rose.

"I'm afraid you just made that even less possible than it was when we disembarked," said David.

"Certainly the prince means us no harm," protested Élise.

"That remains to be seen," said Galiana.

Élise resisted an urge to snap at the whore. Who cared what she thought anyway? She took a deep breath and walked over to Adelie who stared open-mouthed at the city streets ahead.

"Why do I feel like our father's seneschal's guards have finally caught me?"

"You're scared of Antioch?" asked Élise.

"No, of its prince. Why send an armed escort?"

Élise took Adelie's hand. "It is an honor guard, that's all. Come, the others are moving." She gave Adelie's hand a squeeze and they slid into column right behind Gwen and Sir Wigandus.

Élise couldn't help but admire the gates they passed through, tall enough to admit mounted soldiers and wide enough for twelve knights to ride abreast. They gateway led them into a wide columned forum crowded with people, calling out "Unicorn! Karkadann!"

The soldiers cleared the way through the throng, forcing people back with their spears. Beyond lay a wide street, paved with marble worn smooth by centuries of use. The street was lined by columns, topped by broken statues of forgotten men. Lamppoles loomed above the heads of the crowd that continued to follow them.

Élise tried to distance herself from the noise, admiring the view. Buildings of the finest stone—could Antioch be a city of palaces and churches?

A shiver ran up her spine when she realized that these were no palaces and churches at all. These were homes. She gasped. An entire city constructed of stone finer than those used in the cathedral she'd so admired on the Isle de France.

The guards in front of them split into two columns and turned to face each other, forming a path through the crowd for the rest of the group. The captain strode forward and stopped in front of a large ornate door carved with rosettes.

"We are at the residence of the Prince Bohemond of Antioch. I am instructed that you will dwell within these walls as his guests during your stay in Antioch."

Élise wanted to clap her hands. Hospitality at last! Certainly a bath awaited her, and ah, soft hands to rub her sore feet. Her tired limbs ached in anticipation.

"Captain," said Britomar, "I am unused to walls and human dwellings. I would rather wander the many gardens of this fair city."

The captain opened the door with a bow, ignoring Britomar. "The Prince of Antioch is a patient man, but you do him a discourtesy in keeping him waiting."

"Captain, I am a creature of the wild wood. I am ill at ease within walls, even of so beautiful a city as Antioch. Surely your prince would not be so ungracious a host as to force me to leave behind the sunlight and fresh air I am accustomed to."

The captain bowed his head and entered the building. He returned moments later, followed by a corpulent man, dressed in robes that shimmered in the light.

"Good unicorn, my esteemed guests," the man began, "I humbly beg you to put aside any fears for your safety in my humble abode. I am Prince Bohemond, and I welcome you to Antioch. There is a garden within the walls of my palace, in which you may find solace, and my personal attendants will see to your every need."

Élise gripped Adelie's hand tightly, hoping Britomar would ascent.

"Prince," Britomar said, "I am grateful for your offer of hospitality, but I must decline. The importance of my errand is so great that I must only stay in Antioch long enough to acquire the supplies and transport we will need for our journey."

"Then come into my palace and let my servants gather what you need while you rest from your arduous journey by sea."

"Nay, good prince, I would not delay our start even for the time it would take for me to detail my needs to your staff, nor for the time it would take for them to return from the market. I and my companions must leave your fair city before nightfall."

The crowd began to murmur, and Élise heard the words Jerusalem, Edessa, and Damascus clearly through the clamor.

The prince smiled. "Allow me at least to send my most trusted servants with you to the market. The local merchants know them, and you may drive a harder bargain. Just tell me your destination, and I will place them at your disposal."

"That is most kind of you. Our final destination is the Garden at the Roof of the World. We hope to learn the location of this Garden from scholars in residence at Baghdad."

The crowd fell silent.

"Death to those that treat the infidel with other than a sword!"

"Death!"

More voices joined in. People pushed against the guards, faces red with rage. Élise began to whimper. Could the guards keep the mob back?

"Peace! Pacem! Shalom, Salaam!" shouted Gwen.

To Élise's amazement, the crowd fell silent again.

"We are on a Holy errand of healing," Gwen said, "The eldest unicorn is gravely ill and needs fruit found only in the Garden at the Roof of the World! This is a mission blessed by Brother Bonaventure, General of the Franciscan friars, and by Master Albertus, who is a prominent Dominican. These good men of God, holy fathers, have instructed us to seek out men they know and trust in Baghdad. There and only there may we learn where the Garden is hidden. In this, the infidel will be serving God's purpose, and our Holy mission!

"The prince offers us his help. He is a gracious and kind man. We will need his help, and we will need more. Is there a man or woman among you who has not prayed for a miracle, for healing at the illness of a loved one? We have been asked to perform such miracle, to bring healing where otherwise there is no hope. We need your help, and we need your prayers. We will need honest men to take us to Baghdad, a caravan to bring back not goods which enrich a purse but corrupt a soul; but a caravan to bring healing to a creature whose innocence purifies us all."

Gwen then turned to speak to the prince, "If you send your servants with us to the market, and guide us to men of honor, I'm certain that these small things will stand you well in the eyes of the Lord."

The prince stood with his mouth wide open, but he quickly closed it and smiled. "My servants will be yours to command." He clapped his hands and six servants emerged from his residence. Élise quickly surmised that the prince had selected these servants to match their company—four women and two men.

"Captain," the prince ordered, "Disperse the crowd!"

"You heard Prince Bohemond!"

The soldiers raised their halberds, pushing at the crowd. Soon Élise could see down the street in both directions. It wasn't until that moment that she realized she had been holding her breath.

The captain called his men to order and led them away. The prince had retreated to his palace, leaving the travelers with his servants.

Élise said, "We need to arrange for a caravan with sufficient supplies to make the journey to Baghdad, and we will need a trustworthy guide."

One of the servants, an older man with dark skin and gray tightly curled hair, nodded. "Come with us to the market. There we can introduce you to merchants who travel to Baghdad. You may wish to travel within one of their caravans."

"Come close, all of you," Britomar said sharply from behind.

Élise joined the others around the unicorn, wondering what could make her so nervous.

"I don't know how long this will take, but I can't stay in this city. The smells! My nose hurts. The noise! My ears hurt. I'm going to find a place of hiding in the hills and wait for you there."

"How will you find us?" asked Gwen.

"I will watch all the caravans on the roads going east. I will find you."

"I want to go with you," said Gwen, so quietly Élise could barely hear her. She was looking at Sir Wigandus, so Élise could not read her face.

"Yes come with me," said the unicorn. "Climb on my back, I will leave at once."

"I must stay with Britomar," Gwen said to Wigandus, "but I fear to leave you. I'm also afraid of this city and I'm worried I'll never see you again. I love you."

He took her hands and knelt. "Gwenaella, you make me the happiest of men by saying so. I love you too. I will spend my life in service to you. If we live through this, I would marry you, if you would have me for a husband."

She pulled him to herself, embraced him and said something Élise could not hear. She wiped away a tear as Gwen climbed on Britomar's back, wrapping her arms around the unicorn's neck.

Élise said, "Gwen, even if we purchase what we need quickly, we'll need time to get it all together and join the caravan. We may have to spend the night in the city."

"I know. Don't worry, Britomar will find you."

"No, she'll not find me. I've got to stay in Antioch and arrange for an escort to Armenia to meet my betrothed."

Gwen frowned. "You've kept this from us? Why?"

Élise wasn't certain which pained her more, that Gwen looked at her with such pity, or that Britomar did not even glance in her direction.

"Adelie knew, as did Garsenda. I kept hoping that there would be some way for me to take Garsenda's place, help you find the Garden. It was her dream that set us on the path to find Britomar, not mine. My father permitted me to accompany you as far as Antioch, but she was freed of my service so that she'd be able to continue on Britomar's quest."

"That is why she treated you so badly."

"Yes, because I treated her worse."

Gwen reached over and squeezed her hand.

Elise lowered her eyes. "I must go to my betrothed."

"I hope you find love with him."

Élise blanched. "Impossible. He's of the same people that burned those villages in Hungary. How could I love such a demon?"

Gwen hung her head, "My prayers will be with you."

"I'm done with prayers. No matter how earnestly I've begged, fate draws me to a marriage that might be worse than death."

"Élise! Don't think like that. God is good and loving. Something good awaits you, if you just have faith."

Élise smiled at her friend, wishing she was as naive as Gwen. She didn't know what God intended for Gwen, but unless Élise found a way out, God seemed to intend that she marry a monster who butchered women and children.

Britomar reared up and leapt forward, moving so fast that her visage became a blur. The white stones she had trod on cracked, as if her rush to leave shattered the very foundation of the city.

PRINCE BOHEMOND

Élise felt as if she was at the end of a sad song. Tears streamed down her face. Pulling herself together, she turned to the others and said, "Should we divide our efforts, some of us arranging the supplies, the others the caravan, or should we stick together?"

David said, "I fear we must split our efforts, for Britomar needs us to make haste. On the voyage, I learned much of those who bring goods from Baghdad. I will arrange the caravan."

"I will go with you," said Sir Wigandus, "I will help arrange the escort."

Adelie nodded. "Elise, Galiana and I will arrange for the supplies. Let's meet here an hour before sunset." She turned to the servants, "Please lead us to market where such things might be arranged."

In Britomar's absence, the crowds seemed to pay them no mind as they followed the impossibly straight roads down to the market. It was so easy to count the avenues they traversed that Élise had no fear. Yhey would easily be able to rejoin David and Sir Wigandus.

The market was huge. Élise could not see from one end to the other. Multicolored tents stretched to the horizon, their manicured stripes vibrant under the sun. A smell of rancid oil washed over her, mixed with the aromas of strange spices and roasted meats, animals, and excrements. As they entered the maze of merchant stalls, her ears were assaulted by people haggling in languages for which she had no understanding. Élise silently offered up thanks for the thoughtfulness of the prince in lending them his servants.

The tent of a cloth merchant was their first stop. One of the servants, an older woman with brown dried skin, turned to them and said, "The journey to Baghdad may cross the desert, and you will want lighter clothes which let in the air but keep out the sand and the heat."

Élise caressed the top of a soft baudequin, cool golden silk making her shiver with delight. "Adelie, you and Galiana shop for food and drink, I'll stay here and arrange for the cloth."

With the servant to guide her, Élise chose well-woven cotton, undyed and uncut. The servant arranged for it to be sent to the palace of Prince Bohemond, along with needles and thread. Feeling parched and in need of food, Élise had the servant take her to another tent where spits of meat slowly roasted over hot coals. Élise ordered a meal for both of them, and the servant returned with two portions of meat and vegetables covered with a white sauce and wrapped in soft bread. Élise took a bite and found it delicious.

As they ate, Élise heard a loud booming voice speak in Langue d'oc. Trying to catch the words, they meandered through the throng, white sauce dripping on Élise's hands as she continued to eat while she walked. Finally they were close enough to see the speaker and hear what he was shouting.

"Woe to ye, children of crusaders! Woe to ye of the broken vow! Zion stands abandoned, the infidel clawing at her feet! Yea! The very Zion upon which our Lord gave unto us the Law! Zion! The world's center is left to rot while fat princes grow large on the plunder from pilgrims to Zion, to Jerusalem! The Lord's city abandoned like a harlot, not like the bride of Christ she was meant to be!"

Élise gasped. Was Zion truly the world's center? Had Bonaventure been wrong? They all spoke of the roof of the world as the location of the Garden...but what if that monk Gwen had met in the forest had been right all along? If so, they were nearly there already! There was no need to travel to Baghdad, they could just go to Jerusalem, climb Mount Zion, and search for the Garden there. And if it was not there, they could still go to the scholars in Baghdad and learn where the world's roof may be found.

Élise's heart raced. Britomar had been cold with her lately, and this knowledge lay heavy on her conscience. And now, she might finally be of service to Britomar. She had to try! She just had to convince the others! Besides, why else would the old woman at the gate say they were to go to the Holy City? Why else would she have been guided to this market to overhear the man speaking of Zion as the center of the world? She had to act, before it was too late.

Sir Wigandus and David already waited in front of Prince Bohemond's residence when Élise arrived. Galiana and Adelie returned before long. As Élise told them earnestly of Zion and the Garden, the doors of the palace opened and the prince himself emerged, surrounded by servants.

"It is late, do stay the night in my humble abode."

Élise nodded. "We do need some time to sew new garments from the cloth I purchased."

"She's right, we do," said Galiana, "but perhaps the prince would be so kind to lend us the help of his servants? Britomar sounded impatient."

The prince smiled. "I shall see to it myself that your garments will be finished in time for you to start at dawn."

"Thank you, Prince Bohemond," Élise said earnestly.

They followed their host into a large room with inlays of dolphins made from small stones set into its floor. Rugs and tapestries depicting flowers and trees on a deep blue background hung between pillars of red marble.

"My servants will escort you each to your own chamber where you will find baths waiting, as well as fresh garments. Once you have refreshed yourselves, I hope you will join me for a banquet I have prepared in your honor."

"Thank you for your kind hospitality, Prince Bohemond," Élise said.

"The pleasure is all mine, fair lady. But please excuse me, I must attend to my other guest—Prince Leon, the eldest son of the King of Armenia." The prince bowed low, turned with a flourish, and left.

Élise gasped, barely feeling Adelie's hand clasp hers tightly. She would be dining with her betrothed.

What kind of a man was he? Élise wondered as she followed Adelie, Galiana, and the maidservant down a side passage. Was he truly the monster she feared, the kind of man that could burn children? They passed through a central garden filled with fruit laden trees and flowers of every hue and she found herself wondering which of these was his favorite color, and which resembled the color of his eyes.

They entered a hall lit by ornate oil lamps hanging in the center of the arches that framed four doors. The maidservant bowed. "These are your chambers, my ladies. The master has servants and baths waiting for you."

Élise ignored the anxious glances Adelie and Galiana cast her way and strode into the chamber that had been prepared for her. To have a bath again, attended to by maids, oh how she missed that. She'd be able to present herself to her betrothed as a lady, not as a dust-weary traveler cast up from a ship's hull. She resisted the urge to clap her hands with glee when she entered her room, hung with rich tapestries, soft rugs lining the floor.

The servant helped her out of her clothing and bathed her as if she was a child. Élise sighed. This was bliss. If she closed her eyes, she could imagine being at home with Garsenda again.

When she rose from her bath, the maid wrapped a soft cloth

around her, and another over her hair. They entered a larger room where a fire was lit.

"My lady, this fire was set to dry you. I will fetch you some food and drink to keep you before the feast" The maid bowed and left the room, leaving Élise to watch the dancing reflections of the fire on the polished stone. A pillow lay on a rug near the fire, beckoning. She took off the towels and reclined on the rug, leaned on the pillow and relaxed in the warmth.

The floor around the rug had been set with small stones, forming a pattern. Remembering the pictures of the dolphins set into the floor of one of the chambers they had passed through, she pulled back the rug to reveal a picture of a nymph grasping the phallus of a satyr as she guided it into her. Élise gasped, her cheeks lighting up with a blush. So indecent. And yet. . . she couldn't help wondering what it would be like to be that nymph, hips rising to greet him. She closed her eyes, feeling the pulsing warmth between her legs as she raised her hips slightly, as if waiting. She slid a hand down, caressing herself as she imagined the satyr's member sliding up and down inside her. She let her thumb move in circles at the top of her con as her fingers continued to stroke her folds. Her breathing became heavy. She imagined the satyr pulling her close, mixing the memory of Wigandus's smell into this daydream of desire. Deep within her, she heard a voice as if from a well say softly, "Let me take you, and I will free you."

Her heart raced with the heat of her con and the longing for a man. Dazed, she looked down at the picture of the satyr, slowly sliding deeper into her fantasy. "I'd give anything to be her, serviced by such, freed of my betrothal."

She heard the distant ring of a gong and the faint "yes!" as the sound traveled through a thousand chambers.

Sliding her fingers inside, she gasped at the sharp pleasure pain. Warmth rose from her con, rolling up her stomach to her breasts and then to her cheeks. The gong rang again, the vibrations of the sound matching the pulsing heat in her body. The flames from the fire bowed down as if an unfelt wind pushed them. Closing her eyes she imagined strong hands on her hips pulling her to meet his manhood, thrusting hard. She matched the movement, sliding her fingers in and out to mimic the imagined sex. Élise felt a delicious hot stab within her, an exquisite pain. She moaned in delight as she lifted her hips to greet this phantom lover, shaking in waves.

Breathless, she shuddered, moaning. "Yes, please, yes."

The gong tolled a third time.

She heard a soft tapping of approaching feet and sat up, rewrapping herself in the towels. Her cheeks still burned with the heat that rose between her legs. Looking up, she saw that the servant had returned, carrying a bundle of gold cloth that shimmered in the firelight.

The cloth felt unbelievably soft and cool against Élise's burning skin. She held up a sleeve to look at it more closely and was surprised to see her hand through it.

"These are the softest undergarments I've ever worn," she said in genuine admiration.

"My lady, this is your dress for the evening, sent by Prince Bohemond himself."

Élise blushed. "Surely something is amiss. A cyclas or a bliault?"

The servant said nothing, but continued to arrange the clothing on her.

Élise stood up, shaking off the servants' hands. What sort of a household was this? "Return to me the garments I arrived in, at once!"

The servant did not show any reaction as she handed her a pair of silk slippers, bowed, and left the chamber.

Élise sat on the pillow and waited for the servant to return. She found herself daydreaming again. What would happen if she entered a banquet hall dressed as she was, in nothing but the transparent gold silk, all men's eyes on her as the lamps tantalizingly both revealed and concealed her body.

Perhaps all the women in this city dress so in the evening? It was a distant land, after all. They could have different customs. Élise looked down at the gown again. Gold did go so well with her black hair. And its strange, spice-like smell made her feel dreamy, filling her with an eagerness to show off her beauty at the banquet.

She found herself at the door before she realized she opened it, and hesitated. The scent returned, stronger and she thought "Why not, after all my betrothed will be there."

As she stepped into the hall, she heard crying from behind the door the whore's—what was her name—Galiana's chambers were. Desire forgotten for a moment, Élise knocked on the door. She heard Galiana's voice, "Come in."

She entered to find Galiana dressed in a similar silk dress. With the fire behind her, Élise could clearly see Galiana's body through her clothes. Élise licked her lips, but drowned the renewed lust. This was not Garsenda.

"I thought I was done with this when I followed Britomar," Galiana sobbed.

"Let's not judge the prince just yet. For all we know, this is merely the custom in this land. I don't mind so much," said Élise, ignoring the wide-eyed look Galiana was giving her. "Let's go find the others. Imagine how..."

She was interrupted by a familiar bellow from down the hall. "Sir Wigandus!" they both said, and started running in the direction the bellow had come from.

They turned a bend in the corridor, which opened up into another outdoor court, this one surrounded by serpentine columns. The sound of steel upon steel rang from within the grove of fruit trees. The two women ran toward the sound along a stone path, through trees laden with pomegranates and figs.

With his back to a fountain, Sir Wigandus, bloodied but unbowed, was fending off three men, their armor decorated with a red cross of the crusaders on one shoulder and an image of two men on the same horse emblazoned on the other. Knights Templar.

Sir Wigandus was hard pressed to keep up the pace, to match swing with parry. His left arm bled, but so did the three Templars. As one of them slipped on the wet stone, Élise worried that Wigandus might also lose his footing and decided to put an end to this unseemly display of knightly valor. Remembering how Raolett had taught her to project her voice, she called out, "Lords! Is there not enough good Christian blood shed by the infidel that we have sword play between us! Shame! Shame on you!"

They all turned to look at Élise and flushed when they saw her and Galiana. Panting and bleeding from many gashes, they put their swords down.

Galiana whispered, "Cover yourself. Look at the lust in their eyes."

Élise looked at them, and again lust pounded in her heart. Such fine men, so filled with passion. Would that they were fighting for her favor... But why were they fighting?

"Sir Wigandus, explain yourself!" she demanded.

The knight averted his eyes from her unseemly outfit. "My lady, these knights and I were just settling a friendly dispute. That is all." He chuckled. "They claimed that your ladyship, indeed all three women, would be joining the Armenian embassy as a gift to the Crown. On this shaky foundation they claimed that I was therefore free of my oath and could join them in their fight against the infidel. It appears that they are trying to raise an army to march against the Saracen in Jerusalem."

Élise smiled. "Well, that is a dispute I can clear up myself. I am promised to Prince Leon of Armenia as his bride, not a slave to be given by Prince Bohemond. Indeed, as Sir Wigandus here knows, I have been traveling with his company on my way to join my betrothed. Knights, you may redeem yourselves. Go to Prince Bohemond, explain the situation to him."

The knights looked glad of the opportunity to escape their melee against Sir Wigandus. Their leader bowed and said, "As my lady wishes."

"Tell the prince to provide these maidens with more modest clothes!" shouted Wigandus as the knights limped off. "Where are Adelie and David?"

Elise frowned, alarm rising inside her chest.

"We don't know, we were about to search for Adelie when we heard your war cry," Galiana said.

They did not have to wait long before Prince Bohemond arrived with two swarthy men, richly dressed in bright cloth, their oiled black hair glistening in the lamp light. Four men at arms followed in their wake.

Prince Bohemond did not look pleased. "I am told that my guests are ill provided for."

"Guests!" Shouted Sir Wigandus. "You ill treat us as such. Apparently you would give these women in slavery to Prince Leon, have done away with both Lady Adelie and David, and arranged for my abduction." Sir Wigandus lowered his voice. "I doubt that Prince Leon will be pleased to know that one of the ladies you have treated so is Lady Elisabeth du Chauvigny, his betrothed."

The prince drew himself up and turned to his guards, but Sir Wigandus's hand blurred as his sword flew to the Prince's throat before his guards could react. "You will have your servants bring the ladies both the clothing they arrived in, as well as the clothing you promised made. You will also restore Adelie and David to us, so that we may keep our tryst and complete our errand. Until these things are done, my sword will be your pillow. You may dismiss your guards, you will be perfectly safe with me, if you do as we say."

Prince Bohemond blanched. One of the well dressed men, the one with a straggly black beard, laughed, "Well, Bohemond, I doubt much that my father will be pleased when he hears that the slave you offer me is my willing bride. I think you had better reconsider his offer, unless you prefer to suffer Jerusalem's fate."

Élise looked upon the man with wonder. "You must be my betrothed, Prince Leon of Armenia. I am the Lady Elisabeth du Chauvigny. Well met, my lord."

Prince Leon bowed low, but his dark eyes slid over her body with an expression that made her shiver with lust. Whatever was wrong with her? She had never felt this way before.

"My lady," said Prince Leon. "I am honored and delighted to make your acquaintance. Pray tell, of what errand does the good knight speak?"

Élise blushed and lowered her eyes as Galiana told the prince of Britomar's errand.

The prince smiled. "A unicorn! I see now why Bohemond saw in the three of you slaves of great value. Lady Elisabeth, please do not abandon this errand, not when your grace and beauty may be needed in its service. Come to me when you have found the Garden, I will await the healing of the eldest of unicorns to know my bride better."

Élise kept her eyes on the floor. Gwen was right; he was a man she could grow to love. "As my husband wishes."

With a flourish of his red silk robes, Prince Leon strode out of the chamber, followed by the other man also dressed in red silk.

Prince Bohemond said, "Guards, go find these women their clothing, you fools, and find their companions!" He turned to Wigandus. "You don't know what you've done. Outremer is collapsing. Jerusalem has fallen, and we'll be next unless I can secure help from the Armenians! Your foolishness may have doomed the kingdoms won by the holy crusaders!"

Wigandus snarled, "God would rather us see us as honest martyrs than have us purchase our lives with the freedom and honor of good women. Coward! Why not make yourself a vassal of the Armenian king?"

The prince kept his eyes on Wigandus's sword. "He is the grandson of the Great Khan. I was hoping to be his equal, and spare my people the humiliation of looking to that spawn of Satan for governance. Now you've forced my hand, I have no other hope to save what is left of good Christian rule of the Holy Land."

"Good Christians do not buy their lives by selling Christian women into slavery." Sir Wigandus pressed his blade harder against Bohemond's neck. "You are a worthless coward and a slaver who would negotiate with the devil to save his own skin. I'm tempted to kill you outright."

He might have said more but for the appearance of David, escorted by a guard. David's face was darkened with bruises, but his stride was certain and his countenance filled with righteous anger.

David said, "Wigandus, you do well to hold that serpent by your sword. He ordered me beaten and was preparing to ransom me to my kin for gold. Where is Adelie and why are the ladies so poorly clad?"

"Our prince here was hoping to give them to the Armenians—" Wigandus was interrupted by the entrance of another guard, who had a large grin on his face.

"My lords and ladies," said the guard. "We have found Lady Adelie. She will not come, but would have her fellows come to her. Please follow me."

They followed the guard, with Wigandus holding Prince Bohemond tight, sword still at his throat. As they passed through a large room with a stone inlay in the floor depicting a satyr engaged in fornication with a woman, Élise stifled a giggle. What was the matter with her? Why could she think on nothing else? It was one thing to long for a lover to honor her with poetry and valorous deeds, to fulfill her womanly desires, but quite another to wish to throw herself lustily at others. Especially since her betrothed turned out to be a worthy man.

They entered a large vaulted chamber to find Adelie, naked, holding a servant at a knife point. Two guards on the floor crumpled in a crimson pool. A dozen servants at the side of the room were stitching clothes at breakneck speed. Many of them were smiling.

"There you are!" said Adelie. "Wigandus, this son of a sow that bloodies your sword had told the guards to make certain that our cloth was turned into robes for his royal arse! I had to convince the ladies here that they had better get our clothes ready fast."

"Why don't you have one of the women cover you?" David said, averting his eyes.

"That would have meant losing my hold on Miriam here. Now that you are here to make certain of the women's good behavior, could one of you please find me some clothes?"

One of the servants, a young woman with lovely green eyes and deep brown skin, smiled and handed Élise a garment. "This one is finished, and will keep off the desert's sun." She helped Élise place it on Adelie, showing her how it was draped. Soon Galiana and Élise were also better dressed.

The serving women were good to their word. Within the hour the other clothes were ready and bundled up. With the prince still at sword point, Sir Wigandus lead the way to the entrance of his palace.

"What oath may I give you that you will set me free upon my honor?" begged Prince Bohemond.

"I will take no oath from you, and you will see us safe out of the city," answered Wigandus. "Once we join the caravan to Baghdad, I will set you free."

The people they passed on the lamp-lit marble streets pulled hoods or veils over their faces. Élise looked around in confusion. Was it the right decision to leave her betrothed who could bring relief from her frighteningly strong urges? Should she rush back into his arms and convince him to take her?

They took a different path to the familiar blue-striped tent in the center of the market.

"Aaron ben Jeremiah is the brother-in-law of my uncle's cousin," David said. "I've arranged for us to join his caravan." He approached the tent's two sentries and exchanged quiet words with them. One of the sentries disappeared into the tent. A moment later Aaron himself emerged from the tent, dressed in nightclothes. His gray-speckled beard creased as he smiled, the mesh of small wrinkles stretching around his eyes.

"David, I am overjoyed to see you and your companions! Ah, Prince Bohemond, I regret that I am unable to offer you the hospitality of my tent, but we must hurry. I am under strict orders from my employers to leave to Baghdad immediately. David come in; and bring your companions! There is much to do!"

Sir Wigandus lowered his sword and pushed Prince Bohemond away; the nobleman lost no time in running from the market as fast as his legs could carry him. Élise watched his retreat with a mix of relief and wonder. Was she doing the right thing, continuing this quest? Could she afford to stay with the unicorn, when lust overwhelmed her entire being?

What was wrong with her?

Once inside, Aaron's face turned grim. "That dog will fetch his guards and seek to delay us. I've arranged a hiding place where we can stay until the city gates open—" Whatever he was going to say was left unsaid, as Sir Wigandus swayed and sank to the floor. "Miriam, Rebecca! Quick! This knight is badly wounded!"

Two women came from behind a curtain at the back of the tent. The younger was lovely, with long black tresses, dark face, and almond-shaped eyes. The older one, obviously the mother, had gray hair, her face wrinkled with age. With David's help, they removed Sir Wigandus's surcoat and armor.

The knight's torso was covered in blood, his left side badly cut.

A roar filled Élise's ears as heat spread from her con to her face.

Next thing she knew, Galiana was gently slapping her cheeks. She moved her head, realizing that she was lying on the ground. She kept her eyes closed, afraid of the rush of desire that had assailed her but moments ago at the sight of the knight's naked torso; the thought that it might return horrified her.

"I guess the sight of his blood was too much for me," she lied. "Will he live?"

"They think so, but he's lost a lot of blood." Galiana helped Élise to her feet. "They're putting him in a wagon. We still need to move from here, and fast."

Élise climbed into the wagon. Huddled with Galiana and Adelie, she fell asleep to the creaking of the wheels, and dreamt of the satyr.

FALLEN

Adelie could not sleep as the cart rocked and creaked in its slow trek through the quiet streets. The lamps that lined the streets now cast ghostly shadows on the canvas roof of the wagon. She wished she had a veil like the Jewish women who rode with them, to mask the smell of hot oil and metal coming from the outside. She kept peeking out from under the canopy, looking for soldiers lurking in the shadows. She knew it was too much to hope that the prince had not yet mobilized the guards, that they'd see the other side of the gate before the soldiers found them... She hoped Wigandus would live to see Gwen again.

Soon the squeak of the wheels came to a stop, and in the agonizing moments of waiting Adelie poked her face out between the canvas and the wood slats to see Aaron talking to a guard next to the city's massive gates, metal studs shining like pale stars in the flickering lamp light.

Fingering her knife, Adelie took a deep silent breath. Only one guard, his sword sheathed. She could take him if need be. She clenched the hilt, watching the conversation drone on.

Finally, Aaron walked back to the wagon, while the guard slowly opened the gates. The wagon jerked as it rolled forward, and Sir Wigandus moaned in his sleep. Élise slept as well, her face strangely contorted; her lips were moving as if she spoke, though no sound came.

Galiana had told her how Élise met her betrothed and he had given his permission for Élise to continue with them. Adelie was glad. She had grown to love Élise, despite her sister's selfishness. She settled on the floor of the wagon and pulled a blanket around her shoulders, shivering in the cool night air. They'll make it, they had to, Britomar needed them.

Her head dipped forward as the wagon halted. She opened her eyes. She hadn't realized she had fallen asleep. It was still dark but lightening. Adelie shivered as she rose. She touched Élise's cheek to wake her, and pulled her hand back. Her sister was burning hot.

Her lips set, Adelie scrambled to the stack of rags used to refresh Wigandus's bandage, grabbed one, and glanced around searching for some water.

Several water-filled skins were hanging on a pole at the front of the wagon. As she reached for one of them, a hand clasped hers, making her jump. She turned and saw Rebecca, the younger of the two women who had tended Wigandus the prior night.

"Careful with the water, it must last us across the desert," Rebecca whispered.

"My sister has a fever."

"In the desert heat, the rag will dry too soon. Come, let me look at her."

Adelie followed Rebecca back to Élise, wishing she knew something of the healing arts that the Jewish women seem to have mastered.

Rebecca laid her hand on Élise's forehead and pulled it back. "You were right to be worried, this woman burns hot. Help me strip her; exposure to the cool air may help break the fever."

Together they undressed Élise. Adelie suppressed a gasp as her hand brushed Élise's breast. So hot.

"This is no normal fever," said Rebecca. "Have you noticed anything unusual about your sister of late?"

"I've never known her to faint before."

"Yes, I remember she fainted as we tended Wigandus."

Adelie bit her lip. "Is there anything we can do?"

Rebecca shook her head. "Pray. When the heat of the day returns, we'll need to redress her. The clothes will shield her. If she wakes, get her to drink. I'll see if I can get someone else to help, we'll want to sit watch over both her and the knight."

Galiana said, "Can I help?"

"Yes," Rebecca and Adelie said in unison. Adelie blushed at the coincidence, momentarily flustered and confused. She wanted Rebecca to like her. The competence she'd shown the prior night still amazed her. If only she could do these things, she might be worthy to be David's bride.

Rebecca said, "Can you change a bandage?"

"I've done it before," said Galiana.

"Good. Both of you, come with me to the knight and help me with his bandages. Once we're done, we'll each need to take a shift."

The bandages they lifted off Wigandus's torso and arm were soaked in blood, but the neatly stitched wounds beneath were clean and showed no discoloration. Adelie watched Rebecca as she lay down new bandages, paying careful attention to how tightly they were tied. It would do him no good to hurt him while trying to bring him back to health.

Rebecca gave Adelie the first shift, and she spent the next few hours sitting, watching, changing his bandages, dressing Élise, helping her drink in her moments of lucidness. By the time Rebecca returned, Adelie's head hurt. This was harder than any knife fight. While she wanted little more than to sleep, she forced herself to eat and drink before lying down.

The next day brought more of the same, though the air was hotter. Between the heat and her sister's fever, Adelie wondered if she'd be cooked. Watching and waiting as the heat made her temples throb, Adelie longed to be out with the men. Tending the wounded was hard, draining and monotonous, especially when there was little hope of healing. Adelie feared that if Britomar did not find them soon, both Élise and Wigandus would die.

"Jerusalem," Élise mumbled.

Adelie scampered to the water bottles to get her sister a drink. She cradled Élise's head in her lap and put the waterskin to her lips. Eyes closed, Élise swallowed, repeating "Jerusalem". Soon she fell asleep again.

Adelie smiled for the first time in days, glad that her sister's skin no longer burned like flame. If only Wigandus would waken. He'd lost so much blood. She let herself daydream about sparring with David, wondering more and more how could other women bear the tedium of tending others, the anxiety of watching someone they loved waste away, neither aware nor benefiting from their care.

Screams and the clang of metal pulled her back to reality. The Antioch guards must have found them! Scampering over her sister, she shook Galiana awake.

"There's trouble, I'm going to see if I can help."

Galiana clasped her hand. "Be careful."

Adelie nodded and scrambled out of the wagon, leaping to the ground. She was glad to be facing a problem she could handle. Darting around the oxes and camels, she scampered to the rear of the caravan, toward the din. There. Men on horseback, fighting. But which side was hers? She narrowed her eyes, taking in the action. Some of the men's surcoats bore the blood-red crosses Élise had told her were the badges of the holy crusaders. Prince Bohemond's men.

A man toppled off his horse, screaming, clutching his leg. Adelie ran to his mount as it darted out of the melee, grabbing the reins. She ran in stride with the frightened animal, speaking soothing words into its ear. The horse snorted and pranced, coming to a standstill as she held the reins firm. "There's a girl," she said. She patted its hot neck and swung up into the saddle. It felt strange, unsteady; the horse was taller and thicker than she was used to. "Now, let's show them the warrior you are." She pulled on the reins and the horse reared. Drawing her long knife, she rode into the fray.

Her blade caught the one swung at her. She twisted her long knife as it slid down the length of the attacker's sword, and brought her other knife up and in, slashing across his wrist. Her blade caught, nearly causing her to overbalance, but she pulled through. Her enemy's scream rose in the wind and she felt the warm splatter of his blood as his severed hand fell to the ground, still gripping the sword. *One down.*

Steering her mount with her knees the way Britomar had taught her, she rode at another Antioch's soldier. Out of the corner of her eye, she saw David pierce his enemy in the chest, sending him down to the ground. She shivered with excitement—to be fighting with him, side by side!

A blade flashed and her hand rose to meet it. Again, her knives cut the sword hand, and parried another slicing arc of gleaming cold steel. Another blade, duck and stab, slide in and cut. She could dimly hear the screams in her wake. She wanted to cry out in joy, as Wigandus often did when he led them in battle.

As the last of Bohemond's men fell to the ground, someone called out, "Lets get our wounded to the wagons."

Adelie dismounted and ran to the nearest man who did not wear the red cross. He lay moaning, his hand clutched to his side. She cupped her hands under his shoulders, lifting him slightly so her arms slid into his armpits. She set her heels and heaved, pulling him toward the nearest wagon. Her arms felt numb. She wouldn't be able to lift this man as the others did.

"Here, let me help you," said David's voice behind her.

She released the man's shoulders as David stepped around her and lifted him up. Adelie stumbled after him, her legs aching.

Rebecca was in the wagon, busy giving orders and tying hasty bandages. David said something to her in his language as he placed the man he was carrying in the indicated spot. Adelie couldn't help but notice the smile and the blush that spread across Rebecca's face.

Tears stung her eyes and she darted away before he could turn and see them. David was amongst his own, it was only right that he find love here. Rebecca was beautiful, and if her hands were stained with blood, it was from trying to bring others to health, not death.

Loud shouting pulled Adelie from a deep sleep. She shook her head to clear it and slowly realized that the voices were calling excitedly: "Karkadann! Karkadann!" and others: "Re'em! Re'em!"

She poked her head out from under the cart's canopy. Galloping across the barren plain, a white blur sped toward the caravan through the hot shimmering air.

Adelie scrambled over her sister to the rear of the wagon and slid through the opening into the beating sun. *Gwen and Britomar!* She waved frantically to them. Wigandus and Élise would live after all!

She turned to the other women in the wagon. "Let's remove the cover, the unicorn will want to touch both Lady Elisabeth and Sir Wigandus with her horn."

The women pulled back the cover of the wagon while Adelie stood and waved to draw Britomar's attention. The unicorn came straight at them, stopping several yards away. Gwen slid off her back and ran to the wagon. She climbed in and knelt near Wigandus, gently kissing him on the forehead.

His eyes opened and he smiled. "Liebchen!"

"You're hurt!" Gwen sobbed.

"He's dying," Adelie said. "He lost too much blood."

Gwen shouted, "Britomar, please come here. Please, if you can, heal him."

"Élise needs her help too, and others in another wagon," added Adelie, looking at her sister, cheeks bright red from the fever. "We had to fight our way out of Antioch."

Britomar approached the wagon slowly, as if walking against a wind. She laid her horn on Wigandus. Color returned to his face and he reached over and took Gwen's hand.

At that moment Élise stirred, mumbling "Jerusalem". Britomar pranced away.

"Britomar!" Gwen called, but the unicorn did not turn as she disappeared from sight between the wagons.

Adelie looked at Élise who had drifted back into sleep, face still twisted with a strange perverted smile. Her heart raced. Why would the unicorn run from her? Why would Britomar let her die? She jumped off the wagon and ran after Britomar. "Why did you abandon Élise?"

The unicorn looked away. "Lady Elisabeth is not ill, Adelie."

"She burns with fever!"

"I'd rather not discuss your sister."

Adelie ran around and stood in front of Britomar, forcing her to a stop. "She's dying of fever and you won't even *talk* about her? She's left her betrothed to help you!"

Britomar slowly lifted her head and looked straight at Adelie. "I've seen such a fever once before. Lady Elisabeth helped purge it from Gwenaella back in the inn where we met. Except this one is worse. I can't even go near her without feeling sick. She's done something, something unchaste."

"A demon possesses her?"

"I fear so. There is nothing I can do for her."

Adelie hung her head and walked slowly away from the unicorn. Élise has done something unchaste? Well, she had been trying to seduce Sir Wigandus for months, but surely she couldn't have succeeded in that. The knight was so in love with Gwen he didn't have eyes for anyone else. What could Élise have done? How could this be?

When Adelie returned to the wagon, it was empty save for Galiana who slept under a blanket. Alarmed, Adelie shook her awake.

"Galiana, where is Élise?"

"I don't know." Galiana sat up and looked at the two empty cots. "Where is Wigandus?"

"Gwen came here, with Britomar."

Galiana rubbed her eyes. "Then Élise and Wigandus are going to be alright?"

Adelie shook her head. "Britomar wouldn't even go near Élise, she says my sister's possessed by a demon. I've got to find her."

"A demon?"

"Yes. Come, help me look for her. I'll explain as we go."

They found Gwen and Wigandus first, walking with David and Aaron at the head of the caravan. Her heart quickened when David looked at her and smiled. He may be falling in love with Rebecca, but at least she still had his good esteem.

"Please excuse the interruption, but has anyone seen Élise?"

"When we left the wagon, she was still asleep," said Gwen.

"Let me send for Rebecca," said Aaron. "She'll help you look."

"It is good to know your sister is well enough to be up and about again," said David. "I've longed to visit you, but knew you busy with tending this lout," he put his hand on Wigandus's shoulder, "and the Lady Elisabeth."

"I'm afraid she's fever mad and wandering lost," said Adelie.

"Who is fever lost?" asked Élise from behind.

Adelie wheeled, watching with relief as her sister approached them arm in arm with Rebecca.

"Lady Elisabeth's fever broke and she seems as hale as I am," said Rebecca. "I don't understand how this could possibly be, but you can see for yourselves."

I do, but I'm not sure how to tell her.

"This is wonderful news!" David said. "Would someone find Britomar? I have something to say that concerns us all."

"So you've decided then?" asked the knight.

"Yes," said David.

"I will find her," said Rebecca.

"Why aren't we headed toward Jerusalem?" asked Élise.

Adelie looked at her, surprised to hear her ask for the holy city. "You talked about Jerusalem in your fever. Why should we go there?"

"Don't you remember what I learned in Antioch, that Jerusalem is the world's center? We must go there!"

Adelie was confused, Élise was not acting demon-possessed at all. "But this is not new to us, remember? Brothers Thomas and Bonaventure told us that Jerusalem is the world's center. It's just that there is no garden there, the Garden we seek is at the roof of the world, not in Jerusalem."

"Adelie is correct," said Rebecca, approaching them with Britomar. "There is no garden in Jerusalem. Its gardens were destroyed by the Romans long ago, and have not been restored by its current masters."

Élise shook her head impatiently. "But the holy man in Antioch said that Jerusalem is the world's center. We should go there first and make certain. What if the friars were wrong?"

"Élise," said Gwen, "No one is disputing what Jerusalem is, just that the Garden cannot be there."

"I'm sorry, my lady," said Aaron. "We were in Jerusalem before it fell again to the *Muslemi*. My daughter speaks the truth, there is no garden there."

"David, you asked for me?" said Britomar who stayed a good thirty paces from them.

"Yes, Britomar, as what I say concerns us all." said David. Adelie was surprised when he moved in front of her and took her hands. "I have thought long and prayed for guidance. I love you, Adelie. Will you marry me?"

Her ears were filled with a sudden ringing, her head felt light. Her cheeks burned, as she smiled, looking into his eyes. Warmth enfolded her at the tenderness she saw in his gaze as he looked down on her.

Her. Not Rebecca. He loved her! But—

"I'm not of your people," she said. "How can this possibly work?"

David smiled. "Nothing must stand in the way of true love. My people will accept it. Marry me, Adelie."

Adelie hesitated. "Britomar, if we marry, will we be able to continue this quest? Will you still be able to stand my presence if I take a husband?"

"If you are a chaste and loving wife, why not?" answered the unicorn.

"Does it mean you agree?" David asked quietly.

Adelie opened her mouth to give the answer swelling up from her heart but before a sound could form, Élise stifled a cry and ran off.

They all looked after her.

"Something is wrong," Sir Wigandus said, "Something more than not going to Jerusalem."

Adelie felt Britomar's eyes on her. She knew what she had to do.

She sighed. "David, I must go after her. I think I know what drives her from us, and she needs my help."

David kissed her. "Then go to her."

"I'm going too," said Gwen.

"So am I," said Galiana.

They found Élise walking back along the road they had taken from Antioch. Adelie ran to her, the others falling behind, unable to match her speed. "Élise, wait!"

"Why should I? That beast can't abide my presence; why should I risk my neck for her? I have a husband of my own, waiting for me."

"Élise. Please." Adelie paused to catch her breath. "I know what is wrong. Perhaps I can help."

Élise stopped and sank down, crying. Adelie sat next to her, holding her sister.

"How can you help?" Élise sobbed. "I can't be near a man, so much as look at one with out craving him. I've even found myself thinking of stallions, camels, and dogs, and have fought to keep myself from abasing myself! I can't stand it! I should enter a whore house or have them lock me in a convent!"

Adelie knew that if she told Élise that Britomar suspected her possessed, she'd lose Élise forever. "No wonder you ran from us in tears. Come with me, dear sister. You're not like this. My mother was a whore. I know. Let's find a priest. You can lay this in God's lap; He'll help you."

"Do you, do you think so?" Élise sniffed and dried her eyes with her sleeve.

219

"Yes," said Galiana. "If you don't want to end up in a whore house, a priest will help."

Élise wiped her eyes with her sleeve. "Would you stay with me when I talk to the priest? I don't trust myself alone with any man."

"We will not leave your side," said Gwen.

They rose, and walked back to the caravan. Élise sniffled and then asked, "David wishes you to marry him?"

"Yes, though I don't know what to do."

"He is an odd man, and a good one, but he is a Jew. If you marry him, you would forfeit your station and rank, and all that comes with it."

"I want to marry him, but I'm afraid. What if I conceive a child while we still search for the Garden? As you said, he is a Jew. Will he expect me to raise such a child outside the church? How can I? Yet, I'm supposed to pledge obedience to my husband."

"I have yet to see a good wife who does not have her way in the house, when the man is a good man," said Gwen. "David does not strike me as the kind of man who will beat you for disregarding him."

"I know, but this is more than failing to attend to the mending or burning the dinner. This is about following Jesus, the true God he denies."

They walked the rest of the way back to the encampment in silence. A large city of tents rose at the edge of a lush green valley with a river flowing through it—a refuge for the caravans setting on their way across the desert.

As they saw the camp sentries, Élise stifled a groan. Adelie took the clue at once. "Let one of us enter the camp and ask for where we may find a priest."

"I'll go," said Gwen and trotted off.

After she was out of earshot, Galiana said, "Don't worry, lust is not the worst of evils. Jesus himself forgave an adulteress."

"Go and inform Sir Wigandus of our mission," Adelie said to her. "I will stay with my sister."

Galiana and Gwen both returned before the sun had dipped below the horizon. "There is a hermit who has a cell not far from here. He is a Greek, yet still a Christian."

Élise looked up, tears streaming down her cheeks. "Can you take me there?"

"They told me how to get to him, so I'll try."

They soon found themselves on a goat path. As the sun was turning the evening sky a golden red, they came upon a small hut of earthen bricks. Inside they could see a man with long, dirt-matted beard and hair, wearing animal skins. He looked up and said, "Please enter my humble abode and be welcome." He gestured to a small table set with five cups and poured out wine from a skin pouch. "Please, sit, ladies. After you have refreshed yourselves, we can discuss how to deal with the demon that torments you, Lady Elisabeth."

"You know me?" she asked.

The hermit chuckled. "My lady, to say yes would be saying too much. Let us say that I'm informed as to your name and your plight, and I do know the creature that torments you. Please sit."

The women joined him at the table. He lifted up an earthenware cup. "Lord, please bless this cup which we share, and bless those who share it under your roof." He then crossed himself in the manner of the orthodox.

All the women said, "Amen," and then drank of the wine.

"Now, I doubt much that an exorcism is in order, but that depends upon how you came to be so plagued by one of Satan's spawn. That you come to me willingly tells me you are not possessed. Tell me all you know of what happened to you when the torments began, and the state of your soul."

Élise told him all she could remember, and he prodded her with questions to draw out memories and thoughts she had put aside as unimportant. Finally, long after the shadows had turned to cold night, he said, "Lady Elisabeth, I believe you have made a full confession in the eyes of the Lord. Do you repent of the lust you felt, the lust which one of Satan's servants is using to hold dominion over you?"

"Yes."

"You must go into the desert and fast for three days, taking nothing with you except the clothes on your back. You may drink only what you find there, and eat only what the Lord provides you in your ordeal. You must pray, empty yourself into the Lord. By thus denying the body, you will refresh your soul. Return to your friends in three days if you are able, and you will no longer be tormented by this particular beast."

"I will do this, and will start at once." Élise rose.

"No, start at sunrise. First you must fortify yourself with food and drink. I would not see you die in the ordeal you must endure." Adelie blushed, for he looked at her as he spoke. Part of her wondered if the priest could read hearts and minds.

They all ate and drank in silence, and then the hermit found them all a place to lie for the night. He excused himself and went outside to sleep.

Adelie woke with a start; faint light came through the door of the hermit's cell. She looked around and saw Élise had already gone. She stepped over Gwen and went outside to find the hermit sitting on a reed mat, in prayer.

"Has she gone, then?"

"Yes, she has gone into the desert."

Adelie thought of the skins of water she'd helped her sister swallow while she burned with fever. Tending to the sick may be tedious, but waiting for someone you love to come back from an ordeal you can't share was worse.

RETREAT INTO THE DESERT

Élise woke before the sunrise and stretched. The cool and fragrant air, filled with the scent of the women who had shared the hermit's hut with her and the intoxicating smell of the hermit, made her want to kiss each awake, caress the women, be filled with his manhood. She shook her head to clear it and forced herself to step over Gwen. Her knees almost gave way, but she forced herself to walk on. At least in the desert there would be no one to tempt her.

She heard a fluttering and looked up. That bird of Gwen's had followed her. Damned trickster was probably looking forward to feasting upon her bones.

She turned to the rising sun and followed the long shadows toward the east. The raven landed on her shoulder and would not budge no matter how she tried to shoo it away, so she made her way into the desert with yet another burden. Soon she was scrambling down a goat's path, to the shimmering landscape beyond. At the base of the hills, a golden sea of sand opened up before her. Élise fell to her knees.

"Forgive me my iniquity, and accept that which is good, please accept for sacrifice the offering of my lips. As Gomer returned to Hosea, I return to you, if you'll have me. Forgive me, oh Lord, and lead me out of these temptations and deliver me from the evil I've become." She crossed herself and said, "Amen."

Wiping the tears from her face, she rose again and strode into the desert. With nothing but the sun to guide her, she walked for hours, the heat making her head pulse in pain, dry air making her gasp, her legs aching from pushing through the soft sand.

Cresting a dune, she saw Sir Wigandus, naked, reclining in a luscious grove of date palms. He called to her, "Come and refresh yourself!"

She clenched her hands and kept walking, though her eyes stayed with Wigandus.

Gwen emerged from the shadows of the palms, her bare breasts glistening with sweat. She stepped up to Wigandus and caressed his shoulders, calling to her, "Come Élise! Join us!" She squatted and slipped him between her legs.

Her head pounded, her body aching with desire to throw off her clothes and run to them. It could not be, they could not be there, she must... must *not!*

Tears blinding her, she ran from them, pulling her hair, screaming, "No!" She stumbled, rose and continued to run until she saw David and Adelie, naked, engaged in a coitus. With a free hand, Adelie was caressing a goat's penis. She tossed her long dark tresses behind her with a shake of her head. "Join us!" she called.

"No! God help me, NO!" Again, Élise ran blindly, rolling down the dune. She scrambled up and ran until she fell again, her mouth filled with sand. Spitting it out, she scrambled to rise. Her hand found a smooth stone in the sand. Her fingers inadvertently closed around it. She ached to take it, slide it into her; it felt so nice in her hand.

"NO!" She took the stone and threw it as hard as she could, and again ran. The raven flew after her, its "brawk" driving her on, like an accusation.

Britomar stood at the base of a dune. "Élise, come to me, I'll help you." Élise saw the sun glint off the white horn, and wanted it within her.

"No!" Yet it would be a lovely way to die.

She ran again until she fell, too tired to rise. No tears came to her dry eyes. The raven pecked at her cheek gently, then spread its wings to cover her face. Élise felt the sand bite into her as the wind howled "Say yes and it will all be over, surrender to me and taste the joys of womanhood!"

Wind-driven sand cut through her clothes, tore at her flesh and she screamed, "God help me!"

She rose again, arm against her face to shield it. Blinded, she ran until she found herself at a precipice. Turning back, in the middle of the swirling sand, she saw Martis striding to her, naked, his prick erect and glistening.

There was nowhere else to run. Élise turned and threw herself over the cliff, sobbing, "Forgive me!"

Élise woke to the cool air of dawn, her face shielded by the raven's wings. She stirred gently, and the raven hopped away. Next to her was an earthen plate with wafers on it. Nearby stood an urn filled with water.

She almost didn't reach out to take the bread, to drink from the water. She craved it with such intensity, much like she'd craved Wigandus. How can she trust herself? Which of her desires were safe? Shaking, she picked up the urn and lifted it to her lips. The cool water seemed to fill her whole being as she drank it down. How could such a gift be left for her? She had been so much worse than the whore she had despised. In her mind, she had sinned in unimaginable ways. She'd expected to be burning in hell, flesh blackened and boiling in the flames for the sins of her wicked desires, and instead bread and drink was laid out before her.

She broke off a piece of bread, tasted it and began to cry. She wrapped her arms around herself and fell to the ground shaking. "I'm sorry, I'm sorry," she sobbed until she had no more tears. Then she lay, curled like a babe, hugging her knees to herself. That bread, that water, forgiveness. She'd been forgiven, even before completing her penance.

After a while Élise sat and took another drink from the urn, wiping her eyes of tears. She picked up the bread and took another bite, and realized it was nutty as if the whole of the wheat had been used in the making. When she was done, she stood and looked down upon herself. Her clothing was whole. The sandstorm that tore her clothes and flesh was a cheat, a lie, as certainly were the visions of her friends. She must not trust her eyes, not while IT lay coiled within her, twisting everything she experienced.

The sand burned the soles of her feet as she strode from dune to dune, trying to walk to the sun at its point of rising, raven perched upon her shoulder. She figured if she continued east until midday, she could then turn back and find the hermit's hut by the end of the third day.

When she crested the next dune, she again saw Sir Wigandus naked under the palms. Her desire for him came upon her suddenly, like the heat of the sun. She did not run this time. She just looked the other way and kept on walking, ignoring the calls by Gwen and Wigandus to join them.

Soon after midday, she came upon a pillar of salt. Élise turned to the west, to follow the sun, and saw before her a beautiful city she had not passed before. Behind its coral-tinted-walls she could see palms sway in the wind, and the scent of cinnamon made her sigh.

She turned to go another way, and again before her was the city, though closer. Turning to face where she had but a moment ago been heading, she saw none of her tracks across the sand, but that same city, its gates so close she could see the stamped image of a goat's head on the bronze gates.

Élise approached the walls, and began to walk around the perimeter until she found the gate again before her. She felt Gwen's raven alight and nearly stumbled as it flew in front of her face, flapping its wings wildly. Taking the hint, she turned around.

The raven was gone, and so was the desert.

She stood in a large square, a fountain of water in its center. Grapevines ran up the buildings' walls, ripe fruit gleaming in the bright light. Naked boys chased each other, playing some game of tag. Naked girls stood off to one side of the square, clapping hands and chanting a nonsense rhyme.

"Welcome to heaven, Élise."

Élise turned to the voice and saw a tall naked man. His skin shone brightly with an inner light, and his white wings were too bright to look at.

That was not Saint Peter, she was certain of it.

"Did I die?"

"Yes, when you threw yourself off that cliff. Why don't you allow me to remove your earthly shroud, and let your true self shine forth?"

"Shroud?"

"Have you not noticed that everyone goes naked here? We have no need to cover our nakedness. There is no shame here."

"Please," she said, looking down upon her clothing, dirty and torn by wind and sand, "I'm not ready yet to put aside modesty."

"No matter. Come with me, let me show you the delights of paradise."

They passed through an arch and strode down an avenue paved in alabaster. In front of each building was a garden. Some had fig trees, others date palms, and still others pomegranate trees. Yet, no birds flit between those branches, no songs filled the air. She missed the raven, wondered what had happened to it. There had been no sounds at all since they left the square, except for her stumbling footsteps.

They passed under another arch into a court of marble. In the center, a large fountain silently spouted a golden liquid. Around the fountain were men and women, all naked and many engaged in various sexual acts.

Élise froze. This was not heaven. It was just another lie.

"Why do they behave so shamelessly?" she asked.

"Did I not tell you we have no shame here? What need we of shame when we've cast off our mortal shackles?"

Élise turned and looked him in the eye for the first time since she beheld him. "This is all a lie. This is not heaven."

He turned dark as night, and his eyes glowed red. "You dare! Well, if hell is what you see, hell is what you'll have!"

She found herself in a dungeon, men and women standing along its walls. They looked horrible, with flayed skin, entrails wrapped around their faces contorted in pain. They should all have been dead from dismemberment. Dead. Yet, each man had an erect penis as they all advanced on her.

Élise fought the urge to retch, to scream. . . and yet to throw herself upon each penis. There was nowhere to run.

"Repent of your unbelief and be spared their fate!" her guide's voice thundered. Élise looked. His penis stood erect, and the grin on his face was that of hungry delight.

She shivered despite the wilting heat, the aching hunger for him inside her. Repent. Isn't that what she came into the desert to do? She began to sing:

Beatus vir qui non abiit in consilio impiorum et in via peccatorum non stetitin cathedra derisorum non sedit

Sed in lege Domini voluntas eius et in lege eius meditabitur die ac nocte

The demon screamed, reached to her and pulled her clothes to shreds with its claws as she sang:

Et erit tamquam lignum transplantatum iuxta rivulos aquarum quod fructum suum dabit in tempore suo et folium eius non defluet et omne quod fecerit prosperabitur

It started to tear her skin, ripping it off her body. It should hurt, but to her surprise she didn't feel a thing. Not questioning it, she continued:

Non sic impii sed tamquam pulvis quem proicit ventus

Propterea non resurgent impii in iudicio neque peccatores in congregatione iustorum

Quoniam novit Dominus viam iustorum et iter impiorum peribit

She felt a distant pop and realized the demon had pulled off her leg but she let a new song flow over her, becoming one with the words:

Dominus pascit me nihil mihi deerit

In pascuis herbarum adclinavit me super aquas refectionis enutrivit me

Animam meam refecit duxit me per semitas iustitiae

Sed ed si ambulavero in valle mortis non timebo malum quoniam tu mecum es virga tua et baculus tuus ipsa consolaburitur me

Pones coram me mensam ex adverso hostium meorum inpinguasti oleo caput meum calix meus inebrians

The dungeon disappeared without a sound. Where it had stood was only desert. Whole and untouched, Élise sank to her knees and sang one more hymn, sobbing dry tears—a song of thanksgiving.

She heard a "Krwak!" and felt the raven's familiar talons sink gently into her shoulder. Élise rose and followed the sun on its westward trek toward the cool night.

The sun's warmth woke her the next morning. Her skin was red, and she felt blisters on her face. Élise stretched and noticed a glimmering out of the corner of her eye. Again, a tray of wafer-like bread had been set for her. The raven perched upon a large urn of water. She smiled and knelt, then sang a song of praise and thanksgiving.

Translator's note on the hymns:

The Vulgate, the Bible available to people in the medieval era, was originally written in the common or vulgar language of the people, thus its name. It used a different numbering system for the psalms than the Tanakh did. As modern English translations use the same numbering as the Tanakh, the numbers of these psalms would not provide an accurate link to the text of the psalms, it might confuse. Using the vulgate numbering system, Élise quotes psalms number 1 and 22. Using the Tanakh numbering system, she quotes psalms 1 and 23.

ABOMINATION

Adelie looked up from her mending as she heard stumbling foot-steps outside the hut. Relief washed over her as she saw Élise stagger through the door, falling to her knees. Gwen's raven hopped off Élise's shoulder onto the table.

Adelie and Galiana rushed to Élise's side, helping her up and guiding her to the table. The hermit handed Gwen a cup of water and Gwen held it to Élise's lips, helping her to sip gently at first, and then drink deeply until the cup was empty. The women then served her, joining her at table.

When the meal was done, the hermit offered up a prayer of thanksgiving. Without another word, Adelie helped Élise to bed and tucked her sister under a woolen blanket. She lay awake for what seemed endless hours, listening to the others breathe, David's unanswered question battling in her heart.

At dawn, Adelie rose and looked at her sister, still asleep, with a peaceful smile on her face. Stepping over Galiana, she went outside to find the hermit. She was not surprised to find him awake, facing the rising sun.

"You are concerned about your sister?" he asked.

Adelie nodded. "Yes, and about the rest of us. All people lust, yet few of us suffer from a demon's torment."

"Adelie, your errand, of which you have never spoken, has attracted the interest of both Heaven and Hell. You will all face dangers and torments far beyond what most of us sinners face. Lady Elisabeth forgot how Gwenaella easily fell prey to such a demon. You all have to help each other walk the narrow path while seeking this garden, for Hell itself opposes you."

"Will she ever be herself again?"

The hermit smiled. "I can only hope she'll be more herself than she's ever been. What else is bothering you my daughter?"

Adelie swallowed. "Is David giving into lust in his desire to marry me?"

"Child, you ask out of fear. You must trust him, as well as love him. Otherwise, your love will fail. You began this journey when you trusted the priest who took you out of Poitiers. If you can so trust strangers, how much more must you trust David who loves you?"

Instead of voicing her questions, she said, "It is not David I doubt, it is myself. I don't know how to be a Christian bride of a Jew. I would have to give up everything, I would lose my rank and station and once more be despised by those who see me."

"Whose opinion matters more to you, those who love you, or strangers who mean nothing to you? As for being the bride of a Jew, all you can do is be the bride of a man, and place your trust in God that you will never have to carry a burden that is beyond you."

"What if the burden kills me?" she asked.

"Death is not an end, and by far not the worst thing that could happen to you, child."

"You have given me much to think on. May I keep you in my prayers?" Adelie rose, but waited for his answer.

He looked at her and smiled. "I would be honored if you would do so."

Adelie went into the hut and prepared breakfast.

As they ate, Élise told them about the simple loaves of bread, and water she found next to her every morning. "It was as if I was in my own personal Exodus, leaving behind my shattered idols."

Adelie wondered what else she had seen in the desert, but neither she nor the others asked.

After they finished cleaning up from their meal, they bid farewell to the hermit and made their way back to the caravan.

"Do you think Britomar will take me back?" Élise asked.

"She took me back when you drove the demon from me," said Gwen.

"Yes, but you remained chaste," said Élise. "After everything I committed in my imagination, I couldn't possibly—" she blushed, her voice trailing into silence.

"I hadn't been exactly chaste when Britomar accepted me," said Galiana.

Adelie slipped her hand into that of her sister.

Gwen said, "You come to her lovingly, prepared to give your life to help her king. How can she turn you away?"

Élise stopped in her tracks. "I never thought of love that way. When the troubadours sing of love, they always sing of a desire for another, never of giving."

"I've never known love before Britomar, but I've known desire," said Galiana. "I've spent my whole life wanting and taking to meet my wants. I never thought about what I needed, or how to give myself. If Britomar can take me, she'll take you too."

Adelie had no words to add to what the others had said, just held her sister's hand as they resumed their walk to the camp. If love is giving, not desire, then she was well prepared to give herself to David.

Élise squeezed her hand. "Have you decided what answer to give David?"

"Yes. I'm going to say yes to him."

Élise's eyes sparkled in delight Adelie found herself twirled in her sister's embrace. Even the raven, which had lately taken to riding upon Élise, cawed its approval.

"That's wonderful!" said Gwen.

"I'm so happy for you," said Galiana.

Gwen took Adelie's other hand and Élise beckoned for Galiana to take hers. Adelie found herself skipping along with the others as Élise began to sing:

> My love gives me joy of spring
> Birds sing of my love in the trees
> Flower's bloom echoes his beauty
> The warm fragrant breeze brings him
>
> My love gives me joy of summer
> Crickets fill the night with his song
> The golden wheat grows in his light
> The hot winds echo his passion
>
> My love gives me joy of autumn
> Deer dance his grace in the meadow
> The apple ripens like our love
> My heart twirls for him like leaves
>
> My love gives me joy of winter
> Ice glitters in the light of you
> Memory of your smile warms me
> My love is as pure as fresh snow

Blue and white striped flags waved in the wind over their encampment. Gwen and Galiana followed Élise to Britomar, but Adelie excused herself. She had an answer to give.

She found David sparring with Wigandus. A small crowd of men circled around them watching the swordplay. David's swordsmanship had gotten much better than in the early days, on their way to Wien. At the moment he was pushing Wigandus. The knight had a big smile on his face, clearly enjoying the challenge. He twisted out of the way of the attack and brought his wooden practice blade down on David's sword arm.

Adelie watched the two friends embrace, Wigandus patting David on the shoulder heartily. As she approached, David's grin lit her with joy—and doubt. What did he see in her, a gutter rat without even the simple domestic skills? What would his mother say to their wedding? She remembered their embrace as she had confessed to the woman her impossible love for David.

But if Gwen was right, and love was all about the giving, then she would gladly give herself to him.

She reached him and took his offered hand. "Yes, David, I'll be yours."

They wed that night, under the stars. Élise led Adelie through the crowd, arm in arm to a wedding canopy held by Wigandus, Gwen, Galiana, and Britomar, who used her horn where the others used poles entwined with garlands of flowers. David waited for her beside a small table, set with a cup and an illustrated parchment, a welcoming grin on his face. Behind the table stood an old man with a long gray beard, his head covered with a black and white stripped tasseled shawl. He must be the rabbi.

As she walked, she heard angry mutterings from the crowd; "To'eva!" was the most common thing she heard. Others spat at her. Adelie didn't care. David waited for her with a smile. The rest didn't matter, though she wished she knew the meaning of the insult they spat at the dust.

As she had been instructed that afternoon by some women who had come to help her dress, she walked around him seven times. Once she finally stood next to him, the rabbi said, "There is only one moment when our Lord pronounces his creation 'lo tov', which means not good: when Adam had existed alone. The creation of Eve shows us that men are meant to be married. We call marriage: 'kiddushin', which means holy, or to set aside. She is set aside for him; he is set aside for her. David and Adelie, you are two people of different faiths. The challenges you will face will be like those faced by Esther and King Ahasuerus, like Boaz and Ruth. Take heart that as the Lord has blessed those unions, He will bless yours. You will stand unified under the covenant between God and Noah. David, you have found your bashert in Adelie, treat her well."

The rabbi then turned to the crowd.

"I have some words to say to my people. I have heard those who mutter and call Adelie foul names. To you I say: you bring shame on us, on all our people. Esther's marriage to King Ahasuerus was the instrument through which the Lord saved Israel. Who are we to know the wisdom of the Most High? We should not condemn what we do not understand."

The Rabbi then read the marriage contract and blessed the ring. David turned to Adelie and took her hand, placing the ring on her finger. "Be sanctified to me with this ring in accordance with the covenant of the most high with Noah."

David and Adelie then shared wine from the same cup. When the wine was finished, David placed a glass under his right foot and smashed it. A cry of "mozel-tov" rose from the crowd. David took Adelie's hand and led her to a nearby tent that had been set for them.

"David, what does 'to'eva' mean?"

"Abomination. They're worried that you'll be unable to keep one of the prime roles of a wife, that of instructing a husband in Torah."

Adelie looked away from him. "David, how can I be your wife?"

"Do you love me?"

"Yes, with all my heart!"

"That is how. Love is the foundation of everything in the Torah." David reached over and touched her chin, lifting her eyes to his. "We believe that when a male child rests in his mother's womb, the Lord, our God, chooses a bashert for him. 'Bashert' means soul mate. I know I have found my bashert. When I told Rabbi Nathan about this, he found a way for us to be married: under the covenant God made with Noah.

"They're expecting us to join the celebrations in a moment. Before we do, I just want to say I love you."

Adelie answered him with a kiss.

After the hours of joyous dancing, men linking arms in a giant circle with women dancing in a separate one, Adelie and David were separated, not to be alone again with each other until eight days had passed. Each night held feasts in their honor; each day they spent making ready for the journey across the desert.

On the seventh night, two women came to the tent where Adelie,

Élise and Galiana were eating. One was carrying a bundle of clothing. "I am Miriam, and this is Hannah. We've come to help you get ready, for your groom awaits."

As they dressed and perfumed her, they chatted about the duties of a Jewish wife, and the joys of children. Adelie's cheeks burned, especially when Galiana gave her suggestions on how to please a man. Her anticipation at seeing David again mixed with worry as she stood before them, dressed in richly colored robes, her hair covered with a sea-green silk scarf, and rings of silver hanging from her ears. Will she be able to please him? Was she ready to be with a man?

"How do I look?"

"Adelie, you look beautiful!" said Galiana, "I love how the green of your scarf shows off your eyes!"

"You're like a desert flower!" said Gwen. "David will be so pleased!"

"You think so?"

Élise embraced her and said, "He is a good man, your David. Don't be frightened."

"You are becoming a woman in the arms of a man who loves you," Galiana said as she gave her a kiss. "That is a rare and precious thing. Hold nothing back, and he will never look for women like me."

The night air felt warm to Adelie as she followed the women to the tent where David waited. She heard screaming from another tent nearby. A man and a woman, arguing. Adelie felt goose bumps rise up her back. How can she make a good wife? She knew nothing about how to keep a Jewish home. What will he expect of her? Will he be yelling at her in the years to come because she served him the wrong food?

The women took her to a tent set off to the side of the camp. They stood on either side of the flap, drawing it open for her. Adelie stooped to enter and saw David reclining on pillows, his dark hair and beard glistening in the lamplight.

She looked at him, and blushed. He was so handsome. She loved him so much. How could a woman like her be so lucky?

David raised his face to her and smiled, beckoning her inside. She approached stiffly and sat on a pillow. She could not look into his eyes. Her heart pounded so hard it threatened to jump out of her chest.

She had forgotten everything the women told her over the wedding preparations. She would never be able to please him like a good wife should. She had no idea what to do.

He lifted her chin and kissed her. Warmth spread over her as she inhaled his familiar scent. She had never been alone with him before. Never like this, when she could enjoy his closeness with no reserve, when everything she always wanted to do with him was allowed, and good. She was his wife, his other half, his soul mate. She will never have to part with him again.

She threw her arms around his neck. Soon they were pulling off each others robes as they kissed and caressed.

That night they slept entwined, naked and exhausted from their giving love.

THREE BROTHERS

Days dragged on, each the same as the rest. Gwen passed her time staring at the folded cloth, at the other women in the wagon intent on their sewing, at the shadows of those lucky enough to be outside the wagon. She had no joy in the stories Élise told that brought the other women to fits of giggles. She lay awake at night berating herself for the jealousy that stabbed her heart each evening as Adelie bid them a blushing good night with a smile that betrayed her joy in marriage. It felt worse because during all this time she'd seen very little of Wigandus since the wagons resumed their trek across the desert.

They'd lost so much time waiting on Élise, arranging Adelie's wedding. Even though Britomar assured her that she shouldn't worry, Gwen couldn't adopt the unicorn's acceptance of each delay. With a wry smile, Gwen realized that part of her impatience was for her own marriage. If joining her hand with Wigandus must wait until they reached the Garden, they couldn't move fast enough for her.

At least they were not following the easy roads through the fertile valley, but headed south over the desert. She did not look forward to reaching Baghdad. After Antioch, she felt more than ever that she'd rather never enter a city again. She hoped that no one would spot Britomar in the caravan, and that she and the unicorn would be able to slip out under the cover of darkness and wait outside the city, like they did in Paris. She smiled briefly, remembering how she met Wigandus in the forest outside of Paris: his gallantry and bravery in her defense, his bad poetry, his puppyish enthusiasm around her, his vow to defend her chastity and remain virginal until she succeeded in her errand, though it may cost him his life.

Damn that vow, and his accursed resolve to keep it! If Adelie could be both a wife and chaste, why not Gwen? Couldn't their vows of marriage replace a hasty vow taken before they knew love?...

The canter of a horse at gallop pulled her out of her self-pity. Aaron thrust his head through the canvas flap, "Flee! Flee for your lives! There is an army heading towards us!"

Adelie put her hand on her long knife, but Élise shook her head. "Britomar might flee, and Gwen with her, but if they mean to catch the rest of us, they will."

Gwen's heart quivered. Last time she fled a city with Britomar, Wigandus was nearly killed. She couldn't bear the thought of losing him. No, this time she will not abandon him. She will enter Baghdad, no matter the risk.

"We can't flee in secret," she said. "In the open desert they'd spot us. Besides, I doubt that even Britomar can outrun horses bred in this place. No, Aaron, I will wait with the others." The realization of what she'd done washed over her like the desert heat. How could she get free once trapped?

They did not have to wait long before the army was within bow-shot. Gwen, Adelie, Élise, and Galiana peered through the curtains of their wagon, relieved to see Wigandus and David at Aaron's side.

Three men broke off from the army's formation and rode forward; Aaron stepped forward to greet them with a bow. "Aaron ben Jeremiah at your service, worthy one."

"Salaam," one of them said, though he looked not at Aaron but at Britomar. "This humble one brings you the wishes of the Caliph al-Musta'sim. The Chosen One of Heaven desires you to be brought to his presence. I am sent to lead you to him."

"We are honored to be noticed by the Caliph al-Musta'sim, and will graciously accept his invitation," said Britomar.

"My most humble apologies, my command of your language is not very good. Invitation? No, it is his command. You will all come with me at once."

Sir Wigandus stepped forward. "I am Sir Wigandus, Knight of the Holy Roman Empire and sworn protector of this unicorn. What is your name, so that I may address you properly?"

"This humble servant is known as Nasir al-Dawla."

"Nasir al-Dawla, were you not the faithful messenger of your liege lord, I would challenge you to defend yourself, for you have insulted your guests."

"Sir Wigandus, you are a brave and courteous knight. If you were not my enemy, I would be honored to count you as my friend. Please come with me before I am forced to have you brought."

David put his hand on Wigandus's shoulder. "Nasir al-Dawla, I am David ben Yosi, and I bid you remind your master the fate of Sodom and Gomorra, who also spurned guests on a Holy mission."

"Dog of a Jew! Silence, before I have you whipped for speaking thus to your betters! Now, do you follow, or do I drag you to his exalted eminence in chains?"

"We will follow," said Britomar.

"Even so, you will all surrender your weapons to me."

Gwen winced as David and Sir Wigandus handed him their swords. At least Adelie still had her knives. There were some small mercies in their forced separation from the men.

David rode over to the wagon and lifted its flap. "Please, try not to worry. This is all happening as I was shown in a dream. Follow my lead, and no matter what happens, keep silent. Your lives depend on your silence."

Silence they kept, but each peeked through gaps in the wagon's canvas cover, hoping to see a glimpse of their fate.

After several days' ride through the desert they saw a green line of the land ahead, lush with straight channels cut into the earth, bringing water into fertile fields. The roads here led them through large orchards and flowing fields of golden wheat. Gwen couldn't help but feel amazed at the richness of this land on the other side of the desert.

One bright morning Gwen saw the gleaming river, and beyond it, a city. Gwen gasped. Its size and grandeur made Antioch look like a toy. Not one but two walls circled the city, each of them tall, gleaming in the sun with its ornaments of many-colored tiles.

A beautiful prison Gwen's heart dreaded entering. Yet enter it she must.

Beyond the walls, four tall towers rose into the sky with onion-shaped roofs, like spears leveled at the heavens. Many other spear-like towers were scattered here and there throughout this humongous city. They must be the minarets of mosques, where the Saracen came to their unholy prayer. Yet, Élise spoke well of the two Saracen men she'd met near the ruined city after their ship was attacked and the mast broken. Perhaps, these Saracen would be like the Jews: sincerely living the best path to God they knew. Gwen hoped so. When she met the Jews she had learned her lesson not to give in to religious prejudice; she prayed she was brought to Baghdad so that she could do so again.

A glint of light caught her attention, drawing her eyes beyond the towers to a gold onion-shaped dome that towered over them; a beacon to power for all the world to see. She gasped. So much gold. How rich was this caliph they were going to see?

As they drew nearer to the walls, they heard loud chanting. Their escort brought them to gates, wide enough to admit twelve horses side by side. The gate's arch was lined with the lovely tiles adorned with flowers all the way to the ceiling far overhead. Gwen gasped. If even the defenses in this city were so beautiful, perhaps these were a Godly people after all.

The streets were paved with pressed sands, lined with the devout kneeling on mats and rugs facing south-west. Gwen smiled at the irony: with the men prostrate in worship, Britomar's entrance to the city was more hidden than if they had come at night. Gwen only saw one person look at them, a bent old woman whose eyes sparkled through the heavy black veil she wore.

The buildings towered above them as they continued their march to the center, windows covered with intricate wood lattices, balconies capped with canopies resting over ornate frames. Any number of eyes could be hiding behind those pretty nets of wood without being seen. Gwen shuddered at the thought of being a prisoner behind latticework.

Finally, they came to the walls even taller than those around the city. Its arched gateway was covered in brilliant blue tiles, each stamped with a white flower-like pattern. They passed through into a large garden. Exotic animals wandered the groves, many of them known to Gwen only from the pictures in old books she'd seen at the convent school. She recognized giraffes, ostriches, zebras, and some others whose names she did not remember. A colonnade surrounded this animal garden, its onion-shaped arches decorated with more tiles.

The wagons stopped as they entered the garden and the travelers were ushered out into a large hall, lit by large oil lamps hanging by long chains from the vaulted ceiling. In the center of the hall, three women danced to a slow, sensual music. They wore bright translucent silks over their loins, and no other clothes. Gwen blushed as she saw these outfits.

A fat man dressed in costly silks stepped from behind a column and clapped his hands once. The dancers scampered out of sight, and the musicians picked up their instruments and left.

The travelers continued into the depths of the hall, where a portly man reclined on a pile of cushions, eating dates fed to him by a naked slave boy. The man smiled when he saw the newcomers,

"Ah, my unicorn! How delightful!" He spoke Langue d'oc fluently, without any accent. "And who are these others?"

Sir Wigandus moved forward, but David put his hand on the knight's arm and said in a low voice, "Let me handle this, as we planned."

He stepped forward and knelt before the man. "Your eminence. We are this unicorn's companions on a sacred journey, a holy mission of healing. We have traveled far and risked much to come before you and petition for the use of your library. There, we hope to learn the secret of the location of the Garden at the Center of the World. We have all sworn an oath before the Almighty that we will not rest until Britomar the Unicorn has in her possession the fruit her herd needs from the tree that grows at this Garden's center. To this end, we had hired Aaron ben Jeremiah to help us reach your illustrious city."

The caliph pursed his lips. "Dog of a Jew, I consider your oaths not at all. What worth are the oaths of those who do not follow the true faith?"

David bowed. "Your Majesty is just and wise, as He who governs all has decreed. Consider for the moment a father who had three sons, whom he loved equally. He had a ring that had been handed down from father to son for countless generations, and could by no means decide amongst his children. So, unbeknownst to them, he had copies made of the true ring, and so faithful were these copies that he himself could not tell which was the original. When he was on his death bed, he called each son in, one by one. To each son, he told of how he loved him and wished him all the happiness a righteous life can bring. He then handed each a ring. Each son thought he was given his father's ring, each son walked away feeling blessed and loved. On the day of their father's funeral, each of the sons saw that they all wore the same ring. They rejoiced at their father's wisdom and love.

"Most illustrious caliph, consider it is so with the three peoples of the book. Our heavenly father has given us each His word, and none of us can tell which is the original. While we may fight as brothers do, we all know of His divine love and mercy.

"How could my brother, wise as he is, ignore such a sacred pledge taken on by his brothers?"

There were many appreciative murmurs as the courtiers whispered amongst themselves.

The caliph smiled and sat up on his pillows. "You delight me with your story, Jew, and I will permit you this much. You will have access to my library, and bring me the location of this Garden. I will walk its groves and eat of its fruit myself. These others are of no consequence. The raven and the unicorn will be added to my zoo, the Frankish knight will join my guard. The four maidens will be my concubines and entertain me as I will. The merchant and his caravan are of no interest to me, and will be sold into slavery."

David smiled and bowed low. "Would my lord be considered wiser than King David himself?"

"What mean you, Jew? I have spoken my will. Am I not caliph?"

"Yes, and your will shall be ours. But one of these women is my wife. Unless you would repeat the sin of King David, my wife should stay with me."

The caliph reddened, but then laughed. "Your wife! Well it is that you keep me from so grave a sin!"

"I am much relieved, Your Majesty. Would my wife be permitted to visit with her sister, who is one of the maidens you are claiming for your own?"

"Yes, now away with you all! You are trying my patience!"

They all huddled around David, who spoke softly, "I was shown all of this in a dream. Aaron, I know you will find a way to get your people ransomed. As for us, we'll be free before dawn. I've guaranteed Adelie's access to the women's chambers, so she'll be our means to free the three of you." He took three small vials and handed them one each to Élise, Galiana and Gwen. "In the vials you'll find lamb's blood. It will stay liquid until you open the stopper. Use it to pretend of your menses. We'll get out of this, but we must all be perceived as following the wishes of this tyrant."

Gwen nodded. No man would touch them if they had menses... But would they be able to make the deception believable if they were constantly watched?

Adelie gave them each a hug and then hurried to follow David, who walked with an old man. Gwen looked for Wigandus and panicked for a moment when she couldn't see him. Finally she saw him amongst a company of armed men. He looked like a lion in a cage, his eyes darting between his captors. Gwen wondered about Wigandus's silence as she was led to the women's chambers along with Galiana and Élise. Her heart sank as she watched her knight led away by the guards. His head was bowed, and he did not even look at her.

Had he not given his vow of virginity and married her, would she be free like Adelie? Would David's trick have worked twice?

They'd not gone far when two corpulent men in pastel silks approached. One of them pointed at Gwen. "The one with the red curls is to accompany us, the caliph wishes it."

Gwen's hand tightened on the vial that David had secreted to her. Dare she take it with her?

"Might not she be allowed a bath, to properly prepare herself for the caliph?" asked Élise. "It is only fitting."

"The Commander of the Faithful wishes her brought to him at once."

Gwen turned to Élise and Galiana, heartened by the worry on their faces. "I'll be fine," she lied. She turned and followed the two eunuchs down ornate lamp-lit corridors.

They brought her into a garden, where she walked past deer so tame that they did not even glance in her direction, though she could have stroked their coats in passing. She focused on the joy and peace of this place; no sense dwelling on the horror of what could happen to her. Perhaps, after all, the caliph just wanted to discuss her errand. She dare not let go of that hope.

On the other side of the garden were doors that seemed of solid gold but opened to the slightest touch of the eunuch's sausage-thick fingers. The room they entered glowed with colored silks hanging along the walls, its ceiling covered with pearls and gems. As soon as Gwen stepped through, the golden doors were closed and secured behind her.

"You will undress and make yourself ready to receive your master," instructed one of the eunuchs.

Gwen's heart pounded in renewed panic. Perhaps if she mentioned her betrothal this would all go away. "I am betrothed to another. If you inform his eminence of this, I'm certain he'll understand why I must refuse this command."

The other eunuch clapped his hands and a third appeared. In his hands he held shackles and chains. "You will undress and make yourself ready, or you will be made ready."

Gwen started to back away from this third eunuch, but the other two moved faster than their girth suggested they could. Each grabbed an arm, and though she twisted and pulled, she couldn't free herself. She tried kicking at the third eunuch as he closed upon her, but the other two forced her to the floor. Her arms hurt with the strain of her resistance, slowly pulled together until she heard a loud click, followed by three more. Cold metal bit at her wrists and ankles. She was helpless. She wanted to cry for mercy, curse Wigandus for his chivalric stubbornness that robbed her of his protection by the right of marriage, but forced herself to calm down. *Blessed mother,* she prayed silently. *Keep me safe so I may reach the Garden. Give me the strength to endure. Free me from these bonds.*

One of the eunuchs pulled her hair to turn her head, showing her a knife. With a hungry grin, he licked his lips and then licked the blade. "I will cut you with pleasure if you don't lay still."

Gwen closed her eyes, forcing herself to silently say a pater noster, ignoring the ripping cloth, the cold air, the tugs on her limbs and torso as the eunuch roughly cut the clothing from her. Desperately reaching for the discipline the sisters had tried to whip into her in the convent, Gwen focused on each word; *Pater noster,* she was lifted from the floor *qui es in cælis,* she felt herself fall, *sanctificetur nomen tuum.* Pain stabbed her as she landed on her arms, still pulled and bound behind her back, David's unopened vial uselessly clenched in her hand. *Adveniat regnum tuum.* Strong hands clamped on each ankle. *Fiat voluntas tua, sicut in cælo et in terra.* Her ankles were pulled up and under her, another click as the ankle chains were connected to the manacles. *Panem nostrum qauotidianum da nobis hodie.* A eunuch said something harsh in a language she was glad she didn't understand. *Et dimitte nobis debita nostra, sicut et nos dimittimus debitoribus nostris.* A clang of metal, then silence. *Et ne nos inducas in tentationem: sed libera nos a malo.* Bound, naked and alone, Gwen forced the words, *Pater noster...*[1]

---

[1]The prayer Gwen says, the Pater Noster as it was known then, is commonly known today as the Lord's Prayer, or Our Father.

HIDDEN

Adelie wanted to hold David's hand but stayed a few steps back and followed him as an old man led him by the arm. She lost her bearings in the slow steps as the old man shuffled through seemingly endless lamp-lit corridors. Arch after arch passed by, covered with tiles gleaming in the flickering light. Finally, one arch had a door to it, and a small gilded alcove set to the side, holding an oil lamp. The old man fumbled at his rope belt until he brought out an iron key, which squeaked in the lock as he turned it. The door creaked open; the old man grabbed the small lamp from the alcove and shuffled inside. Adelie followed and closed the door behind her.

More spry than she'd thought he'd be from his shuffling, the old man went from lamp to lamp, lighting each from the small flame he tenderly touched to the wicks. The room smelled of rancid oil and dust, but as it emerged from the darkness Adelie had to suppress a gasp. Books lay everywhere, from floor to ceiling, stacked against columns and filling the gaps of arches.

Searching through this library was not a night's work, but a lifetime's. It could take years to find anything here that might lead them to the Sacred Garden.

The old man said something she couldn't understand, but his tone sounded urgent. She looked up and saw that he was gesturing for them to follow. He took them behind a curtain, into a smaller chamber. A table in its center was covered with broken clay tablets that someone must have been trying to fit back together. The holes in the lattice-like walls held scrolls, with more scrolls piled on top of a small table in a corner.

The old man said, "You did well to remind the caliph of his duty to Allah. His disregard of a sacred oath will bring disaster upon us all. I will seek out the chief of the guards, the zookeeper, and the head eunuch. I will persuade them that following the Quran is more important than following the whims of a corrupt monarch. In the mean time, you must do your work. If the answer to where the garden is can be found in this city, the secret lies in this chamber.

I will return to you shortly." The old man left through the same curtain.

Adelie's eyes darted to David. "Do we dare trust him?"

He took her hands. "If he is sincere about his devotion to the Quran, I would trust him with all of our lives. Now, let's see about these texts." David sat and began looking through the scrolls. Adelie brought him new ones, careful not to pass the fragile documents near the flame that was their light and her only comfort. She felt as if the walls of this library were closing in on her, like the walls of the cave back in Hungary.

Something soft ran across her foot and she squealed.

"Adelie?"

"Sorry, David, a mouse ran across my foot and startled me." She looked down and saw the mouse disappear behind the small table. As she followed it with her eyes, a glint caught her eye. A dirty-white corner peeking out from behind the table leg.

She pushed aside the table. The wall lattice extended behind it, empty except for just one hole with a scroll in it. Why has it been tucked away? Or was it just forgotten?

She carefully pulled it out. Its edges were ragged and cracked, and she was afraid the paper might crumble. Curious, she brought it to the large table and slowly rolled it open. To her surprise, the writing was in Langue d'oc. She started to read and gasped.

"David, I think this is important."

David looked up. "When did you learn to read Hebrew?"

"This is in Langue d'oc."

"Langue d'oc? Let me look closer." He bent over the scroll, moving his fingers across the words as he saw them. His hand trembled as he looked up at her, wide-eyed.

"Adelie! This is it! It tells us where the garden is and how to get there! Listen:

> At the roof of the world waits the garden
> For those who are His children and walk the way
> Hidden behind walls of ice and fields of stone
> Where the four sacred rivers burst upon the world
> In the shadows of the three tallest peaks
> Only the pure of heart may tread its paths
> Only the pure of body may enter
> Nothing of death will be found within its walls
> For the Lord is the Lord of the living
> His name is to be praised above all names."

There was a knock and the curtain parted. Sir Wigandus stepped through the opening.

"Wigandus! How can this be?" said Adelie, turning to him with a grin.

"It would seem that as the caliph's new guard I've been assigned to guard the library, and to make certain you are not disturbed in your research. The captain of the guard is most upset at how we were treated by the caliph, and means to restore our freedom to us. I also have a message for you to send to Gwen, Élise and Galiana. Tonight a boat will be waiting for us on the river."

"And Britomar?"

Before he could answer, the librarian returned. "Ah, good. Al-Rashid has kept his word. I've had words with the zookeeper and the chief eunuch. They're sympathetic, but will not do anything to help."

"Al-Rashid promised he would get Britomar out," said Wigandus.

"Where can we find this boat?" Adelie asked.

"I'm told it will be a mile down river. Tonight, just get the others to a safe house that Al-Rashid will tell you of, and wait for us there."

"How will I get to the others?"

"Al-Rashid will come here and take you to the harem himself. He'll knock when he arrives."

"David." Adelie took his hand. "If I don't succeed..."

David held her gaze. "God will go with you, Adelie, trust in Him." There was a soft knock.

"Adelie, one more thing please," said Wigandus, looking down at the floor. "Just in case the worst happens, tell Gwen I will love her till my last breath."

David gave Adelie a kiss. She stepped through the curtain to find a tall muscular man with skin as dark as night and a short beard equally dark waiting for her. He was dressed in the armor she'd seen in the throne room, that of the caliph's personal guards.

Captain Al-Rashid bowed. "If it is the will of Allah, I will serve you as befits a queen. Please permit me to escort you to your sisters."

As they walked, Al-Rashid told Adelie of two hidden ways out of the palace where he had stationed loyal guards with orders to aid the women. He also told her of a safe house, to which they should flee and wait for the others.

Al-Rashid's long legs set a stiff pace. Adelie was winded by the time he stopped beside a stout wooden door with a grate in the center. He knocked. The cover to the grate slid aside to reveal a pasty-faced man on the other side.

"What does the captain of the guard wish from this humble one at this late hour?" said the eunuch.

"I bring Lady Adelie, sister to Lady Elisabeth who is lodged within. She wishes to be taken to her sister and her dear friends Gwenaella and Galiana."

"It shall be as you say," answered the eunuch, who opened the door wide enough for Adelie to slip through.

"When you wish to return to your husband, my lady, have the eunuchs send for me, and I will bring you to him." Al-Rashid bowed and strode away.

Gwen tried to turn her head in the direction of the voices she heard but she couldn't twist her bound body far enough to see. They voices were getting louder. As words became distinct, she groaned in frustration. Arabic. No chance of deliverance. Death would be preferable to what came with those voices.

The voices ceased, but a cool air moving across her skin spoke of a door being opened. She closed her eyes, itchy and swollen with tears. She heard a deep murmur of satisfaction from a man she would not look at and held in a scream of pain as she felt her breasts squeezed and kneaded like dough. Tears filled her eyes at the sharp biting pain of her nipples being pinched. Renewed words of prayers poured into her mind. She tried not to think of his wet lips pulling on her nipples, his teeth nipping as his coarse beard tickled her tender skin. She would not look at her rapist as he ran his hands over her bottom, pinching and gripping tightly. Large smooth hands gripped her knees. She held her breath as she strained to keep them together, sending her silent pleas to God. She would not dignify her assailant with the pleasure of her suffering. She clenched her legs but could not resist the strength of the hands that slowly, painfully, pulled her knees apart. Her legs stung with pain as they opened. Gwen screamed through clenched teeth and tried to rock herself free.

"Hiyād!"[1] a voice growled.

Her knees snapped shut as the hands let go. Gwen sobbed, but would not open her eyes. If she couldn't see him, it would be easier to forgive him.

Rougher hands rolled her on her side and the chains that had held her feet and hands fell away. She curled into a ball, listening to a man yell and stomp away, the anger of his voice the only thing she

---

[1] Translator's note: "Menstrual blood!"

understood.

No one touched her again. After a while she dared to open her eyes, wiping away the tears as best she could with her hands. She stood up and looked about her. The room was empty, save for the cruel-faced eunuch who had so eagerly chained her. He lay on the floor, eyes open, mouse curved in a snarl, blood pooling around his body. Dead? She recoiled from him. What happened here? Had the caliph, her rapist, released her, killed his own eunuch, and stormed out of here? It must have been, because she did not sense anyone else's presence...But why?

A red gleam on the bed caught her eye, inside the impression her body must have made upon the cushion. Blood?...She frowned. Had David's vial opened? She looked at the vial she'd clasped so uselessly. No. She looked down, seeing a red smear on her upper thigh, between her legs. Her virginal blood? But she was certain that her assailant, however terrible his handling was, had not disturbed her maidenhead. She looked at the blood on her thigh again. There was only one explanation. Somehow, her own menses had started, without pain or cramping, and nearly a week too early. But how?

She startled as she heard the soft padding of slippered feet upon the stone. She looked around the room for a place to hide, something to cover herself with. Nothing. Who or whatever came, she would have to face it as she was.

Gwen turned to the noise, covering herself with her arms. The door in front of her opened, letting in the scent of sea air. Two women bent with age hobbled in, carrying folded clothing. They approached her and wiped her clean, then began dressing her in the translucent garments. Too tired to fight, Gwen submitted to their hands and let herself be lead from the room. She had no idea where any of the others were. If these women did not lead her back to her friends, if Adelie failed to free her, it was only a matter of time before she would be brought back. Gwenaella sobbed as she was led away.

Adelie followed the eunuch through silk-draped corridors filled with the smells of spices she could not identify but enjoyed very much. She was brought to a beautiful room; satin cushions scattered on the floor beneath silken hangings, walls painted with images of the same flowers that were set out in urns around the room.

The eunuch bowed. "If my lady could make herself comfortable in this poor chamber, I will fetch the others."

Adelie walked to the lattice-covered window and looked at the stars glowing in the clear evening sky. Perhaps all women in this land were kept so, hidden from the world, pampered behind bars.

Galiana, Élise, and Gwen soon came into the chamber, dressed in clothing so translucent that it was easy to see their blood-stained loin cloths. They huddled together, their cheeks glistening with tears, especially Gwen whose eyes were red and face blotchy as if she'd been crying for some time. Adelie gave each of them a hug, and whispered in each ear, "We're getting out of here tonight."

She then turned to the eunuch. "May we be left alone, we have women's things to discuss."

The eunuch pursed his lips. "I am not a man, my lady, and so I am used to women's things and will pay you no mind. Feel free to talk in my presence."

Adelie stepped closer, hand slipping into the fold of her clothing to grip a dagger's hilt. "I'm certain you would pay us no mind, but I'm certain there must be things worthier for your attention than our poor chatter." The wires of the hilt dug into her skin as she tightened her grip.

"It is my joy to... uh!"

Adelie's foot hit the eunuch in the gut, making him double over in pain. She grabbed his hair, pulled back his head and slid the dagger across his neck. His ponderous body collapsed upon the ornate rug.

"Come, we have no time to lose," said Adelie, as she wiped her dagger on the eunuch's clothes, then cut his keys from his belt. The pleading in his eyes haunted her. He was annoying, but he hadn't done anything to harm her. Had she turned into a cold-blooded killer? Wasn't there another way to deal with her enemies?

"But our clothes?" asked Gwen.

"No time." Delay would only mean more death.

The women hurried back along the passage Adelie had recently taken. She reached the door first and peered through the panel behind the grate. The lamp-lit hall was empty.

Adelie used the eunuch's keys to unlock the door; she let the women through one by one, then relocked it behind her. "There, that should slow things down a bit. Now, for the way out."

"As we came up, I saw servants coming through that door over there," offered Galiana.

"Then we should avoid that way by all means; the servants are the most likely to be up and about at this hour," said Élise.

"Follow me, and hush!" whispered Adelie, hoping she remembered Al-Rashid's instructions. There. The tiled wall to the side of the hall. She strode to it, counted seven tiles from the top, seven tiles from the right, and pressed. The tile gave slightly under her fingers and a section of the wall slid open, revealing a passage. She ushered everyone through and closed the wall behind them. So far, so good. If Al-Rashid was honest about the loyal guards waiting for them on the other side, they had hope of escape.

She led the women down ill-lit passages, counting turns until they came to another wall. This time, it was too dark to see the tiles. She slid her fingers over the wall, tracing and counting tiles from the bottom and then from the side. There. She pressed, and again a section of the wall slid aside. A cool breeze swept through the opening, bringing smells of fish and muddy water.

The women stepped out in to the starlit night and found themselves on a riverbank.

Two guards were pacing along the water. They must have been instructed by Al-Rashid, for they ignored the four women, deliberately looking the other way as they passed. Adelie led them through the dark city streets to a small house made of mud bricks. She knocked and the door opened to reveal a woman wearing a long blue garment and white veil, only her eyes and her hands visible.

"Báyt-naa báyt-kum," said the veiled woman as she hurriedly gestured for them to enter.

A TALE, INTERRUPTED

Gwen kept her eyes on the floor as she followed the young woman into the house. In the dim lighting of the oil lamps, the flowers and leaves of the rug covering the hall seemed gray. From the corners of her vision she could see men staring at her; she could feel their eyes on her skin. She forced herself not to burst out crying again, cringing at the thought of their eyes on her. She knew her translucent clothing hid nothing, even in the soft lighting of the oil lamps. She shivered, forcing herself to follow the velied woman to a back chamber.

It was a cozy, scarcely lit room with pillows scattered across the floor. Against one wall a large shelf held books and scrolls. An older woman greeted them as they entered. "You can rest here. Only my husband comes into these rooms, and he will honor my guests by staying away for as long as you enjoy my hospitality. I am Rayhana, and am pleased to welcome you. Food and clothes more suitable for a journey will be brought you, and I will meet any of your other needs with delight. Al-Rashid's message said that the others of your group may arrive at any time, and that upon their arrival you must all be prepared to flee."

"We have nothing to pay you for the clothes, or food." said Élise.

The woman bowed her head. "It will be our honor and privilege to feed and clothe you in the service of Allah." She slipped beyond the door curtain at the entrance.

Gwen shivered. "I saw men watching us as we entered. Our clothes display us for these men's eyes like toys…I can't wait to change!"

"When I saw the unicorn, I thought I'd be leaving this behind forever," said Galiana.

"You have." The other three women looked at Élise who was relaxed, sitting on a pillow. "This was not your choice. When so much depends on you living, what matters if you choose life and give up your modesty for a moment."

"Élise is right," said Adelie. "It's not as if either of you wanted to become the caliph's slaves. In any event, it's over now. In a few hours, we'll be free of this place."

"Adelie, what happened with David?" asked Galiana, joining Élise on the pillows. "Where is he?"

"He's with Sir Wigandus." She told them how they found the document they were looking for and how the guard captain Al-Rashid brought her to them. "They're supposed to get a boat and come for us, but I don't know how, or when."

Soon, Gwen hoped. She looked at the rug, but did not really see the birds resting in the woven trees. She wanted nothing to do with Wigandus. If it hadn't been for his foolish oath to remain virginal, her ordeal with the caliph wouldn't have happened. They would have been married now, like Adelie and David. And yet, she desperately longed for his hand in hers.

Rayhana returned with a pile of clothes in her arms. A young girl followed her, carrying sandals.

"It is a pity you don't have time for a bath. Food is being prepared," said Rayhana. "Here are some garments to clothe you rightly in the eyes of Allah."

Gwen felt relieved as she donned a simple, loose-fitting dress girded with a rope belt, and mercifully non-transparent. A scarf covered her hair. Rayhana helped all the women dress, replacing their loin clothes with the clean ones, and removed the translucent silks, while a child helped the women tie on the sandals. Gwen longed for a bath, to wash herself clean of that monster's hands, but she'd have to find time for that later.

Gwen's thoughts were broken as Rayhana returned with a tray of pastries. They all sat on the cushions and ate in silence. Gwen, quite at sea between rage and yet more tears, found a moment of small pleasure in watching as the young girl very seriously poured each of them a drink, sweet water with a hint of honey. This made her think of her own girlhood, when she would bring her Tadig his stew by the fire. If only she was there now, by his side.

The young girl yawned and Élise picked her up, setting her in her lap. "You're a big help for your mother, and I want to give you a gift my mother gave me when I was about your age."

"Mama? May I?" asked the girl. Her mother nodded, and Élise smiled.

"I no longer have my harp, but my mother used to play on her harp and sing this to me:

> *Little one,*
> *The birds are asleep.*

Rest your ears,
Their songs are done today.

Little one,
The lambs sleep now.
Rest your eyes,
Their skipping is done today.

Little one,
The flowers are asleep.
Rest your nose,
Their fragrance is gone at night."

Gwen noticed Adelie had a tear in her eye. Since when did Élise take an interest in children? She didn't have time to wonder long, as her host began to speak.

"Now, so you don't think us all monsters, would you care to hear a tale of a caliph who lived long ago?"

"Yes. I for one would love a story of your land," said Élise, cradling the child who had fallen asleep in her lap.

Gwen was surprised by her smile. One thing had not changed. Élise would look for a story at the gates of Hell itself.

"There was once, a long time ago, a caliph who had had no children. Every day he would spend an extra hour in prayer at the mosque, begging for a son. Finally, his youngest wife became with child. When the child was born, the caliph rejoiced, as he had been given a son. He named his son Camaralzaman.

"The young prince was raised by the best of tutors, and became well versed in the Quran, the arts and sciences. When he came of age, the caliph was approached by one of his viziers. 'Oh Esteemed of Heaven, it would be good for your son to marry.'

"The caliph agreed with his vizier, and called for his son.

"'What is your wish for me, Anointed of Heaven?' his son asked.

"'Son, it is my wish that you take a wife.'

"'Father, as much as it pains me to dispute your will, I have no wish to marry at this time.'"

Gwen winced. Was this what Wigandus felt? Gwen shook her head at her thought. Why was she doubting him? She knew the knight loved her, why such anger?

Rayhana continued her story. "He dismissed his son, and called for his vizier again.

"'My son has no wish to marry.'

"'Son of Heaven, give him a year. His mind will change.'

"The caliph thought that this was wise counsel. After a year had passed, he again summoned his son. 'It is my wish that you take a wife.'

"'My objections to taking a wife are unchanged,' answered the youth.

"Again the vizier was summoned. 'Beloved of Heaven, place your son into the tallest tower and keep him there for a year without access to any amusements. After a year, return him to your presence before the entire court and ask again. I assure you, he will have changed his mind.'

"The caliph did as his vizier recommended, and brought his son to him a year later in a public audience with all the court in attendance on his eminence. The caliph then ordered his son to take a bride.

"To this the son replied, 'There is no God but Allah, and there is no law but through you, my father. However, I will not take a bride at this time.'

"The caliph was enraged, and ordered his son thrown into the deepest dungeon. That very night, the djinn who was responsible for the torment of the prince's soul ran into a fellow tormentor.

"'You would not believe my bad fortune! I have the most beautiful man, but I cannot get him to even look at a woman, let alone be seduced by one.'

"To this the other djinn replied, 'That is nothing to my pain. The woman I must torment is the most beautiful creature under heaven, and I too cannot get her so much as to gaze in the direction of a man.'

"'I cannot believe that your woman is as beautiful as my man.' said the first djinn.

"'Let us put them together and compare.' So the second djinn returned to China, where the daughter of the king slept in a dungeon cell. He brought her back to the first djinn, who placed her next to the prince. The two djinn could not agree on who was more beautiful, even when they were side by side. Then one of them had the idea of judging their beauty by their reaction of each to the other. First, they woke the prince.

"Upon his awakening, the prince saw the beautiful maiden asleep by his side and declared, 'If this is the woman my father wishes me to marry, I withdraw my objections. I will readily marry her.' He tried to wake her, but to no avail. Finally, he removed her ring to wear as a token. After his djinn returned him to sleep, the second djinn woke the princess. She saw the sleeping prince and was struck by his beauty. 'If this is the man my father wishes me to marry, I will gladly do so.' She also tried to wake him and failed. The second djinn returned her to sleep.

"The first djinn said, 'There is no judging between their beauty. Alas for us.'

"The second djinn returned the princess to her cell. Upon awakening, she announced that she would be willing to marry the prince she had seen that night. Her father was delighted, but no one knew of where he could be found. Her brother agreed to search the world for him, knowing he would be wearing her ring."

Gwen grimaced. All that had happened to her had come from her venturing forth to save her own brother from the consequences of her father's sin. People were better off solving their own problems.

Rayhana continued her story. "The princess's brother finally heard rumors of the prince and of his story, and decided that this foreign prince may be the man he sought. He set sail, knowing that he could travel faster by ship. He was in sight of the palace when a terrible storm arose, grounding his ship on rocks—"

A young woman slipped through the door curtain in to the room. "Excuse me, mistress, there are two men at the door, sent by the master of the palace guard."

Gwen jumped up, quickly followed by Adelie.

"Thank you." Rayhana gestured toward the door. "Follow me."

"Thank you for the lovely story," said Élise. "It is a shame you didn't have time to finish it."

Gwen looked about her as they passed back through the corridors, listening to Élise and Rayhana discussing what happened to the brother of the princess with loud chuckles. She looked at the lovely spiraled columns, illuminated by oil lamps hanging within a colored glass mosaic. Beauty she had distanced from in her shame, beauty that made her long for Wigandus to share it with.

They passed through one of the arches into a large garden, lit by oil lamps hanging from metal poles cast to look like trees. Gwen wished it was daylight and she could see if any of the plants bore flowers. Palm crowns fanned overhead, casting many-fingered shadows across their path.

Wigandus! Gwen's heart raced. He stood next to David under a palm tree, both men breathing heavy, splotches of blood on their clothes. Was he hurt? Gwen's gaze followed Adelie as she rushed to David and embraced him. Gwen swallowed. She wanted to kill Wigandus for leaving her to go to the caliph. Yet, she longed to rush to him and hold him in her arms like Adelie did. She hesitated, tossed into the stormy sea of her feelings.

"Where's Britomar?" Galiana asked.

"She's gone straight for the boat," said Wigandus. "Al-Rashid went with her, to make certain all is ready for us. We should leave right away."

David and Adelie, hand in hand, rejoined them. "We'll need to go quickly; there are patrols all over the city," said David.

Rayhana led them to a door in the garden wall. Stepping into the alley, Wigandus drew his sword. "Follow me, and keep your weapons ready."

Gwen wished she had learned to use a knife or sword. At least this city had no street lamps like Antioch—perhaps they'd slip through under the cover of dark? She could sort out the joy and the rage she felt toward Wigandus later, when they were safe.

They trotted down the meshwork of streets, until the wall became visible in the gray moonlight. As they neared, David called to them in Arabic, and the guards opened the gates.

They passed through the gate, which closed behind them, into the warren of shacks and warehouses that sprawled between the southern gate and the two rivers. As they trotted, Gwen could hear Sir Wigandus counting intersections, changing direction when he reached the number he was looking for. They turned one last time and saw the river, gleaming in the moonlight.

"Allah Akbar!" A small patrol stepped from a side street and drew their scimitars.

"Al-Rashid!" bellowed Sir Wigandus as he rushed the patrol. David and Adelie were just steps behind him, weapons at ready.

Gwen held her breath as Wigandus's sword brought down two of the guards in one blow, one bleeding and one shaking his head trying to rise. The scimitar from the fallen guard slid to Élise, who stooped to pick it up. Two guards slashed at Wigandus. He parried one, pushing him into the path of the other. David fell to his knee as he blocked a scimitar. Rising, he pulled on the arm of his assailant, stabbing up and in. Adelie caught a scimitar with her knife, slid under it and stabbed. She whirled to catch another blade as a scimitar sliced at her head but fell to the ground as another's blade caught her on the legs.

Gwen saw movement out of the corner of her eye.

"Élise, what are you—?"

Motion seemed to have slowed to Gwen's eyes... A scimitar lifting over Adelie's shaking head... Élise diving over Adelie's body, her scimitar raised to strike...

"No!" screamed Gwen.

The scimitar aimed for Adelie sliced into Élise's neck. Her blood erupted in a fountain, covering Adelie in a crimson rain.

"Élise!" Gwen cried.

Adelie rolled out from under her fallen sister, screaming as she rose. Knives flashed, catching the scimitar and tearing it out of the man's hand. She slashed at his belly, sending the man writhing in the crimson dirt.

Gwen crawled to where Élise lay. Ignoring the slashing and screaming of the ongoing battle, she lifted Élise's head into her lap, pressing her skirts against the slice in her neck. *Oh, Élise.*

"Britomar!" she shouted, raising her head to search for the unicorn. The battle was dispersing around them as Gwen watched in relief Britomar running toward her. *It will be fine. The unicorn is here. Nothing is impossible for the healing power of a unicorn.*

Britomar trotted over, then hung her head. "I'm too late."

Gwen froze, silent tears welling in her eyes.

"No!" Adelie ran to Britomar and started hitting her with her fists. "No! You're a unicorn! You're pure! You healed Wigandus! You abandoned her once, I'll not suffer it again! Heal my sister!"

Britomar laid her horn on Élise.

Nothing happened.

Adelie picked up her knives, wiping them clean on the robe of a dead guard. "Don't wait for me, I'm going to slit the throat of their caliph!"

David blocked her path. "Then kill me too. You know you will not survive if you attempt this revenge. I cannot live without you."

Adelie dropped her knives, fell to her knees and began to cry. David knelt and held her, Adelie burying her face in his shoulder.

Gwen looked up as she heard the pounding of feet.

"Al-Rashid!" called Wigandus.

"Wigandus!" shouted Al-Rashid running toward them. "You must come at once to the boat! It's our only hope! There's another patrol coming, larger than this one."

"Élise," said Gwen, "We can't leave her."

"No, Gwen, we won't." Wigandus lifted Élise's limp body from Gwen's lap. The bleeding had stopped. Elise's face was creamy white, her eyes closed as if in sleep. Gwen stifled a sob as she rose from the ground to follow Wigandus.

"One of the Maidens?" Al-Rashid shook his head. "Allah forgive me, this has been an ill day. I lost two of my closest friends taking the boat. Come, we have not a moment to lose."

Wigandus placed Élise on Britomar's back and they all ran to where the boat lay waiting.

As they settled on the boat, Gwen saw the blood on the hem of her skirt and started to cry, unable to hold back tears anymore. A miracle had saved her. Where was the miracle for Élise? Galiana put an arm around her, but she couldn't stop crying. Élise shouldn't have come. She should have run off with Martis like in the songs she was always singing, she should have gone to the husband who would now wait for her in Armenia in vain. A woman's death, her love broken—all to save a unicorn? Was this quest truly worth it? No one should have to die for a beast!

The boat rocked against its moorings. Al-Rashid took Élise down from Britomar's back, and then leapt onto the boat. He laid her next to two slain men and folded her hands over her chest. Gwen heard a familiar flutter of wings and braced for the Raven to land on her shoulder, but instead the bird landed on Élise.

Once all were on board, two men wearing the armor of the palace guards untied the ropes and pushed the boat away from the river's edge, waving their farewell. Al-Rashid sat at the tiller, while others hoisted the sail. As the sun rose over the banks of the Tigris, they sped away from Baghdad with no other boat in sight.

"I'm not going on," said Gwen, staring at Élise's corpse. "I'm going home."

"Liebchen!" said Wigandus.

"I can't," sobbed Gwen, "I can't."

"Then you take away the meaning of her death," said Galiana.

"No I don't. She died so Adelie could live for David! I want to live for Wigandus. I want to raise his children." She turned to face the knight, and took his hands. "Let's go home, marry, and have a daughter to remember Élise by. Why can't we know happiness when even that horrible man, the caliph, has a home, wives and children?"

Wigandus knelt and put her hand against his heart. "Liebchen I call you, my little love. I swore on all that was holy to protect you and to remain virginal until you entered the Garden. I can't break that oath. I swore to keep it with my life. I love you, Gwenaella. Right now you're angry. We all are. But if you and I turn around right now, I won't be the same man who saved you from Sir Bryon. I'll become like he was when I fought him, without honor. You won't be the same woman I saved; you'll become what he accused you of being, someone who puts self before others."

Gwen found herself shaking. "That Godforsaken promise of yours! What wouldn't I give for a man who breaks his word to God to keep his word to me. Because of that promise you value so highly, I was taken, stripped, chained for the caliph's pleasure! I was nearly raped because of your damned vow!"

"But the vial David—"

"That vial stayed clenched useless in my hands as I was chained to the bed. Damn you! Damn your promises!"

Wigandus turned and walked away, head hung low.

Galiana stood up and slapped Gwen on the cheeks. "How dare you! You had a miracle to save you that day! Where was the miracle that could have kept me from a lifetime of being raped for coin? Where was the miracle that caught the blade that sliced Élise's life from her? And you dare to damn the man who went brokenhearted into slavery because he believed David, because he believed that blood would keep you safe? Damn you! Blood kept you safe!"

Gwen slid off the bench to the deck of the boat, holding herself as she sobbed. She couldn't explain to Galiana the rage she felt towards Wigandus, she didn't understand it herself. David lifted her and set her back on the bench. "Don't turn your back on the good you are doing because Élise died. People die every day, and less nobly. You need to live, not to run. It is up to you to preserve the last living fragment of Eden, a holy task bestowed on you by Heaven. Don't run from that because some of us may die along the way. We all knew the risk when we decided to come."

Gwen looked out to the riverbank as the sky turned the pale blue of dawn. As tears dropped from her eyes into the river, causing small ripples that were soon lost in the boat's wake, she silently cursed Wigandus for being right. For always being right.

Adelie slid next to her, placing an arm around her shoulder. Gwen turned to Adelie and embraced her. Adelie broke down sobbing. "I never knew what she felt like when I saved her life. I never knew how small it made her feel."

Gwen shook her head. "I don't think it did. You saved my life and that did not make me feel small. I think she was in awe of you and how capable you are with those knives."

"I'd give that up to be able to sing like her." Adelie wiped her eyes.

Galiana's voice from behind them startled Gwen. "No you wouldn't. Not if you think about it. David loves you for who you are. Don't you realize how precious that is?"

"I'm just a gutter spawn," said Adelie. "We all knew how to fight. That is how we survived."

"You chose to be that, instead of taking the easy way, like I did. There isn't a day that I don't see you and wonder what my life would be if I had chosen to hide in the gutters and fight, instead of selling my body for false comfort and security. In the harem, while Gwen was with the caliph, Élise told me that you were an inspiration to her. You gave her the courage to admit that it had been Garsenda she had loved, and that Garsenda had broken her heart. You helped her see how to take a situation most would look down upon with disgust and make something good of it.

"As for you, Gwen, what makes you think you can just give up on us like that? What right do you have to say that we can't choose to give up our lives to save the eldest of unicorns? What gives you the right to walk out on all of that hope?"

Gwen forced herself to look Galiana in the eyes and was surprised by the anger she found there. "Any one of you can do this. Any one of you can reach the Garden, walk its paths. What makes you think it must be me? You can go on without me. You don't need me to save the eldest unicorn."

"We need each other. Yes, any one of us can do this, but not if we don't help each other. You were called in a dream, so was Garsenda, so was I." Adelie looked Gwen in the face. "Élise was never called, but she gave her life so that we all could go on. When Élise saved you from the demon, you begged us to come with you. Now we're begging. We can't do this without you, Gwen."

Gwen wiped her eyes. "I'm sorry. You're right, Galiana is right. Wigandus is right. I'll go on."

She looked for Wigandus but couldn't find him. Could he forgive her angry words? Could she forgive him for not being there when she needed him? Could she forgive him for always being right?

Could she bear to live if she couldn't? Her heart was at sea and she was lost in the storm.

BEING AND BECOMING

Adelie wrapped Élise in white cotton, translucent from the wet of her tears. Gwen and Galiana helped her move the body so she could wrap the torso, each silent in their sorrow. They had no priest. Her sister would be laid to rest in the brown waters of the Tigris, unshriven.

It bothered Adelie that her sister's harp graced the halls of the caliph. She hoped it would cut the hands of any who tried to bring music to its strings. She kissed Élise's cold still lips, a final farewell. It was strange to her that in death Élise bore a smile she never had in life, a smile of peaceful joy. Adelie remembered how twisted her sister's face had been during her illness, those long days in the wagon as they fled Antioch.

Her sister's head enshrouded, she tore off the cloth and tucked it under a fold. Would her betrothed prince, would her father ever know the sacrifice Élise had made? If Adelie could, she'd send them word. Élise should be remembered with words raised in song, not with tears lost in the river.

She stepped away from the corpse and felt David take her hand. She squeezed it. Élise had been so happy at their wedding. And now, she will never see her sister again.

As Wigandus lifted Élise's shrouded corpse from the deck and gently lowered it over the rail into the river water, she sobbed and buried her face in her husband's shoulder.

Galiana sat at the prow of the boat, away from the others. She had spent most of her days alone, eating little and not talking much, other than polite nothing when she picked up her food. The words she had used to help Adelie and Gwen recover their self-worth had eaten at her own sense of self. Had she ever made a choice she could be proud of, before Britomar came into her life? And even since the time she had chosen to follow Britomar, what had she done beyond following?

Could hell be worse than what her life has been?

261

"What do you see, when you look at the waves?" asked Al-Rashid, who had come to join her.

"Oblivion," she said without turning.

A pause. "Do you mind if I sit and talk with you?"

She shrugged. "It's your boat."

He settled down next to her, crossing his legs with the ease of someone used to sitting on the floor, "Amongst my people, a woman of your beauty would never be alone. She would have the pick of lovers."

She looked up. "I have found my beauty more a curse than a blessing."

His smile made her blush.

"This is a terrible thing," he said. "Would sharing your story help?"

Her mouth twitched. "What could the former captain of the palace guard find of interest in a whore's story?"

"You were not always a whore, and you're not one now. I was once a slave, until my former master, Allah bless his name, rewarded me with my freedom. I am familiar with degradation."

"A slave does not choose his slavery."

"This is not true." Al-Rashid frowned briefly. "I could have tried to escape, but I found my life too dear to risk it. I have seen too much death to mistake it with freedom."

"How so?"

"My master was a powerful sorcerer. He commanded demons of unimaginable terror, and would summon the spirits of the damned to serve him."

"What use would such a man have for a slave?"

"He used me to gather what he needed from the market, to protect him during his incantations and while he slept." His countenance faded into a scowl as his voice lowered. "I could have slain him any night, and there were many times when I wanted to."

"What stopped you?"

"To do murder is not right in the eyes of Allah, even though it were to gain me my freedom."

"Did it not ever occur to you that removing a sorcerer from the world may be pleasing to this Allah of yours?"

His smile returned, and Galiana was surprised by the joy it brought her. "I wondered at that, but thought perhaps that the injunction against doing murder was too strong to ignore."

She opened her mouth to mock him by pointing out that he'd rather obey some fool god than seek freedom, but something stopped her.

"So what great deed did you do to earn your freedom?" she asked instead.

"My master used to frequent a number of whores. One of them was sleeping in my master's bed when he summoned a demon of terrible strength. It was too strong for my master and broke free of his control. It went for the woman, and I gained this in her protection." Al-Rashid opened his shirt to reveal three long scars across his abdomen. "My master sutured me with his own hands, and wept as he did so. When I was strong enough to move about, I learned that he had destroyed all his equipment and burned all his grimoires. He had also married this whore, and freed me as his thanks for saving her life. He told me that he had never known what love was until he almost lost her, and that in knowing love, he could never again practice the dark arts."

Galiana frowned. "Why are you telling me this?"

"You asked me how I could be interested in you."

"But—I didn't ask... You're interested in me?" She drew away. "Go away, I'm not going to be your whore."

He shook his head. "I don't want you to"

"Nor your lover."

He smiled. "I am not interested in you that way." He blushed, pink rising over his thick black beard. "I can't. I'm no eunuch, but amongst women I am cursed, unmanned. No, I came to you because I find you interesting. You alone of your companions puzzle me."

Galiana looked at him with curiosity—and pity. Such a handsome man, cursed so evilly. It must be terrible for him. And yet, she felt safer around him after his confession. It was nice to have a companion on this boat who found her interesting and did not resent her for her past.

The water started to get choppy and the boat began to rock. Al-Rashid grabbed onto the ship's railing to steady himself.

"I truly respect you for being so unique in this group. Everyone else was chosen for a purpose—Gwen as the leader of this quest, Sir Wigandus as her champion and protector. Elise was the visionary and poet, the best of the aristocracy, Adelie is the knight errant and the doer, and David is her champion and wise councilor. You—you joined them of your own free will, and have stayed with them despite two opportunities to become associated with a royal house."

Galiana swallowed. "In Britomar I thought I saw something pure. She accepted me without question. How could I not follow her?"

Al-Rashid smiled. "Ah, so you are the mystic, the dreamer."

"I'm sorry, I don't understand," she stammered. "I have never..."

"You alone are following the purity, instead of being on a mission to return the eldest of unicorns to health."

They were both quiet for a few minutes, staring at the waves breaking on the prow. The sea had become quite rough, despite no clouds, and little wind.

"You told me something I did not know about myself," said Galiana.

At that moment, a huge form emerged from the waves in front of the boat. Galiana screamed.

Gwen heard a scream from the prow and looked up to see a colossal creature covered with stone-gray scales rise from the depths of the see. It had four eyes and two hideous mouths surrounded by many tentacles.

Gwen gasped. She had heard of these monsters from the fishermen's tales.

Al-Rashid shielded the screaming Galiana and drew his scimitar. Wigandus pushed his way past Gwen and strode to Al-Rashid's side, his sword at the ready.

"Stop! Wait!" Gwen shouted. "You can't hurt it with swords!"

"Then what in Allah's Holy name would you have us do?" asked Al-Rashid. "Offer it one of my men as sacrifice for safe passage?"

Gwen scrambled toward them over the yawing deck. "I think it wants me. My father did something terrible to a mermaid. The merfolk have been trying to avenge her on his children. And it stops *now*." She pushed the men aside and lifted her hands to her mouth. "Creature of the sea, hear me!"

A tentacle froze before her.

"I am Gwenaella, a maid on a sacred quest of healing! I swear on all that is Holy that when I am free of my errand for the eldest of unicorns, I will serve whatever penance is needed to atone for my father's deeds!"

"No, Gwen!" cried Sir Wigandus.

"I have to. Look!" She pointed and they all saw the creature disappear into the waves.

She sighed. So much for her hopes of marriage and peaceful life. Still, she was grateful to the monster for one thing; at least Wigandus was talking to her again.

"You must make amends for what your father did?" asked Galiana.

Gwen lowered her head. "My father took a mermaid as a lover, and then stole from her. I don't know exactly why the thing he stole was so precious to her, but they tried killing my brother because of this. That's why I first sought Britomar, to restore his health. I think they're now angry at me for preventing their revenge. My father's debt to the mermaid must have passed to me, and they are trying to collect it whenever I am near water. A creature attacked me on the Danube, and threatened our ship as we journeyed to Antioch. I guarantee you that if I had not made this vow, those tentacles would have come for me and me alone."

"You never told us of this," said Sir Wigandus. "It was reckless of you to speak to this creature. You could have been wrong."

"Yes, I could have. I hoped and prayed I was. I hoped to keep my father's shame his own." Gwen looked at Adelie, locked in David's embrace. "I will not have anyone else die, if by any deed of mine it can be prevented." *I'll also not have any more secrets hidden.* David had told Wigandus of his dream, and still Wigandus had let her go unwed into the caliph's hall. Had Wigandus acted as David had, she'd be holding him too.

Astonished and shaken, Galiana held Al-Rashid close. Warm, safe. Since when did she find comfort in a man's arms? She looked up into his eyes and said, "You've told me what the role of the others is on this quest; what is your role, Al-Rashid?"

He smiled. "Galiana, that is simplicity in itself. I am your champion and defender."

He stepped away from her, bowed, sheathed his scimitar, and joined the others. She was alone again. She shivered, looking at his retreating back. She didn't come on this quest to find a champion and defender; she needed a reason for being. Yet, having this dashing, capable man proclaim himself her champion made her feel strangely warm inside.

That night, Galiana woke while the stars were still bright in the void. Chilled, she wrapped her blanket around her. She looked at David curled beside Adelie and thought of yesterday, when Al-Rashid held her. She had never been held—taken often, but never just held. She turned to look at Al-Rashid who slept further aft, and wondered if he'd hold her again.

She made her way aft and lay down next to him, sliding her hand under his tunic. Once she found his penis, she began to gently stroke it with her fingertips. After a while she started to drift back to sleep, but was startled as she felt a strong hand grip her wrist and gently move her hand away. She looked into his eyes. He smiled as he placed her hand on his chest, and turned to hold her. Rolling over, so his arms were wrapped around her, she fell asleep.

Galiana woke to see dawn creeping over the prow. Al-Rashid's arm was still wrapped around her, his hand still held her wrist, though gently. She cuddled closer, his stiffness pushing at her through her skirt. She smiled. Unmanned with women indeed! The liar!

She pulled away from him. His eyes opened.

"You've broken the curse!" he said softly, looking at her with wonder.

"I did not believe you," she confessed. "No man should ever be cursed this way. How did it happen?"

"While in my former master's service, I angered a witch who was visiting him. She cursed me that I'd never again be able to be a man with a woman. My master took pity on me, but to no avail. I've tried ointments, herbs, fasting, and whoring... Why did you lay with me last night?"

"I wanted to be held."

"That's no reason to caress me."

"I guess I also wanted to..." Galiana felt her cheeks blush and tried not to chuckle at her incredulous embarrassment. How could a whore be embarrassed about sex? "I guess I wanted to see if what you said was a lie."

He shook his head. "Men must have hurt you so much if you felt the need to test my words. There is no God but Allah, and what has happened to me now is nothing short of a miracle. But you probably won't believe that. Allah forbid, but I fear that you must now think me a liar instead of marveling at my cure."

She drew back. "How can I believe that a whore like me could do a miracle? It is easier to believe you lied to me."

"Is it indeed? Why couldn't a whore who changed her life to follow purity do miracles?... Is there any way to win your trust? How can I prove to you that what I say is true?"

Galiana was surprised to find tears at the corners of her eyes. "I have spent my entire life expecting lies, for that is what I lived."

"Yet when you saw Britomar, you followed her blindly. You neither knew nor cared where her path leads you. Galiana, open your eyes. Can't you see that you've become holy?"

"A sinner like me? No."

His frown unwound into a smile. "It is your humility alone that makes it true."

"I am no more a holy woman than you are. I want you, Al-Rashid.

I want you the way a woman wants a man. This is why I lay with you, caressed you. Please don't let my doubts keep you from me. Last night, I woke and found myself alone. I don't want to be alone again."

Al-Rashid bowed. "Both my sword and I are at your service."

Galiana looked at him with wonder. Yesterday all she wanted was oblivion. Today, she wanted to live again. Could this be love? Could a whore learn to love?

Gwen stood next to Adelie, peering from under the canopy stretched across the deck to keep away the rain. She strained her eyes, hoping to see anything distinct on the gray horizon.

"I think we are lost," said Gwen. "We have not seen the stars for days, nor the shore. If this rain does not end soon, we may never see land again."

"Have you talked to Al-Rashid about this?" asked Adelie.

"Yes. He showed me an iron rod set in a piece of wood floating in a bowl. He claims that this rod always shows him which way north lies. Even if what he says is true, that does not tell him how far from the shore we are. I don't think he understands how dangerous it is to travel by sea."

"Hoi!" came the call from David, who was sitting at the prow serving as a lookout. "Light in the distance!" He lowered the long tube he was looking through and handed it to Al-Rashid.

"It is a harbor," Al-Rashid said. "Everyone grab an oar! Lets steer toward that light!"

Gwen went to the prow, stumbling as the boat pitched and yawed in the heavy surf. "Al-Rashid, you're much stronger than me, and I'll spot the rocks faster. Let me sit lookout, go and take an oar."

He offered her the tube he had placed at his eye, but she wanted no part of it. Ever since Galiana had told her of his slavery and how he gained his freedom, Gwen secretly suspected him of sorcery. She sat and wrapped a rope around her left hand, in case she was washed overboard. Sorcerer or not, Muslim or not, he had saved them all in Baghdad. She looked over at David, and remembered her talk with the rabbi in his village that made her feel ashamed about her prejudice against the Jews. It should be easier this time to put aside her doubts about a man of a different faith.

It took hours of rowing through the storm-swept seas, but before nightfall they finally passed the breakers and entered the quieter waters of the harbor.

As the boat stopped rocking so violently, Al-Rashid once again came to the prow and held that tube to his eye.

"This is not the harbor on the banks of the Indus river. Gwenaella, I would value your judgment, please look through and tell me what you make of this place."

Sighing with resignation and forcing herself to trust him, Gwen took the tube and placed it to her eye, as she had seen him do. "Eeek!" she screamed, dropping the tube. "How did it make everything so close!"

"Look," he said, picking up the tube and showing her an end. "There is a glass at each end. These are shaped so that they make things far away appear closer. Here, look again."

Her hand shaking, Gwen again lifted the glass to her eye. The streets and houses of the harbor town rushed toward her, so close that she felt she could touch them if she stretched her hand.

"This is a marvelous device. With this and that iron pin, I could easily believe you a sorcerer."

"Thankfully, this humble one is not cursed with such skills," said Al-Rashid. "These things are common to our sailors. What do you think of this place ahead of us?"

She looked closely at the city she had seen. "I see a large bay with a chain of sizable islands at the entrance. Most of the lights are on the islands. We should wait out the storm here and the bring the ship closer to those islands."

Al-Rashid nodded. "I see the same thing. We're much further south than I was trying to take us. I don't know these waters. Should we land or should we set out north?"

"Let's talk to the others," she said.

After Gwen had acquainted everyone with what they knew of their location, David asked, "How many days of rations do we have left?"

Adelie, who had taken on the role of the ship's cook, said, "We have a week's worth of human rations, but only two days' worth of oats for Britomar. Unless the Indus river is close by, we must go ashore to purchase provisions."

"I can go some days without eating, if that would help," offered Britomar.

"I don't know how far south we've come in the storm," said Al-Rashid. "The trouble is that none of us speak the language of these barbarians. How can we purchase anything if we can't speak with them?"

"We should make an attempt," suggested David. "We may succeed. Failing that, we can still try to make our way north."

There was a loud splash to the aft of the vessel. They all turned to the sound, Adelie drawing her knives as she did so. In a moment, Sir Wigandus and Al-Rashid stood next to her, their weapons drawn.

A slim woman climbed on board at the stern of the ship, dressed only in a loincloth. She was brown of skin, with long black hair clinging to her wet body, and a red dot in the middle of her forehead. She brought her hands together before her bosom and pressed them together, as if in prayer.

MUMBAIDEVI

Galiana could not take her eyes off the woman who stood before them. Water streamed from her long wet hair over two small firm breasts. She showed no shame at being so exposed.

"Namaste," she said, bowing. "Lakshmidevi said I would find amongst you a one-horned mare in need of my guidance to the Roof of the World. I am Kavundi, and I place myself at your service."

Galiana found herself suddenly embarrassed, as if being clothed in the presence of this almost naked stranger was an obscenity. She hastily grabbed a blanket and brought it to Kavundi, wrapping it around the woman's shoulders.

"Thank you." Kavundi smiled but unwrapped herself, handing back the blanket. "I am foresworn against, and have no need of garment."

Gwen stepped forward. "I am Gwenaella, and I am the one-horned mare's chosen maid. Her name is Britomar. How is it that you know our destination, and speak our language?"

"The Goddess came to me and touched my lips. She told me of your need, and where I could find you. I rose from my meditation and swam directly to you so I could offer my services."

Britomar stepped forward so that Kavundi could see her. "You serve your Goddess well. I am Britomar, and I do seek the World's Roof. I will be glad of any help you can offer in reaching it."

"Don't follow this immodest heathen, Britomar," said Al-Rashid, "What she claims as a goddess is a demon, and she is of a proscribed people, an anathema to Allah. Besides, have we not a document that tells us where the Garden is?"

Galiana wondered how he could find Kavundi immodest. The woman looked so pure, any sexual thoughts about her seemed impossible. Then again, could a man ever look at a scantly clad woman without desire?

"That document can't help us buy food or find the best path through the mountains," said Gwen turning to Al-Rashid. "I know nothing of Lakshmidevi, but the friar who set Britomar and me on

270

this errand said that we should seek help along the way, and that we should trust those who are willing to help us. We did not reject your help, Al-Rashid, though you are a Muslim. Nor did we reject David, though he is a Jew. How can we reject Kavundi, even though we don't understand how it is she came to stand before us, offering what we need?"

"Gwen is right," agreed Adelie. "Britomar, we should accept her help."

"And what do the rest of you think?" asked Britomar.

"David and I will abide by your judgment," said Sir Wigandus.

Adelie looked at Galiana, who shrugged. This stranger had more right to help than she did, how could she voice an objection?

"I also know nothing of Lakshmidevi," said Britomar. "Such things are for humans to reveal to us. Kavundi, I will follow you. How would you have us proceed? We understand that the World's Roof is in the north of your land."

"I suggest going over land through the Delhi Gate."

Al-Rashid shook his head. "Land routes are dangerous and slow. Isn't there a way to go by water?"

Kavundi hesitated. "It is possible to take this craft to the Indus river and follow it north. However, I do not believe it is the best way for you."

David said, "I agree with Al-Rashid. We should take the water route, after we provision ourselves. It has the advantage of speed and will bring us close to our destination before we need to risk exposing Britomar to human settlements."

Kavundi winced. "The sacred river runs through a large waste-land, through which we will have trouble finding pasture for Brito-mar at this time of year. If you were traveling soon after the yearly flood, you might manage it. I don't believe your ship can carry enough food to keep Britomar in good health before you find good pasture." Kavundi paused for a moment. "I see skepticism in your face, Al-Rashid."

"They have already passed through a large wasteland on their way to Baghdad," he answered. "They did this over land, following known caravan routes. Why could we not do this again?"

She sighed. "Because there is war in the Indus valley, between the children of the great Khan who have made Persia their own, and the Sultans who rule from the Delhi gate. The needs of this war have brought famine to the land. I did not wish to mention this, as it only speaks ill of your people, Al-Rashid."

Al-Rashid turned red, but said nothing.

"Then we will take the land route," Britomar said.

Gwen said, "I don't think it wise for all of us to go with Kavundi into the city to purchase supplies. Britomar's presence should be kept as secret as we can. A small group of us should go on the ship's boat and purchase what we need."

"How shall we pay for the food?" said David. "We're beyond the reach of my family's trade network."

"Have no worry on this account," Kavundi said. "Lakshmidevi will provide. Nor will we have to go into the city. Food awaits us in a nearby temple."

"I will go with Kavundi," said Adelie. "I know what we need."

"Al-Rashid and I will also go," said David. "If nothing else, you'll need us to help carry the supplies."

"It is settled then. Let us all get some rest," said Al-Rashid.

Shortly after dawn, Adelie climbed into the prow of the small boat. Kavundi sat next to her as Al-Rashid took the oars, David taking the tiller.

The large town they approached consisted of square brown buildings standing close to each other. A mountainous structure of stone towered over them, every inch of it carved with statues. As they got closer, Adelie noticed that many of the statues portrayed naked women with large melon-shaped breasts. Some of them wore necklaces of skulls and skirts of severed human hands. She shuddered in horror, wondering if Al-Rashid was right. Was this Lakshmidevi some demon that devoured people?

Kavundi instructed the men to row past the city to a smaller island further ahead. As the boat passed by, Adelie watched the crowds in the city streets with fascination. The women wore outlandish garments, long strips of bright-colored cloths in vivid reds and purples, wrapped around their bodies and draped over one shoulder. Many had a red dot painted on their foreheads; others had vertical red stripes. Men were dressed more sensibly, in light purple trousers and loose shirts. Red and white vertical stripes adorned their foreheads. Some had shaved their heads; others wore long hair and beards. Many men were bare from their waists up, their bare torsos often covered in white powder... Ashes? Adelie gasped, barely able to turn her head fast enough to take in the amazing sights.

"Why do these cows have bells on their horns?" she asked as they passed by a small herd of cows driven by a young man.

"Cows are sacred to us," Kavundi replied. "They bring life."

To Adelie, anxious to get back on the ship, it felt like it took forever to reach the island Kavundi insisted they make for. Adelie
peered ahead, searching for any buildings or settlements, but the
place seemed all but deserted. Why did Kavundi take them here, instead of going to the city which was much closer to their ship? How
would they acquire the supplies they needed in the absence of people? Adelie started to suspect the worst as Kavundi directed the boat
to a small dock.

As they pulled up to the pier, Kavundi leapt onto it and lashed
their boat to a piling. She reached down and helped Adelie climb out
of the boat. David followed, averting his eyes.

"How can you walk about in just your loin cloth?" he asked.

Kavundi smiled. "I am a sannyasi, what you call a nun. I have
rejected all material things in my devotions, including clothing. I
used to wear a kavi, but as I've progressed toward enlightenment,
I've abandoned even that and am content with just this kaupinam.
The world is my garment; my hand, my begging bowl; the earth, my
bed."

"Is there no risk of rape?" Adelie asked.

"Sri Vishnu will protect me. I have no reason to fear the world's
violence, as I do no violence within the world." Kavundi smiled.
"Besides, Madhvacharya teaches his students to wrestle."

They made their way up the stone path cut into the rock of the
island until they found themselves before a set of arched entrances
to what appeared to be caves. Beneath one arch sat a well muscled
man, bare from the waist up, his legs crossed. His shaven head had
a red line painted above his nose.

He rose, brought the palms of his hands together in front of him,
and bowed.

Kavundi returned the bow. "Namaste, Madhvacharya. These are
some of the companions to the one-horned mare, David ben Yusef
and Al-Rashid."

"Namaste. I greet the god within all of you."

Al-Rashid put his hand on the hilt of his scimitar. "There is no
God save Allah."

"Al-Rashid, Sri Vishnu told me of your skepticism," said Madhvacharya. "Your God is also our God. For you, He is Allah; for
me, He is Narayana. Address Him by any name you choose; the
Lord will answer your prayers."

Al-Rashid frowned. "You blaspheme."

"If you are unable to let go of your anger against those who call
Him Narayana, Vishnu, or any name other than Allah, you will cause

the failure of your errand. Aren't the names of Allah innumerable?"

Al-Rashid drew his scimitar and placed its edge against Madhvacharya's neck. "Allah teaches us not to worship idols, but only He. How can Allah and Narayana be the same?"

Madhvacharya smiled as if he had a blade at his neck frequently and it was of no concern. "Doesn't Allah say in the Quran that you are permitted to befriend those who don't attack your faith?"

"Al-Rashid, put down your blade," said David. "Though I might ask the same question of our host. While we also call Him by many names, we know Him as He who is, and make no graven images. Do you really claim that you worship the one true God, and yet make images and offer them sacrifice?"

"Is not the nature of your soul different than that of God? He makes all things holy, even the very stones. It is in the contemplation of these things that we learn more of His nature. It is not the stone we worship when we do reverence to Shiva Linga, but to Sri Shiva as he is revealed to us in the stone. It is much the same as when you, Al-Rashid as a good Muslim, stand before the holy Qabaa in Mecca. It is not the building that you do reverence to, but nevertheless, you find Allah there."

Al-Rashid lowered his blade, but did not sheath it.

Madhvacharya said, "Please, come inside. We have gathered food for you and your one-horned mare."

A large statue of a dancing man with many arms dominated the cave. Woven baskets filled with rice and lentil were set around it, next to large bales of hay. No meat, Adelie noted as her stomach churned with hunger. There were other baskets filled with things Adelie didn't recognize, but Kavundi had been honest with them. They were well provided for.

Kavundi followed her gaze. "I hope you and your friends find it sufficient. I know that your people usually pack meat rations on their travels, but we do not have any meat to offer you. Eating flesh is not good Karma."

"Thank you for this gift," said David.

"We are glad to help," Madhvacharya said. "The plight of the one-horned stallion is one that rends the hearts of all good people. Kavundi will take you to a place not far from here where you can offload from your ship in secrecy. You will find beasts of burden waiting for you there."

Gwen looked up from mending a rent in the sail and saw Galiana staring at the distant town that the boat had gone to. She put down the canvas and went to her, putting her hand on Galiana's shoulder.

"What?" asked Galiana.

"You looked lonely."

Galiana sighed. "Is it that obvious? Gwen, I've never missed a man in all my days."

"Al-Rashid?"

"Yes. Half the time he's around I want to scream at him to make him go away. When he's not around, I feel empty and without purpose."

Gwen nodded. "I often felt this way when I first met Wigandus. It took me months of traveling with him before I realized I loved him." She wished she'd never spoken the angry words that still rang in her mind.

Galiana looked up at her. "You think I'm in love?"

Gwen smiled. "I think you're falling in love, yes."

"Damn him!"

"Why?"

"When Britomar came, I had hope I could leave men behind forever, forget what I'd become—"

Gwen put a finger on Galiana's lips. "Galiana, there is a difference between sex and love. He can't pull you back into what you once were, he can only help you fulfill yourself."

"I always wanted to think I could find fulfillment without sex, without a man."

"You can. Look at Kavundi, I doubt much she's ever needed a—" Gwen stumbled as the ship made a sudden jerk. She looked up. The sea was becoming choppy.

Galiana extended a hand, pulling Gwen to a seat next to her. "She strikes you that way too?"

Gwen smiled at the memory of Kavundi standing on the deck unashamed and nearly naked. "Yes. I just don't know how she manages."

Galiana grimaced. "I've stood naked before strangers, but never felt as self-assured when I did. I was always using my nudity, always flaunting it. She—she just stood there as if she were clothed."

Gwen heard Wigandus singing in the stern. She looked back, hoping to catch a glimpse of him, but she couldn't see him. The ship was tossing wildly, though there was not a cloud in the sky.

"I see you are also lonely," Galiana said.

"Yes, but having him near makes things worse. He promised me marriage, but has done nothing since."

"Why not go to him as a wife?"

Gwen didn't know if she'd forgiven him for letting her go to the caliph, but was not ready to admit that to another. "He is a very proud man. When we met, he swore a vow to protect Britomar and her companions and to remain virginal until I entered the Garden. This vow makes our marriage unthinkable to him until our quest is completed. I don't know how he'd react."

"That's fear talking," said Galiana.

"I know." Fear and panic, whenever she was near him.

One of the sailors cried out, the horror in his tone conveying all his words couldn't. Gwen looked up to see gray tentacles rising from the sea.

How could this be? She'd sworn a vow! The monster had backed off at her vow!

The sailors scrambled from their tasks to the deck cabin, drawing their scimitars. Gwen looked around wildly. Where was Wigandus?

She pulled Galiana away from the ship's rail as a tentacle whipped toward them.

"Gott im himmel!" Wigandus swung down a rope from the mast. His sword flashed, and the severed tentacle fell on the deck, thrashing and splattering blood. In a moment, the other sailors were by his side as more tentacles reached out to the women. Gwen heard a loud thump over the screaming and Britomar sped by her, rearing up on her hinds, hitting the tentacles with her hooves and slashing at them with her horn.

A tentacle had wrapped around Wigandus's waist, lifting him off the deck as he hacked at it. He severed it and fell to his feet, sword flashing to meet others reaching out from the murky depths.

"Wigandus! Behind you!" Gwen cried. He turned just as a large tentacle landed on his head, sending him down to the deck.

Gwen barely noticed the battle around her as she scrambled around and under the flailing tentacles, trying to reach Wigandus. Something cold and wet grabbed her on her ankle. She screamed and kicked at it, but it tightened its grip, lifting her off the deck.

"No!" she pleaded, kicking as she rose into the air. Her raven flew next to her but Gwen's eyes were fixed on the battle below, where Wigandus lay, where Britomar struggled against the five tentacles that tried to lift her off the boat.

Suddenly Gwen's foot kicked emptiness. The hold on her ankle disappeared, the hard wood of the deck rushing at her too fast. She closed her eyes and sobbed a plea to God.

Strong arms caught her and set her down upon the deck. Shaking her head, she opened her eyes and saw a naked woman with ash-gray skin and black feathers woven into her matted gray hair. She had the most beautiful face—a face Gwen remembered from somewhere.

The woman leapt over a tentacle, rolled and lifted a scimitar from a dead sailor's hand. Gwen backed away and froze as all the scimitars on the deck rose into the air and flew to the strange woman who caught them in... each of her seven other hands.

Eight hands? Gwen felt sick but fascinated as the woman lifted the scimitars and rushed at the tentacles with a growling scream that sent shivers down Gwen's spine.

The woman moved impossibly fast, slicing through the tentacles as others rose from the sea. One moment Britomar was being dragged overboard, the next the unicorn slashed with her horn, free again to fight against the monster from the depths.

As if realizing it had no other hope, fresh tentacles rose from the sea and grabbed hold of the ship. The woman turned to Britomar and shouted something to the unicorn. Gwen couldn't understand the words, but something in her heart broke at the sound, picking the edge of meaning, as if she had heard this language before. Britomar nodded and started slashing at the tentacles along the rail while the woman leapt from the ship's deck into the water.

Gwen pulled herself to her feet and grabbed a scimitar. Running to the other side of the ship she began to hack at the tentacles. Out of the corner of her eye, she saw Wigandus at her side, hacking at the tentacles that pulled at the hull. The ship shuddered, knocking Gwen to the deck. "Grab a rope!" she yelled, rolling along the deck until her hands clasped a rope. She held on for dear life as the ship shook violently.

Just as suddenly, the ship went still—and then resumed its gentle rocking with the waves of the bay. Gwen shivered and pulled herself to her feet. Wigandus edged toward her, sword raised. She looked at the deck. Here and there the sailors were rising to their feet, staring at the bodies of their comrades who would never rise again.

Britomar was nowhere to be seen.

David and Al-Rashid loaded the baskets and hay onto two carts that Madhvacharya provided, and began to pull the carts out of the temple. Adelie found herself walking back to the ship next to Kavundi.

"Are there many nuns like you?" asked Adelie.

"In the ancient days, there used to be. Madhvacharya is trying to restore to us that the way to live relates more to one's nature than to one's body, or to whom we are born."

Adelie nodded. "We also have women who dedicate their lives to God, but our nuns are different."

"How so?"

"Like you, they give up the world to serve God. But they cover their bodies to hide their sex, and live chaste, as virgin brides of God."

Kavundi smiled. "We too live chaste lives. Please don't confuse my rejection of clothes with sensuality. Such a life is for wives who honor Parvatidevi, or for dancing girls and prostitutes, devotees of Naitratmadevi."

"You may find that wearing clothes while you travel with us is an easier burden than to go as you are."

"Are you worried that much about your husband?"

Adelie lifted her chin. "Why would you think I'm worried about David?"

"Would you worry so much about the others?"

Adelie let out a sigh. "Yes, I suppose you're right. I worry about David."

"Why do you doubt yourself so much?"

"Kavundi, I grew up in the gutter. I am not of his people. He is the son of the second most respected man in his village. Why should he choose me?...No, do not interrupt. I am convinced that he married me only to save me from a fate worse than death."

"Is David the kind of man who would marry just to save someone's life? Would he have married Galiana for the same reason?"

Adelie paused, and then softly said, "No."

"See, when you think on the situation, all you have left are unfounded fears. I know nothing of the differences between your people, but he does. He still chose to marry you. You still chose to marry him. These are choices that are not something you do once. Keep choosing him and trust that he, in his love for you, will keep choosing you."

"Élise told me that. God, I miss her," said Adelie.

"Élise?"

"My sister. She was killed saving my life."

"Adelie, I believe you have lost your sense of self-worth because you grieve for your sister, and question your life with David because it does not feel right to you to enjoy happiness with him when it was her death which secured it."

Adelie walked next to her in silence for a moment, and then began to cry. Kavundi put her arm around Adelie's shoulders and held her as they walked.

Adelie wiped her eyes with her sleeve, and then said, "I wish I was wise, like you."

"You are a warrior, I am a nun, it is my Dharma. Both are valid paths. We each have need of each other, much like the head needs the hands."

After they arrived at the boat, they each helped move the baskets on board. The journey back to the ship was quiet, only the splashes of the oars cutting the water broke the silence.

When they rounded the cape and entered the harbor, Adelie's mouth fell open. Their ship in the middle of the bay rocked violently, engulfed in tentacles.

Al-Rashid dropped the oars and lifted his sighting tube to his eye. "What in the name of Allah is that?"

"What do you see?" urged Adelie.

"I see Wigandus and Gwen on deck chopping at the tentacles. Where are my—?"

Something bright rose from the ship and fell into the waters. Adelie gasped.

"What was that, Al-Rashid?" asked David.

"A multi-armed demon with scimitars. My men must have driven it into the sea." Al-Rashid put down his tube, lifted the oars and gave a strong pull. "I must add my scimitar to their defense."

Adelie's heart quickened at the thought of facing such a monster, her knives against the tentacles.

"That won't be necessary," said Kavundi. "Look."

The great mass of tentacles convulsed and released the ship, causing it to rise and fall again into the rough rhythm of the sea. The tentacles submerged, and in moments the bay was clear again, waters rippling peacefully to the slight touch of the breeze.

Nausea swept over Adelie. She leaned over the side of the boat, breathing heavily as she tried not to vomit.

Gwen rocked back and forth on her haunches. Britomar was gone. They failed to protect her, and now their quest to save the eldest of the unicorns was doomed. It had all been for nothing. All the death, all the suffering...Oh, Britomar. If only she had been strong enough to protect her.

Someone touched Gwen's shoulder...Wigandus.   "Leave me alone."

"Gwen—"

"Don't touch me." Fighting panic, she rose and ran from him sobbing, arms wrapped around herself. It was all wrong, it was all for nothing. How would she be able to live on after this?

She stopped sharply as loud raps echoed on the deck behind her. It sounded so much like...hooves! Britomar?...

Gwen turned, relief washing over her as she saw the unicorn prancing toward her over the deck. On her back sat the mysterious woman who had saved her—now with two arms, each of them still holding a scimitar...Of course, Gwen must have imagined it. No one could have eight arms!

The woman looked much older than Gwen initially thought, her face eerily familiar. Where could she have seen her before? She forced away the questions as she ran to the unicorn and embraced her, sobbing. Galiana appeared at her side.

They heard a sigh and the woman sitting on Britomar's back slowly collapsed. They rushed to her and tried to lift her, but the woman cried out in agony.

"Wigandus, please help us," called Galiana.

Gwen looked away as he approached. Only after she heard his footsteps fading did she look back to the woman sprawled on the deck, her head cradled in Galiana's lap. Gwen knelt and took the woman's hand, meeting her eyes.

A familiar sea smell washed over her, fresh and clear even on the deck of a sea-ridden ship. She remembered...the pain writ on the old woman's face...these clear blue eyes that haunted and guided Gwen's dreams ever since that unforgettable day when she returned home from the convent...

This was the same woman she had helped in Redon.

And, with this knowledge came another realization, so certain that Gwen shivered at the thought that she had failed to realize this before.

This was the First Woman herself, the one who called her to take on this unicorn quest.

Lilith.

"I've touched her with my horn, but her wounds won't heal," said Britomar.

Gwen stroked the unicorn's sea-wet mane. "You tried, that is all any of us can do."

"I'm sorry." Britomar hung her head.

"Oh, Britomar!"

"All these people dead when my touch can bring life. I've failed Garsenda and Élise, and now I've failed Lilith herself."

"You haven't failed me, dear girl," said the old woman faintly. "I made a choice. The merciful sister will be here soon, I won't regret giving her my hand."

"Ahoy!" came David's shout. "Is anyone alive up there?"

"Yes, I suppose we are," said Wigandus in reply. There was a thud and Gwen recognized the sound of a rope falling to the boat. The sorrow in the knight's voice made her shiver. She wished she could run to him, bury her face in his chest, and cry.

Footsteps echoed over the deck as Wigandus, Kavundi, David, Al-Rashid, and Adelie joined them around Lilith's broken body.

"Namaste, Mumbaidevi," said Kavundi.

"Namaste, Kavundi," whispered Lilith.

"She saved us all," said Gwen with a sob. "This is Lilith."

"Lilith!" gasped David.

The old woman smiled weakly. "Yes, David ben Yosi, I am Lilith."

"You know her?" asked Gwen.

"We tell stories of Lilith, Adam's first wife, mother of demons and devourer of uncircumcised babies."

Gwen looked at David, alarmed by his words. Did he really think the woman who had saved them was a devourer of babies?

"The Father of Lies has had much joy at my behalf." Lilith coughed up some blood. "I was Adam's wife when the world was new. I fled him in anger, out of pride."

Kavundi knelt down and kissed her on the forehead, "Rest, Mumbaidevi, let it go."

"I must say this. You must understand. Barren, I used to hate all Eve's children, turning those who sought me out into sorcerers, delighting in each of their deaths. Then the eldest of all unicorns, who alone shared my exile, fell ill—and I, who had breathed the air of unstained paradise, could do nothing. My one remaining student, Nimuë, spent herself in a mighty spell for nothing. Then she did something hateful—she turned to a servant of that divine fool.

"Do you know what it was like, hearing Nimuë beg for help—and *Eve* promising aid? Eve! My long-dead rival would send help for my friend!"

Lilith coughed, bubbles of blood breaking upon her breath. Gwen edged over and clasped Wigandus's hand.

"I watched as almost all of you were chosen by Eve. I watched as life was torn from Garsenda. I could have stopped it, her death held no joy for me. I did nothing. I watched as the demon took Elisabeth, showed her Sodom restored, and did nothing as he tormented her. I stood amazed as she chose to let herself be destroyed rather than give in to her desires one more time, so I brought her food to sustain her.

281

"When I saw the caliph's plans for you, for Britomar, I decided to help at last, and sent David that dream. I never imagined that Elisabeth—" Lilith coughed. "I watched as she took a sword that would have missed her sister, thinking she was saving Adelie's life. I could not have stopped her death—it happened too fast, and it shocked me to the core." Lilith shook with coughs, splattering blood.

"Mumbaidevi, rest," said Kavundi, placing her hand on Lilith's shoulder.

"No. I must say this. I will not die until I've said everything, and I long for death. When I saw the Father of Lies convince a leviathan to destroy you despite its acceptance of Gwen's promise, I couldn't stand by again. Elisabeth was right, if you love someone, you lay down your life for them. I remembered then that I can love.

"Gwenaella, you among all who travel with Britomar, you were my choice to reach Eden. After you helped me in Redon, I sent you to meet Nimuë. I beg you, don't let my friend die. I give his care and keeping into your hands. Let him walk amongst the children of Eve."

Gwen could only nod her ascent, tears streaming down her face. Élise hadn't died for nothing. Her death had saved them all.

Lilith's voice was very faint, Gwen had to strain her ears to hear her. "Eve? Is that you? Have you come for me?"

A voice in the wind said, "Lilith, sister, you know my other name."

"Yes," was Lilith's response. Her eyes closed and she sighed. Her lips mouthed a final "Yes."

As the First Woman let out her last breath, her body shifted, and Gwen briefly saw light pass through her. As the light faded, her body was gone, leaving nothing but a trace of red dust where Lilith had lain. A breeze filled with a voice beyond Gwen's hearing lifted her hair. The dust swirled in the breeze and disappeared.

Gwen turned to Wigandus and buried her face in his chest, sobbing, dismayed at how his hand on her back terrified her so.

Galiana felt Al-Rashid's warm hand clasp hers as Lilith became dust before them. Tears rolled down her face. Lilith had lived a life without men. It took an untimely death to remind her of love. Did Kavundi have love in her life? Was it possible to have love without opening yourself to the terrible risks of another within your life? Was love worth the price?

She turned to Al-Rashid, sinking into his embrace, sobbing for the death of a woman she never knew. She felt him sobbing too, and realized how many men he had lost today, how much blood had been spilt on the deck of his ship.

Only later, as they lowered the wrapped still bodies of his dead sailors into the placid waters, did she realize that she would not have been able to bear it if he too had died. She broke away from his embrace and ran to find a quiet spot to grieve over the death of Lilith, over the death of all those men, over the death of the woman she had once been.

NATEṢA

The following day they made for the far shore of the large bay. Galiana sat next to Gwen in the prow. She did not have Gwen's patience in the search for rocks and looked up frequently at the land they headed toward. She was desperate for anything to keep her mind from a good-bye she feared she was about to face. Al-Rashid had agreed to see them safely out of Baghdad, and had done that at a terrible cost. She couldn't see any reason he'd want to continue the journey, especially now that Britomar had agreed to follow Kavundi. The worst of it was not knowing her heart. Did she hope that he'd continue on with them, or that he'd go home?

The land before them was certainly diverting enough. Lush, with tall vine-covered trees growing as far as her eyes could see up the river they sailed. As she peered into the greenery, she became aware of a movement up in the branches along the banks. Looking closer, Galiana gasped. Furry little people leaped from branch to branch in the crowns overhanging the river, shaking them up and down.

"Look, Gwen!" she exclaimed, grasping her friend's hand.

"Those are rakshasa,"[1] said Kavundi, who must have quietly come to stand behind them.

"They're adorable!" said Gwen. "Look, that one carries a babe on its back. Do you know our word for them?"

"I don't know if your language has a word for them. They are good creatures; in ages past their king, Hanuman, aided Rama, and recently he came to Madhvacharya with word of your errand. It was he who arranged for the beasts we'll be riding. We're near them now," said Kavundi, "Al-Rashid!"

Al-Rashid called from the stern, where he held the rudder. "This humble one is needed?"

"Do you see that place to the left of the river where the trees are

---

[1]Translator's note: Rakshasa is the Sanskrit for monkey. There was no cognate word in Langue d'oc in the 13th century for this adorable creature. Since rakshasas would have been new to all except Kavundi and Al-Rashid, I chose not to translate the word.

284

further from the shore?" asked Kavundi.

"By the grace of Allah, the trees pull back from the shore just beyond that large rock."

"Yes. We will disembark there," said Kavundi

"Be it the will of Allah it shall be so," promised Al-Rashid.

Gwen giggled. "A rakshasa just climbed that rock and is jumping up and down as if excited to see us."

"It's so sweet," said Adelie, who had come to stand next to them.

As the ship neared the shore, the rakshasa on the rock leapt to the ship's rigging. It scampered down and climbed up on Gwen's shoulder, where it sat and chattered.

"Gwen, it likes you," said Galiana.

Gwen opened her mouth to respond but the words slipped away to a frightened gasp as the ship rounded a bend in the river. On the shore stood seven huge gray beasts, each with a nose like a snake and ears like sails.

"What on God's earth are those?" asked Adelie.

"Those are our beasts of burden, I think 'elephant'[2] is your word for them," answered Kavundi.

Gwen's voice sounded strained to Galiana. "Beasts of burden?"

"Yes."

Galiana had heard tales of the gray beasts from customers of hers, but had never believed them. Perhaps the tales of men with mouths on their stomachs would also prove true?

It did not take long for Al-Rashid to pilot the ship to the shore where the elephants waited. With a mixture of admiration and envy, Galiana watched Gwen leap ashore with one of the ship's ropes, tying it to a tree on the edge of the clearing. Two of the sailors lowered the ramp and the rest of them climbed down to the sand and formed a line. The sailors brought the supplies up from the hold, passing the baskets carefully from the rocking ship to the men on the shore.

When all was unloaded, Galiana saw Al-Rashid approaching her. She held her breath. Partings had always been welcome to her when men were no more than prey. This time she felt so very different, so conflicted in her emotions.

"Salaam," he said with a flourish and a bow.

"Good day to you, Al-Rashid."

"There is something I must say, but Allah has not granted this humble one with means to say it."

"Then let me say it for you. It has been a pleasure, but life is too

---

[2]Translator's note: A 13th century speaker of Langue d'oc would have known an elephant as an "elefant". I used the English spelling of this word.

short. You are grateful that I've restored your manhood, and wish me a safe and successful journey."

"It is not my wish to contradict you, but I have not come to say farewell. I come as a supplicant. I would travel with you, if you would accept me as your protector."

Galiana opened her mouth wordlessly. She couldn't believe what she heard. It must be because he truly believed that she'd given him back his manhood, there could be no other reason a man would want to stay with her.

She lashed out with sarcasm, filled with her own self loathing. "Do you continue to claim that your interest is to protect me and not to bed me?"

He bowed slightly. "It is as you say. You are precious and I fear for you on this journey."

Precious? This had to be another lie, and she'd had a lifetime of men's lies. In the end they were all the same, all they wanted was sex. "Precious? Because I restored your precious manhood, more like. Get out of my sight. I am not your whore. I will not have you as my protector."

Al-Rashid bowed his head. "It is as I feared, you continue to doubt my motives. I had hoped...no matter. You leave me with a dilemma. I can either leave and confirm your suspicions that my motives are as you fear—or I can stay against your will, and prove my worth." He raised his head and looked her in the eyes. "This I do swear, to bring you safe and unharmed to the Garden at the Roof of the World, though it may cost me my life." He bowed and left her wide-mouthed, staring at his walk with unexpected joy.

Gwen found Britomar in a circle of elephants, each touching her horn with their absurd snake-like noses.

"They are such magnificent beasts," she said with wonder. "How will we keep up with them?"

"Kavundi tells me that each of you will ride."

"Ride? How could we even climb on to the back of such creatures?"

As if the elephants understood, they each bowed. Gwen returned the bow. "They are amazing. Do they understand what I'm saying?"

"No, but Natesa does. Natesa told them to get ready for you to climb up."

"Natesa? Who is Natesa?" Gwen narrowed her eyes, noticing for the first time a small furry shape crouching between an elephant's ears.

Britomar exchanged a few screeches with the rakshasa. "Your new friend. She asked me to tell you she can understand most of what you say."

"Do the elephants also understand us?" asked David, coming up to them with Wigandus and Al-Rashid in his wake.

"No," Britomar said. "The elephants can understand people, but they don't know Langue d'oc. Nimuë gave that gift only to Natesa."

"Who is Nimuë?" Al-Rashid asked.

Gwen said, "She is a sorceress who lives in the forest near my home, the student Lilith told us about. She helped me find Britomar." She tickled Natesa under her chin. "Are you also a friend of Nimuë?"

Natesa nodded her head and squealed.

"Well, let's load up these beasts and get moving. The mountains we seek aren't going to come to us," said Adelie.

Natesa chattered and Gwen felt sharp pain on the side of her head as the rakshasa grabbed some of her hair and pulled.

"Ow! Stop that!" she scolded.

Still chattering, Natesa scampered down her back and up Wigandus's leg, handing the knight the stolen strands of her hair.

"What's this?" he muttered as he looked at the strands and then to Gwen. She could feel her cheeks redden, and smiled at him. Wigandus yanked some strands out of his own head and handed them to the rakshasa. "Here you are, Natesa."

The rakshasa gave Wigandus a big hug and scampered back down. As the rakshasa reached her, Gwen bent down to pick her up. Instead of climbing up, Natesa handed her a bracelet of woven hair.

That night, Gwen lay awake playing with the bracelet. Above her in the sky, the stars were slowly disappearing behind what Gwen presumed were clouds. Even in the desert, she'd never known the air to feel so hot. With any luck, those clouds meant a cooling rain. She looked over to the fire and saw Wigandus sitting watch, using a stone to sharpen his sword. She rose, determined to find words to get past the panic she felt each time he touched her.

"Liebchen?" Wigandus looked up at her as she neared.

"Wigandus, I'm sorry."

"So am I. When I heard that you were nearly ra—"

"Don't, please. Lets not talk about it."

"As you wish." He hung his head.

She swallowed, uncertain of her words. "I feel I must explain myself. I've been unfair to you. It's just... Each time we touch, it brings it all back—the panic, the anger, the fear. I don't want to feel *him* when I'm with you, but I can't help it."

He looked up at her again, his eyes hidden in shadow. "I love you."

She hesitated. She ached to embrace him, to cradle in his strong arms—but she couldn't. Not yet.

"I love you too," she whispered. "Please give me time."

He bowed his head. "Until my life ends, I am yours."

Galiana never knew a smile could hurt, and hurt it did. She couldn't help the wide grin that made her cheeks ache as she looked around her.

The torrential downpour that began at dawn had continued throughout the day. Along the roads, people ran from their houses into the rain, dancing, embracing, and opening their mouths to swallow the water. Men swung up their giggling children, women closed their eyes and let the torrent stream down their beaming faces. Couples embraced, wet clothes plastered to their bodies. Men lifted women in their arms, squeals and laughter slitting the pounding of the rain upon the hard earth.

She looked over at Al-Rashid where he sat awkwardly on the back of an elephant. She couldn't understand her longing to have him hold her. She'd never known such delight in being alive, in being in the presence of any person, especially a man. Was Gwen right? Had she started to love him? She thought on the words that she'd spoken to him days before, when he swore to her to protect her at the cost of his life, words she had come to regret many times over. How did you unsay something? How did you move beyond your fears?

MANY PATHS

Loud swearing shook Kavundi from her meditations. Not bothering to sort through the voices, she lowered her hands and slipped out of the lotus.

She followed the voices to the fire, where Adelie, Galiana, and Gwen scurried around in a heated argument.

"What is wrong?" Kavundi asked.

They all turned their flustered faces to her. "It is this food," said Gwen. "None of us can figure out how to cook it."

"And the men, they couldn't help?"

Galiana giggled. Gwen said, "They offered, but Adelie told them to be off. This is our day to cook, and we're going to *cook*."

Galiana said, "Our brave protectors scrambled away. If they were dogs, their tails would have been between their legs."

"Well, I don't blame them. Your swearing pulled me out of my meditation. Here, I will show you what to do."

Kavundi picked up three coconuts and took them to the frying pan. "Adelie, hold these over the pan and cut them open with your knife. We need to collect the water inside into the pan. Where is the mortar and pestle?"

"I'll get them," Galiana said. She scampered over to the packs and took out a wooden bowl and a rounded peg. Kavundi took them and set them down before her. "Now, bring me some of the small spice jars that you set by the coconuts."

Gwen handed her the first jar. "This is coriander," said Kavundi. She took some of the seeds out and placed them into the mortar. "These are mustard seeds." Galiana handed her the next jar. "Pepper, it adds spice to the food." Kavundi dropped some peppercorns into to the mix of mustard seeds and coriander. "And this is ginger root. Please find a grater."

"Grater?" asked Galiana.

"I saw one," said Gwen. "I'll get it."

"Good. We'll need a piece of ginger the length of your fingernail grated into the pan."

Adelie and Galiana brought the other jars, with saffron, tamarind, cumin, and fennel. Kavundi mixed them in her wooden mortar and began to grind them. "You want to make as fine a powder as you can," she said. "You can mix it with butter, but that spoils too easily on a journey, so we'll use the water from the coconuts instead. Adelie, could you find some onion and chop it into small pieces?"

The smells of the spice mixture she was grinding reminded Kavundi of the last time she had helped her mother cook. When she was just a girl, she had stirred the curry carefully, knowing her father would come from work hungry, thinking of how he liked the vegetables in the curry as whole chunks, not broken.

One night, her father had brought a young man with him. He had called to her, "Tirulamanan, come here." Tirulamanan, that had been her name once upon a time.

She had entered the dining chamber, her eyes on the ground. The man who was with her father had struck her as handsome despite his bald pate. His shoulders were broad and the muscles in his arm rippled as he scooped the rice from his bowl with his fingers.

"Tirulamanan, this is—"

It was at that moment that her father, his guest, all that surrounded her disappeared from her sight. The smell of the spices overwhelmed her and she lost all sense of being. She came back to her senses to find her face soaking wet, her arms bruised from pinching, her worried mother fussing over her. It was night and her father's guest was long gone.

The next day she was sent to the nearby temple. From what she'd overheard of her parent's argument, she was to stay there and never come home.

On her way to the temple, she'd met a woman dressed as a princess who pranemed to her.

"Tirulamanan, you're going the wrong way."

She bowed, astonished that such a noble woman would address her. "Namaste. I go to the temple my parents have sent me to."

The woman smiled. "You are no longer Tirulamanan. You are Kavundi. You will go to Madhvacharya and ask him to be your guru. You will learn from him, you will live as a sannyasi, for I will have need of you one day."

She had been Kavundi ever since, and she'd not prepared curry since that day. It was strange to be doing so again.

Kavundi's hand slowed as she felt the right consistency in the spices she ground. "You'll want to ground the seeds to a fine powder. Now, I'll place the pan on the fire and make the coconut water hot.

Adelie, where is the onion?"

"Here."

Kavundi took the chopped onion and placed it into the pan. Once the water boiled, the onion started to sizzle. She then poured the spices into the hot pan. "Now, we'll add the lentils and let them simmer. When they're soft, but before they break up, we'll add some other vegetables."

She rose and went to the baskets of food, selecting the most fragile vegetables, cauliflower, eggplant, and some spinach leaves. As she directed the women to chop these into small pieces, Kavundi's thoughts wandered back to her mother and the day she'd had her first visit with Lakshmidevi.

That day Lakshmidevi had asked her to serve the unicorns.

Kavundi had just joined Madhvacharya as his disciple. At first some of his male disciples had made fun of her, but Madhvacharya put a stop to it. Reminding his students how Sri Krishna had taught that anyone seeking him, man or woman, would find him, he had Kavundi take the same vow of poverty that all the others took. He taught her better than the Vedas; he also taught her wrestling. As her skill grew, so did their respect. Some joked that she was Durga in their midst. Thankfully that kind of joking was not something that Madhvacharya tolerated amongst his disciples.

Kavundi came back to the present, directing the women to pour the cut vegetables into the pan, and demonstrating how to stir without breaking them. She wondered if her father would be proud—not of how she made the curry, but of her life as a sannyasi. What was it about cooking that brought her out of her detachment to the thoughts of her parents? For the first time in years she felt confused. How was she to keep her vows, and live as Lakshmidevi asked of her, and also serve the cause of the one-horned mare? How could she both be sannyasi and serve those within the world?

It was enough to know her Dharma was to serve the unicorn in need, she reminded herself. No need for concern if sometimes on her journey she must also prepare food. Hadn't Sri Krishna taught that any action, if done as an act of worship, would bring you to him? Teaching and serving would not violate her oath any more than Madhvacharya's teachings had violated his own.

The trouble was that she, as a sannyasi, was supposed to beg for her food. How could she beg for the food she helped prepare?

"There, it is ready," Kavundi said.

Galiana called for the men to come and Kavundi served each until none was left. Galiana, who had been served last said, "But Kavundi,

291

you left none for yourself?"

"I am a sannyasi, I am supposed to beg for my food."

Wigandus started to choke, "Mine Gott, es heisse! Wasser! I need water!"

Gwen waved her hand in front of her open mouth gasping, "I've never had anything so hot. It is delicious, but—"

"She is trying to poison us!" said Al-Rashid. "This is why she doesn't eat of it herself."

Kavundi held out her bowl. "If any of you would spare some, I will show Al-Rashid that this is not poison. It is a recipe I prepared for my own father when I was a girl."

Adelie moved some of the curry back to Kavundi's bowl with her knife. Kavundi ate gladly; it was the taste of youth, of love, of home. It had been too long since she'd tasted more than dried rice and table scraps.

David said, "Al-Rashid, it would seem that she lives, though I doubt much my tongue will ever be the same."

Kavundi was surprised to feel a rush of blood to her face as they all laughed heartily. The memories of her parents and the taste of the food she'd often prepared for them had broken down her carefully built wall of detachment. She rose and excused herself; it was time to return to her meditations.

She sat, but before she could begin to chant the mantra, she heard footsteps behind her. She reopened her eyes and turned to find Galiana.

"We were not laughing at you, Kavundi."

Kavundi shook her head. "I didn't think you were. I was just seeking to return to my meditations."

"What does that mean? Are meditations a prayer?"

Kavundi took a deep breath. "Meditation is letting yourself become one with God's word—which is the essence of a prayer."

"God's word?"

"Om. That is God's voice. Through its repetition, one joins one's voice with God's."

Galiana squatted, her face wrinkled with a mix of concern and curiosity. "But what does it mean?"

"Om doesn't have a meaning, it *is* meaning. Through its contemplation, you remove yourself from the misery of entanglement and let God become the motive for all actions."

"How I would love to remove myself from the misery of entanglements. Is this something I could learn?"

Kavundi paused a moment to consider. She could either continue to answer these questions, or question the reason behind them. Clearly, Galiana had deeper interest in this than just curiosity. Maybe she was ready to take the next step? "Yes, this is something you can learn, but it is not something to pursue just to rid yourself of the misery of entanglements. Are you seeking to find God, or to evade something else?"

Galiana lowered her eyes.

"There are many paths," Kavundi went on, "all of them valid. It would not be right to set your feet upon the path that is wrong for you."

"The path of a whore is a valid path to God?"

Kavundi was taken aback. She'd never thought of it that way. Yet Krishna had told Arjuna that even prostitutes would find him.

"If you do so as an act of worship, yes. Even the path of the whore can bring you to God. There was once a whore who lived in a large house, and a sanaysin who lived across the street in front of a temple. He chided the whore for her sins, and she repented deeply. Daily she would pray for forgiveness—but by night she had no choice but to continue her trade. It was the only way she could eat. The sanaysin would count her customers, placing a small pebble next to her door for each man. Through the years, the pile grew tall. They died the same day. He was taken by Sri Yamma to hell, she by Sri Krishna to heaven. The sanaysin was furious but Sri Yamma told him that while her body sinned, her mind was with God, but all he did was dwell on the sins of others, and did not seek God, though he gave up all the sins of the body."

Galiana listened with her mouth open, like a child.

"I never prayed," she said quietly.

"Go to Al-Rashid, ask him to teach you."

"Why not you? Will you not teach me?"

Kavundi smiled. "I did teach you tonight, with spices, vegetables, and fire."

"But I want to learn how to pray."

"And that, Galiana, is what I did when I cooked."

As Kavundi watched Galiana return to the others, she wondered at her words. She'd always heard Krishna's words in the Gita, but before tonight, she'd never acted in worship. She'd meditated, but had tried to avoid all action. It was odd to consider that cooking and whoring both could be surer paths to God than prayer alone.

From the back of her elephant, Adelie looked up at the white stucco squared-cone towers that towered in the distance above the canopy of trees. They looked out of place, as if someone had tried to bring a mountain range into the heart of the jungle.

"Britomar, are you certain there are no other villages nearby?" she asked.

"None within a few days travel. Our food supplies are low, we should replenish here."

"Do you intend to enter this place?" Gwen asked.

"No," replied the unicorn. "I will wait in the jungle."

"May I wait with you?"

"Yes."

Gwen slid off her elephant, and said something to the rakshasa which rode on her shoulders. Natesa immediately leapt from her back and scampered across the elephants to Wigandus's shoulder.

He looked over to Gwen. "Thank you, Liebchen."

Gwen climbed onto Britomar's back, her copper curls shining as if the sun lay only on her. "Each time we part, something bad happens. Please take care of yourself, my love."

Adelie sniffed back a tear. It was the first time since Baghdad she'd heard Gwen remember she loved the knight.

Kavundi said, "I don't know what this place is with so many temples, but I am certain we can easily find the supplies we need there. Remember one thing. If you're ever asked to enter a temple, it is right and proper to remove your shoes, and once you are inside—to circle the God three times."

"Our shoes?" asked Galiana.

"Circle the *what?*" demanded Al-Rashid.

"The shoes are the most unclean of garments." Kavundi slid her glance over Al-Rashid but did not reply to his words.

Adelie looked down at her shoes. They were dirty, but no more so than the hem of her skirt. What did this God have against dirt? When she looked back up, she saw Al-Rashid fingering the hilt of his scimitar. She put her hand on her long knife, and wondered if she'd have to fight him to protect Kavundi. Then again, if Gwen and Élise, both of them good Christians, could become possessed, perhaps Al-Rashid was right to be suspicious about Kavundi?

The jungle thinned and they entered a large clearing. Small wooden buildings ahead of them clustered together like children beneath the towering temple peaks. The ground near the houses was brown and well trampled. Women sat on shady porches beside the hanging garlands of drying cow manure, spinning cotton into rolls of thread. They watched the travelers with interest. Some rose to

greet them, hands clasped in a gesture Kavundi called a Namaste—
greeting the god within them. Returning the greeting, Adelie thought
it strange that these pagans also worshipped God incarnate.

Next to the women working their spinning wheels, cows pulled a
horizontal beam attached to a pole sticking from the ground. Children gently drove onward with long thin sticks, causing the pole to
turn, which in turn rotated a large wheel bearing a chain with buckets attached to it. Adelie watched as the wheel turned, raising bucket
after bucket of water, tipping them one by one over the trough before the wheel pulled the buckets over the top and back down into
the ground. The main trough brought water to smaller troughs that
carried water to the green fields surrounding the village.

Adelie looked back upon the laughing children as they reentered
the jungle. The sun on her back had been a welcome change from the
jungle gloom.

No more than an hour's ride through the jungle, sunlight again
burst upon them. Ahead rose the walls of the strangest city they'd
ever seen. A doorless gateway in the short stone wall gaped ahead,
flanked by tall pine trees, like sentinels. Beyond the wall towered
the tall white peaks of the temples, blazing in the sunlight. The road
leading into the city was empty and clean, as if it did not see much
traffic.

As they rode through the gateway into the shadow of the first
temple Kavundi signaled to stop the procession. They all gasped at
the buildings looming over them.

"Is it usual for your temples to be so adorned?" asked Wigandus.

Adelie could not suppress a blush. The walls as far as the eye could
see were covered with carvings of naked men and women engaged in
many variations of the intercourse. She gasped. The blatant sexuality
depicted on these walls was much more disturbing than the women
with skull necklaces she saw back at Kavundi's temple.

A group of young men came out of the nearest temple with broad
grins on their faces, talking excitedly amongst themselves. One of
them looked up at Kavundi and said something too quiet for Adelie
to overhear. Kavundi's reply was stern, louder than Adelie ever heard
Kavundi speak:

"Even were I the whore you take me for, your behavior is unbecom-
ing. Do you think the God resident in that temple will take kindly to
this?"

"Woman, the God within that temple would love your holy arse!"
one of the men shouted as they scampered away, laughing.

Kavundi frowned. "There is something amiss. Not with the statues, Sir Wigandus, which were placed there to ward against lightning, but in the behavior of those men. I can only suspect what is going on in there. In case I'm wrong, Adelie, I would be glad of your company, and your knives, if you're willing."

Adelie blanched. "Why not Wigandus, David or Al-Rashid?"

"I think they should guard the elephants while I seek the supplies. Besides, none of the men have learned our language as well as you."

"Can I be of help?" asked Galiana.

Adelie had never seen mirth on Kavundi's face before, though it was quickly replaced by the emotionless detachment the nun always wore. "Perhaps you can; come then."

Adelie slid down her elephant, helping Galiana remove her shoes when they reached the temple gate. "Do you want a knife?" she whispered to Galiana, as she helped her with her own shoes.

"Yes, if you've one to spare."

Adelie handed her a knife, keeping for herself the one her father had given her. Barefoot, the three women entered the temple.

It did not take long for Adelie's eyes to adjust to the dim lighting of the interior, illuminated by candles scattered along the hall. They approached a pillar in the center of the room and Kavundi prostrated herself before it. It felt odd lying down in front of a pillar, but Adelie followed Kavundi's lead, not wanting to offend. At least at the ground level, the heavy smell of incense that dominated the air was less obvious. Kavundi rose and they followed her into the main chamber.

Adelie suppressed a gasp as she saw men and women on the floor, entangled in various sexual positions beneath the brightly painted statues of men and women similarly engaged. After a moment her shock faded into wonder at the variety of positions and the lack of passion of the participants, most of them chanting rather than panting as they moved rhythmically against each other.

Kavundi stood frozen in front of Adelie, staring at a statue in the center of the chamber, depicting a man and a woman in a sexual embrace. She slumped her shoulders, bowed to it and then began to walk around. Adelie followed, glancing at Galiana to gage her reaction to the scene. Galiana's eyebrows were pinched, as if she were more puzzled than shocked by what she saw.

From the shadows in a far corner, a woman approached them. A golden chain hung in a graceful arc between her nose and left ear. It was the only thing she wore.

This woman brought her hands together and said, "I welcome the goddess in each of you. Have you come to join in our worship?"

"No, we come begging food. Lakshmidevi sends us to do her work."

The smile never left the woman's face. "We have no such provisions. Join us in tantrayoga, become one with the Devi as she remakes the world, and set aside your need for food."

Adelie could not believe that this priestess had disregarded the most basic of temple rules, always have provisions at hand for those in need, and that she justified this unforgivable lapse with such a base reason.

"You follow the lowest of the paths," said Kavundi, "And my companions seek a higher way, as do I. We will seek the provisions we need in another temple."

"If all you concern yourself with is filling your bellies, you needn't bother. Here we all learn to let go of the illusion of self, surrendering to the dance of creation."

"You are not an illusion, but a woman lovingly created," began Kavundi, but as her speech became faster, filled with emotions Adelie had not expected from the normally placid nun, she could no longer follow the alien words. She let her attention drift to the statues along the walls—a more comfortable place to rest her eyes than the couples on the floor. One statue showed a maid pulling a thorn from her foot, another lifting her leg over her lover's shoulder while he slid into her. She wondered at some of the positions, and decided to try them with David the first chance she got. Then a thought occurred to her, and would not go away, no matter at how many erotic sculptures she gazed at. Where was God in all of this? What would David say? Perhaps all this was an abomination—and she had the means to destroy it? Her right hand rested on the hilt of her knife.

Kavundi shouted and wheeled, striding toward the temple's exit. Adelie snapped back to reality, rushing along with Galiana to follow the nun out of the temple.

"What's going on?" asked Galiana. "Those were not whores."

Kavundi shrugged. "This whole complex is dedicated to a preposterous idea, that they'll find the way to God through prayerful sexual union. Willingly deluded fools, likely from noble houses, come from far away, lured by the promise of sex without responsibility."

"Should we destroy them?" asked Adelie.

She had to skip back a step as Kavundi stopped in her tracks and turned, her face showing shock.

"Why would we destroy those who follow a different Dharma? *I* may think that what they do is an anathema, and those like me will try to steer people away from that path, but each of us must make our own choices. Not even Kalidevi destroys just to destroy, but destroys so that renewal and newness may emerge. Besides, even what they do in there can be a path to God if done in worship, and love."

"Does this mean that your people do not kill at all?" Adelie asked skeptically.

"No. We all must die, and killing or not killing is all about making the right choice. Choosing not to kill someone does not keep them from death. However, if you don't kill rightly, then you will also die an unrighteous death. That is Karma. When Kalidevi destroys, it is not in anger, but to bring about something new."

Adelie looked back at the shadowed entrance to the temple, wondering who or what this Kalidevi might be. If killing was not destroying, wouldn't it be right in the eyes of God to kill these pagans?

Something touched her shoulder and she turned to see her elephant lifting her hair with its trunk.

"You startled me." She laughed. The elephant knelt and she climbed up behind its enormous ears.

"So, what's the big secret?" asked David.

Adelie turned to him, cheeks hot with a furious blush. "I'll show you, later."

As they returned to the village, an old man covered in ashes approached them, palms together. "You are not giving Kalidevi her due," he said. "Do not deny Kalidevi."

Kavundi said, "We do not deny Kalidevi. We honor Lakshmidevi."

"You seek to keep Bethiel from death. All things must honor Kalidevi, all things must die."

"Who is this Bethiel?" asked Galiana.

The man frowned. "You mock me, and you disparage Kalidevi. Know you not the name of the unicorn you seek to keep from Kalidevi?"

Adelie narrowed her eyes. "How do you know so much about our quest, old man?"

He looked at her with a triumphant gleam in his eyes. "Kalidevi speaks to me. She told me much about you, strangers. You must not interfere in the order of things. You must let the eldest unicorn die."

"Love does not die," said Wigandus as they directed their elephants past the ashen man.

"You are wrong, knight. Even Sri Kama let himself die, for the sake of Sri Shiva and Kalidevi. Do not seek to deny Kalidevi in this."

"It is not Kalidevi who speaks of this to you, but a demon who pretends her visage," said Kavundi. "Both the First Woman and the First Wife have sent these people to care for Bethiel. The first woman gave her life so that Bethiel might live. I was asked to help them by Lakshmidevi herself."

"I warn you! Deny Kalidevi at your peril!" The man began to trot after them, but Kavundi said something to the elephants and they sped up, leaving the ashen man far behind.

"Who is Kalidevi?" asked David.

"She is the destroyer," said Kavundi.

"See, I told you these people follow demons," said Al-Rashid.

"No, Al-Rashid, I don't think you have the right of it," said David. "All things must pass away in the fullness of time. The embrace of the angel of death is not a punishment. If the seed does not die, new wheat will not grow. Everything has its season; only the Lord endures forever."

"That is so," said Kavundi, "Though I will give this much to Al-Rashid, some of Kalidevi's followers delight in killing, thinking to serve as her arm within the world. We should hurry from here."

They were not far into the jungle when they met up again with Britomar and Gwen. The rakshasa chattered happily as it scrambled down from its perch on Wigandus's shoulder and up Gwen's leg.

Adelie looked behind them at the many peaks of that most inhospitable town, and wondered at that ashen man. Did they do the right thing in putting their lives at peril to save this eldest of unicorns? Perhaps it would be best to let him die after all.

Galiana asked, "Britomar, why did you never tell us that the name of your king is Bethiel?"

"Do you speak the name of your father? How did you learn his name?"

Galiana told her of the ashen man.

Britomar hung her head. Gwen slipped off her elephant and embraced the unicorn. "What troubles you?"

"When I last saw the eldest of unicorns, he was in great pain. The herd begged him to allow us to find a remedy. I guess I never questioned it when I chose to act as I did. Could we all be wrong?"

"All we can do is to do what good we see, and trust to Allah to permit what is truly good," said Al-Rashid.

That night, as they made camp, Adelie went to David who was sifting through the legumes, making certain none of the remaining beans were rotten. "I'm bothered by what Britomar said. How can we know what is the right thing to do?"

David put down the bag. "We are taught that the Torah was given to us to follow, so that we'd always know how the Lord wants us to act. We always give to those who don't have means to provide for themselves, the widows, and the orphans. This is much the same. The unicorns can't do this for themselves, so we must provide for them."

"Yet since you've joined us, you've broken the laws for your Sabbath observation."

"The commandment is to keep the Sabbath holy. If I were to permit death on the Sabbath through my non-action, that would not keep it holy, no matter my intent. There is a time for everything, my love, and right now is a time for us to seek paradise not for ourselves, but for another."

"David, I wish I were wise like you. Lately, all I seem to want to do is fight and kill."

"My father always wanted me to be wise. I always wanted to be like my uncle—adventurous, daring. I would stay up all night, thinking on the stories he told us of his adventures. When you came to us, you lived a life I had only dreamed of. I have learned of adventure and daring from you. If you wish, I will teach you what I know of Torah and the Lord's wisdom."

"Are you asking me to become a Jew?"

"Understanding the Lord's wisdom and His Torah does not make you Jewish. The Nazarene who you follow loved and respected Torah."

Adelie took his hand in hers. "I thought Jews didn't acknowledge Jesus."

"In general, we do not think of him. However, my father and I were in frequent correspondence with Friar Thomas in Paris regarding the teachings of Moses Maimomedes. We couldn't help but respect many of his ideas."

"I wonder if it is the same friar that Élise and I met in Paris."

"It is possible. Now, what did you see in that temple?"

Adelie giggled. "Let me show you."

Shortly after dawn the next day, as Gwen's elephant bowed for her to mount, Adelie saw something red out of the corner of her eye.

She turned. In a flash of red and sable, a gigantic cat sprang from the jungle. Adelie drew her long knife as she leapt from the elephant's back onto the cat. Together they fell just short of Britomar. Adelie rolled onto the ground, returned to her feet, knife at ready, facing a cat whose body was longer and more massive than that of a horse. It growled, its ears flat against its red black-striped face.

It lowered itself to spring, and Adelie met it head-on, a rage boiling within her. Claws raked her and her body exploded in burning agony. She felt faint, her vision blurred. *I am dying.*

Strangely distanced, she watched her hands tighten on her knives. She wrapped her arms around the beast's neck as it clawed at her back. Delicious pain. Her knife bit flesh. Claws tore at her and she fell, rolling to rise again between Britomar and the cat, dimly aware of the blood dripping down her burning back, of the agony in her leg, of the foam on her chin.

The tiger slunk back and forth, looking for a way around her. It growled in defeat, then turned and bounded away into the forest.

"I never heard the beast coming," said a beautiful voice behind her. She knew that voice, just couldn't quite place it at the moment. "Thank you Adelie, you just saved my life."

A sharp jab of pain pierced her shoulder. She wheeled, knife flashing at a horn touching her. Its blazing white pulled at her thoughts. She knew that horn. What were those voices, calling her name? What was that roaring sound?

Everything faded into darkness.

Galiana watched in horror as the huge black and orange cat leapt past her at Britomar, as Adelie sprung upon the cat, rolling, slashing, a flash of steel and the spray of blood. Wigandus, Al-Rashid, and David jumped off their elephants, their swords raised—and unneeded. Growling, Adelie backed away from the cat, which turned and bounded into the undergrowth.

Galiana froze as she heard the agony in Gwen's voice crying out Adelie's name. She rounded her elephant and saw David cradling the bleeding Adelie in his arms. Her body was limp as she leaned against his shoulder.

Britomar stood over them, confused. "Why did she slash at me?"

Galiana looked at the unicorn and back again at Adelie. "You touched Adelie with your horn and she still bleeds?"

"Yes," said Britomar. "And she attacked me after I touched her."

Galiana remembered how Britomar touched Élise to heal her, and nothing happened. "A demon's got her," she blurted.

David looked up from his wife, tears welling up in his eyes, "You may be right. She didn't seem to know us... How can we drive it out?"

"First, let's get those wounds bound so that she stops bleeding," said Gwen as she rummaged through her packs looking for the gauze Élise had purchased in Antioch.

"Al-Rashid, you're the swiftest of foot," said Kavundi, "Run back to the village. Do you remember the cow dung hung upon the porches to dry? I need you to fetch me three pieces."

"If it is the will of Allah, I'll return with what you need."

Galiana tore her gaze from Al-Rashid as he ran back up the path to the village, and helped Gwen bind Adelie's wounds. Before long, Al-Rashid returned, panting, holding a string of the dried cow dung.

"By Allah, bargaining without speaking is hard," he said between breaths.

Kavundi took a piece from the string, cradling it in her hands she lifted it, and began to sing. To Galiana's surprise, the dung burst into flame in Kavundi's hands. The nun placed it gently near David and Adelie, knelt and blew the smoke toward them.

Adelie's body started to shake. David held her tight and also began to sing. Gwen knelt to one side to help him hold Adelie's twitching body in the stream of smoke. Galiana wrapped her arms around herself watching Adelie's body twist and writhe in their arms.

She looked at Kavundi and the burning dung, anxious for any sign of hope in the nun's face, but it showed no emotion, not even anxiety. Galiana shivered, though she wasn't cold. She found herself walking up to Kavundi and kneeling beside Adelie. An unknown force drove her hand as she touched the burning dung with her forefinger, then reached to Adelie and traced signs on her forehead, cheeks, lips, pushing aside the bandages to make a final mark between Adelie's breasts. A smokeless blue flame burst from each sign. Adelie's lips parted and she shook in one great scream.

Finally she went still. The flames were gone.

"The demon is gone," Kavundi said, wide-eyed. "How did you know to do that?"

Galiana felt suddenly light-headed. "I didn't. Suddenly I found myself doing it." She looked at her right hand. The finger she had written with was black. What power had used her to free Adelie? How could this miracle have come through her?

An unreasonable joy filled her as Britomar brushed past her. The dear beast touched Adelie with her horn, and from that touch light spread across Adelie, illuminating her body through the bandages, letting Galiana see her deep cuts close, the red swelling dissipate, until the light faded and Adelie was whole again.

Adelie heard a low singing and opened her eyes. David's face looked at her, upside down. She shook her head to make sense of it and realized she lay with her head in his lap. It was his singing that had woken her.

"I'm alive?" she asked.

"We almost lost you." He gently caressed her cheek.

"I felt myself dying—and then a strange force took me. I guess I let it, feeling like either I killed or would be killed."

David pressed a finger to his lips, then to hers. "We don't always know how to make the right choices. This is why God forgives so readily, He knows we don't."

"David, what should I do next time?"

"Do you really think there'd be a next time?"

Adelie sat up and looked him straight in the eyes. "I'm afraid to die, and we've seen so much fighting. I'm not always going to win."

"I know. One day we may both die." His smile was sudden and whimsical. "Until that day, let us enjoy what days we have."

He reached out his hands to her, and she took them, pulling herself into his embrace, twisting so that his arms wrapped around her as she sat against him. "What would you do if you were losing, and facing certain death?"

"Again?" He chuckled. "You've no idea how many times Wigandus saved my life. I always start a battle with a prayer for help. So does Wigandus, by the way."

Adelie paused on the edge of her question, and then with a deep breath let herself fall into it. "David, teach me to pray."

That night, as Galiana snuggled into Al-Rashid's welcome embrace, he whispered to her, "See, you can work miracles."

Galiana thought of the burning signs her finger had inscribed upon Adelie. "It wasn't me. Someone was using my finger."

"By Allah the merciful, you still doubt. I love you for this doubt, Galiana. Yet, after all that, it was your finger. Do not forget that."

Galiana closed her eyes, hoping to do just that, forget, but one particular sign hung before her closed eyes, burning upon her memory. Not for the first time in her life she regretted she had no idea how to read. Perhaps she'd ask if anyone could tell her what she'd written, tell her the meaning of the signs that drove the demon from Adelie. Perhaps.

THE TRUE FAITH

Galiana woke stiff and sore from yet another night's sleep on the hard ground. She was tired, tired of their journey, tired of sleeping under the trees, on roots, rocks and hard turf. She felt Al-Rashid cuddle closer as she stirred. She wanted to wake him, scream at him, and forced herself to walk away before she said anything harsh. Disgusted with him, with herself, with all the world, she went to the stream. Looking at her reflection as she splashed some water on her face, she saw small lines next to her eyes.

She spat into the water. "Shit! I'm getting old and ugly!"

"Ugly is when you don't like what you see."

Galiana whirled around and saw Al-Rashid.

"You! Won't you ever leave me alone!"

"Do you really want me to?"

"Yes! God damn it! We've traveled for months and you won't look at me, you won't touch me, and I'm tired of you following me around like a great big puppy!"

Al-Rashid bowed his head. "My apologies. I have tried to be the devoted lover of which your poets speak."

He turned to leave, but Galiana screamed at him:

"Poets! They wouldn't know now to treat a woman! I want your hands on me, not your words!"

Al-Rashid spread his hands. "Most humble apologies, but did you not just say..."

"Every morning for the past four months I wake up next to your stiff penis. But do you do anything about your interest in me? No! All you do is..." Whatever else she might have said turned to a muffled *mmmf* as Al-Rashid stepped forward and kissed her. She struggled for a moment, then wrapped her arms around him and the two of them sank to the ground. Kisses turned to caresses as they tumbled, struggling out of their clothes.

Later that morning, after they had washed in the cold water of the stream and dressed, they walked back to the others, holding hands. They stopped at the edge of the clearing, Galiana's cheeks burning as she saw the others look up at them and smile.

Gwen giggled as she handed them each some flat bread that she had prepared for their breakfast. Wigandus put down the sword he had been sharpening with a whet stone.

"Ah, good!" he said. "The two of you finally worked it out."

Al-Rashid gave her hand a squeeze. "Have we been that obvious?"

"Rather loud, too," said Adelie as she removed clothes from the branches where they had been hanging to dry.

"We were beginning to wonder if we should draw lots to see who would have the honor of disturbing you," said David, placing the folded cloth Adelie gave him into a pack. "Britomar's back, and tells us that she found the ford Kavundi spoke of. Unfortunately, there is a rather large encampment right next to it."

"Let me guess," said Al-Rashid swallowing quickly. "They're the caliph's troops?"

"Ah, then the rumors aren't true," said Sir Wigandus.

"Rumors?"

"That you put aside women to preserve your intellect."

"Why you pompous—" Al-Rashid stopped when he saw that all the others were laughing, including Galiana.

"See, Wigandus?" said David, "I told you she'd be good for him. He's learning not to take himself so seriously."

"I do not!" Al-Rashid began to protest but when this was greeted by yet more laughter, he shrugged and laughed too.

Galiana loved riding through the jungle on the elephant's back, gazing at the sunbeams as they broke through the canopy to reveal lush greenery and make the damp air shimmer. A shrill "Chee" echoed overhead and a flash of red and gold shot into the canopy of leaves.

"Look at that tiny bird," Galiana exclaimed. "Its beak is longer than its head."

"Those are kingfishers. We must be close to the river," said Kavundi.

"Should you not cover yourself?" Al-Rashid called to her. "We're about to enter lands ruled by those of the true faith."

"All faiths are true, Al-Rashid," she retorted. "It is the men who follow them that are sometimes false"

"Still, it may save us all trouble if you wore clothes," said Gwen.

"Would you put aside your clothes to save yourself trouble?" asked Kavundi. "I have taken a vow of poverty."

"Did you not also promise Lakshmidevi to help us reach the Garden?" asked Britomar. "Would it not be a breaking of that promise if the Muslims did you harm because of your refusal to wear clothes?"

Al-Rashid said, "Let me tell you a story. Once there was a princess who was promised in marriage to the Sultan of Granada. Her father, the Sultan of Tunisia, called his best knight to him and said, 'I wish you to escort my daughter to Granada, where she will marry the sultan.'

"To this the knight replied, 'I will protect your daughter and her virtue with my life. I myself will not touch her at the peril of my soul. Though it may cost me my life, I will see her married to the Sultan of Granada.' Satisfied with the knight's oath, the sultan called for his daughter, and sent the two of them on their way. They arrived in the city in the middle of a tournament. At the request of the princess, the knight entered the lists, took on all, and by the grace of Allah he triumphed. When the tournament ended, he was shocked to discover that the tournament was held at the command of the old sultan to choose his successor, as he had died without issue. He found himself presented with the throne of Granada as his prize. Without waiting a moment, he immediately married the princess.

"Now, I ask you, when the knight was made sultan and married the princess, did he not break his first vow, not to touch the princess? Yet, had he not married her, would he not have broken his second vow, to see her married to the Sultan of Granada?"

Kavundi snorted. "Sri Vishnu will protect us."

When they came in sight of the river, they all got off their elephants. Sir Wigandus pushed past Galiana and Al-Rashid to the head of the column and gazed out of the edge of the forest. "They know we're coming, and have a guard at the other side, waiting. Gwen, you and Britomar should cross upstream. We don't dare repeat what happened in Baghdad."

"But how—" Gwen began, when Britomar interrupted.

"He's right. Come, climb up and let's fade into the forest."

Gwen ran to Wigandus and threw her arms around him. "Be careful!"

He stroked her long auburn hair, then kissed her. Flushed, Gwen leapt onto Britomar's back and together they sped off into the forest.

Al-Rashid said, "It would be best if Sir Wigandus and I cross the ford first, with the women behind us."

"I will not be counted among the women, Al-Rashid," said David.

Adelie placed her hand on her long knife, but said nothing.

"A thousand apologies, but you are no warrior."

"David walks with me," said Wigandus, placing his hand on the pommel of his sword.

Al-Rashid bowed to Wigandus and said, "Then the Children of Abraham walk together into the water."

"Shouldn't we ride?" asked Galiana.

"No," said Wigandus. "None of us knows how to fight on the back of such a beast, and none of our weapons would reach."

As they crossed the water, Galiana looked down to see fish swimming through her reflection. Wrinkles! Who cared about wrinkles! She hadn't felt this good in years!

As they got closer to the other shore, Galiana noticed that one of the soldiers waiting on the other side held a coil of rope. Al-Rashid called to them in Arabic, exchanging a few short phrases.

"I told them that we're on a mission Holy in the eyes of Allah," he said. "He replied that if we valued our lives, we would lay down our arms, as we were now the property of His Eminence the Sultan of Delhi."

"Shall we teach our hosts some manners?" asked Wigandus.

"First, let me remind them of the Quran," said Al-Rashid. He called back to the waiting soldiers, who exchanged words with him, laughing as they did so. Galiana watched Al-Rashid's face anxiously during the exchange, and it was obvious from his eyes that whatever they said, it was not good. By this point, David, Al-Rashid, and Wigandus almost reached the shore of the river.

"They intend to take us as slaves," Al-Rashid said quietly, "They care nothing for the instructions in the Quran against enslaving guests, or fellow Muslims for that matter, and believe our dear Kavundi to be a whore. As for me, I do not intend to ever be another's property again."

Kavundi said in a low voice, "Madhvacharya told me that he met their sultan, and he is actually very devout. He offered Madhvacharya a palace. I'm surprised his servants would be instructed to disregard the Quran."

David said, "I'm certain then that if we remind them about the laws of hospitality, they will seek guidance from their sultan."

"It is worth trying. Allow me." Al-Rashid shouted, so the guards on the shore could hear. This time Galiana kept her eyes on the captain for the guard, who blanched, bowed and left.

Al-Rashid said, "Allah be praised, he has gone to seek instructions."

"I am sorry I did not listen to you," Kavundi said. "You were right, I should have put aside my vow in my service to Britomar's errand."

Galiana said, "It is less a sacrifice than that which two women have already given. In fact, I seem to be the only woman amongst you that has gained rather than given on this journey. I can only imagine what price I have yet to pay. Whatever it is, I hope that I will be willing."

Adelie took off her pack. "I've got something here that should fit you. It was Élise's. Take it. She'd be happy to know she was still helping."

Galiana saw Kavundi hesitate and said, "Don't think of it as owning; it is a loan. You can return it when you no longer have the need."

Kavundi smiled. "It is the need I'm uncertain of, and the need in which I find much danger. Keep it for the moment; these guards might take my dressing as a sign that Al-Rashid lied, and I would not risk that. I may wear it once we are beyond these soldiers."

Galiana glanced anxiously at the soldiers. They had relaxed, and were talking in small groups. She shivered, standing in the water that made her feel cold for the first time in months.

Finally, the captain of the guard returned with another man besides him. This second man spoke the language that Kavundi had been teaching them. "I, Ulagh Khan Balban, humble servant to His Eminence, Nasir-ud-din Mahmud, the Sultan of Delhi, welcome you to the Sulinate in his name. While the sultan has other matters to attend to, I am certain he will wish to greet you and hear all about your errand, which is holy to all the Children of Abraham."

Galiana smiled as she saw that the guards behind Balban were snickering.

Al-Rashid bowed. "We are honored by your welcome in the name of His Eminence, the sultan. It is with heartfelt regret that we must decline your invitation. The nature of our errand is such that all haste must be made in its service."

Balban bowed. "I insist. Come, I pledge my word to you, in the name of Allah the Just, you have nothing to fear from accepting the hospitality of His Eminence." He signaled to the guards, who sheathed their weapons.

David said, "We pleaded our cause in the name of the laws of hospitality. It would be more than rude to refuse the invitation in the name of the sultan."

"Come, let us meet with this sultan and see how those of Islam keep their word," said Wigandus.

Galiana was glad that Balban and the guards marched ahead of them, giving her hope they meant no treachery. She stepped next to Al-Rashid as they strode up the bank to follow the guards. "I'm glad you were able to persuade them. I would have hated to lose you, after finding love with you for the first time in my life."

"While my sword is thirsty for action, I, too, am relieved. I am also saddened that good Muslims stood in our way."

"Is it better to face and kill those who are not?" she said as she looked at his feet.

Al-Rashid lifted her face gently with a finger under her chin. "No, it is just less sad when my foe is not of the true faith. I delight in no one's death."

"Does it sadden you that I am of no faith?"

He raised his eyebrows. "You're not a Christian?"

"If I was baptized, it was before my family was slaughtered and I found myself sold into slavery. I have no memory of it. The priest who would visit us was a frequent customer, and never cared about the state of our souls."

Al-Rashid gave her hand a gentle squeeze. "Have you no thoughts on the nature of God?"

"Until I met Britomar, I would have laughed at such a question. Her purity called to me through my filth. Her father walked with Adam and Eve in Eden, yet she looks to people to reveal God to her. I suppose I'm waiting as well."

Al-Rashid laughed.

Galiana frowned at him. "What?"

"I've been upset at having a Hindu in our midst, and now I find that I fell in love with an agnostic."

She gasped, "You love me?"

"With all my heart," he answered, and then bent down to kiss her.

It was dusk when they reached a city of tall stucco-covered walls and gilded gates. Just beyond the gates a dark column stood like a thin needle pointed to heaven. Balban turned to them and said, "It is said that if you can stand with your back to this column, reach behind, and clasp your hands around it, you will have you heart's desire. Do any of you wish to try?"

Galiana took Al-Rashid's hand. "I already have my heart's desire."

Balban looked to the others, but they all shook their heads.

"What, not even you, Wigandus?" Al-Rashid said.

Wigandus laughed. "My heart's desire will come freely given, or not at all."

"Since when have you become wise, good friend?" asked David.

"I failed Gwen once in Baghdad. I'll not fail her again."

"What about you, Kavundi?" asked Galiana.

The nun shook her head. "I seek to free myself from desire, finding only God. All this could do is to take me from my dharma."

"Then, let us proceed," said Balban.

In the gathering dusk, Balban led them into a large palace, through halls and courts dimly illuminated by lamps, until they came upon a large garden. As they followed under lamp-lit boughs, Galiana heard running water and the notes of a string instrument. A small breeze lifted the ends of her tresses, filling her nose with the scent of fresh fruit. The sultan lived well.

They rounded a bend in the tree-lined path to find a small canopy near a fountain. Under the canopy lounged a thin man wearing gold robes and a turban, absorbed in a book that was held in front of him by a kneeling young man clad only in a white loincloth. She found it odd that she'd seen no guards through the entire palace, as if the sultan had complete confidence in his safety.

Balban stepped forward and said, "Your Eminence, may this humble one be permitted to introduce the former guard captain of the Caliph of Baghdad, Al-Rashid, and his companions Sir Wigandus of Thuringia; the Jew David ben Yosi with his wife, Adelie; Galiana Passavanti; and Kavundi, who claims to be a Hindi ascetic. They claim an errand holy to all the children of Abraham." He then turned to them and said, "Bow, for you have the grace to be in the presence of His Eminence, Nasir-ud-din Mahmud, the Sultan of Delhi."

They all bowed, and Al-Rashid also salaamed.

The man in the gold turban looked up and smiled. "Welcome to Delhi! Come, esteemed guests! Gather near. I am reading my favorite passage in the Most Holy Quran."

Balban bowed low. "Your Eminence, I must ask your leave to take the patrol to their barracks."

The sultan waved his hand, his attention already back in the book. "Yes, yes. Off with you. Now, my guests, gather round and let me read to you."

Galiana sat next to the others on the plush rug, listening to the strange words, wondering why the sultan had not inquired as to what their errand was. She could no more understand what he read than she could discern the colors of the rug's pattern in the torch light. She focused on the tones instead, accented by the distant sounds of a string instrument and the trickling sounds of the fountain. It was only when the boy who had been holding up the book collapsed that she realized she'd been half asleep.

The sultan looked up. "Oh, dear, have I been reading that long?"

Al-Rashid said, "Your Eminence reads so beautifully that we'd not noticed the passing of the hours."

"Where are my servants? I must have this boy whipped."

"They sleep, Anointed of Heaven, just beyond the canopy. Your reading must have graced them, as a mother's loving lullaby," said Al-Rashid.

The sultan nodded. "Just so, just so. Still, I cannot permit them to so disregard the words of His most blessed prophet."

"Not everyone is blessed with your stamina, Anointed One," said Al-Rashid. "Even this poor servant must find sustenance and rest before I can fully appreciate more of those most blessed words. May we be excused to seek sustenance at your table's bounty?"

Picking the book from the arms of the collapsed boy, the sultan waved his hand in dismissal, leafing through the book to find the right place. Galiana rose as Al-Rashid signaled for them to move away quietly. As they passed under the arched gateway out of the garden, Galiana was struck by a singular thought. As incomprehensible as the words of the prophet were to her, one thing was clear. For the first time in her life, she'd met a man who never even glanced at her body or asked of her anything other than her name.

"Nasir-ud-din Mahmud missed his calling," said David. "He would make a remarkable Imam."

"David ben Yosi, I must beg to disagree," said Al-Rashid. "Nasir-ud-din Mahmud should have been a court fool. I've never heard the Quran so poorly read, intonation and accent in all the wrong places. Mark my word, Balban will be the next sultan. His men followed him without question. It is only a matter of time before he decides that Delhi needs a leader not a holy fool on the throne."

"He struck me much the same," said Wigandus. "I'm just glad for the sake of our mission that the Lord of Hosts saw fit to keep Nasir-ud-din Mahmud enthroned until we passed through Delhi."

Galiana felt a shiver run down her spine. Upon the hilltop, horn shining brighter than the moon, Britomar waited with Gwen at her side.

Thanks to the courtesy of the sultan, Galiana felt for the first time as if she might belong with the others. Right as the others may be about that man as a ruler, he found her worthy of sharing what was most precious to him. For that alone, she'd be ever grateful.

LO MANTANG

Kavundi looked back down the roughly cut mountain stair they just ascended and let out a heavy sigh. Only Wigandus seemed to be able to keep up with her on the narrow mountain passes, and he stayed mostly with Gwen, leaving Kavundi to lead the way. Their slow pace, nightly complaints from the others, the fact that this was the fourth sacred river they'd followed to its source without finding the Garden, was annoying Kavundi—and she was supposed to be beyond such things.

To clear her mind, she looked back at Kali Gandaki. Silver in the sunlight, the sacred river would merge into the Ganges on the way to the sea. In places it reflected the snow-capped peaks, the home of the gods. She took a breath of the fresh mountain air. Certainly they would find this Garden soon.

She resumed her climb. She had no desire to hear the complaints she was certain would greet her when the others were in earshot. At least this mountain path was better than the others, with steps carved in the stone as if someone had tried to make the way easier.

"How dare you trespass on my road!" said a voice from above her in a language she'd mastered when, as a novice, she'd spent time learning the teachings of Siddhartha Gautama.

"Go slowly," she said, remembering the traditional greeting of these lands. "I bring no threat, and those that follow are on a sacred errand."

"It would be a sacred thing," the voice said, "to bring those tits here to warm my hands."

Kavundi sighed again. She was doing that far too often lately. She stopped, waiting for the others to catch up. The swords of Wigandus, Al-Rashid and David would silence such a foul tongue.

"Fool, put down your weapons," said another voice from above. "She follows the Sanātana dharma."

Kavundi looked up, squinting in the bright light, hoping to see the speakers and learn something of their nature.

"Yet she flaunts her tits in my eyes," said the first voice. "Let me

313

bring her to my tent. I would show her how the world's greatest lover honors those tits."

"You don't become the world's greatest lover from consorting with goats," said a third voice. "She shall be mine, and we will make the mountains shake with our love."

The second voice said, "Both of you, go back to your patrol."

Kavundi could now see a tall man dressed in saphron robes standing next to a small pile of stones high above her. His bald head gleamed in the sun and his narrow slanting eyes held a smile. His two companions loomed at his back, both dressed in plain robes and shabby fur-lined coats typical for mountain shepherds.

"Thank you for your help," she called up to him.

"If I had known you traveled without clothes, I would not have set those two to watch for you. I am Jigme."

She took a deep breath. Why was her nakedness such an issue for each man she met?

"I am Kavundi. I wear no clothes because I have sworn an oath of poverty."

"Yet you are not a mule, why act like one?" His gaze trailed to her companions, working their way up the stone steps. From this distance Kavundi could hear Al-Rashid's panting and Adelie's muffled cursing. "You should tell your companions to place small pebbles under their tongues and to suck on them. It will help relieve the sickness they feel and make walking easier."

Kavundi nodded, even though it did not make sense. Pebbles under the tongue? She looked again into Jigme's laughing eyes, but there was earnesty in them that told her this was probably not a joke.

When the others finally caught up she told them of the trick with the pebbles, wondering what Jigme meant by comparing her to a mule. After they had all caught their breath, she led them up to the top of the steps where Jigme and the two other men waited with wide grins on their faces.

Kavundi was mildly surprised when Jigme greeted her companions in Langue d'oc. "Welcome to the Kingdom of Lo Mantang. Britomar, word of your errand has reached the ears of this humble lama—"

"Humble, my ass!" said the man who had earlier spoken first, also in Langue d'oc.

"Heh!" laughed the other man. "Then again even the greatest lamas have fleas."

Adelie suppressed a giggle, but Jigme continued as if the interruptions had not happened. "Lo Pal, the king of Lo Mantang, wishes to honor you and your errand and give what aid he can."

"I will be glad of any aid that can be offered," said Britomar.

Kavundi hung her head. "The Garden we seek is not at the source of this river, is it?"

"No, but that speaks to what Lo Pal wishes to share with you. Come, we have a long journey still."

Kavundi had to admit that she felt disappointment at his words. She shrugged. That too was something she should be beyond.

Over the next two days, Jigme led them through mountain paths into a large valley with many gleaming rivers cutting through fields of barley. His two companions would not cease pestering Kavundi at night, boasting about their manhood.

On the second night, she found Jigme as he squatted near the small fire Adelie had used to cook with. She sank to the ground next to him. He moved over, giving her space next to the warmth of the fire.

"Is there nothing to be done to silence those two?" Kavundi asked.

Jigme's eyes creased with a smile. "It would not be easy. They are brothers, and neither has found a woman willing to take them for a wife."

Why am I not surprised? "They have no father to arrange their weddings?"

Jigme's smile widened. "Haven't you heard about our customs? Here, women choose their husbands. As they are brothers, a woman who chose one would gain both men, and such men as these two don't easily win a woman's heart."

Tell me about it...But—what an unusual custom. "Your ways are strange to me," said Kavundi.

Gwen's rakshasa, Natesa, chose that moment to climb onto her shoulder. Its tail tickled as it settled in.

Jigme said, "We wait for Maitreya, and in our waiting try to do honor to the Buddha. Since these two are not bothering any of the other women, perhaps you may find the answer to your question in this fact?"

Kavundi's eyes widened. *Is he suggesting that she silenced these men by taking them as husbands?* She forced her voice even as she said, "I have no need of a man to protect me."

Natesa screeched at Jigme. Kavundi wondered if the beast sensed her emotions and was taking her side, or just mocking her.

Jigme picked up a stick, looking at the embers as he stirred them. "Is that what David is to Adelie—her protector?"

"I have sworn an oath of chastity."

Smoke from the stirred embers swirled into her face, stinging her eyes. The rakshasa leapt off her shoulder and scrambled away. Kavundi sighed. She will not so easily leave the questions that burned her more than the smoke. What was happening to her self-control? How could smoke make her eyes sting so much? How could her heart race?

Jigme kept his eyes on the embers. "Has not Wigandus sworn such an oath? If you do not choose a companion, these two will continue to pressure you to choose amongst them."

"Then I will pray some other woman falls for their enthusiasm." Kavundi stepped away, too troubled to continue this conversation, hoping to renew herself in her meditations.

Toward the middle of the next day they neared a small city enclosed by white walls. The surrounding terrain was bare of crops, only small wisps of grass pushed up through the rocks. White flags wavered on the roofs of many buildings, like a sea of clouds.

As they neared the gates, Gwen approached her with Natesa perched on her head. "Kavundi, this city has the Devil's emblem on its gates. Could Jigme be trying to trap us?"

Kavundi looked. "Do you mean the images of goat heads?"

"Yes, that is the emblem of the evil one." Gwen pushed the rakshasa's tail away from her eyes.

Kavundi shook her head. "Goat images don't mean the same thing to these people. Here evil has different emblems, emblems appropriate to the people that dwell in such hardship."

Gwen nodded and resumed her walk, seemingly satisfied with the explanation. Kavundi followed her through the city's gate into the vibrant market plaza.

As they entered the city, she looked around in wonder. Hardship? Was that the word she'd used? She wished she could take it back. How could she possibly call what she beheld hardship? Women scurried around with smiles on their faces, wearing bright blue capes closed with peacock-shaped broaches, their leather head-dresses adorned in front with large turquoise studs and hanging in a long flap down the center of their backs. Those with larger head-dresses also wore ornate silver and gold boxes hanging around their necks on the chains of orange and turquoise stones. Men wore long fur-lined coats similar to those Jigme's companions wore, some dyed red, others white.

The anxiety Gwen felt stirred up in Kavundi as she saw people they passed sticking out their tongues at them. She hurried up in their column to catch up with Jigme walking in front.

"Jigme, why do they stick their tongues out at us?"

A smile shimmered at the corners of his eyes and mouth. "They are showing us that they have much respect for us." Something in his tone suggested her question was childish, and she decided not to follow it up with others. Anxiety should be one of the feelings long behind her. Still, this was an odd way for respect to be shown, and the muttering she heard from Wigandus likely meant that the others were also bothered.

She took a deep breath to force away her worries. There was nothing evil about Jigme, she was certain of it. In fact she felt that she rarely had such trust in anyone.

He led them through the tangled mesh of crowded streets, up a flight of stone steps, to a large flat terrace which afforded them a view of the entire valley. In its center was a large three-story-tall white square house with a massive but simple wooden door. It opened as they approached. Two people came out of it toward them—a man wearing a simple fur-lined coat, and a woman in a red silk blouse under a sleeveless red fur-lined tunic. Neither wore any of the fancy headdresses or jewels that had seemed so popular with those they'd passed on the streets.

Jigme said, "May I present to you Lo Pal, the king of Lo Mantang."

Kavundi pranemed as the others offered similar signs of respect. Jigme exchanged words with the king and then said to them, "I have been given His Majesty's permission to translate our conversation."

Jigme approached the king, who spoke softly to him. Kavundi stifled the brief wish that he'd speak up, so that she could validate Jigme's translation. Finally Jigme turned to the rest of his companions.

"Please allow me to share His Majesty's words with you. He said: 'I am grateful to you, Britomar, for the opportunity to lend you aid. We of Lo Mantang have not forgotten the unicorn that appeared before the army of the great Khan, dissuading him from destroying our fair city. Word has come to these ears not only of your errand, but that demons and Yeti are gathering in the shadows of Sagarmatha. I fear that they gather there to oppose your entrance into the Garden.'"

Kavundi said, "None of the sacred rivers flow from a source near Sagarmatha. My companions have a document that says 'from the Garden the four sacred rivers flow'. Though Sagarmatha might be one of the tree pillars the document also mentioned."

"Perhaps the rivers travel underground before they go to the source you've tracked," said Jigme.

Kavundi's eyes widened. "I never considered that."

She felt a gentle hand on her shoulder and looked up. Al-Rashid whispered in her ear, "Do not lose heart."

Britomar said, "I am grateful to Your Majesty for this news. Please forgive us if we leave right away, we have a long journey ahead of us."

Lo Pal again spoke to Jigme, who translated: "So far I have offered you only news, but I also promised aid. I have provisions to offer you, garments designed for the upper mountain passes, and mules to carry these things for you. You'll find these things awaiting you at the city gates.

"Also, my second son has asked to join your group. He is a monk, member of an ancient order of monks dedicated to keeping the Garden safe, and he knows the mountain paths. I will give him my permission, if I know him to be welcome to you."

Britomar said, "I am grateful to Your Majesty, and to your son. I would be glad of his guidance."

Lo Pal's face beamed with delight, and he embraced Jigme, kissing him on both cheeks. Jigme then pranemed to Britomar, "Forgive me, but I couldn't reveal myself to you until my father gave his permission. I am he who would be of service."

Kavundi realized a blush had stolen her cheeks, and reared herself. It should mean nothing to her that this monk would be the one to lead them to the Garden. She would permit herself no jealousy. That was a worse failing than anxiety.

"Forgive my questions," said Gwen, "but I must know. Friar Maeldoi told us of an order of monks that protects the Garden, one founded by Saint Isa. How can you be of that order? You are no Christian."

Jigme bowed his head. "Saint Isa founded our order, and lay upon us only one rule: no matter who came to serve the Garden, such person would be welcome, no matter the path he walked to get there, or the faith he followed. We are few in number, but it is a number constantly renewed from amongst the world's faithful."

"Yet you dwell in a city that sports the emblem of Satan and amongst a people who stick their tongues at us in mockery," said Wigandus. "We have followed you here in good faith, but how can we trust what you claim?"

"Jigme, what brought you news of our errand?" asked Britomar.

"The ravens carried news of it to us last moon, in a missive from my good friend Sri Thomas. Here, feel free to read it."

Britomar nodded. "I am satisfied. Will you please extend my gratitude to your father. We must be on our way."

Jigme once more spoke to his father, turned and translated, "He extends to you his blessing."

That night as they all ate Kavundi approached Al-Rashid sitting next to Galiana.

"Thank you for your encouragement today," she said.

He nodded. "You have been taking our failure to find the Garden in these mountains very hard, as if it were a failure of your being. Sometimes the road that Allah sets underfoot is a hard one."

Kavundi sighed. Lakshmidevi had certainly set a long road before them. Would they get to the Garden in time? "I have learned that when you love, it is hard to keep focused on your actions, hard to let go of their results." There, she'd admitted it to herself. She loved. She'd loved Britomar since the first time the mare had glanced at her on the boat. She was supposed to be beyond that too.

Galiana said, "Perhaps the result of our meandering is that now we have an eighth person again. Perhaps you have given us what we needed, not what we thought we needed."

"Eight is an auspicious number," said David who came over and sat next to Al-Rashid.

Kavundi looked into Al-Rashid's eyes. "I also want to thank you for finally accepting me, for no longer fighting me."

Al-Rashid smiled. "It is written in the Quran that you should not fight with those who do not threaten your faith. It took me a while to see that you and your people are no threat to Islam."

Galiana rose and gave Kavundi a kiss. "You brought us through much to get us to these mountains. We never would have gotten this far without you."

Kavundi's heart pounded, her breath short and heavy, the light air becoming suddenly hard to breathe. She rose to seek a place to meditate. Strange that of all the things that had happened to her, Galiana's kiss should shake her so much.

Later, as she was lying down to sleep, Jigme came and sat next to her. "Are you not cold?"

She closed her eyes. He of all people should know better. "If you cannot control yourself, self becomes your worst enemy."

Jigme smiled, settling into a lotus position. "Isn't self an illusion? Why waste your time on things that keep you from enlightenment?"

She'd forgotten that the followers of Siddhartha Gautama denied the reality of self. She sat up to face him. "My body is real, and is a gift. Enlightenment is not hiding from reality, but its fulfillment."

"So, if your body is real, and its needs are real, why take the path of the aesthetic? Why deny yourself?"

Kavundi shook her head. "I don't deny my body; I control it."

"Have you had sexual relations?"

Kavundi felt a blush creep up her cheeks. She peered into his face, but saw nothing but quiet curiosity. She wanted to respond that desire was not something she knew, but Galiana's kiss told her the lie of it. There was something of the divine about that woman, she felt it in her kiss, and longed to know it more. She wished Madhvacharya was here. It was hard, sometimes, being without her guru.

"No, I have not," she answered at last, remembering the argument she'd had in the temple with the devote of the tantrayoga. "Enlightenment through sex is possible, but forces you to depend on someone else who seeks the same. In my journey I need only depend upon me."

Jigme's smile softened. "Thank you, this helps me understand the path you walk better. One thing still confuses me. I understand not wanting clothing because you exercise control over your body. Still, garments could provide you comfort and protection. I asked you this before, when we first met: you are not a mule, why act like one?"

Kavundi rolled her eyes. "I don't act like an animal by walking unclad. We take oaths of poverty so as not to become dependent on things, and on people for providing them. Like Sri Shiva, the world is my bed, my hands my rice bowl."

"It is one thing not to be dependent on others, it is another to be immodest. You wear a loin cloth, hence you are not ready to shed all covers and expose yourself. Why not a sari?"

Why such a fixation on her breasts? "I'm a sannyasi," said Kavundi. "No sannyasi wear more than I do, some wear less. Why should I seek to differ?"

"Ah, but you are a woman. You are by your nature different. I am quite surprised that your swami took you as a student."

She let her anger slip, and chuckled instead. Did he feel threatened by her? Threatened by her sex? "Sri Krishna once said that those who take refuge in him, even women, will reach the supreme goal. Lakshmidevi herself sought me out and sent me to find Madhvacharya, and then to serve Britomar. There have not been many women who sought to become sannyasi since the time of the Vedas, but we exist."

Jigme said, "Tell me this, is it still taught that one must be a Brahmin and keep ritually pure to achieve enlightenment? And how may a woman keep ritually pure?"

Kavundi tried not to gloat as he retreated to a critique of the way things were a thousand years ago. Gloating should also be beneath her. "Madhvacharya teaches that one's true caste relates more to one's nature than to one's birth. A Chandala who treads the spiritual path is a better being than a Brahmin who is ignorant of that path and puts on an artificial appearance. Besides, did not Sri Krishna say that all those who love and trust in him, even prostitutes and beggars, would achieve the ultimate?"

"I would like to meet this Madhvacharya," said Jigme. "Apparently much has changed since the Buddha's time in the south. We don't get much word from below the mountains. Perhaps, when Britomar's errand is done, you will take me to him?"

Madhvacharya would be glad of another student. Kavundi looked at him with curiosity. "Do none of your order follow Dharma?"

"Some do, but strangely we don't discuss our different ways with each other. It is considered impolite. I hope you don't take offense at my questions, curiosity was ever my weakness."

He's curious? Perhaps he wasn't threatened by her sex at all. Perhaps she was right to begin with, he was just following a different dharma. If so, then all her thoughts betrayed her own failings. "I take no offense, and would enjoy learning more of those who follow Siddhartha Gautama. It has been long since his followers walked the lands south of the mountains." She leaned back. "I am tired, Jigme. We should talk more of these things as we travel. If you don't mind, I would like to rest now."

"Why do you sleep so far from the others? Are you not worried about the snow leopards?"

"I seek silence for my meditations, and have no fear of any beast."

He frowned. "As we near Sagarmatha, you may wish to sleep closer to the fire. The Yeti are about."

Kavundi saw the concern in his eyes and felt resentment rising in her chest. Hadn't she told him she had no need of a protector? "I will not live in fear of man or beast, but in peace in my search for God. That I might die is of no consequence."

"I must disagree. I think your death would keep Britomar from succeeding. If you will not come near the fire, will you at least accept my company? I will not disturb your meditations, as I've my own."

Kavundi had no easy answer for this request. She couldn't shake the misgivings that he didn't see her as a sannyasi, but as a woman, but she had no desire to insult him with her suspicions.

"Sleep where you may," she said.

KATHMANDU

Kavundi stood with the others at the crest of a hill looking down into a large and lush valley. Around its edges, forests darkened the base of the mountains higher than even those near Lo Mantang. Spacious fields opened before her. Beyond them rose the jagged mass of walls and towers of a city, too distant to see the details.

"That should be Kathmandu," Jigme said. "We'll be able to get what we need there to travel the high mountain passes."

"The Garden is supposed to be centered between the three tallest peaks," said David.

"I have never seen mountains taller than those surrounding this valley," said Adelie. "If what the parchment says is right, we'll find the Garden near here."

As the city grew closer, they passed women in the fields beating drums while the men tended the crops.

"Why do they do that?" Adelie asked

"To keep away the rakshasas who delight in stealing the crops," Jigme said.

"It's not scaring Natesa away," said Gwen.

"She is no thief," said Kavundi.

The constant and regular beat of the drums followed them in their descent through the fields to the central plateau of the valley. Kavundi was surprised at how her feet had picked up the rhythm. She frowned. Was she going too far and surrendering her self-control?... Why was she so anxious?

As they neared the city, Gwen said, "I see golden roofs, but no wall. How can a city have no walls around it? Even Lo Mantang, which was so much more remote, had strong walls to protect it."

"Kathmandu is a sacred city to both people and beasts," Kavundi said. "Who would want to do it harm?"

"Sacred to beasts?" asked Britomar.

"Beasts are honored, as our playfellows and our helpers. Sri Shiva especially looks in favor upon beasts, and Kathmandu sits in the shadow of his mountain."

"Is Sri Shiva not the destroyer?" asked Jigme.

"His dance is a means of renewal, not destruction," answered Kavundi. "Those who see in him or in Kalidevi only a destroying force forget what Sri Krishna said. There is no time when you or I did not exist, nor will there ever be such a time."

"We believe differently," said David. "We believe that everything has its season, even death, and that only the Lord is eternal."

"This is why my people see demons in this Shiva and Kalidevi," said Al-Rashid. "Though if I understand you, when you say destroyer you mean it as, for instance, autumn that destroys the flowers only for spring to return them to us."

"Yes, that is a good way to understand what we mean when we talk about Sri Shiva and his dance," said Kavundi, relieved that Al-Rashid no longer saw a threat in Dharma.

As they neared the city, its tall and brightly painted wooden square towers became distinct. Built in levels, their gilded roofs glittered in the sun brighter than the snow-covered peaks in the distance.

"Do they build their roofs out of gold?" said Gwen.

Kavundi nodded, narrowing her eyes against the blaze. "Madhvacharya told me of those buildings. They're temples; one is in honor of Kathma, one of Shiva the protector of animals, and one of the Buddha. I heard that guests to the city are housed there, hence their size."

"No mosques?" asked Al-Rashid.

"No, but both imams and Christian priests are permitted in the city," she said, and then noticed David grinning. "I don't know if there is a rabbi, but I know he'd be welcome."

David said, "From what I know of my uncle's trade network, I'd be surprised if there weren't a few."

"Will you enter this city, Britomar?" asked Sir Wigandus.

Kavundi looked back at the unicorn and saw Gwen next to her, pain evident in her face. She offered, encouragingly, "Beasts are honored in this city."

Britomar shook her head. "No. I will wait in the wilds."

Gwen said, "I think that I'll enter this city. For months I've avoided cities, and so I've not been able to find a priest. If I can find one, there are things I'd like to confess."

Britomar hesitated. "I have not been alone for so long that I find myself dreading the prospect of a night without you. Perhaps I should enter this city wherein beasts are sacred, so you and I are not separated."

"Is it safe?" asked David.

"No, it's probably not," said Gwen as she looked down at her feet, twirling her hair with one hand behind her back. "But I need a priest, if one may be found."

"Then we will try to find you one," said Kavundi, not knowing why her heart quickened.

Kavundi found entering the chaotic din of the city helped her restore her sense of self-control. The central square was large and crowded. Merchants spread their wares over large colorful blankets. Hot peppers were displayed in enticing rows like red Shiva Linga, each pointing to the tiered pagodas of the temple that dominated the square. Thick round posts of dark wood set on a step pyramid that was taller than most surrounding buildings, lifted the tripartite tower into the sky.

Kavundi led the way to the temple, intending to be the first to honor Kathmadevi, the patron of this city. She climbed the smooth stone steps to the plateau at the pyramid's top.

Three times they circled the dark and quiet temple with its open doors, with a pile of shoes tossed carelessly to the side. Kavundi finished the circle and bent to remove her shoes.

"Please respect Kathmadevi, and bare your feet before entering," she reminded the others. Al-Rashid opened his mouth to speak, but stopped as Galiana fell to her knees and began to undo the straps on his sandals.

Unshod, Kavundi stepped into the temple, properly bare of any ornaments save for the black statue of Kathma at the rear. Large glowing braziers set on tripods at the sides of the hall emanated heat, filling the room with thick, fragrant smoke. In their dim light, she could barely make out large open arches to the chambers where she knew they could lodge if they desired.

She heard a shuffling noise and turned to see an old man with three stripes drawn from the top of his nose up and across his bald head. He had painted his chest and arms red. He brought his hands together and bowed slightly. Kavundi returned the greeting.

The man nodded. "Ah, yes, as promised. You seek the Garden. Good, good."

Kavundi stiffened. She shouldn't be surprised that this man knew their destination so well, yet she felt her skin prickle in anticipation. Was he going to show them the way?

"You're near," the man went on, as if hearing her unspoken question. "It is north and east of here, beneath the shadow of the three mountains. The tallest one is Sagarmatha, where Lord Shiva perches. In Sagarmatha's shadow, you will find them waiting to take you to

Kalidevi."

Them? "It is not Kalidevi we seek," she said, no longer so certain of herself, or her conviction.

"So you say."

Kavundi lifted her chin. "I am disappointed. I had hoped for the hospitality of Kathmadevi, and instead I find her devotee directing us to Kalidevi."

The man smiled with his mouth, but not his eyes. "You may avail yourself of the hospitality of Kathmadevi for a night or two, but you are for Kalidevi."

"No. I am for Lakshmidevi."

"So you say. Follow me, I will show you where you may spend the night."

"Did you follow what he said?" Kavundi asked Gwen quietly, watching the man disappear in one of the side passages.

Gwen nodded. "Yes. I wish we had not come...Yet, I couldn't help wondering: could those three mountains he spoke of be the three pillars mentioned in the scroll?"

"They may be."

"Perhaps it would be safer to leave the city?" asked Gwen.

Kavundi shivered. She had such a bad feeling about this place. What happened to her usual detachment? Could the one the priest called Kalidevi be a demon robbing her of what she was? They'd already faced demons on their journey, perhaps it was her turn to confront her darkness?

"I promised to help you find a priest," she said. "I will keep that promise."

"Thank you."

Kavundi wondered if perhaps the search would help her as well.

"Is it wise for the two of you to go alone through the city?" asked Wigandus.

"None of this is wise, Wigandus," said Gwen as she took his hand. "It is not wise that I'm in this city with Britomar, it's not wise that we seek the Garden. No, not wise, but hopefully merciful."

"Take care, both of you," said Adelie.

Gwen delighted in the smells and colors of the market. Everywhere she looked she saw rakshasas, some stealing from the food vendors, others chasing each other or being chased by merchants. Natesa sat on her shoulder, tail curled around the back of her neck, hissing at any rakshasa that came near. Gwen smiled at the thought that Natesa was trying to protect her. She did her best to keep close to Kavundi, who strode through the streets with determination, stopping every once in a while to talk to some locals. So far none had been forthcoming.

A group of men ahead of them gathered around a flat board. Like a chess board from back home, this board was laid out in a grid, but painted with snakes and ladders all the way across. Five different stones rested on the board. Not for the first time Gwen wished that she knew more of the local languages, as she longed to understand what the men were so excited about as they chattered rapidly in their language. She stretched her neck, watching.

A young man with a red line painted on his forehead picked up a blue stone from the board and moved it one square at a time until it rested at the base of a ladder. His fellows murmured appreciably as he then moved the stone along the ladder to rest on the image of a man's face with three open eyes.

"Namaste," said Kavundi as she pranemed.

Each of the men rose, pranemed and returned her greeting. The eldest, with a face as wrinkled as the mountains, spoke in one of the languages Kavundi had so painstakingly tried to teach her. To Gwen's relief she understood the words:

"Holy One, how may we be of service?"

Kavundi briefly glanced at Gwen. "We seek a priest of my companion's dharma. One who would speak of God as one, but with a son who became a man, died, and conquered death in finding his divinity. Do you know of such a priest in the city?"

The man who had moved the stone said, "I know of such a priest, and would be honored if you permitted me to take you to him."

"What of your journey on the board?" asked another man.

The older man rose from his seat. "It is my dharma to bring this Holy One to the priest she seeks. If I turn from it to follow my path on the board, surely I would find myself beset by snakes." He stepped around the board and gestured for the two women to follow him.

He kept a slow pace, allowing them to easily follow him through the crowded streets and alleys. Soon he stopped next to a small house, expectantly waiting for them to approach.

"Is this the place?" asked Gwen, wondering at the absence of a crucifix.

"Enter and see, enter and see," said the man, gesturing to the door.

"I'll wait outside," Kavundi said.

Gwen pushed the door open and stepped into a room dimly lit by an incense burner. The familiar scent of smoldering frankincense welcomed her. She looked around, relief washing over her.

In the dim ember glow she could barely make out an image of Christ raising his hands to reveal the holes where the nails had been. Gwen started to kneel before the image, but a soft voice said, "You know He'd not want you to prostrate yourself. He's your brother, not a tyrant."

Gwen peered into the gloom, trying to see the owner of the voice. "You speak Breton?" She was suddenly very homesick.

"It is a gift of the Holy Spirit, no?" The priest chuckled and stepped into the light, a thin elderly man in the simple brown robe of the Franciscans with a tonsured head and kind, smiling eyes. "This gift has allowed me to minister to many of our faith, from many lands. What brings you here?"

Gwen looked at her feet. "Father, I wish absolution from my sins."

"You know He's already forgiven them."

"I was taught we must seek a priest for intercession. . ."

He nodded. "I've engaged in a lively correspondence on this issue with a Friar Thomas. A truly holy man, he, but a peculiar one, too. He agrees with you."

Friar Thomas? Gwen wondered briefly if it could be the same priest that Adelie and Élise had told her about.

"But I think," the priest continued, "that anyone can be our confessor. Are we not His adopted? Anyway, let's not debate theology when you're hurting. Tell me what is troubling you. While forgiveness comes from God, I can at least offer comfort."

Gwen took a breath. "I've blamed a blameless man for my near rape at the hands of the Caliph of Baghdad."

"Have you spoken to this blameless man, have you asked his forgiveness?"

"Yes, father," said Gwen.

The priest smiled to her gently. "When we're hurting, it is easy to seek a reason, someone to blame. Don't be too hard on yourself. Forgive yourself."

"Forgive myself?"

The priest stepped closer, his thick gray beard gleaming like spun silver in the dim light of the censure. "Yes. If you have sought forgiveness of God and man, your last step must be to forgive yourself."

"But—" Gwen stammered. "Is there no penance to do? No gift to give?"

"Child, don't you think forgiving yourself is enough penance for anyone?"

Gwen had no answer for this question, it was enough just to try to wrap her thoughts around such a novel idea.

The priest touched her arm gently. "Go, and pray if you need. Forgiving yourself is not easy, yet it is what you must do."

Gwen nodded. "If you please, father, there is another who seeks to speak with you. My companion, she's waiting outside."

The priest nodded. "Send her in."

"She's not Christian..."

"Child, that is not an issue."

Gwen took a step back and pulled open the door. Kavundi, who was seated with her legs crossed, resting her open palms upon her knees, opened her eyes and rose in a fluid motion, bringing her palms together to praneme.

"Come in my sister," said the priest before Gwen could extend the invitation.

Gwen made to exit, but Kavundi touched her on the shoulder "Please stay."

"Namaste," the priest said to Kavundi.

"Namaste." Kavundi pranemed again.

"What is it that troubles you?"

Kavundi swallowed. "I need a new mantra; I'm no longer finding the mantra my guru gave me sufficient."

"This is not uncommon. How is your mantra failing you?"

"I've become impatient, I lost my temper at two men who would not relent in their offers of marriage, and found my body stepping to the rhythm of the drums as we walked through the fields on our way to Kathmandu. I just—I seem to react to many things that should be beyond me."

Gwen shifted from foot to foot, wishing that Kavundi had let her leave; this was too much like a confession, she had no right to listen to it.

The priest shook his head. "Your guru teaches self-control as a means to enlightenment?"

"Yes, that is what he teaches."

"Why come to me with these questions, when our way is different from yours?"

Kavundi glanced at Gwen. "This maid, Gwenaella, is the reason I stand before you. She lives as if love is about giving, rather than a desire. This is not what Sri Kama teaches in his sutra. Yet, I feel that it is love that has disrupted my meditations, much like love disrupted those of Sri Shiva. I would learn a new mantra."

The priest regarded her. "Who is it you love?"

Gwen held her breath. Could Kavundi have fallen in love with

Jigme?

"Britomar."

"Is this Britomar a good man?" asked the priest.

Gwen set her breath free in a hearty laugh. "Britomar is a unicorn, father."

Kavundi took a breath. "When I'm near her, I feel complete, in a way that my meditations only hint at. Lakshmidevi herself asked me to help Britomar, bring her to the Garden so that her father may have his health restored. Helping her is slowly destroying me."

The priest smiled. "Then, my daughter, let yourself be destroyed. Let yourself love. Is that not the message in the story of Shiva?"

"It is hard, giving up all I thought I was, my journey to the divine."

"God created you in love. Love is of your being. You will not find Him without it. Go, my child, love, and in your destruction find renewal."

As they returned to the temple complex, Gwen wondered if at long last she had found a way to renew her own love. Was it selfish of her to long to find the Garden so that Wigandus may be released from his vow of virginity? Would she be able to enter the Garden, with such mixed motives? Or would God look into her heart and find her lacking?

DEVI

Gwen woke from a dream that Wigandus was calling her name. She sat up and looked around her in dim light accorded by the braziers. Shadowed mounds of her sleeping friends on the floor—Adelie and David, Britomar, Galiana and Al-Rashid, Kavundi and Jigme... Where was Wigandus? Gwen's heart raced as she strained her eyes to see through the shadows. She could see Wigandus's armor piled by the wall, his sword reflecting the fire... Where would he go without his sword?

Gwen stepped over her bundle and tiptoed through the shadows to Britomar. She gently touched the unicorn. Britomar opened her eyes at once.

"What is wrong?"

"Wigandus is not here," Gwen whispered urgently.

The unicorn sat up. "Let's wake the others, we should search for him."

"No." This time Gwen's voice was firm. "I'm going to go looking for him alone."

Britomar peered into her eyes. "Is that wise?"

Gwen averted her gaze. Wigandus needed her. There was no time to lose. She grabbed her cloak, too warm in the oppressive heat of the temple, but she knew it would likely be freezing once she stepped into the open air.

"I've the strangest feeling that it is. I just did not want to go off without telling someone. Wake the others after I'm gone, I think we'll need to leave the moment I return."

"Gwen, please be careful."

"I will. We're too close to the Garden to fail now."

Adelie rubbed her eyes and yawned, pulling away from David's sleepy grasp. In the dim light she could see Britomar walking through the chamber. She sat up, looking at her waking companions. Her skin prickled when she realized there were fewer of them.

"Where are Gwen and Wigandus?" she asked, grasping David's hand.

"Gwenaella woke and found him missing," Britomar said. "She's gone off in search of him."

Kavundi put her finger to her lips. Adelie drew her long knife and David reached for his sword. Al-Rashid held his scimitar at ready, even Galiana held the knife Adelie had given her so many months ago.

She heard a muffled *umph* in the passage leading into their room. Al-Rashid and David nodded to each other quietly and slid to either side of the entrance. Adelie clenched her dagger.

After a long, painful pause, men in red garments with broad curved swords poured into the room. Al-Rashid cut down the first through his door, David the second as Adelie met the third one with her blade. She quickly emasculated him, but the next man was ready for her and caught her knife on his sword.

Snarling, he sliced at her. She stepped back, pushing up with her knife, until his sword was over her head. She twisted out of the lock, thrusting at his chest. He stepped away, hitting her knife hand with the pommel of his sword. The sting knocked the knife from her hand. She leapt after it, falling into a roll, pulling away from a burning cut on her back. She grabbed the knife before it landed and rose to her feet catching the man's blade on hers as he sliced at her. Holding the lock she kicked him in the belly and he doubled over. She sliced his neck and pushed him to the ground.

Galiana was down! Adelie stepped under the blade aimed to re-move Galiana's head, catching it with her knife. She nearly tripped over Galiana's leg, but let herself fall into a roll, picking up her old knife from Galiana's limp hand. In one motion she rose and tossed that knife at the attacker's face. He fell, the bloodied hilt quivering in his eye socket.

Adelie looked for another opponent, but saw that their assailants were all either dead or fleeing. Her back stung. She reached up with her hand to see what it was and barely registered her fingers sinking into thick, warm liquid. Her ears roared, and the ground rushed at her.

Kavundi stood over her two fallen enemies. Her chest heaved as she let her breathing relax, slowly calming down. She looked over at Jigme who also had two men at his feet.

He bowed to her. "You did not mention your control of self being extended to an ability to fight."

Kavundi's lips twitched. "Madhvacharya also taught us wrestling ... How is it that I found myself in your arms when I awoke?"

His smile was innocent, his eyes gleaming with merry sparkles. "I am as ignorant as you. Are you angry?"

"Do you swear that you did not waken and come to me in the night?"

"By the Maitreya, I do so swear." His eyes told her the truth of his oath.

"Then, I am not angry. Let's see how the others fared. We will speak more of this later."

"Britomar! Quick, over here!" yelled David.

Kavundi let her gaze find him in the shadows, kneeling over Adelie and Galiana. The unicorn was there in a heartbeat, Kavundi and Al-Rashid not far behind.

As Britomar leaned down to touch her horn to the fallen women, smoke rose from the blood on the floor, gathering into thick tendrils around their bodies. Britomar's eyes rolled but she lowered her horn again, touching the women through the smoke.

"Don't!" Kavundi shouted, recognizing the demon.

Tendrils of smoke clasped her, throwing her across the room. Their touch burned like hot iron. She brought her hands together, centering herself, and her flight stopped. Letting go of the momentary astonishment at hanging in mid air, she brought her legs up to settle into a lotus position, focusing. She prayed.

The burning tendrils of smoke burned, pushed against her, but she would not let go of her center, her mind focused in a plea. "Great Mother, help."

Crash!

A gust of air blew past her. Kavundi opened her eyes. Holes had opened in the walls, filling the room with chaos. Wood and stones swirled through the smoke, sparkling in the moonlight cast through the divinely cut windows.

Steel flashed as Al-Rashid and David raised their blades. Kavundi concentrated. Steel would be useless against the Vetal. She dared a glance away from the battle of wind and smoke to spot Britomar, her horn gray, her eyes closed where she lay against the wall.

A voice colder than ice spoke to Kavundi. "Will you reject me again, sister, or will you let go of self and let me in? You were told I would come for you."

Kavundi ignored the speaker as she closed her eyes and sought her center. She let her conscious wander out of the room, through the wall, to where the Dark Mother stood outside the temple, her necklace of stones dripping fresh blood on her black breasts. She fought panic as she pranemed to Kali. "Please, enter and help us, Great Mother."

A wall of the temple burst apart. Kavundi watched, entranced, as Kalidevi stepped through the gaping hole into the chamber, walking in measured steps through the smoke to stand over the two fallen women. Kavundi tried not to wince as the Dark Mother reached down. Her black hand touched the blood, from which the smoke came. The smoke gathered around Kali, swirling inward and upon her. Kavundi glimpsed a face twisting in a silent scream—the face of one of the fallen men. Then the smoke disappeared. The winds slipped into a breeze, lowering Kavundi back to the ground.

She ran to Britomar, placing her hand on the unicorn's side heaving with her shallow breathing. Kavundi could find no wound.

David and Al-Rashid stepped before Kali, swords drawn. David said, "Do you serve the Lord of Hosts, or the adversary?"

Kali's lips twitched into a smile. "I brought the last curse to the pharaoh because of Moshe in Egypt, David ben Yosi. Who do you think I serve?"

David's eyes widened as he lowered his sword.

Kali nodded. "Put down your swords and comfort these women. The spell of the Vetal is broken and they're awakening." She stepped aside to let David and Al-Rashid go to Adelie and Galiana.

"Take me, Mother," Kavundi pleaded. "I am ready." She knew it was a lie. She was not ready. But she could not bear the thought of anyone else dying.

Kali shook her head, her face grave. "No, sister. This sacrifice is not yours to make."

"Who is to die then?" asked Jigme.

Kavundi stifled a sob and looked down at Britomar, gray and still against the temple wall.

After climbing down the cold stone steps of the pyramid, Gwen looked around the square. The gibbous moon allowed her to see much of the empty field. *Blessed Mother, please help me find him.* Pulling her mantle closer to fend off the cold night air, she set off with no clear direction in mind. She had not gone far when a familiar squeak sounded faintly from the shadows. Natesa! She hurried in the direction of the squeak to find the rakshasa pulling herself along the ground with her forelimbs, her hinds dangling, twisted beyond use.

Gwen stifled a cry and lifted Natesa gently, kissing her on the head. Natesa reached out, her paw clenching a small object Gwen couldn't make out in the dim lighting. Natesa hissed, they way she always did when Wigandus was returning. Gwen looked in the direction the rakshasa gestured to. "Did Wigandus go that way?"

To her relief, Natesa nodded.

Cradling the rakshasa in her arms, Gwen ran in that direction. At some corners, the rakshasa hissed and Gwen changed her path as Natesa pointed the way. Each hiss a little fainter, each corner a little darker, as the moon slipped down and the shadows lengthened. As Gwen trotted down a street too narrow for the moon to lighten, the rakshasa groaned. Gwen stopped, looking for a new street to take, for Natesa to point the way, but Natesa's head hung limply. Gwen felt the rakshasa's chest, failing to feel a heartbeat.

Natesa had taken her last breath.

Gwen's eyes filled with tears. The dear creature had done so much to help reconcile Wigandus to her, had spent her last breaths trying to help Gwen find the dear man. She closed her eyes briefly, uttered a silent prayer of thanks for Natesa and a plea that she'd find Wigandus, and continued through the shadows in the last direction the rakshasa had shown her.

GIVING

Galiana heard someone calling her name. The voice was joyous but hollow, as if coming from far away. She wanted to answer, but a strange smoke enfolded her, choking her. She couldn't breathe through that smoke, couldn't remember the last time she took a breath. Was she dead?

She must be dead, this must be hell, with so much smoke in it. Yet why did the voice calling her name sound so gentle, so caring?

Her nose tickled. Galiana sneezed and found herself breathing freely. The smoke dissipated, replaced by the smells of blood and incense oil, heavy in the air. She opened her eyes, but all she could see was haloed black and brown shapes, swirling. She closed her eyes again, rubbed them and reopened.

Al-Rashid's face emerged from the chaos, leaning over her. His skin looked ashen gray in the pale light, his brow knit in worry.

"Allah be praised, you've come back to me," he said.

She could see a shadow looming behind Al-Rashid. *Who was it?*

"I was hurt," she heard herself saying. "There was smoke, I couldn't breathe. What happened?"

Al-Rashid said, "A demon hurt you and Adelie. When Britomar came to help you, it threw her like she was no more than a feather. Allah be praised, somehow Kavundi destroyed the demon, but she can't do anything to help Britomar."

Galiana sat up and looked around.

Dead bodies littered the blood-covered floor. Great holes gaped through the temple's walls, letting in moonlight that pooled upon the floor. Her eyes were drawn to a shape lying against the back wall, beneath the feet of a broken statue. *Britomar!* Galiana's heart raced. Even in moonless nights, the unicorn had never looked so gray and disturbingly still, her horn losing its usual glow to become a dull bone-white. Galiana stood up and swayed, her head spinning. A hand slipped under her arm to steady her. She looked up, expecting to thank Al-Rashid for his help, but it was not his arm that held her up. It was Kavundi—and she was crying!

"Galiana," sobbed Kavundi, "It is in you to heal Britomar, if you choose."

Galiana stared at her. "What do you mean?"

"The Vetal—it is something that should be dead, but isn't. It hurt Britomar and tried to kill you and Adelie. Kalidevi destroyed it, but told me you alone knew how to save Britomar."

Galiana looked at Al-Rashid, hoping to find in his face an answer for the question that tore her mind. How could she save Britomar? She searched his smiling eyes, dancing with the same light that sparkled there when he first talked to her on his ship, when he had told her she was holy.

I can do this. Galiana looked at Britomar then back at Al-Rashid. A shiver ran through her, warmth filling her with a sense of rightness she'd never known before meeting Britomar. "I love you," she said to him.

He embraced her. "I love you too."

Kavundi gave her a kiss. "There was never a time when you did not exist, nor will there be."

Galiana wondered what that meant, but put aside her question. She had no time for Kavundi's odd ideas, Britomar was dying. She approached the unicorn and knelt next to her. What did Kavundi expect her to do? Britomar was always healing others, healing with a touch. She looked at her hands, and saw the blackened finger that had traced the signs on Adelie.

Galiana closed her eyes and saw again the one symbol that had haunted her since the tiger had attacked Adelie. She reached down to the unicorn and touched her, tracing the sign upon her silky coat. Pain shot up her hand. She screamed and pulled her hand away.

She steadied herself and opened her eyes. Britomar was less grey, like the moon in a cloudy sky, but her horn was still dull. Galiana knew she had to trace the sign again. With a sob, she reached out. Each stroke of her finger burned, slicing up her arm with unbearable pain. She screamed, sweat pouring down her forehead, tears flowing from her eyes. But she kept going. She could not afford to stop.

She barely registered it as an arm wrapped around her, a hand gently taking her free hand. The sign hung before her, glowing brighter and brighter until she had to close her eyes from the hurting brilliance.

Finished, she fell upon the ground, sobbing. She felt a gentle squeeze on her hand and opened her eyes. The sign she had traced on Britomar was fading, its brilliance bearable, but Britomar was still gray, though less so. Her horn no longer looked like a clean bone, but still had no sheen.

Galiana clenched her teeth. She had to do it again. But did she have the strength?

"Help me." Her voice cracked.

Two pairs of arms helped her up, a hand caressing her back. She turned to say thank you and Al-Rashid kissed her on the cheek. Warmth spread through her and she shivered.

Taking a deep breath, Galiana reached out to take in Britomar's agony and trace again the sign that burned urgently before her eyes.

As Gwen crossed each road, she looked down both ways, hoping for some sign that would bring her to Wigandus. Finally she saw a large shape lying on the ground up ahead. As she got closer, the hairs on the back of her neck rose. The moon slipped behind a cloud. She held her breath hoping it would return soon, fearing what it would show.

The darkness was short-lived, and her breath returned with a sob. Wigandus lay face-down not twenty paces away, naked and still. She fought off panic and ran to him, gently laying down Natesa's broken body and lifting Wigandus's hand. It was cold, but she could feel the steady rhythm of his breath as she put her arm on his back. Alive. Relief washed over her. She rolled him over and noticed a thick rope around his neck, clutched by his other hand as if he had been trying to pull it loose.

She unwound the rope, and threw it into the shadows. Hoping to warm him, she lay next to him, trying to cover as much of him with herself as she could. She kissed him on the cheek and neck, calling his name as she rubbed her hands on his shoulders and arms. He stirred slightly against her legs and she blushed as she continued rubbing, kissing his face, his neck, pleading for him to wake.

He moaned, and she shivered and started to cry. The hope that swelled in her was too much to bear. She shifted again and rubbed his shoulders more vigorously, pleading for him to wake.

Finally, he opened his eyes. "Liebchen?"

Gwen kissed him. "Wigandus! What happened to you?"

The knight gasped, steadying his breath. Leaning on Gwen, he slowly sat up, dazed. "I couldn't sleep. As I lay awake, one of the rakshasas slipped in, crept over to David and pulled a parchment from his pack. Natesa and I followed it out of the temple, and ran into some rough company. Strange men, I'm not sure why they attacked us. All I had with me was my knife, but I took out a few of them. Then one of them jumped onto my back and wrapped a rope around my neck. I couldn't shake him..." He rubbed his neck absentmindedly, tracing the raw imprint of a rope against his throat.

Gwen kissed him again. "I'm so glad you're alive! I don't know what I'd have done if I'd lost you." She snuggled in closer to him.

He stiffened. "Mine Gott! I'm naked!"

Gwen fought back a smile. Even in the moonlight she could see him blush. "I found you that way. They must have stolen your clothes."

Wigandus rubbed his head. "I didn't... I'm sorry."

Gwen hid her face against his shoulder. "Your manhood awoke and greeted me before the rest of you."

Wigandus chuckled, then put his hands gently behind her head and pulled her face to his. She drew closer, letting her hips slide down to meet him, his sweet smell washing over her. Her breath quickened as he brushed her face in a brief, chaste kiss and released her.

"Come," she said, drawing away from him. "Let's get back to the temple and tell the others of the theft."

"How did you find me?" he asked as he rose to his feet.

Gwen bent to lift Natesa's body from the cold earth. "Natesa lived long enough to bring me here."

Wigandus lowered his head. "She leapt onto one of the men, clawing at his eyes. Dear thing, I feared her dead when she was thrown to the ground. What's that in her paw?"

Gwen slipped the scrap from the rakshasa's paw. The parchment! She handed it to Wigandus who smoothed it out.

"Mine Gott! Es ist eine, sorry, a fragment of the manuscript David found, and look: the text is all here!"

Gwen nodded, relieved. They still had their guide to the Garden. More to the point, those who had set the rakshasas to steal the manuscript didn't. She noticed Wigandus shivering and unwrapped her mantle, draping it over his shoulders.

"You're only in your shift?" He removed the coat, holding it out for her to take.

"I didn't have time to dress. We'll share it, You wear it until I'm too cold."

"No knight of the empire would permit his love to be cold."

Gwen's eyes inadvertently slid down and she blushed. "You should cover yourself. Let's get going."

As they walked, Wigandus slipped his hand into hers. She gave it a gentle squeeze as she took it.

"Thank you for searching for me. I have failed you in every way, hurt you... my vow... if only I'd—"

Gwen interrupted him. "So, marry me, Wigandus. Replace your vow of chaste chivalry with that of chaste matrimony."

He suddenly stopped, forcing Gwen to stop with him. She turned to face him, still holding his hand.

"I do receive you as mine," Wigandus said solemnly, "so that you become my wife and I your husband."

Gwen's eyes widened as she recognized the ancient wedding vows. She lay Natesa's body on the ground, rose and took both of his hands. "I do receive you as mine, so that you become my husband, and I your wife."

They embraced and kissed, holding each other close. Gwen sighed, inhaling his familiar scent, losing herself in his warm, strong embrace. An intense feeling of happiness washed over her. Whatever perils they faced, whatever they had to do to complete their quest, she felt it was all worth it. She felt complete.

Finally, they drew away from each other, lifted Natesa, and resumed their walk back to the temple, hand in hand. On the horizon, the sky began to lighten, a deep blue rising from the black.

Galiana's body screamed in agony as she forced her hand to trace the sign upon Britomar for the third time. Her head started to feel queasy, but she knew she must finish it, whatever the cost. She couldn't afford to stop. It took all she had to keep her hand steady. Spots swirled before her eyes, her lungs screaming for air as she tried and failed to take a breath. Her whole being concentrated on pushing the one last agonizing line along the unicorn's fur.

Fur! As her finger reached the end of the stroke, all she felt was fur. The agony of the touch—all gone. Air rushed into her lungs as her chest heaved with a much-needed breath. Strong arms lifted her, and Al-Rashid's musk scent washed over her.

"Britomar!" she heard Adelie say. And another, glorious sound—hooves scraping on the wood floor.

She felt a sharp touch to her shoulder, filling her with overwhelming joy, painfully pushing aside her sorrow until the only thing she knew was the warmth of Al-Rashid's embrace.

Gwen could feel Wigandus shivering long before they reached the temple square. The sky brightened, touching the streets with the first light of dawn.

Three men ran past them. Even in the faint light Gwen noticed one of them clutching an arm, bleeding heavily. Wigandus and Gwen glanced at each other and ran the rest of the way up to the square, up the stairs and into the temple.

The braziers that had formerly lit the hall had been knocked over, cinders steaming through wide pools of water. In the distance, they could hear a woman weeping. Wigandus pushed Gwen behind him and stepped into the room where they had all slept. She followed close and stopped in shock.

A pile of corpses lay in the far corner of the room. Three couples huddled by the wall around Britomar. Adelie and Kavundi were sobbing. Galiana lay in Al-Rashid's embrace. Her arm hung limply at her side, its skin ashen gray, covered with black soot and blisters.

"What in the name of all that is Holy happened here?" Wigandus bellowed.

"Wigandus! Gwen!" Adelie rose from David's lap and ran to them, embracing Gwen. "Oh, poor Natesa! What happened?"

David grabbed a blanket and hastily draped it around Wigandus's shoulders. "What happened to you? Did you decide to become a sannyasi?"

"I found him like this," said Gwen, who lay Natesa down and helped him pull some clothes from his packs, then donned her own clothes. "A rakshasa stole David's scroll. Wigandus followed it and was attacked by a group of men. I think they left him for dead, after they stripped him of everything he had. Natesa gave her life so that I could find him and save the scroll... What happened here?"

Al-Rashid said, "After you left to look for our naked knight, Britomar woke us. By the grace of Allah, we were ready when these men entered our room." He glanced at the pile of corpses in the corner. "We fought them, slaying some before the others fled. One of them harbored a demon—"

"A Vetal," sobbed Kavundi.

"We saw them retreating on our way back," said Wigandus as he pulled his shirt on. "Any idea what they were after?"

A clear voice from behind Gwen said, "They were after the mare."

They all turned to see a young girl standing in the doorway. She wore a woolen coat over a saffron-colored dress, her forehead marked with red paint. In its center gleamed a gold ellipse in the shape of an eye with an onyx set in the middle, like a pupil.

Kavundi brought her hands together and bowed. "Kumaridevi, you honor us." Her voice was hoarse from tears. So unlike Kavundi,

Gwen reflected.

Kumaridevi calmly acknowledged the greeting. "They will be back, and in greater numbers. They think that they serve Kalidevi in sending the eldest of unicorns to his death. They are much mistaken, but will not listen to reason. Gather your things. I'll take you through the city on the paths they don't watch."

"How can we trust you after everything that happened in this temple?" asked Adelie.

David put his hand on her shoulder. "I think we must."

"There is no time," Kumaridevi said. "We can talk later. Quickly, finish dressing, gather your things and follow me."

"Can you travel, Galiana?" asked Al-Rashid.

Gwen looked at Galiana again. Though her face glowed of health, her arm looked deader than burnt wood. *What happened to her?*

"I can try." Galiana's voice was cracked and shallow, as if she had trouble to find enough breath to speak.

"Once we're out of the temple, she can ride on me," said Britomar.

Gwen grabbed her pack and followed Kumaridevi out of the temple. Dawn was rising, turning the horizon into a glowing pink. She felt Wigandus take her hand as they strode through the quiet dawn-lit paths. Though the doors and windows seemed to hide danger within their shadows, Gwen felt like skipping. Even at the face of the would-be followers of Kali who had turned this lush valley into one of death, she knew no fear. She held the hand of her husband.

Kavundi's tears kept rolling as she walked through the streets of the city. It was as if all the tears she'd never let herself shed would fall on this cold gray morning. She watched the sun crest the mountains before them, where the shadowed peaks loomed in front, pointing into the sky. Only after it cleared the mountaintops, touching her skin with the warmth of a new day, did Kavundi find a way to stop her sobbing.

The farmers were already in the fields, beating their drums as they worked. Kavundi let her feet fall to their rhythm. She felt an unusual clarity, once again certain of what she must do. She had let go of herself. She had given herself to Kalidevi to save Britomar.

She had had no idea how much it would hurt. Listening to Galiana scream as she drew forth the Vetal's spell had pierced her to the core. She'd been so wrong before. Out of all of them, it was Galiana who followed the true path of holiness.

That night Kavundi went to Jigme where he sat in meditation.

Normally, she would have joined him, but this time she just sat next to him and waited. She needed to talk to him before she could try to reach for God.

After a while he opened his eyes and turned to face her. His face was serious, but that soft smile was playing in his slanted eyes again as he regarded her.

"You were remarkable," he said.

"What do you mean?" she asked, taken aback. She did not expect this.

"I watched you stand in the midst of the swirling smoke, your face terrible to behold as you lowered your hand and grabbed the Vetal, sending it to death."

Kavundi frowned. "That wasn't me; that was Kali."

"Yes, you became the Dark One, terrible and beautiful. I will never forget the anguish in your face as you said that it was Britomar who was to die, or when you stood next to Al-Rashid, holding Galiana up during her torment, lending her your strength."

Kavundi, shook her head. "I don't know what you mean. I didn't do all these things. I watched Kali as she stood over the Vetal, pronounced Britomar's doom, and held Galiana." She clenched her teeth as she felt the treacherous tears rise in her throat again, and swallowed them back. She would not cry again. "Did you not hear me beg her to let me die instead of Britomar?"

"No. I only saw you." Jigme reached to her cheek and gently swept off a tear. "I envy your strength."

"What strength? I've not been able to stop crying, like a babe for its mother."

"You brought Devi into our midst."

Kavundi lowered her head, closed her eyes. She wished he was right. And yet, she knew what she saw. It wasn't her doing all these things—it was Kali. All she did was realize how wrong her path had been before this day.

"Like Siddhartha, who learned that self-denial is no path to enlightenment, I've learned that dispassionate giving of self is a false path. I found only joy as I surrendered myself to Devi."

They both sat quietly side by side. It was nice to find quietude with Jigme. After a while, Kavundi found a smile surface from underneath her tears.

"Can you forgive me?" Jigme's voice broke the silence and the stillness within. "I failed in my promise, and I have failed you."

Kavundi lifted her head, staring at the monk. "In what way have you failed?"

Jigme lowered his eyes. "I touched you, and even though my touch was not intentional, you can no longer be a woman untouched by man. I have taken this from you, and it matters not that I did so in my sleep."

Kavundi reached to Jigme's cheek and brushed away a tear. "And yet it was you who held me when I broke down, after Britomar rose. It matters much that you did not let me be alone."

Jigme looked back at her, his eyes welled with tears. "It was easier to renounce the world as an illusion without you in it. My fingers can still feel the silken softness of your breasts. I can no longer find longing to be illusion."

Kavundi fought back a smile. "Have you become a mule, Jigme?"

Jigme shook his head. "I have become a man. And now... How can I seek both enlightenment and you?"

Kavundi didn't know how to answer. She'd never been loved before. How did one respond to someone's desire, when you had none yourself?

"Are you telling me you've fallen in love with me?"

"Please forgive me, yes." Jigme hung his head.

Kavundi embraced him in his sorrow, and he held her. After a long moment, without a word exchanged, they both settled into their separate meditations. Later each lay down to sleep, Kavundi settling some distance away from Jigme. She missed the closeness she had felt that morning when they awoke. Was that what Galiana, Adelie or Gwen looked for in their men?

She thought back on how it had felt, his hand on her breast, his body wrapped around her, his lingum raised for her. Was this what the Christian monk meant for her to think on as he reminded her of the dance of Shiva and Parvati? Did she want to be held again? Or would she, like Shiva, destroy the love that brought him to her, to regret it later?

Must she love more than she already felt for Britomar? Was this something she must surrender to? She put aside her worries, opened her inner eye and sought Kali as she slipped into sleep.

Kavundi woke before anyone else. She rose and looked at the sleeping couples and then at Jigme. In the cold light of morning, it was easier to understand herself. While she had to admit she liked being held, she had no longing for him. Her true desire was for Lakshmi, for Kali. Her tears yesterday were shed in no small part for their parting. She sighed.

She did love more than Britomar. She had fallen in love with Kali.

A soft hand on her shoulder broke her from her thoughts.

"He's loved you from that first day we met him on the pass to Lo Mantang," said Galiana.

Kavundi frowned "How could you tell?"

Galiana smiled. "Trust me, I know men. His face lit up as the two of you sat up talking, and his gaze lingered on you whenever you were near."

"What do I do? I have no more love for him than I do for you. I never asked for his love. Yet, I don't want to hurt him."

Galiana took Kavundi's arm and pulled, leading her away from the sleeping monk. "I never knew love until I saw Britomar. I think it is impossible to be around her and not become open to love, to being loved."

Kavundi nodded, understanding dawning on her. "Madhvacharya always told me something was missing from my devotion to Lakshmi. He was right. It was love. When Lakshmi came to me, asking me to help Britomar, I think she also saw it as a way to help me find how to love."

"What are you two talking about in secret?" asked Adelie, coming up to them.

"Men," Galiana replied, as Kavundi said, "Love."

Adelie smiled. "Don't tell me you and Jigme are in love."

"No. He claims to love me, but I don't love him—not as a woman loves a man."

"But that doesn't mean you don't love him," said Adelie.

"Say more," said Kavundi.

"The other day, when you were talking with David and Jigme about meditation, you came alive. I've never seen you so filled with joy."

Galiana stopped walking. Kavundi looked at her aging but still beautiful face as it filled with joy. "Of course you love Jigme for who he is. He is a monk—that's what he is all about, the true Jigme. You see that in him, and love that in him, calling him to be more true to himself."

"But," stammered Kavundi, "Doesn't loving a man mean desiring him?"

"No, that's silly," said Adelie. "That is the mistake Élise used to make. You desire him to be true to himself. David is most true to himself when he's giving himself to me." Adelie blushed. "Jigme is most true to himself when he's emptying himself to listen to God."

"Let yourself love him, don't be afraid of it," said Galiana. "This love doesn't need to mean you must become one with him as a wife with her husband. After all, you love Britomar, and you wouldn't want to lay with her. If he's professed his love for you, help him see that to be true to his love he must help you become truly who you are, a sannyasi."

Kavundi looked at Jigme, still asleep in his red robes, his shaved head like that of a babe. If Adelie and Galiana were right, his love for her would not mean giving up who she was. But he also desired her as a woman. He had made that clear last night. That would just have to be a sacrifice he would need to make, if he truly loved her.

I must confess that I had to put down my pen and cry for some time after writing these remembrances. Sri Thomas, I do not know if you have ever loved a woman, but in loving Kavundi, I found an echo of Nirvana. I have never known such joy, and such sorrow. I miss her terribly and must put down my pen until I can face my memories of the terrible days that followed.

LORD SHIVA'S SEAT

With Wigandus's hand in hers, Gwen walked behind Jigme, who led them via secret paths marked by plants with clusters of spear-like leaves. Jigme had told her that in the spring they spouted lovely flowers, pink, red or white. Each time they found such a bush, he examined it for cuts made by members of his order to choose the way. Eventually the bushes gave way to scrub grasses—also marked in secret.

After more days of travel, even these plants disappeared and the air grew thinner and colder. Each of the travelers now held a pebble under the tongue to help with the thin air. In silence, they climbed up the secret way Jigme traced from faint patterns in the stones.

The silence was broken when they came upon a sheer cliff of ice.

"Allah preserve us, our way leads up *that?*" exclaimed Al-Rashid.

Jigme walked up to the ice and along its edge for a few paces. "Yes. Here are the markings, see the three lines pointing up?"

Wigandus removed his pack, pulling out a small hammer and a sack Gwen knew to contain small spikes. "I've not climbed the ice since I was a boy, but I've not forgotten the trick of it."

"Then you and I shall go up together, setting the spikes," said Jigme. "The others will follow."

"Galiana, are you strong enough?" Al-Rashid asked.

Galiana's bright eyes traced the ice cliff. She frowned. "No, I don't think I can."

Gwen did not doubt it. Galiana's arm was still shriveled and ash-gray. She had trouble walking and rode daily on Britomar, whose horn had no healing to bring to this strange ailment.

"How will Britomar climb such a cliff?" asked Adelie.

"There are cracks and crags in the ice. I will make my way up those. I am not certain, though that I could climb with Galiana on my back."

"She and I will stay here then, and await your return," said Al-Rashid.

Galiana slid off Britomar's back and gave the unicorn a hug. "It is

347

hard, parting from you after all these months."

Britomar bowed her head. "Thank you for giving me my life."

Tears glistened in Galiana's eyes. "And thank you for giving me a new life."

"I will await the rest of you at the top." Britomar took a step or two backwards and leapt. Gwen gasped as the unicorn landed on a shelf of ice she could barely see and then leapt again. Up and up she sprang, until it became hard to see her white fur against the white of the wall.

Jigme and Wigandus took out their tools and went to work. Each put on special shoes they had purchased in Kathmandu, with spikes along the edges and soles.

Gwen helped Wigandus lace his boots.

"Please be careful." she said as she pulled the raw hide.

"Ach, du, mine liebe. I've climbed ice before." He put his hands under her arms and lifted her to her feet as he stood. Gwen threw her arms around him and hugged him tight.

"I know, but what kind of a wife would I be if I didn't worry?"

He kissed her, stroking her cheek. She helped him wrap the rope around him and gave the ice another glance. Strange that something so deadly and cold could be so bright, so beautiful.

Gwen tore her gaze from the glittering summit of ice as she heard the cling of metal. Jigme was using the small hammer, tapping one of the many small spikes into the ice.

Once set, Wigandus placed his foot upon the spike and heaved himself up, pressing against the ice, tapping in the next spike. Up the ice the two men scrambled, climbing and setting the spikes. Gwen held her breath only once, when Jigme's legs swung free, a spike Wigandus had set sparkling in the bright sun as it tumbled away uselessly. Wigandus reached down and their hands clasped, so small to her eyes, so high, and pulled Jigme to safety.

Gwen sat on the ground next to Kavundi, donning her own ice shoes, watching David and Adelie next to her helping each other with the laces. She kept glancing upward to where Wigandus and Jigme were barely visible against the gleam of the ice. She prayed that they all reached their goal safely.

After what seemed like an eternity, a rope tumbled from above. David grabbed the end, helping Adelie to climb up. Once they were out of sight, Gwen clasped the rope to begin her ascent when a hand touched her on the shoulder. She turned to see Kavundi. Tears stood in the nun's eyes, her thin brown body shivering.

"I know they purchased clothing for me in Kathmandu. It's too cold, please help me."

"Of course," said Gwen, letting go of the rope. She suppressed a smile, hoping Kavundi would not think she was laughing at her. In truth, she felt relief at the excuse to delay her climb—she was not looking forward to it.

Together, they rummaged through the packs they were going to leave behind, things they hoped they'd not need on this final leg of their journey. Gwen found the furs and pulled them out. "Here they are."

Tears streamed down Kavundi's cheeks as she yelled something so fast Gwen couldn't catch the words from one of the many languages the woman spoke. She had never heard Kavundi speak so harshly.

"What is the matter?"

Kavundi swallowed. "Furs. They're dead. It's one thing to wear clothing—but quite another to put on something dead. I'd sooner die."

Gwen shook her head. "I fear you might, from this cold, if you won't wear them. Look, we're all wearing normal clothing underneath. I'll find you some, and you can dress the same as everyone."

Kavundi looked up at the ice. "I'm afraid you're right. But I can't, sorry. I don't know what to do. Ever since I met Britomar, I've slipped away from who I thought I was. Go on ahead. I must deal with this alone."

Gwen nodded, and once again grabbed the rope. The picks on the shoes made the climb easier, but still, every muscle in her body screamed in protest as she pulled herself up. Her hands burned even through the thick gloves she wore, until she remembered to wrap the rope around each hand before pulling up, using her shoes to keep her weight off the rope when she couldn't easily reach the spikes Jigme and Wigandus had driven into the ice.

She never looked down, keeping her eyes on the rope, on the spikes, on the merciless ice as it numbed her fingers, turning her legs into leaden weights. Reach, grab, step, wrap, and pull. Nothing else mattered, nothing else entered her thoughts. Reach, grab, step... Her legs gave way as she felt the ice slip away below her. Her hands burned in agony as she clenched the escaping rope, trying to break her fall. Heart pounding, Gwen scrambled to dig the spikes on her boots into the ice. Arms aching, she finally steadied herself, her breath ragged as she began to pull herself up again.

Kavundi looked down at the bundle of furs at her feet, at the leather spiked boots, not knowing if she shook from anger or cold. Both would have been an anathema to her, before she answered the call of Lakshmi to help Britomar, before she knew love. Since she let Kali in, she'd not tried to control herself, surrendering herself to the Devi in her meditations, hoping to see the dark face again, feel one with her.

Why did Kali not take her, in the temple, when her death could have had some meaning? She could have spared Galiana all that pain. Why let her die here, in the cold, an empty and pointless death? Must she degrade herself? Must she become like a Chandala, and wear dead things? What next? Eating flesh? To sink into rebirth in the service of Lakshmi when all she sought was to become one with her goddess? To stay naked was to die, to abandon her service—but to die as who she was. To clothe herself in these dead things would take her from Lakshmi, reduce her to rebirth, at best as a Chandala.

"A Chandala who treads the spiritual path is a better being than a Brahmin who is ignorant of that path and puts on artificial appearances," said a voice.

Kavundi looked up. No one was there except Galiana and Al-Rashid who had moved away from the ice, out of earshot. Yet, she heard the voice so clearly. She settled into the lotus position, opening her inner eye, her mantra setting aside all anxiety, all indecision.

She saw a naked blue-skinned man standing before her on one foot. He held a flute near to his lips.

"Why do you doubt me?" he asked.

"I don't doubt you, Sri Krishna." A frown of disappointment passed over his face. "I didn't think I did," she amended.

"If you love me, trust me." Krishna put the flute to her lips and played a song for her, a song she'd heard David sing every seventh night. The sounds washed over her, and somehow the song had cleared her mind even better than any meditation. She opened her eyes and looked up at the ice, and then at the clothing Gwen had left for her. Suddenly, she understood. Wearing clothing came from fear of not being adequate. She didn't need clothing if she was certain about herself.

Kavundi removed her loin cloth and centered herself. She would climb as she is. She must trust that if she died by doing this, her death would not be meaningless. She surrendered her being, let the music Krishna played for her fill her heart. She found joy in her new freedom, and it hurt, beautifully.

She set aside her fear and reached for the rope.

Wind and muffled breathing was all Gwen heard as she followed Jigme up the barren pass. Around her was rock and ice. Even her fur-lined coat was no match for the bitter cold wind that whipped around the curves of the pass. She looked back and caught Wigandus's eye. He smiled at her, lifting her spirits. She returned the smile, her cheeks warming at the thought of him. His love could do that, even in this barren place.

"Gwenaella you must flee with Britomar! The Yeti come," urged the winds.

She stopped. "But how can I leave the others?"

"What is it?" asked Adelie.

"I heard a voice telling me to flee—" *And I know that voice, but from where?*

A roar echoed against the gray cliffs, stopping her words... and a shimmering form stopped her breath. Élise and Garsenda stood before her, hand in hand.

"Run!" urged Élise.

A second roar split the air, this time from behind. Wigandus grimaced, reached over and lifted Gwen, placing her on Britomar.

"Run!" he urged.

Gwen heard the metallic ring of a sword pulled from its sheath. *David.* "Wigandus, I can't leave you!"

"Liebchen, they want you, not us. Flee!"

Gwen watched in horror as he drew his sword and ran to the aid of Adelie, who was backing away from a huge white beast taller than any man. The beast swiped at her with claws as long as knives. She tried to dodge, but the beast caught her on the shoulder. Adelie crumpled as David swung his sword at the creature.

"Adelie!" cried Gwen.

"Gwen, it is your choice," said Britomar, who pranced and snorted. "We can join the fight."

Gwen looked longingly at Wigandus, who swung his sword at the beast attacking David. It broke her heart to leave her friends like this. But she had to go. If she failed, the eldest of the unicorns will die.

"I'll return if I can!" Gwen shouted. " Britomar, let's go!"

She nearly fell off as Britomar reared up and leapt over Jigme. The unicorn's hooves landed on the Yeti's head, spraying the air with its blood. Sparks flew from the rocks as Britomar galloped up the pass with the agility of a mountain goat and the speed of an antelope.

As they rounded a bend in the pass, two more Yeti sprang from behind rocks and Britomar charged them with her horn. One fell into the abyss, screaming, as she pierced the other. Its roar deafened as it fell, and Britomar again began to run. Gwen pulled her knife from her belt. Another Yeti leapt at them as they rounded a corner, and Gwen threw the blade, the way Wigandus taught her to. The Yeti howled in agony, Gwen's knife quivering in its eye.

Britomar stumbled, no longer running. Gwen looked behind and saw that her leg was bleeding badly.

"Stop, and let me bandage you!" she urged.

"Not until we get to the Garden!"

"You will die if we don't stop the bleeding soon."

"Then let's hope we get there soon."

Gwen would have missed the pass if she had not been on Britomar's back. At first she saw only a wall of solid rock, but above it the marks Jigme had taught her indicated a narrow path rising to her right. Its base was a good twenty feet higher than the path.

"There's the pass!" she shouted to Britomar above the wind. "To your right! You'll have to leap to get to it."

"I'll try." Britomar turned to face the wall. Gwen gazed upon the green lichen covering the entrance to the path, hoping she was right.

Britomar stepped backward one step and leapt.

Gwen flew off Britomar's back, tucked, and rolled as Wigandus had taught her, landing on the lichen. She rose and ran to Britomar who lay on her side.

Britomar's hind leg was torn badly, strips of flesh hanging from the large gashes. Gwen dropped her furs to the ground, frantically tearing at her dress and shift. She wrapped Britomar's wounds with the shift, wishing she had some way to wash them first. Pulling her knife from its sheath, she used it to cut strips from her skirt and reinforced the bandages. Hopefully that would stop the bleeding and let the wound close.

"Can you rise?" she asked.

Britomar tried to stand, fell, and tried again. That time she stood. "I feel weak; but I think I can walk. Thank you."

Gwen pulled her furs back on. "Good. Let's go up the pass."

As Gwen walked, she realized that her legs were not cold, despite being bare. Soon she opened the furs to let in the fragrant balmy breeze.

The path took them around a bend of the mountain. Without a word exchanged, they both stopped.

They stood at the edge of a fragrant meadow, filled with flowers, its golden grass swaying gracefully. In the middle of the meadow rose a long and tall wall of reddish brown stone. It had no seams or cracks, as if cut from a single piece, too tall to see over. An open archway gaped in its center, and Gwen could see trees though the opening.

The Garden at the Roof of the World.

Could this be the right place?

If this wasn't, no place was.

Gwen wished Wigandus was here with her, holding her hand. She felt small beside the wall, like a child looking for the first time upon the adult world, realizing she was not ready for what she beheld.

"I will wait for you here," said Britomar.

THE GARDEN AT THE ROOF OF THE WORLD

Gwen gave Britomar a hug, turned toward the gate, and stopped. She couldn't bring furs into that place. It would be wrong. Gwen removed her mantle and stood naked before the walls. As she walked, she found herself humming the prayer that she had heard David teach Adelie. *Baruch atoi...* she wished she knew the words. She neared the gate, her spirits lifting as no one barred her way. Perhaps it was all worth it, perhaps she'd be permitted to enter and retrieve what Bethiel needed. She took one more step forward and stopped, freezing in fear.

Before her stood an angel holding a flaming sword.

"What would you, Gwenaella?" he asked, his voice rich but foreboding.

She lowered her gaze. "I seek to bring healing to the eldest of the unicorns."

"Are you pure of heart?"

Gwen blushed. It was no time for a lie, though speaking the truth broke her heart. "No, I am a sinner."

"Put aside what separates you from God and enter."

Gwen knelt and prayed.

"*Pater noster, qui es in cælis, sanctificetur nomen tuum. Adveniat regnum tuum. Fiat voluntas tua, sicut in cælo et in terra. Panem nostrum qauotidianum da nobis hodie. Et dimitte nobis debita nostra, sicut et nos dimittimus debitoribus nostris. Et ne nos inducas in tentationem: sed libera nos a malo. Amen.*"

She poured her soul into these words, which had acquired new meaning to her. She prayed for her soul, and those of the brave, innocent people who gave their lives to bring her to this gate. She prayed that her sins will not prevent her from doing the right thing, so that their death would not be in vain—so that the eldest of the unicorns would live.

Rising, she turned to the angel. This time, she raised her eyes and looked him in the face, pale and beautiful, with eyes so dark she felt her head spin when she met his gaze.

He nodded and put aside his sword. With her heart pounding, Gwen walked past him into the Garden.

Once inside, the walls were no longer visible. She glanced around, briefly wondering how she will find an exit from this place, and strode along a quiet lane beneath the trees. Their rich green limbs filtered the sunbeams, dissipating them into a lush, soothing golden shade, brightening her way. She turned to look behind her, and saw through an arc of the tree's boughs Britomar grazing upon a field of grass.

Gwen crested a small hill and stopped, holding her breath. Glory be! She stood on the threshold of another meadow, but the colors of the flowers growing here were richer, deeper. Its beauty made her want to cry. Britomar should have come in, this was made for her too.

"No, Gwenaella, no beast will enter the garden. None have since Adam left."

Puzzled that someone had heard her thoughts, Gwen turned, but saw no one. She noticed for the first time how quiet the air was, devoid of the humming of bees and chirping of birds one would expect in such a lovely place. But who was this mysterious speaker?

"Do you really need to see me?"

Gwen paused. She recognized His voice. She wanted to, but did she really *need* to?

"No, Lord," she said truthfully.

"The tree you seek is before you."

Gwen looked across the meadow and saw a tree unlike any she had ever seen. Its bark was smooth and silver, its broad, long leaves a deep green with reddish veins. On its boughs were large golden flowers and round-shaped fruits. They were all green, save for one, which had ripened to a blood-red. It emanated a sweet, rich smell that filled her nostrils as she approached the tree.

The smell made her hungry, longing for its taste like she longed for Wigandus's hand in hers. How was she ever going to take it without eating it? How could this delicate fruit survive the trip back? Even if she could preserve it by a miracle, the same men who couldn't resist trying to take Britomar, would surely claim it. On the other hand, if she ate it, if she tasted its delicious sweetness, filled her mouth with its rich, juicy flavor...Gwen stopped herself. How could something so good as this fruit make her want to abandon all she had fought for, all that her friends, and even Lilith, had died for?...Did Eve feel like this?

She paused in her tracks. "Lord, now at last I understand Eve.

The temptation to eat this fruit is more than I can bear. I have never wanted something for myself so much."

She imagined a smile in His voice. "I'm glad you understand Eve. This was in part why I allowed Lilith to send you on your journey. You also have a choice to make."

Gwen walked to the tree, and bowed to it. She lifted her hands to the fruit, to find it fall into her grasp without her needing to pluck it.

As she held it in her hands, her longing grew. She wanted to make that fruit a part of her. Now she understood what Élise had told her of that Muslim mystic Shams she and Adelie met before they reached Antioch, who had told them of the beautiful agony of ecstatic joy. How could this be paradise when there was such longing?

"Has your longing for Wigandus diminished since your wedding?"

Gwen blushed. "No."

"What have you learned from this?"

"I never thought about it," said Gwen. She paused. "Do you mean... being in paradise is not the same as being at peace?"

"My peace is not an end to longing, but its fulfillment. It is just that longing here is no longer tainted with anxiety."

Gwen thought of Wigandus, wishing that she was with him. He may be dying... or worse. She looked again at the fruit in her hands.

This fruit would restore Wigandus.

"To fulfill my quest, I also have to let those who love me die. How else can I give meaning to their lives—or their love? How else can I give dignity to their choices?"

Is he dead?... She wanted to wail, but found herself remembering the way his hand felt as they walked to the temple, newly wed. "I should bring this to the eldest of unicorns, but I long to bring it to Wigandus. How can I keep myself from giving it to him?"

To this, there was no answer, but she felt the wisp of a breeze caress her shoulder. She remembered Élise rolling under the scimitar, Lilith diving into the waters, Wigandus wrestling the Yeti.

Cradling the precious fruit in her palms, Gwen turned and walked back to the gate. She was confused and surprised that instead of the meadow where Britomar was waiting for her, she found herself in another meadow. A small and painful mercy, she could not give in to temptation.

This one was surrounded by tall trees, and in its center lay a unicorn—larger than Britomar, with a coat as gray as the moon. His head rested on the grass, his eyes closed. Next to him sat Nimuë, stroking his mane.

Gwen walked to them. She felt relieved—at least the fruit would not spoil or fall into the wrong hands before Bethiel could eat it. Still, she wished she could have at least shown it to Wigandus.

As she neared, Nimuë rose. "You come in time. Would you like to feed it to him?"

Without answering, Gwen sat before the old unicorn, and lifted his head to rest in her lap. Unlike when she touched Britomar, she felt no spark, no sense of joy or revelation. She felt his shallow breathing as he kept his eyes closed. *So old. So sick.* Gently, Gwen fed him the fruit that the Garden had given her. Only after he finished did she realize she was crying. She looked past him, trying to see through the garden to where Wigandus fought for his life, but she knew it was too far.

The old unicorn lifted his head, brushing against her cheek in a brief caress. She lowered her eyes. She felt meaningless, empty. She was glad to have fulfilled her quest, but at what price?...

"Thank you," Bethiel said, his voice deep and musical. Hearing him speak woke every fiber of her being. "You saved my life. And now, it is time for you to return to yours. Would you like to go back to your family and safety—or to my daughter and danger?"

Gwen swallowed. "I will return to Britomar, and to my companions."

The old unicorn smiled. "Go then. Bring Britomar my love, and my gratitude to all."

Nimuë helped Gwen to her feet, and led her back to the Garden where the angel holding a flaming sword stood, waiting at the gate. Gwen turned to the sorceress. "Did you know all along that the Garden is wherever we walk?"

Nimuë's voice was barely more than a whisper. "No. If I had, I would have sought its gate myself."

The angel said, "Nimuë, you would have known, if you had but listened. Open your heart, and let go of your power."

"Give up all Mother Lilith taught?"

Gwen reached for Nimuë's hand. She owed Nimuë the tale of Lilith's death. "I met Lilith on our way to the Garden. She came to our aid when a monster would have otherwise destroyed us."

Nimuë nodded. "She is wonderful to behold, such power!"

"Nimuë, she died fighting the monster from the depths that attacked our ship. She gave her life to save us all."

The sorceress's eyes widened. "Dead?" she whispered.

Gwen told her the details of the fight, of Lilith's confession, of her embrace of sister death. "She told us that she gave her life because she remembered how to love."

Nimuë's face contorted in anger. She shook her fist at the angel. "It's all your fault! Yours, and your God's!"

The angel shook his head, but his face was sad. "No, Nimuë. Lilith made her own choice."

"She chose to die? To submit herself to Eve's curse?"

Gwen grasped Nimuë's shoulders, turning the sorceress around to face her. "She chose to give of herself. If she hadn't, Britomar would have died and I never would have made it to the Garden. How could anyone, even God Himself, deny that?" She took Nimuë into her arms as the ancient sorceress broke down in tears. Gwen cried too, for Lilith, for Garsenda, for Élise, for Wigandus, for the rest of her friends who gave their lives for this quest. Like Lilith, they had saved the eldest of unicorns—but not for themselves.

THIS CUP WE SHARE, THIS BREAD WE BREAK

Gwen did not know how she found herself on a different path through the garden. The worst thing was how much she wanted to stay here forever. How could she bring herself to leave paradise when every fiber of her being cried out that this was made for her, that she belonged here—how could she leave? And then another thought haunted her. Perhaps she would not be able to find the exit until she found that answer?

She made her way through the silent flowers and trees, until she came upon a spring. Four streams ran from it, meandering through the Garden. How was it she had not seen this before? She drank deeply, quenching her thirst and feeling the cool, refreshing water wash into the depths of her soul. How to leave? She rose and strode across the stream.

Midway across she felt a cramp inside. She looked down, and gave out a sob. A small trace of red faded into the flowing water. She ran to the far shore, fell down on her knees and cried out in an agony of grief. She'd always been taught her monthly bleeding was part of the punishment for Eve's sin—and here, in this Garden, she felt this sin weighing so heavily upon her. This blood made her impure, not worthy of this place.

To this there was no answer. To bleed was part of being a woman. She couldn't stay here without soiling the grass, the flowers, the beautiful perfection, with the blood of a child that was never to be. She wanted that child. If she left, she might bear children.

She rose, tears streaming down her cheeks, watering the grasses with her grief. She ran, sobbing, stumbling, until she found herself leaning against that tree. She looked up, its leaves whispering around her.

Should she take another fruit? Should she bring it to Wigandus?

Gwen sobbed again with the honest realization that if she took another fruit she would eat it before she was six steps to the gate.

She stepped back from the tree and bowed to it, hands pressed together as she had seen Kavundi do. Then she turned her back to it and followed the paths she remembered. There, ahead of her, Britomar lay in the grass, and seeing her friend made her own sorrow wash away, forgotten.

Ashen-gray, save for a crimson leg wrapped in a fur-lined skirt, Britomar lay on her side in the meadow. Gwen barely felt the ground under her bare toes as she sprinted to the unicorn. She lifted Britomar's head into her lap and leaned over to kiss the unicorn, tears falling on Britomar's face. Her hope all but gone, Gwen buried her face in the unicorn's fur and wept. If only she could pluck another fruit. Could she go back? Would it be permitted?

She kissed the unicorn's face, lay her head back down in the dewy grass, and stood, looked back at where the garden had been but moments before. Before her was only a wall of rock and ice.

Gwen lowered her head. She couldn't go back. That way was closed.

She walked the path marked by Britomar's blood to the base of the pass. Turning back to where her friend had lain, she saw that Britomar too was gone, hidden by the tall grass. Gwen swallowed her tears and gingerly climbed down to the main pass, knowing that before her was only death and heartache.

A bitter wind whipped around the heartless mountain pass. Gwen crossed her arms over her chest and trod down the path. As she rounded a corner, she saw that the sun was setting on the horizon. This night she would die. If she pressed on, she would surely fall to her death. If not, she would freeze, huddled against the heartless pillars of the world's roof, naked as the snow-capped stone.

She had to go on.

As the light faded, Gwen crept on all fours, feeling for the path with her hands. She had to find her friends and learn what happened to them. Perhaps some of them had survived. She would certainly die if she gave up that hope, if she stopped trying to return to those she loved.

Reach forward. Put her hand down, move the knees forward. *Ow! That was sharp! I can't stop shaking.* Reach. Emptiness. *Try again.* There. *Move. My tears are frozen to my cheeks.* Reach, no rock. Reach—

Someone's coming.

Yeti?

What does it matter, I'll die either way. No, I won't give up. Perhaps I can crawl faster. Reach. *The thing's drawing closer. I can hear its breath.* Crawl. *I won't make it.* Reach. *Dear God, it's almost here, forgive me my choices in the Garden.* Crawl.

A sharp point touched Gwen between her shoulders and an agonizing warmth spread across her back as she curled up in a ball to surrender to death and doom.

Kavundi heard the commotion ahead of her and raced up the path. She fell to her knees when she saw the Yeti, the blood, her fallen friends. She cleared her mind and centered as she brought up her guard. She must stop the Yeti, save the others. Slam! The Yeti's claw hit her, swiping aside her arm. Kavundi felt herself rise through the air, her arm burning where the Yeti's claws had raked across her, lifting, tossing her aside like a rag doll. Center! She let go of the pain, let herself become limp as she slammed into the mountain. The world swirled before her. Her back felt as if a thousand knifes cut her. She could not breathe. Center! Sri Lakshmi! Help your daughter! If only she could treat pain as the illusion Jigme talked about.

Jigme! He's fallen!

The whirling of colors and shapes before her eyes faded into anguish. She opened herself, surrendering to the pain—calling again to the Devi.

As her pain faded into joy, Kavundi knew her prayers were answered.

Adelie screamed as the tower of fur and claw brushed aside Wigandus, racing after Britomar, screaming in frustration as the unicorn leapt over its fellow who turned in pursuit. Jigme blocked its path. Adelie held her breath as the horrible claws that had torn her shoulder into ribbons of hot pain swept down upon the weaponless man. Her sobs were joined by a scream that started in grief and rose to fury.

Kavundi's brown skin blurred as she moved faster than Adelie's tear-filled eyes could follow. Blood burst into the air, and with a horrible scream the monster fell over the precipice.

Unwrapping herself from the ball she had huddled into, Adelie ran to David. He lay limp and bleeding, but he was still breathing. Pulling apart her clothing, she wrapped his wounds, not giving herself time to cry.

Another ghastly scream. Adelie turned her head and saw Kavundi push the second Yeti over the edge. She crawled over to Wigandus and began to bind his wounds. He coughed up blood. "Live! Damn you!" she screamed at him. "Give Gwen something to come back for!"

"We have to move them, or they'll die in the night air," said Kavundi.

"Yes, we need to try to get low enough to find wood for a fire," said Adelie. "But how? All three men are hurt. How can we carry them?"

"I think I can walk," said David. Adelie's heart beat faster. She heard a scrape of stone upon stone, turned to see Jigme trying to sit up. *Thank you!* She sang in her heart, the way David had taught.

Gwen heard a voice, soft and distant, as if high above her, filtered through a tunnel. It was gentle, but insistent. If only she could understand what it was saying. She stilled her thoughts and strained to hear.

"Gwenaella."

Britomar's voice! She must be in heaven!

Gwen fought to rise. If she was dead, Wigandus might be near! She felt warm. She curled in like a babe and something soft—fur—covered her back. She opened her eyes.

She was sitting on a cliff's edge next to Britomar. In front of her was emptiness. Had she gone any further in the dark, she would have died for certain.

She looked at Britomar, relief mixing with disbelief as she met the familiar, warming look of the unicorn's eyes. "But how?" she whispered. "When I left you, you were dead."

Britomar shook her head. "I don't know. I woke to find myself whole, with a voice urging me to go to you. Are you strong enough to climb on my back?"

"I think so."

"Come, then," Britomar said as she stood.

Gwen climbed on the unicorn's back. The wind lashed at her bare skin but she felt no pain. The glittering light of dawn burned off the white peaks, but her eyes were not blinded. The joy she usually felt when riding Britomar did not fill her this time. In the core of her being was an emptiness that she knew could not be filled—not even by Britomar. Was Wigandus alive? Had any of the others survived?

The path was empty. Gwen looked around, searching for any signs of what happened here. All she saw was dried brown blood on the gray stone. Had they all perished? Did they become food for the Yeti that the followers of Kali had sent after them?

Perhaps she was still dying on the cliff, cold and alone, and dreaming of riding—not her friend, but a nightmare into hell?

Britomar sped down the paths to the ice they had climbed just yesterday. "Hold on tight!" the unicorn said.

Gwen wrapped her arms around Britomar's neck and clenched her knees like she'd been taught in their first gallop through Brocéliande. Britomar leapt, and Gwen shut her eyes as they fell together to land, leap, and fall again. Gwen felt the wind lift her hair behind her and she opened her eyes to see that they were down the glacier, the walls of the pass blurring as the unicorn galloped by.

Around a bend of the path Gwen saw a large white tent with a red flag flying over it. A stream of smoke rose from within. She remembered the white flags of Lo Mantang and wondered. Jigme had told her that white flags were prayer flags, but he never mentioned the red. Was this a flag of death?

Britomar stopped and Gwen slid off the unicorn's back, into the bitter cold wind.

Next to the tent's entrance was a small pile of furs and shoes. Gwen was tempted to put on one of the furs, but somehow it did not feel right to enter that tent wearing something dead. She remembered how Kavundi had told her there was no shame in nakedness. She squared her shoulders, pushed open the flap of the tent, and stepped inside, into the warm gloom.

"Gwen!" she heard in a blended chorus of voices.

Her eyes stung as they strained to see into the tent's shadows. A bony arm wrapped around her waist and led her to a bed.

Wigandus! Gwen's heart leapt.

The knight was lying on a cot, covered with a woven blanket. His cheeks were hollow, his breathing shallow and his eyes closed. He lived, but only just.

A tear slid down Gwen's face to splash upon his as she bent over to kiss him. As her lips met his, she felt his arms rise and pull her into him. Her head swam as she lost herself in the timelessness of his kiss, in the joy of seeing him alive.

As his arms let her rise, she opened her eyes to see his, shining with joy. Gwen smiled and felt within the same joy she had felt in the Garden.

At that moment, she knew. She had not left paradise; paradise was within. Something of it had passed to Wigandus when she kissed him. That must have been what restored Britomar! She'd breathed in the air of paradise, drunk from its fountain. Some of that grace must have stayed with her.

She looked around and saw that Adelie, Kavundi, and David were also badly hurt, lying on fleece-covered beds. Galiana and Al-Rashid sat beside David and Adelie. She looked at Jigme, and realized that the flag she had seen was his garment. Wearing only his loin cloth, he sat by Kavundi's side, his body a mass of bruises and red welts from where his skin had been torn by a claw that had mercifully only scraped him.

Gwen went first to Adelie, then to David, then to Kavundi and Galiana. To each she gave a kiss and felt life return to them in her embrace. Feeling overwhelmed, lightheaded and drained, she sat on Wigandus's cot. He sat up and held her.

"I don't understand," she said. "How did you all get down here? Where did you get this tent from?"

Galiana, who looked up from her now healthy arm with tears glistening at the corners of her eyes said, "First tell us, does Britomar live? What happened?"

"I live," said Britomar as she pushed aside the flap of the tent and entered. "And, like everyone, I am anxious to hear Gwen's story. What happened when you entered the Garden?"

Gwen told them of her walk with God in the garden, of how she met Nimuë and fed the fruit to the eldest of the unicorns. "Now please tell me, how did you come to find this tent?"

Adelie said, "I think the tent was set here for us. After you and Britomar raced up the pass, the Yeti forgot us and tried to follow you. We knew that a night on the mountain would be the death to those hurt and bleeding, so we carried those who could not walk down into this valley, where we found Al-Rashid and Galiana waiting for us with this tent."

Al-Rashid said, "After you climbed the ice, Galiana and I retraced our steps down the mountain path, looking for a good place to build a shelter and wait for your return. Through Allah's grace, we found this tent already erected, but we could find no evidence of anyone about, so we decided to use it."

David said, "When we got here, exhausted and on the edge of death, Jigme felt that our prayers for help and the restoration of health would be better heard if we had a prayer flag, and so he hung his garment from a pole. I told him that there was no need, but collapsed before I could explain. Come here and look for yourself."

Gwen rose and went to where David pointed. Near the pole that held up the tent was a large chest adorned with the carving of two angels, wings pointing to a central seat. Gilded rings held the two poles supporting the chest. Next to it on a simple wooden table stood an earthen dish holding flat round loaves of bread, and a simple cup filled with wine.

"Is this what I think it is?" Gwen asked.

"Shhh, listen," said Kavundi.

The flap of the tent fluttered in the breeze, making the flames in the brazier flicker. Words echoed in that breeze, beautiful words right at the edge of meaning.

David bowed, Kavundi and Jigme each pranemed. Al-Rashid salaamed, and Wigandus crossed himself.

Then the air became still.

Sri Thomas, in the days that followed, each of us was restored in mind, body and soul. As we recovered, each of my fellows made their plans. At Adelie's request, Gwenaella, Wigandus, Al-Rashid and Galiana would go first to Armenia to tell its prince that his bride waits for him in heaven. From there they agreed to journey to Jerusalem. Wigandus and Gwen would then seek the sea and fulfill her promise to the merfolk, though they had no idea what that would entail, or even if it was still necessary after the leviathan's attack.

Kavundi told me she would seek Krishna's city beneath the waves. I offered her my company on the journey, but she would not hear of it.

"Perhaps, you and I may yet meet again, but I need to walk this path alone. You and I have both learned that love is real, and to truly be is to love, and to truly love, you must also love and be true to yourself. Who I thought I was is gone, I go to find who I am. Perhaps, one day I will return."

Not a day goes by when I don't wonder what happened to those good people, where their lives took them. Not a minute goes by without hoping to hear Kavundi's voice again.

Kavundi was not the only one torn by Kali, and I long since put aside my saphron robes. I am king of Lo Mantang now, my elder brother died soon after he took the throne. No longer finding the world an illusion, I must live within it. The longing for God may be an echo of my longing for Kavundi, but it is for Kavundi that I wait now. I know God will find me. Will she?

It is a terrible thing that among my final reflections on all that we accomplished, the reconciliation of the First Woman with the First Mother, the destruction of the monsters and demons, the saving of the eldest of the unicorns, all I can dwell upon is my own failures, loss and longing. While I helped to bring the women to the Garden as I promised, I also brought myself into the world, which for a follower of Siddhartha is a terrible thing.

Sri Thomas, I wish you peace. Om Shanti, Shanti, Shanthi, Om.

APPENDIX

Translator's note:

I was skeptical when I was contacted about a Sanskrit manuscript unearthed in an archaeological dig in Lo Mantang. Especially when the archaeologist told me that the document was in nearly perfect condition, and had whole sections in medieval Church Latin and Langue d'oc. This sounded very much like a hoax, but there was no harm in seeing the manuscript. Since the archaeologist's expedition would foot the bill, I readily agreed.

No one besides my wife would be interested in the trip to Nepal and the journey by foot through the mountain passes to the small isolated Kingdom of Lo Mantang. I lost some of my skepticism when the manuscript was placed in front of me. The ink was well faded upon the leaves, but the writing was clearly Sanskrit as it was written 800 years ago.

If this was a forgery, it was the work of a dedicated scholar who had access to aged hand made Tibetan paper. Carbon dating of a fragment would place the manuscript in the mid 13th century.

While the manuscript was almost complete, the leaves were fragile, so we took digital photographs of each and printed the results. Copies were provided for the current King of Lo Mantang and his royal library, as well as for my own use as a translator. I then began the laborious process of translating the text from the photographed images.

I was immediately struck by the unusual content of the text. The first leaves contain a letter from Prince Jigme of Lo Mantang to Thomas of Aquinas in Paris. I did some quick checking to discover that St. Thomas Aquinas had been a student at the University of Paris for a brief period from 1245 CE through the middle of 1248 CE when he accompanied Albertus Magnus to the University at Cologne, though he later returned to Paris to work on his Masters and teach, dwelling there from 1252 through 1261. This was too much for me, and I began to suspect the text again. I knew of no recorded communication between medieval Tibet and Europe, and had no cause to believe that St. Thomas Aquinas was known outside of Europe at the time.

After much ranting at my gullibility, I approached the text again and began to read the letter of Prince Jigme. In his letter, Jigme refers to a kartayan, which is the Sanskrit word for a unicorn. This renewed my skepticism, but I no longer suspected a modern forgery of no purpose. I now suspected that I had in my hand a medieval romance written in Sanskrit. Much like the romances of Chretien or Wolfram, the narrative refers to mythological figures such as the sorceress Nimuë from Arthurian literature, the demon Lilith from Hebrew mythology and creatures such as unicorns, griffins and leviathans found in medieval bestiaries.

In many ways, the manuscript is very similar to the medieval Tamil epic the Shilappadikaram, in so far as there are a fair number of historical personages who appear in it. Also, unlike European medieval romances, this romance is not littered with anachronisms, metaphor and analogy. Perhaps the author was inspired by the Shilappadikaram, in that there is a character in the Shilappadikaram named Kavundi.

Some of the persons mentioned by Jigme were giants in their day. I've already mentioned St. Thomas Aquinas. Jigme also mentions St. Thomas' good friend St. Bonaventure. In the text you find St. Margaret Arpáds of Hungary, Rambam, the poet Rumi (Mevlana Jalal al-Din is his real name), Shams, Madhvarchya, Eleanor of Aquitaine, St. Louis of France, King Bela Arpáds of Hungary, Prince Bohemond the last Prince of Antioch, Caliph al-Musta'sim, as well as both Balban and Nasir of the Delhi Sultanate. Whoever wrote this romance knew a lot of peoples and lands far from the Silk Road.

During the translation, I uncovered that the author also knew some medieval Church Latin, Hebrew, Arabic, Hungarian, Breton, and Langue d'oc, and was astounded to learn that the street names Lady Elisabeth mentions in Paris were still in existence as late as the French revolution. Such accuracy is most unheard of in a medieval romance.

I made two translations of Jigme's manuscript. The first translation is a scholarly effort that is heavily footnoted and tries to capture both the meaning of Jigme's words and the meter of his poetry. The second is a prose narrative of his story suitable for mass publication. To capture the flavor of the many languages spoken in Jigme's narrative, I've translated most of the Sanskrit into English, but have kept the prayers and songs in their native languages.

Translating Lady Elisabeth's songs proved a unique challenge. Her first is much like the songs of Beatriz de Dia. Lady Elisabeth wrote with ten syllables per line and an ABAB rhyming scheme. The others are more like that of other known women troubadours. Women troubadours tended to write in the first person singular, something that was unique in medieval literature. I've done my best to translate them into English and preserve the structure.

I've spoken at length with my colleagues and have found no references to either the monastic order that both St. Bonaventure and Jigme make reference to, nor could I find any reference to the Garden at the Roof of the World. It was not uncommon for medieval romances to invent things and places, so I was not at all surprised by this.

However, I did find a surprising number of borrowings from texts that we have no record of ever making the journey across the Silk Road into Lo Mantang until the modern era. Jigme references le Fresne, by Marie de France; le Roman de la Rose, by Guillaume de Lorris and Jean de Meun, Eric and Enide by Chretian of Troyes; Parzifal, by Wolfram von Eschenbach; The Decameron, by Giovanni Boccaccio; and one of the tales commonly associated with the Arabian Nights cycle.

There were also quotes either in part or in whole of various songs of the twelfth and thirteenth century troubadours and trouvères. The ones I've been able to identify include:

"Quant voi la flor novele," by an anonymous trouvère.

"Ab joi et ab joven m'apais," by Beatriz de Dia.

"Ar em al freg temps vengut," by Azalais de Porcairages

"Amours, ou trop tart me sui pris", by Blanche of Castile, Queen of France.

It is the plethora of unexpected accuracies that continue to make me wonder about this manuscript. I want it to be true, but how could it be?

I've looked for the convent mentioned as Gwen's school in Vannes; it was destroyed when the cathedral was expanded. Antioch and Baghdad were both sacked within a decade of the events this text depicts, and very little of the Paris of Lady Elisabeth survived the changes to the city ordered by Napoleon III. The India and Nepal of Jigme's manuscript also suffered badly the ravages of time. Shortly after their stay in Kathmandu, the city and its temples were destroyed, later to be rebuilt in the style we know today. Khajuraho, though never named in the manuscript, was abandoned shortly after their visit to sink into obscurity and ruin. Even Mumbai was overrun by the sea, to be later rebuilt. I can find no evidence outside this manuscript for the events it depicts.

Still, if a unicorn ever ran in the world's forests, what better place to find one than where Gwenaella looked, in Brocéliande where according to legend, Nimuë snared Merlin in love. Alas that I am not pure of heart.

Bernard Mondschein, PhD., translator.

ACKNOWLEDGEMENTS

I wish to first thank my beloved wife, Margo, and my darling children Kayla and Hannah who put up with meetings of the Boston Critters in their kitchen, reading through drafts of the manuscript, and all the time they let me have to write and edit the story.

I must sincerely thank Dragonwell Publishing team, especially my editor, whose collaboration brought out the best of the story.

The list of people to whom I'm indebted to for their advice, critiques and encouragement during the many drafts is absolutely huge. The worst thing is that I know that I've forgotten folks. Still, I am profoundly grateful to Leo Korogodski, Tracey Stewart, Pamela O'Brien, Lisa Bouchard, and Helen Mazarakas, all members of the Boston Critters. This manuscript would never have reached publication without you.

To the many members of the Online Writer's Workshop who reviewed the manuscript, I owe each of you a tremendous debt. Thank you to: Adrian Krag, Al Riney, Alex Van Rossum, Alice Spicer, Alisa Goode, Amos Peverill, Ariana Cordelle Sofer, Betty Bivins, Bonnie Freeman, B. R. Hollis, Carlos J. Cortes, Carol Bartholomew, Carole Ann Moleti, Carsten Kroon, Cat Collins, Chance Morrison, Charles Coleman Finley, Chris Reynolds, Christiana Ellis, Christine Hall, Clarissa Geffon, Clover Autrey, D. Melissa Bowden, David Ackert, David Booker, David Busboom, Duff McCourt, Dustin Neff, Earl Dean, Elizabeth Schechter, Emily Kinsman, Eric Bresin, Eric Priuska, Gerard Harrison, Greg Byrne, Haylie Norton, Heather Marshal, Heather Nagey, Helen Hyndes-Snodgrass, Ian Salt, J. R. Elkins, Jarucia Jaycox Nirula, Jason Venter, Jerry Murray, Jessica Miller, Jo Anderton, Jo Van de Walle, Joab Stieglitz, Joanne Steinwachs, Jodi Meadows, John Clifford, Jone Sterling, Justin Parente, Katheryn Allen, Keith Katsikas, Kevin Miller, Kirk Rafferty, Kirsten Kohlwey, Kurt Hausheer, Kyri Freeman, Ladonna Watkins, Larry Pinaire, Laura Comerford, Laurie Sandra Davis, Linda Dicmanis, Lisa Smeaton, Lizzie Newell, Luke Kendall, Margaret Fisk, Marguerite Reed, Mark Reeder, Martha Knox, Matt Doyle, May Iversen, Mike Blumer, Mike Farrell, Miquela Faure, Parker Owens, Patty Jansen, Penelope Kert-Kuzmich, Randall Humphries, Randy Baker, Ranke Lidyek, Raven Matthews, Raymond Walshe, Renee Otis, Robert H. Butler, Rochita

Loenen-Ruiz, Rhonda Garcia, Sandra Panicucci, Sarah E. Short, Sarah Trick, Simon Rhodes, Suzann Dodd, Tammi Hyde, Terri Trimble, Terry Weide, Tim Brommer, Tom Harris, William Clay, Willis Couvillier, and Zachary Davis. To those whose names I've lost over the years, I thank you as well.

ABOUT THE AUTHOR

W. B. J. Williams holds advanced degrees in anthropology and archeology and is an avid historian, mystic, poet, and author who manages an information security program at a prominent New England start-up. He is noted for his bad puns, and willingness to argue from any perspective. He is endured by his beloved wife and two daughters, and lives in Sharon Massachusetts. When he is not at home or at his computer, he can often be found haunting the various used bookstores of Boston.

More from Dragonwell Publishing:

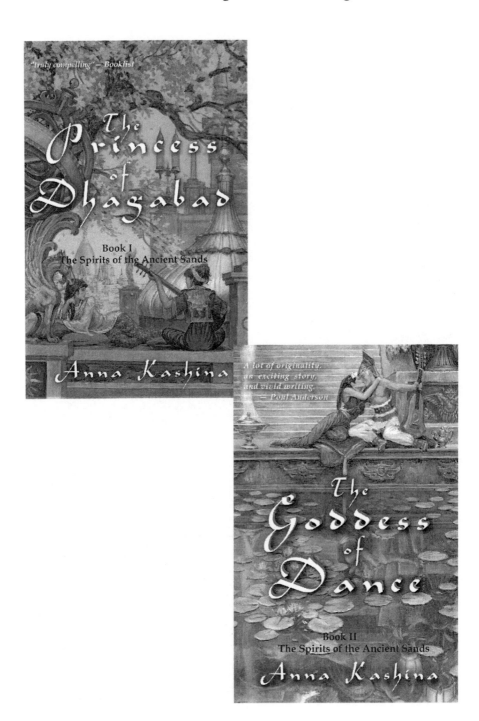

More from Dragonwell Publishing:

More from Dragonwell Publishing:

CPSIA information can be obtained at www.ICGtesting.com
Printed in the USA
BVOW08s1029040913

330218BV00002B/51/P